EX LIBRIS

Jack Baltic

O RIVER, REMEMBER!

O RIVER, REMEMBER!

By

MARTHA OSTENSO

New York

DODD, MEAD & COMPANY

1943

PRINTED IN THE UNITED STATES OF AMERICA

CONTENTS

Author's Note

The background of *O River, Remember!* is historical.
The town of Wing, and the characters used, are fictitious.
Any resemblance, in name or personality, to people living
or dead, is purely coincidental.

SPRING—1941

I

THEY stood in the chilling April rain under a street light on the corner, and waited for the bus. Once in a while they exchanged fretful glances, as if each thought the other might hurry the bus along somehow. There was no smile of sympathy between these two strangers, for neither the man nor the girl possessed at the moment any sense of mirth.

In the pocket of his top coat, a stubborn English tweed, reposed half a pack of limp cigarettes, an uncrowded keyring, and ninety-seven cents. His eyes stared bluely at the wet glitter of the pavement, where the raindrops arrowed up like tiny jumping fish.

The girl wore a cherry-colored wool suit with a gray squirrel collar. A pill-box hat of cherry felt sat atop her long, turned-under bob that glistened in the street light with the hue of a bronze coin. She was erectly slender, and her eyes swam darkly in the tense pallor of her face. From moment to moment she lifted the black leather music case she carried, as if in an effort to keep it dry. The tiny lock on the case was evidently at fault.

"Would you like me to hang onto that for you?" the young man asked on impulse. "You seem to be having trouble with it. I can keep it under my coat till this damn' bus comes along."

She seemed startled at the sound of his voice, and glanced up at him uncertainly. "Why, thank you, but that's too—"

"Here, give it to me."

Their bare hands touched in the transfer, and they hastily drew a step farther apart with faint, mutual embarrassment.

[3]

"I should have had that lock mended today," the girl said as if in apology. "Or at least brought an umbrella with me. I can't afford to get my music wet."

"You've been taking a lesson this evening?" he asked with reluctant interest, wishing to hell the bus would arrive. He was without rubbers, and there was a sluice in the sole of his right shoe.

"No." Her smile was shadowy, but the plaintive sweetness of her lips caught at him in a disconcerting way. He frowned with a shrug, not caring; but then she added, "I've been *giving* a lesson. Two, in fact, this evening."

"Oh." He felt disproportionately conciliated. "A nasty night to be out in." Then, after another glance down the street, his wits assembled themselves. "Here comes the old ark now!"

There was another minute or two before the bus anchored near the curb in six inches of water. In the glare from the headlights the young man looked down at the slender inverted spires of the girl's legs. It was still April in Minnesota, he thought irritably, and she might have worn galoshes—rubbers, at least.

"I'll take the case now, thank you," she said as the bus door sprang open.

"Hang onto it, then, and I'll give you a hoist up."

She was about to demur when he clasped her about the waist and stepped forth into the small torrent of the gutter.

Any average girl, he thought, would have giggled and been profuse in her thanks, but she was calm and matter-of-fact as he set her on her feet in the vestibule. Her coolness, as she dropped a bus token into the cage, nettled him somehow—and not because he was soaked halfway up the shanks, either.

He was fishing out a dime from his pocket when the bus driver, throwing his vehicle into complaining gear, said with a grin at the girl, "I'd 'a' hopped out and picked you up, Miss

[4]

Shaleen, if you didn't have your friend along. Bilge of a night, ain't it?"

"Terrible, Jim!" The girl smiled and moved away to take a seat.

Shaleen! The young man's color changed, and he clamped his teeth down on his tongue just in time to prevent himself from exclaiming to the driver, "What was that name? Shaleen?"

Seated across the aisle from the girl, he stooped to make a mock attempt at wringing out his trouser legs. Shaleen! The name was so uncommon, and yet the coincidence was not impossible. He might not have heard accurately, of course. He stole a sideways glance at the girl, whose face was half averted in the cheerless light of the bus. The pure modeling of her jaw and throat quickened a pulse within him. Even if she weren't one of them—but no, with that extraordinary hair and coloring she *must* be! And if she were, what an omen!

Somehow he would have to find out—and immediately—or something would snap in the center of his brain. There was only one other passenger aboard—a fat woman sitting far back, chewing gum. He removed his sodden hat and knocked it against his legs, remembering with irrelevance that he had paid twelve dollars for it two years ago, before Alice went off in a huff to her "beloved France."

The girl looked across at him with big-pupiled eyes, with eyes like the heart of darkness. *Hold on, Brill Wing—you aren't Joseph Conrad yet!*

"You're soaking wet," she said. "I shouldn't have let you— oh, I'm so sorry!"

"Huh!" He grinned leanly. "You needn't be. I'm all wet —from the inside out. Have been for quite a while. Will you forgive me if I ask you a question? I've got to know the answer, or I'll blow up!"

[5]

"Goodness!" A ghost of a smile touched her lips, and then a curious regard of him came over her face. She frowned and looked at the top center of his bare forehead, where the dark hair grew in a peculiar obstinate cowlick, counter-clockwise.

Self-consciously he ran a hand over the short-cropped lock. "Is your name Miss Shaleen?" he asked, his heart thumping.

Her long, straight lashes fanned down and up again in surprise. "Why—yes. How did you know? Oh—the driver, of course!" She blushed. "Jim lives near—near us, in Rosedale."

Brill Wing had detected a hesitancy in her manner and wondered about it sharply. She lived in the suburb of Rosedale, twice as far away as he was going to his own furnished room. He had only another twenty blocks in which to learn her first name.

"My name is Brill Wing," he said bluntly, on a long chance.

Her lips parted as if in sudden fright, and the color ebbed from her cheekbones. "That *is* your hair, then," she said breathlessly.

He laughed. "It's not a wig!" Excitement possessed him. "Are you Norma?"

"Yes. I saw your college graduation picture at your grandfather's, but of course that was taken years ago. Still, you had that twist in your hair when you were fourteen, too."

The animation of discovery was drawn taut between them now like a singing wire; and searching the fragile shell of her face, he was astonished to find in it no shrinking from him, no long-nurtured resentment or contempt for what his father had done to hers. Of course, she had been so young at the time. Still—

"Funny, isn't it?" he said. "And yet—no, it isn't. It was bound to happen some way like this. Nothing was ever prosaic between the Wings and the Shaleens."

"No." Her voice was just audible above the hum of the

[6]

motor. "I was nine and you were fourteen. You tolerated me, though, in your lofty way." She laughed. "Even when you called me a brat I was grateful."

A preposterous smarting struck his eyes. Good God—in a city bus hurtling through black rain—a nostalgia for the sunlit years! And in another minute he would have to get off the bus. No, by Jeepers, he wouldn't! It was only nine o'clock. If he appeared at Ivar Gossman's swank party by midnight, it would be time enough to collect the two hundred his cousin owed him for that publicity job.

"You're still living with your Aunt Maude, Norma?" he asked.

"I'm still living in her house. Aunt Maude died two weeks ago."

"Oh, Lord, I'm sorry! Just like me—clumsy ox!"

"You couldn't have known," she said gently. "How long is it since you were back at your grandfather's farm?"

"Too long. Look here," he hurried, "the next corner is mine. But I'm not getting out. I'm going home with you, Norma. It's important—you can't say no!"

"But your shoes—you ought to change—"

"Never mind my shoes. I'd rather catch pneumonia than miss talking with you tonight." He stopped blankly. "But perhaps you have guests, or—"

"No, Brill. I'm all alone. That's just it." She looked away, and he remembered the expression of her face when he had first seen it under the street light, vividly strained and forlorn. Poor kid—poor, little, long-legged, nine-year-old kid, grown up to such tenuous, haunting beauty, with sadness over it like a—like a patina. No, that was pretty trite. Like the dim effulgence of some crypt—

"Alone? No maid, or anything?"

"Why shouldn't I be alone? There was no one but Aunt

[7]

Maude and me. I've taught music and—we got along all right."

Here was his corner, and a number of people came aboard. He might have moved over to her seat, but for some obscure reason he could not bring himself to do so. An assumption of familiarity, perhaps, might reside in the move, and he was still too unsure of himself, of her, and of what she was thinking of the past. A youth with pimples lounged next to Norma, whistling offensively between his teeth.

When she got up to leave, Brill followed her. It had stopped raining.

"Have you an oven in your house?" he asked. "I could dry out my shoes in it."

"Oh, yes. And we'll have a hot drink."

They walked two short blocks and came to a small bungalow fronted by a lilac hedge. At the corner of the hedge a real estate company's signboard was staked. It bore the words "For Sale."

"Aunt Maude left her property to me," Norma explained simply. "I don't want to live here alone. There's already a prospective purchaser."

She put the key in the lock, opened the door, and turned on a light. They were in a comfortable, nondescript living room of overstuffed furniture and the bric-a-brac of a maiden aunt. Between the lace curtains of a bay window hung a canary's cage covered with green chintz. From a cushion a fat maltese cat bridged its back up in welcome, its face splitting into a yawn like a ripe pod. An alcove was occupied by a baby grand piano. An archway revealed the dining room, at the opposite end of which stood an old-fashioned organ of the type that used to be called a "melodeon."

Brill recognized it at once, though he had not seen it since he was fourteen, when Aunt Maude Shaleen moved away from the Shaleen farm at her brother Loren's death and took her niece with her.

[8]

The melodeon had belonged to Great-aunt Kate Shaleen, and in Brill's mind it stood as a symbol of the generations of somber and preposterously archaic yet somehow dusk-and-sun-lighted drama of the Shaleens and the Wings. He wondered how much the young Norma had come to know of the story.

He went to the ancient instrument and laid his hand on the worn golden wood.

"This was your Great-aunt Kate's, wasn't it?" he said.

"Yes. You remember it? It's the only thing Aunt Maude and I brought with us from the farm. She gave me my first lessons on it. We'd better go right into the kitchen," Norma said as she removed her hat and jacket. "Hang your coat on the kitchen door. It may dry out some there."

She lighted the oven of the gas range and lowered the door.

"Set your shoes there, and I'll rinse out your socks and iron them dry," she said.

It was all trancelike and improbable to Brill Wing. The last time she had seen his bare feet was when she had gone wading with him in the creek at his grandfather's farm, eighteen years ago. Now he was thirty-two; she must be twenty-seven. She did not glance at his feet, but drew up a chair for him near the oven. Then she went to the cupboard and took down a bottle and a sugar bowl.

"We had hot buttered rum here after a skating party last winter," she said. "I have four grownups among my piano pupils, and one of them had a birthday. He brought the rum. I'll try to fix it the way he did."

Brill's eyes went to her feet. "Hadn't you better change to something dry, first?"

"Yes." She lighted the gas under the teakettle. "I'll just be a minute."

When she had vanished, he looked at his long, bony toes.

[9]

They seemed to belong to somebody else. His wet socks lay on the floor. No, he would certainly not permit her to wash those, after he had worn them for three days!

He was scrubbing at the socks under the sink faucet when Norma returned. She made no comment except to tell him to lay them on top of the oven when he was through.

Her casualness doubled his conviction that he must be dreaming.

"Do you like lemon or nutmeg in the rum?" she asked as she poured hot water into two old-fashioned cut-glass punch cups. "I like both. Harold made them that way."

Harold. He found himself disliking the name. A "grownup" pupil of hers. As he watched her, she moved with the deceptively idle grace of a river. *The* river!

"Sure," he replied. "Whatever *you* have."

She smiled at him, and he noted the faint depression in her full lower lip. Someone might have held a larking finger there, to tease her.

"I used to say that," she said, "when you treated me to ice cream soda at old Gimp Featherstone's, back in your town, in 1923."

"*My* town?"

"Wasn't Wing your town? You used to tell me it was. They named it after your family, didn't they?"

Brill got up on his bare, homely feet and took the hot drink from her hand. She was much shorter in her bedroom slippers.

"You don't have to rub my family in, Norma," he said with a sour smile. "Take a look at my socks there, and you'll see what one of the Wing family has come to."

The corners of her mouth shaped to stillness. "I didn't mean it that way at all. And you know I didn't. Let's sit down and have our drinks. How are your shoes doing?" She lifted one of them and looked at its sole, then set it back without a word.

Brill felt no embarrassment, but rather a perverse pride. She must have known that he had married Alice Hartmann, the brewer's heiress, back in '35. The wedding had been greeted with enough fanfare in the papers.

"Well—I may as well come out with it," he said, the drink aromatically hot on his palate. "I've written a play. The first draft of one, at least. Based on the tangled skeins of our two families—yours and mine."

"A play. I don't see how you could get it all into one play, Brill."

"Well, not all of it, but—aren't you even a little surprised that I tried it?"

"Not very much. You used to talk about writing a play some day. Besides, I couldn't be surprised at anything tonight—after meeting you like this. I'm still a bit dazed."

He thought about that for a moment. "I have a feeling that we've met quite often in the rain during the past eighteen years."

"Maybe we have," Norma said.

He wondered if she knew what he meant. It was a sensation that he could scarcely explain even to himself. He had felt it first when he looked across at her in the bus and told her it was important that he should go home with her. It was as if another voice had spoken through him—a dim host of voices clamoring as one.

He brushed his hand across his brow. "You know the story, of course—the story of the Wings and the Shaleens?"

"Aunt Maude told me a good deal. I remembered some, and the rest I pieced together."

He searched her eyes with a hardiness that seemed to come from his very muscles. "I know your aunt went to see my grandfather a couple of years ago. He wrote me about that—and was so proud and glad about it. So you don't hate *him*. But

[11]

you must have hated my father—all the time you were growing up."

Her long, expressive hand, not as feminine as the rest of her, lay tranquil upon the bright wool of her skirt. "I never had any such feeling toward your father—or any of you. We Shaleens were brought up to forget at once any injustice done us. Remembering and hating—that was what Aunt Maude called unconstructive. When she talked about our family and yours, it was always in an impersonal way, as if we all belonged in one big picture. She had a way of looking at it as if the figures in it might have been others, not ourselves at all."

A sigh went through Brill, a sigh that was like a deep wash of tears. *God*, he thought, *I can't get maudlin—not on one hot rum! But I've had such a hell of a time—am having it—and to learn that this child of my own childhood bears me no malice, no little-scaled bitterness, when she has every right to—*

"Lord, I'm glad of that, Norma!" he said. "Thank you."

"It isn't easy to live with hate," Norma said quietly. "When your father foreclosed the mortgage on my father's farm—well, it was a matter of business, after all. Your father was president of the bank and had its interests to protect. My father was a farmer trying to get past the slump in wheat prices. Farmers were having a hard time of it in 1923. The bankers had their hard times later. And your father wasn't harsh, by any means. He left us the house and buildings, and forty acres. It was as much as my father was fit to handle after he lost his hand in the threshing accident the year before."

Brill closed his eyes. Did she think it necessary to be so stubbornly considerate of his feelings? She knew his father, Arne Wing, had been a crook, even though he had been mayor of the town that bore the family name. He hadn't given a damn what happened to anyone so long as he saved his own

[12]

hide. He had been the embodiment of everything that was hard and despicable in the Wing family. Norma knew that. She must have known.

He tried another approach. "It all goes back beyond your father and mine, of course. My old grandfather Ivar has told me enough about that, in his own gentle way. There was a richness in the Shaleens that the Wings never had. Our stinking materialism against your intuitive religion of beauty. When I say *our*, I'm not including those of us who were spineless victims of my grandmother's ambition. A few of us had a dream—but never had the guts to follow it and make it real." He paused and lighted a cigarette. "Do you know, Norma, from old Ivar's description of the bygone Shaleens, I was certain tonight that you must be one of them? Your great-aunts—Kate and Delphy—and your Aunt Rose—old Ivar brought them all alive for me when he talked about them. He was always wistfully attracted by the very thing in your family that my grandmother hated and feared. Grandmother Magdali had him licked from the start!"

"When did you see your grandfather last?"

"Well, I haven't been back since I married Alice Hartmann. That was six years ago. The depression was still on then, and I couldn't get a decent job. College degrees were going begging. My grandfather Ivar paid my way through college, you know—after my father was killed in that automobile accident. Mother married an old dodo with money, out in California, and my sister Dorothy hooked up with a guy named Tridd, a mercantile princelet in Wing. The Tridd Glass Block—you know. Their youngsters gad about the countryside in their jalopies, and throw the old man's money around in beer joints and roadhouses. You know the kind. Hell, their name is legion —all over the United States. Their grasping pioneer ancestors spawned them—and here they are!"

"I never thought of your grandfather Ivar as a grasping pioneer, Brill," said Norma.

"No—but my fabulous grandmother Magdali made up for what he lacked in that respect. The heroic pioneer women—good God, what a sample of them *she* was!"

"Maybe she was just as essential to the picture as—"

"Did you know that my brother Allen is a popcorn salesman now?"

"No, I didn't, but I can't see anything wrong about that."

"You probably can't see the pattern, because you're a Shaleen," Brill retorted, with rising impatience.

"Maybe I just see a different pattern," Norma replied, with irritating gentleness.

"The Wings of 1870 or thereabouts were all steamed up to be something great in America, the land of plenty. Something great like land speculators or bankers or lawyers or railroad thieves. Artists and scientists were crack-pots who'd never make a dollar, so they weren't in the scheme of things. If the two strains had been blended, we might have had something to be proud of. As it is—" He crumpled his empty cigarette pack.

"I have some more in my purse," she said, and smiled. "Same brand."

"That's funny," he laughed. "The two families got together at last—on cigarettes."

"And there's enough rum left for two more hot drinks, if you want another," Norma added, and touched the iron with a finger moistened on the end of her tongue. "You make them while I iron your socks."

He pattered about in his bare feet. When he looked at his watch it was nearing eleven.

His socks and shoes were dry, and he put them on. "I've got to drop in at my cousin's place some time tonight," he said, "to collect some money he owes me for a publicity job. Ivar Goss-man—you probably know about him. Quite a big shot!"

"Who wouldn't know him in this town?"

Loneliness descended suddenly upon Brill Wing. "I don't suppose you'd feel like coming along with me? They're throwing a party, but we'd have to stay only a minute."

She hesitated, considering him oddly with her strange eyes that were like a twilit sea—blue to gray to fleeting olive.

"I hate to think this evening is over," she said frankly. "And there's probably more you want to tell me, isn't there?"

Brill drew hard on his cigarette to steady his thoughts. *I hate to think this evening is over!* It was all somnambulistic and illusory still—and it might mean nothing. Just her way of seeming to capture something as irretrievable as a lost sun-mote out of their childhood.

"There's plenty, of course," he said, "and plenty I want you to tell me; but we don't have to crowd it all into one evening. If you'd like to come along, we'd better start catching a bus."

"Aunt Maude's old car is out in the garage. I haven't driven it since she—"

"Would you mind if I drove it?" He felt a complex awkwardness and a lightening of his mood.

"I really wish you would. And I think Aunt Maude would like you to, if she knew."

"Then we don't have to leave for a few minutes. I'm in no hurry to see Ivar Gossman." He settled back in his chair, his feet toward the open oven. "You were pretty young, but perhaps you remember that my sister Louise drowned herself in our river in July 1918, when word came that your cousin Tom had been killed in France."

"I was four years old. It's the earliest thing I remember, just about. Tom was Uncle David's son. Aunt Maude talked about it after I was grown up, so I'm not quite sure what is memory

[15]

and what is an impression of her account of it. But I have a distinct recollection of seeing my grandparents crying. Especially my grandfather storming across the kitchen floor and swearing, with the tears streaming down his face."

"That was old Steve Shaleen," Brill mused. "Your grandmother was Selma Engebrigt Shaleen. They both died in the flu epidemic of 1918."

"I remember that very well. The smell of sulphur burning on the stove."

"And how they tried to account for what happened to Louise—after she walked into the river that July night, in her graduation dress! Even her school principal had his theory—said she'd been studying her Shakespeare too hard, and got herself confused with Ophelia." Brill laughed shortly. "The damned old fool!"

"I don't think I remember that. There was a lot of talk, of course, but Aunt Maude said she didn't believe the stories that were going the rounds."

"Your Aunt Maude was right. My grandmother and my mother were both dead set against Louise having anything to do with Tom Shaleen. He was studying something silly at the university—something called chemistry—in which there couldn't possibly be any money. They forbade Louise to have anything to do with him. I remember the last time she saw him. It was at Easter, when he was home on leave before going overseas. There was a dance at the Odd Fellows' hall, and my mother sent me along with Louise on the understanding that I was not to let her out of my sight. I didn't. I watched them waltzing together. I was only nine, but that song—Smile the While You Kiss Me Fond Adieu—I still can't bear to think of it. They were the most graceful couple on the floor—Tom dark and tall, my sister fair as moonlight. After the waltz, I sneaked out behind them and saw them clinging together under a leafless tree in the shadow of the hall. That was their good-by. That's all there was to it. The gossip about why Louise drowned herself months later didn't have a word of truth in it. Hell, how could there be any truth in it? It was months since Louise had seen Tom—and people have eyes in their heads! But the Shaleens and the Wings were under a cloud, of course, and the gossips grabbed at every chance—"

"You mean after what happened between my Aunt Rose and your Uncle Karsten, don't you?"

"I think the trouble started long before that awful affair," Brill said. "It goes back sixty years, to my grandfather and your Great-aunt Kate."

"Maybe so. Aunt Maude was always uncertain about Kate, though she told me all about Rose and Karsten."

Brill's laugh was not as brusque as he hoped it would be. Rather, it held a note of wistful sadness. "I'll bet you'd like to think there was a romance between Kate and my grandfather, back in the '70's, wouldn't you?"

"Of course I would. Do you remember our old album, and how we used to go into stitches when we looked through it?"

"We didn't laugh at Kate, though. She was too beautiful to laugh at. We'll have to look through that album again some day." He lighted another cigarette. "Do you mind if I change the subject? I suppose you know that my wife Alice has disappeared somewhere in Europe?"

"There have been items in the papers about it," Norma said. Her tone was so impersonal that they might have been discussing something as remote as the Cater case, Brill thought. "You don't know where she is? Whether she's—"

At her pause he allowed himself a grim laugh. "It has cost me most of what I've been able to earn in the past year or more trying to find her. Through embassies and consulates and private agencies and God knows what all! My lawyer told me long ago that I could file suit for divorce, serve papers at her last-known address, and advertise the suit in the local papers if I got no reply. I'd be free in six months, unless she turned up to contest the suit. But it hasn't seemed quite decent—quite the square thing, somehow. She may have got into some mess after France fell. She was reckless—and she really did love France. Certainly more than she did me! Or perhaps she's ill and hiding out in some place where she can't get word to me." He stopped to put out his cigarette and light another.

"Your grandfather told me you hadn't been back to the farm to visit him after your marriage," Norma said quietly. "He thinks you were afraid *he'd* think you married money."

"I did marry money, but I was in love with Alice—or thought I was. She had all the smart qualities my family had brought me up to believe were important because they were inseparable from money. We spent our first six months gadding about Europe on her coupon clippings, until I saw that her money was beginning to lead me around by the nose. We came back home, and I got a job in the advertising department of the Hartmann Breweries. Very edifying! I made five thousand a year, but that was chicken feed alongside what Alice took from the estate her father left her. I couldn't travel her pace, so we battled constantly. When she finally reminded me that I owed my job to her, I quit the job. That was in the summer of '39. Alice tore off to Europe and took her money with her. I haven't heard from her since."

After a silence, Norma said, "You couldn't have done anything but what you did, Brill. Old Ivar's grandson couldn't."

"Oh, no?" His laugh had a gritty edge. "Ivar Gossman is his grandson, too. And isn't he a swell namesake for that grand old man! It gripes me every time I think of it."

"You should have been the one to bear his name," Norma said. "Why don't you go and visit him, as soon as you can?

[18]

He talked so warmly about you when Aunt Maude and I were there. He always expected good things of you."

Brill stared down at the empty glass cup in his hand. A line like a stretched rubber band moved down his cheek as his teeth clenched.

"Sure—I know. Why do you suppose I haven't had the crust to go back and see him since—?"

"Don't, Brill," Norma murmured, touching his arm. "You've still got your self-respect. And besides"—her smile was radiant from lips to eyes—"you have written a play."

"It's rotten." He got up and looked at her. "I've done one admirable thing—just one—in my whole life. And even that may not benefit anybody but me. I've put in my application to the Naval Officer Procurement Office for an A. V. T. commission as flying instructor. I've done a good deal of flying—in Alice's plane, naturally. She sold that before she went abroad the last time, but after that I had a job for a while with a flying school. Since then I've flown a luxury cabin plane that belongs to a rich old codger friend of mine who loathes trains. I've piloted him all over the country. He put in a good word for me, and I have the required number of flying hours, so I think it's set. Before long, if this fracas goes on, I'll be teaching youngsters how to get off the ground and get back again without breaking their necks. It isn't much, but it'll be something."

Norma's dark-sea eyes widened, her lips parted with that very young, sweet surprise that he had seen upon them before, and she said, "Why, Brill—I think that'll be wonderful for you!"

"Oh, don't try to make a hero out of me," he said, coloring. "I'll probably never get anything to do but routine work."

"How soon will you know?"

"I'm hoping to hear in about a month. My credentials and everything have gone to the Bureau of Navigation in Washington. They finecomb my record, and if I'm lucky they'll make me a junior grade lieutenant. I'll get in somehow or other. The old writing is on the wall."

The home of the Ivar Gossmans, on the Lake of the Isles Boulevard, was French château in style, appropriately landscaped with Lombardy poplars and terraced lawns. A little later in the season a colored fountain would be playing among the trees, with the glistening lake as a background. Janet Clifford Gossman admitted with disarming facetiousness that she was the fortunate daughter of a profiteer of the last war. The house had been her father's wedding present to her and her husband, Ivar Gossman.

It was brilliantly illuminated, and the socially elite of the city swarmed within its walls. In Janet's "Watteau" music room somebody was playing the piano, a sultry, deep-south melody of the "torch" variety, while a girl incoherently wailed the words of the song.

"Brill, my pet!" Janet cried, embracing him. "You did come!" And then in pretty confusion she saw Norma and telescoped her from head to foot with her narrow eyes. "Oh—"

"This is Norma Shaleen, Janet," Brill said. "Ivar must have told you about our home-town Shaleens. Norma, this is my cousin's wife, Mrs. Gossman."

"My gracious—you're not the great sculptor's sister?" Janet gasped, clutching Norma's hand.

"David Shaleen is my uncle," Norma said.

"Heavens—of course! You're too young. I must have had one too many. Come, both of you, let's have another, and I'll see if I can remember people's names. That's our mayor over there, Miss Shaleen. He's a lamb—"

"Yes, Mrs. Gossman, I've met him, and he is," Norma agreed. "We were on a committee together once—to stimulate interest in good music among school children. He seems deep in conversation just now. Wouldn't it be better if I talked to him later?"

Janet Gossman was taken aback. "Then you must know our Dody Crane, too, if you're musical! He's playing the piano. He's in demand everywhere, but *simply!*"

"Norma teaches music," Brill said neutrally, and glanced about for Ivar Gossman. *Get your money and get out, my boy! You had enough of this nonsense before Alice decamped.*

The musical orbits of Dody Crane and Norma Shaleen were spatially remote from each other, but Janet was confident that she must nevertheless have heard of him. Dody was five years younger than Janet, and had been her lover for some time. Ivar Gossman knew it and, caring little or nothing about his wife, amused himself elsewhere as impulse prompted. He was anxious that his twin sons, Hubert and Homer, now in college, should feel none of the embarrassment of discord between their parents when they brought their school friends home with them. The truth was that Hubert and Homer knew all about what they called the "set-up," and thought it amusingly naïve.

The narrow black blades of Janet's eyes cut questioningly across the milky pallor of her thin face as she waited for Norma's reply.

"No, I haven't met Dody Crane," said Norma politely, as she accepted a highball from one of the extra flunkeys Janet had hired for the occasion. "He plays very well. Who is the singer?"

"The singer?" Janet said with bright effort. "A darling girl! Hallie Something-or-other. My husband met her the other night at a—"

"She sings like a tin pail full of acorns," Brill said.

"Why, darling!" Janet cried indignantly. "Ivar thinks she has a lovely voice."

"In her sleep?" he asked.

[21]

Ivar Gossman slapped Brill on the back. "Been lookin' for you, Brill, ol' boy! Want to tell you what a good job you did on that promotion stunt. The radio contact was tops—absolutely tops! Look—I got the little something I promised you —in the library. How's about a few of us leavin' this mess and havin' a quiet get-together in the library?"

Janet had drifted away, her curiously fluted sherry satin train suggestive of a great centipede. Brill introduced Norma to his cousin. Perhaps it was the drink he had had, but he found himself resenting Ivar's oily survey of Norma.

"We weren't going to stay, Ivar," he said, and glanced at Norma.

"How you talk!" Ivar laughed. "Look—there's Bob and Rinky. You know them, Brill. Collect 'em, eh? You come with me, Miss Shaleen. Any kind of get-together needs decoration."

He grinned affably above his meaty blob of chin and took Norma's arm.

The Gossman library was medieval, almost monastic, in tone, paneled in dark woods with a gigantic fireplace at one end that looked as if it had been hewn out of a rock cliff. One did not feel conscious of books, although they were indisputably there. Golf trophies abounded, and there were mounted fish and two antlered heads to relieve the ascetic atmosphere.

As soon as Brill entered with the two men, Ivar Gossman took an envelope from a drawer in a table that stood against one wall, gave it to Brill, and smiled. "There you are, you ol' stiff! Betcha I couldn't 'a' dragged you in here tonight with horses if you didn't have a good reason for comin'. Well, sit down, sit down. Rinky—Bob—take a load off your feet. And —oh, just a minute, *just* a minute!" He led the two men to where Norma was already seated on a couch. "I want you to meet my new girl friend—Norma Shaleen. Now go and sit down while I get you all a drink."

[22]

They were seated at last in front of the fireplace, and Ivar Gossman launched forth at once, pontifically, upon the war in Europe and the golden opportunity it offered to the peaceful-minded citizens of the United States.

"The greatest chance in a generation, and if we have any brains left in this country we'll cash in. I have a little stock in a company that's shippin' plane equipment to the Argentine as fast as we can turn it out. Where it goes from there is nobody's business. Who cares? If we play our cards right this time, we'll have the world by the tail when the war is over. But first of all we'll have to put this man Roosevelt in the cooler. If we don't do something about him, he'll have us in the war before another year."

Bob and Rinky concurred with satellite fidelity. Brill sipped his drink and glanced at Norma. She smiled and stroked her right eyebrow with her finger, and out of the long past Brill remembered the mystery sign that meant, "Don't shoot till you see the whites of their eyes."

He held himself in check. "You don't seem to realize that we *are* in it—now," he said.

"Not the way he'd like to have us in it," Gossman retorted. "If we mind our own damn' business—"

Brill felt a slow boiling within him. "I'm joining the Navy —if they'll have me."

Ivar burst out laughing. "I heard a crack along that line the other day—but it can't be told in the presence of a lady. You don't mean a word of it, of course."

Brill reddened. "I do mean it!"

Ivar Gossman's eyes frogged out. "Well, I'll be—you *do* mean it!" he exclaimed. "I believe you do. Stickin' your neck out, eh, young fella? That"—he slapped the carved oak arm of the high-backed, red-velvet-cushioned chair that might have belonged to a cardinal—"that is exactly the kind o' thing that's goin' to get us into it. A lot of hare-brained young fellows like you with cockeyed notions about patriotism. Flag-wavin' instead of gettin' down to business!"

"I'd rather not discuss that right now," Brill said coldly.

"Well, I'll tell you one thing—when those two boys of mine finish college this June, I'm goin' to see to it that they get into harness before they get any fool ideas about joinin' the Air Force, or whatever. Hubert and Homer will have a place right beside me in the Gossman Investments, and they're goin' to stay where I put them. If the war in Europe and China lasts another ten years, so much the better. Them boys'll be in their prime by that time—and sittin' on top of the world!"

Brill stood up and set his empty glass carefully aside. Then he turned and looked at his cousin. "I said I didn't want to discuss this right now, Ivar. I'm a guest in your house, and you have me at a disadvantage. But I'm fond of your boys, and I hope to God they'll have more sense than to let you turn them into leeches like yourself to suck on the blood streams of the country that gave them birth."

"Hurray!" Gossman shouted. "Brill, you're an orator. Carry on, m'lad!"

There was one fierce moment in which Brill wanted to send his clenched fist into the soft face of Ivar Gossman. But he saw Norma lift a hand in a gesture of warning. He turned away from his cousin.

"Come on, Norma. We're leaving," he said abruptly.

In the car, with Norma sitting straight and speechless beside him, Brill said, "Would you like to drop over to Charlie's for a bite of supper before I take you home? I've got enough to take care of it. Ivar paid me in cash. He likes that sort of gesture. If I hadn't needed it, I'd have rammed it down his throat."

"That wouldn't have helped any," Norma replied.

"No—you're right. Well, how about a little—"

[24]

"I couldn't eat anything just now, Brill. But—you know that lookout on the Shakopee Road, don't you? Let's drive out there and sit a while. We won't be able to see anything, but—"

"That's an idea. I'd like to drive around a while and cool my temper." He felt an elation, a lightness, and an anticipatory quickening that magically erased Ivar Gossman from his mind.

In half an hour or less, with little talk between them, they arrived at the point on the highway where they turned and crossed the misty headland and came to the stone parapet overlooking the valley. They got out of the car and stood close together while Brill struck matches so that they could read the stone-framed inscription:

Minnesota Valley

Carved out several thousand years ago by the vast torrents of water of glacial River Warren flowing from glacial Lake Agassiz in the Red River area, this Valley eventually became a great highway of travel for traders and settlers, by canoe, steamboat and ox-cart. Near here Sioux and Chippewa fought the battle of Shakopee on May 27, 1858.

"Time has somehow been sealed up in things like these," Norma said. "This valley grew out of our valley, Brill—the Red River Valley of the North."

Without replying, he took her arms and brought her up to him and kissed her, a kiss reverent with the memories of their sunlit childhood before any bitter knowledge had come to either of them.

"You're sweet," he said, deep in his throat.

"You haven't changed, Brill," she whispered.

He put his arm about her so that she must face the valley below, and the valley was a sullen and impenetrable expanse of murk.

[25]

"The future," he said.

"I'm not afraid of it, Brill. Hold me a while."

He felt swept up now. The current of the river again, in spate—no foothold there, no overhanging branch within reach, no shore rock to cling to. The generations had swept them both on to this finality. . . . Norma Shaleen's mouth was warm and mistily soft beneath his own.

"We'll go to your grandfather's farm," she murmured. "We'll wade in the creek again."

"I'd like that. And I'll start fixing things right away. We won't talk about it now, but you know what I mean. This time it's going to come straight for the Wings and the Shaleens—for us!"

Over her head, with his arms about her, Brill stared down into that black void that had once been pathed by thousands of moccasined feet, and the fear that she had denied was deep within him; the fear that any brevity of time might still be long enough to destroy their happiness, for she was a Shaleen and he a Wing. He pressed his eyes against the rainy fragrance of her hair.

II

It was May now, and time had not yet become the enemy.

Dawn would come soon on the northern river, and like a blood-red shallop the waning moon hung low in the west, among the trees.

Norma Shaleen pressed her cheek down to Brill Wing's head, cradled against her shoulder, and murmured, "We ought to go back to the house, darling, don't you think? Old Eudora is a strict housekeeper. She'll be shocked if she hears us sneaking in so late. I wouldn't mind so much about your grandfather. Anyhow, you'll have to leave early in the morning."

Brill stretched, yawned in the luxury of content, and brought his arms up about Norma to draw her down awkwardly upon his breast. She laughed, her teeth nipping at his throat.

"You needn't break my neck this last night we're together," she said. "I might have use for it while you're away."

"Somebody else might have use for it, you mean," Brill said, kissing her. "Necking is—"

"Ugh! Honestly, the moon is setting. And there's dew on this blanket."

"There's *you* on this blanket."

"Ugh, again! I can't endure your brilliance, Mr. Wing. Sit up and look at the moon before it's gone. The Red River moon. Sometimes I can't believe it—that you and I are here, I mean, on your grandfather's farm again."

Brill hoisted up on one elbow. " 'And the star dials pointed to morn.' I wonder if the star dials are pointing to any morn in this benighted world. I wonder if, when I am married to you and this war is over, I'll be able to write anything worth reading."

"Of course not, darling! Even the second draft of your play is terrible."

"I wish you really meant that. Then I'd scrap it. But it's pretty good, and it's going to be better before I show it to Stevens. Wish I knew him better. You can't trust a producer you've met socially just once, and then where you're in the company of a rich—"

"We promised not to talk about her tonight. Don't speak her name until the moon is set, Brill."

"Right! Anyhow, producers are all swell and cordial over champagne, when they're damn' sure a hick from the Middle West won't bother them again. I wish I'd been assigned to a training base somewhere in the East instead of out West. I'd be a little closer to the center of things."

"You wouldn't be any closer to me," Norma said.

He drew his arms about her. "Tell me the truth, now. We've had this week together up here, and I've been too happy to figure out how you really feel about staying on with Grandpa while I'm away. The old boy is so tickled to have you, but maybe you'll be bored—"

"Bored! You know I won't be bored. I'm going to start building up a piano class as soon as you leave. It'll work out fine. And I've been thinking—do you know what? I'll have the storage people send the old organ up here and give my pupils a sense of the long ago by letting them play it."

"Oh, Norma, sweet, you're so damned idealistic!" He held her thin fingers against his lips. "If you find one kid with that much sensitiveness among the crop that's growing up now, you'll be lucky. It's a nice idea, anyhow."

"You're too hard on the youngsters of today, Brill," Norma said. "They're not so different from the youngsters of any day.

Maybe it'll take a war to prove it, but—" She paused abruptly. "The moon is gone. I can't see it now."

"I can see you, though. I ought to say something about the queer light on your eyes and your mouth—something lyrical. But I love you too infernally, Norma! Do you know what I think? If I'd met you again a little sooner, I wouldn't have enlisted. It takes something to say that, but it's true."

"It's better this way, darling. It will mean so much more to both of us, afterward."

"Afterward? Then you believe there will be an afterward, don't you?"

"Of course! I'd die if I didn't believe it."

Brill was silent a moment. "You have nothing to worry about. Michelson says the divorce will come through by October. So promise me—" He tilted her face in his hands and kissed her gently. "You won't worry about anything at all—I mean *anything*? This time it's going to be *right*—between a Shaleen and a Wing!"

She hesitated only a moment, and yet in anxious suspense he pressed his hand to her heart and felt its quickened pace.

"I won't worry—about anything," she said, clinging to him with all the fierce, soft vehemence of her body. "I'm not afraid —of anything! And I won't be. I promise you, Brill. Dearest, dearest, I *do* promise!"

"Even if by any chance—Alice should turn up in the meantime?"

"Even so. I'm not afraid. You must believe that."

A chill breeze moved in under the starlit sky, brushing the trees with a secret whispering. It came from beyond the river, beyond the valley, a ghost wind crowded with the hurt memories of forgotten years. Beneath its touch, in other days, young courage had faltered and young faith had clutched at its dreams with a sigh. . . .

BOOK ONE

The Seventies Begin

I

THE red and white oxen, the breaking plow, and the broad-shouldered young man with the dark shock of hair were wrought into one by the evening majesty of the sky in this late May of 1870. The sunset included one thing more in its silent welding. The long grass, veering slowly away from the plow-share, sighed over and fell forever, and the earth came to dark and vivid life, the black top-soil breathing out toward the luminous arch of the sky its naked amazement. Thereupon the setting sun took the ragged, inky scars in the earth and joined them with the image of the oxen, the plow, and the man. All, now, were one.

The man's name was Ivar Vinge. He was but twenty-five years old, yet the steady blue-gray of his eyes as they dwelt over the five acres he had already broken and harrowed with a harrow he had himself fashioned out of ash wood from his own land held a contentment, a warm, tired pride that might have shone from the eyes of a much older man. Any other man might have felt boastful of his achievement, for the five acres had already been seeded to oats and barley.

But Ivar was not the boasting sort. It was luck—or God, perhaps, looking down from some cold star during the long spring nights of the oxen's trek—that had guided him to the pre-emption of this amply wooded quarter section on the river they called the Red, one hundred and sixty acres for which he would acquire a patent in due time.

This day's end and another, and if the weather held he would be able to count two more acres of the astonishing loam bared by his plow to the prairie sky. Here, within a stone's-throw of his dugout, he meant to plant the seed potatoes and the carrot and turnip seed he had brought with him from Wisconsin. He smiled as he thought of the scoffing stage driver he had met at a hostlery fifty miles south on the trail, where he had stopped to rest his oxen after a laborious day through the mire of spring thaw.

"You mean to tell me you're going to try to raise *vegetables* in that sour muck on the river?" the driver had snorted. "Man, you're crazy! Why—when the government surveyors got through with that country, they turned in a report that it wasn't good for anything but buffalo and Injuns. Now even the buffalo have cleared out!"

But the tavernkeeper, a gnarled little Scotsman who had been patient with Ivar's broken English, tossed off his peppermint toddy and said, "I'm no' so sure aboot that, Joe. A soldier cam into Stark's saloon one day last summer wi' a dorlach o' garden truck he'd raised over Fort Abercrombie way. He dumped the stuff on the bar, and a stranger cam up and took a look at it, and told the soldier he was a liar if he said he raised it in the Valley. You heard what happened, like as not. The soldier up and shot him dead as a crappit head. He wouldna shoot a man for nocht, now, would he?"

A single handful of this soil, stirred from slumbering ages beneath its silver-green tide of grass, had told Ivar Vinge what no man need tell him. Here was work for the idle, food for the hungry, peaceful sleep at night for the worn in heart; here was dark, living gold. His eyes saw the blue of the empty northern horizon cleave the sea of spring grass, but he knew only the strong velvet of the earth in his hands; it was more than a feeling in his hands, it was almost a taste in his mouth.

Now, as the oxen's sweating flanks strained toward the creek that ran back of the dugout peering from its gentle shelf of ground, Ivar fretted at the shortness of the days. They were approaching their maximum length; yet, by rising before his body could cast a shadow and by going to bed long after the first star had pierced the sky, he would still be unable to complete all he thought was necessary before the arrival of Magdali and the children.

The plowing, yes; he was satisfied with that, and the seeding which he had done by hand, broadcasting the grain from the canvas bag slung at his waist. But Magdali would never be able to understand a one-room dugout, and it was against her coming that he had felled the oaks in the timber along the river. He had lopped the branches off the sturdy trunks and sawed them into even lengths; and the pile of logs stood now against the front wall of the soddy with its one small window.

The logs, built forward from the soddy and chinked in with the sticky river clay, would make an additional room, something more in the way of a house than the molehill he had lived in this past month. But it would all take time, even though he used the logs with the bark on them after their brief weathering.

Then there was the turning over of another acre or two for his dream—his dream of wheat. One plowing for that would not be enough. There would have to be another plowing in the fall; after the rich grass had rotted into the soil for a sunny space of time, there would be the backsetting, the preparing of the ground for the spring seeding when the frost would be out of the top soil to a depth of three or four inches. He would probably have to send to St. Paul for the seed wheat, and it would be costly. His heart seemed to skip a beat when he thought of it, for in the end he might find it to be only a harebrained experiment. Nobody had told him that wheat could be grown in this valley. And once grown, where would he market it, or where have it ground into flour? It was a week's

[35]

journey southward to Alexandria, and even farther to St. Cloud.

But the time would come—and it was as if the myriad voices of the grass told him this, the voices of the doomed grass—when threshing machines and mills would be the new and resounding life of this land. With means as crude as his own, they had been raising wheat for years in the Selkirk Settlement far to the north, in the region of Canada. Of this he had read in the *Nordisk Folkeblad*, while he was yet working for wages on his brother-in-law Karsten Bratland's farm in Wisconsin. It was that reading that had caused Ivar to set his face westward. Yes, a time would come. Even now, in the immeasurable loneliness of earth and sky, he could sense a passing as of wings over him, the mighty passing of time. He stood for a moment in awe and humility that so great a thing should be passing over a man alone, a man as common as he, with only his dumb beasts to share the wonder of it.

He set his hands again to guide the plow, and watched the sod yield and split into a moist, dark wound, the grass recoiling from it. But now the oxen's ponderous, slow heads turned ever leftward toward the chuckle of the bright little creek close by. In the pasture beyond the soddy, where Ivar had tethered her, the cow he had acquired from the German settler in Georgetown in payment for the digging of a well, lowed companionably at his approach. From here, there, in the width of the red sundown, came the song of meadow lark and bob-o-link, the hurried whistle of killdeer, and farther away in the timber the liquid urgency of the brown thrasher's mating call. Where the grass thinned toward the creek bed small flowers grew, buttercups, violets, and anemones.

"Ya, Storli! Ya, du Hans!" Ivar called to his oxen. "You have done enough, you two. Now you shall eat and drink, while I do likewise. I must lead Bluebell to water too. Shortly, now,

Bluebell will have her calf, and that means something here in the Red River Valley, my dears. Well, everyone to his own ability!"

His laugh was wholehearted and strong. Though he spoke in Norwegian, the oxen swung their heads as if they understood.

II

AT THE station of Burbank, a half-dozen miles up the river, the August sun smote down upon the shrinking gray-green of the trees and the prairie, upon the sallow and indolent flow of the stream between its tawny banks. The stage was hours late—even allowing for possible washouts somewhere in the south, it should have arrived long ago—and Stafford, the fat little agent, was in a temper. He was expecting a can of buttermilk from Alexandria, part of which would be hung in the cistern back of the log depot until his wife turned it to culinary uses in her kitchen. A goodly portion of it, however, would be reserved for a purpose much more to Stafford's liking. Combined with certain leavening ingredients, and given a little time . . . The little man sighed and tugged downward on his trousers. His wife had somewhat too diligently patched his underwear in a place where he had for some time treasured a sizable hole, and the patch was making his discomfort in this heat well-nigh insupportable.

To add to his irritation, Gresham, the sutler, was lying under his wagon, sound asleep, his hat over his face. Was there a lazier man anywhere this side of the Gulf of Mexico? The only person showing any sign of life about the place was a thin, blue-eyed young Scandinavian, whose name was something like Vingy, and who kept up an abominable, long-legged stride up and down the road while he waited for the stage that would bring him his wife and children. If the fellow at least had some sociable talk in him! Stafford had done his best by mentioning the Endicotts, who had pre-empted just east of Burbank and

[38]

now had title to their land. The Endicotts had come before this Vingy had, and you'd think he'd be interested in hearing how they were almost starving to death, what with the mother coughing herself to skin and bone, three little ones looking on, and Charlie Endicott no hand for farming, wondering if he'd planted his potatoes with their eyes shut!

Ivar Vinge stalked up again, his brow furrowed with anxiety, and Stafford nodded wearily and eased the crotch of his trousers with a bent thumb.

"Listen, young feller, she'll be here all right. You better sit down, or you'll be gettin' chilblains."

Ivar glanced at his oxen under a tree across the dusty road. Perhaps he should lead them down to the river again to drink. It was pleasant to think of Bluebell and her calf Dokka in the willow shade beside the creek at home. What a surprise Magdali would get when she saw the calf! He had purposely reserved the news of Dokka's advent so that, if Magdali should suffer dismay at the sight of her new home, she would take cheer in the knowledge that the Vinges possessed two cows now instead of one. Milk and butter for the children had been Magdali's chief concern when Ivar had first proposed venturing into what she regarded as a grim and uncharted wilderness. Curiously enough, once resigned to his decision, she had been disposed to belittle the real hazards they were bound to encounter in their life on the frontier, and make much of the lack of small luxuries and comforts. Ivar smiled in tender reflection on the queries her letters had contained: What sort of water was to be found in the Red River Valley, hard or soft? And how far would they have to drive to the nearest Lutheran church? Dear, pretty Magdali! His heart drummed with impatience while his ears strained again vainly for the first sound of the stagecoach on the trail from the south.

After leading his oxen down the river bank to drink, he stood and watched three or four barges being poled downward with the slow current along the opposite shore. Earlier in the day, the stern-wheeler *International* had splendidly churned up the golden water in her wake, her whistle blowing a shrill greeting to the handful of people who watched her go by. Along her gleaming rail had stood eager-faced men, women, and children, settlers bound for the new province of Manitoba. Ivar, standing apart from Stafford and the others along the shore, had waved his big straw hat at the passengers, and when they had waved back with rollicking shouts he had felt an odd tightening in his breast. Where they had come from and what fate awaited them at their journey's end, he could not know; but for those moments of their passing down the bright, slow river, their life was mystically his life; for both they and he were joined now in the will of the river, to survive or die upon the bounty of its soil.

When he went back to the station, Gresham, the sutler, crawled out from beneath his wagon, yawning prodigiously and blinking against the sunlight. He scratched his left armpit in a morose quest for a sand flea, then cast a melancholy eye at the load of goods on his wagon. He turned and ran an appraising glance over Ivar.

"There's a half-dollar in it for you, brother, if you'll haul them boxes into Stafford's place for me," he offered.

"Gresham, you're the laziest man this side of hell!" Stafford burst out suddenly from his bench.

Gresham squinted at the agent. "I've hauled that load forty miles—and I've got another sixteen to go with a box of dried apples for Fuller, up to Georgetown. I've a damned good mind not to do it! He can get his truck by boat after this and pay the freight."

"And save himself money!" Stafford grunted.

The sutler stepped toward Stafford and looked down at him

with something like contempt. "Listen, you toadstool! I'm gettin' spot cash off'n you for this load. I ain't settlin' on no crooked game o' pinochle, like the last time. That buttermilk grog o' your'n put me clean out o' my head for three days. When I think back on it now—"

Stafford yanked angrily at his trousers. "Nobody forced you to drink it."

"You promised to give me the receep for that grog, too," Gresham reminded him, then turned to Ivar again. "I'll make it a dollar, partner—an honest-to-God dollar—if you'll shift them boxes for me."

Ivar had been staring down the trail to the southward. He had taken his heavy silver watch from his shirt pocket, and was winding it needlessly with the key on its chain. It was only a matter of ten hours between the halfway house and Burbank, the journey commencing long before sunrise. What could have happened? A tipsy driver . . . horses frightened by a bear lumbering out of the brush . . . the sudden illness of one of the children, of Magdali herself! He gnawed at his lip and spoke politely to Gresham.

"I will unload it for you," he said.

In a quarter of an hour he had transferred the boxes and bales to the storeroom at the back of the depot, and Gresham gratefully handed him two half-dollars. It seemed to Ivar a disproportionate amount for so little work, but the sutler sleepily waved aside his protests and crawled back again under the wagon.

Stafford's rangy, wooden-faced wife emerged from the tavern and shaded her eyes with her hand.

"The stage is outrageous late," she observed in a shrill, peevish voice. "I've had the stew on now two hours longer'n need of been, keepin' the fire goin' in this tarnation heat! Donahue like as not got drunk somewhere down the line and throwed the whole shebang into the crick!"

Ivar went pale, but Stafford fanned the air toward his wife's rear with a gesture of rich derision. "Don't listen to her. What she hates most about this place is there ain't a graveyard handy —just to look at."

Across the prairie air that shimmered like hot tin came the prolonged blast of the stagecoach bugle. Ivar's heart leaped, and an involuntary cry of relief sprang from his lips. Scarcely aware of what he did, he took half a dozen bounding steps down the dusty trail, and then laughed shamefacedly as he returned to where Stafford was sitting.

"Take it easy, partner," the agent said. "She's a couple o' miles off yet, and Donahue ain't one to lather his nags."

A wiry, long-limbed man driving a yoke of oxen ridiculously hitched to a fringe-topped surrey approached from the open prairie to the northeast, where there was no road.

"Hello, Ole!" Stafford greeted the man as he jumped, red-faced and sweating, from the vehicle. "Keep your shirt on. That off ox looks like he might be in for a heart attack any minute."

Ole Sondstrom and his brother Pete had taken up land on the Buffalo River. Ole had sent south for his wife and had been expecting her every day for the past week.

"Heart attack, bedam!" Ole spluttered. "He was stuck in a muskeg this morning, an' I near broke his damn' neck tryin' to haul him out!"

Suddenly the stage lurched around the poplar bend in the trail, the four horses careening forward as if catapulted out of an explosion of dust, the stage itself shuddering at last to a standstill in front of the station.

"Good Friday!" Stafford ejaculated, his eyes bulging. "Donahue *must* be drunk!"

But Donahue was sobriety itself. He leaped down from his

[42]

seat in front of the brown and yellow coach, and as Ivar hurried forward, straining his eyes to catch a glimpse of the passengers behind the small windows, he saw that the driver's face was gray with sweat and dust, and that there was a glitter wild and not quite sane in his eyes. In the instant Donahue threw open the coach door, Ivar saw Magdali's radiantly smiling face at the window. He could have wept with relief. Whatever the distress of the driver, it had nothing to do with Magdali and the children. In a moment, Magdali stepped down, her little flowered straw bonnet unbelievably askew. In her arms there was a bundle swathed in a woolen shawl.

"Be careful, Ivar!" she cried gaily, restraining his embrace. "It's a baby I have here!"

Magdali was a little island of sunny calm, while around her everybody was talking at once and getting into the way of everybody else. Ivar had taken little Magdis from the arms of a silvery-haired, flustered gentleman, and was holding young Karsten's hand when Stafford and Ole Sondstrom carefully lifted a woman on a makeshift pallet out of the coach. On her face was a weary but blissful smile.

In his astonishment, Ivar had barely time to glance at his two children. Little Magdis, flatteringly, seemed to remember him, while Karsten clung to his legs with wild joy.

Mrs. Stafford, clucking to herself, bustled indoors to carry out Magdali's orders. Ivar, forgotten now in the confusion, drew away and sat on a bench, his two children clambering over him.

Gresham, yawning and rubbing his eyes, approached from his wagon. "Anybody special come in on the stage?" he asked.

"Ya," Ivar replied. "A new generation for America, on the Red River of the North!"

Low voices came from the inner room of the Stafford place, and among them Ivar could distinguish the voice of his wife, soothing yet forceful. Across the bobbing heads of Karsten and Magdis, he saw the other passengers who had got down from the coach: the stooping, white-haired gentleman who had held Magdis in his arms, and a modish young lady who cast her eyes about, settling them as if by accident upon Ivar.

The gentleman ventured forward and said diffidently, "You are—you must be Mr. Vinge."

"Ya, that I am!" Ivar replied.

"Your wife acquitted herself nobly when Mrs. Sondstrom's baby was born along the trail. A very notable experience indeed! We live in a remarkable time, sir. You have two very fine children there, Mr. Vinge."

"Yes," said Ivar modestly. "I have not seen them since spring. The boy, he know me. And the girl—I think she remember my clock chain!"

The young lady, scarcely more than a girl, stood back a little in her drape-fronted skirt and bustle of lavender bombazine and held tightly to the elderly man's arm. "Oh, papa, how adorable!" she exclaimed. "Is he a *pioneer?*"

The dignified gentleman frowned on his daughter and said nothing, but the girl laughed in a friendly fashion and said to Ivar, "This is our first long journey—from eastern Canada. Father has an appointment in the new province of Manitoba, and we're going to live there." With a naughty laugh at her father, she added, "I'm going to take a peep at the baby."

"Frances," her father rumbled, "your conduct is unseemly, to say the least. We have some hours between supper here—if we are fortunate enough to get it—and bed at Georgetown. Please do not make a disturbance until—"

"Very well, father," Frances sighed. "I should have gone down to the river with Miss Kate. But just think of all I'm going to write in my diary!"

Magdali appeared in the doorway then, her bonnet off and

[44]

her smooth, sun-colored hair tidily imprisoned in a chignon at the nape of her neck. A great white apron, borrowed from Mrs. Stafford, enveloped her bright blue linsey dress entirely except for the tight long sleeves and the prim round collar at which was fastened a gold Norwegian brooch wrought with many little pendant concave disks that tinkled musically when she moved. Her eyes were the exact summery blue of her dress. She had a faintly arched, fine nose, delicately curved brows beneath a high, white forehead, and small, straight teeth which her smile only rarely disclosed, so properly did she control the plump redness of her mouth. The bright rose strain of the North looked almost artificial in the transparent whiteness of her skin. Her neck was rather short, and to correct this she held her head always tilted upward and a little to one side, giving the impression that she was ever alert for some half-expected sound. The posture gave her also a rapt and charmingly absent-minded appearance which was misleading, for Magdali was never unaware of what was going on about her. Her feet were pretty, and her sense of decorum did not extend to any undue concealment of them—especially when they were shod in soft, bright leather. In repose Magdali's hands were not graceful, even though they were small; her thumbs were somewhat clubbed, the fingers blunt. But except when she slept, her hands were seldom in repose. Their swift and dexterous movements in the tasks of the day lent them a vital intelligence of their own, something almost apart from Magdali herself. Her hands were like small and efficient machines, and no one could think of them as ugly.

Ivar had risen when Magdali appeared in the doorway, and he stepped forward with an impetuous word on his lips. But Magdali checked him, smiling, and said:

"You can all come in now. Ivar, do not tramp too loud in those hobnails. The mother sleeps, but you can see the little girl all washed and swaddled. She is a beautiful little baby! I gave her warm barley water in the bottle, and she drank it good, poor little thing. She is some weeks early, but she is strong, and with the hot stones I put under in her basket, she will be all right. The people are Swedes, Ivar, from Iowa. Sondstrom is their name. They are settled east of us, on the Buffalo River. You didn't know we have good neighbors only ten miles away, Ivar?"

At the humorous reproof in Magdali's voice, Ivar flushed.

"Might be," he laughed, "I was working too hard to see so far. But—it is good to have neighbors."

Then the children grasped him by the legs, clamoring in shrill voices that they wanted to go and "pink-pink." Their appeal to him in this urgent need made Ivar grin with almost fatuous pleasure, but as he stooped to lift little Magdis his wife said primly, "I'll take care of her. Karsten, you go with papa." The color in Magdali's cheeks had deepened, and she kept her eyes averted from the strangers who stood about. *Herre Gud,* Ivar thought, abashed, I've forgotten all about Magdali's sense of propriety! I'll have to learn all over again.

Karsten was running ahead of him along the lengthening tree shadows on the river bank when Ivar saw the girl seated alone there in the dappled light beneath a great elm. She must have come off the stage with the others, but in all that to-do it was not strange that he had failed to notice her when she strolled away by herself. She was in her early twenties, Ivar judged, and was dressed in a simple flowered dimity laced tightly at her slender waist. Her dreaming attitude said plainly that she had come here to be alone, and Ivar would have retreated hastily had she not just then turned her eyes upward and full upon him. He could do nothing now but stand confusedly and stare at those long, deep-lidded eyes that were dark and moistly blue as rain on a horizon.

"I didn't know you was here," he said apologetically.

The grave friendliness of her smile was a relief to Ivar, even before he heard her melodious, soft voice.

"I came to look at the river. And I thought one less in there" —she nodded toward the station—"might help a little."

"That is right," Ivar agreed. "So I come too, with my boy."

"Your wife delivered Mrs. Sondstrom's baby," was the girl's next remark, so simply uttered that she might have been speaking of the weather. Ivar couldn't believe his ears, though he felt them reddening. For a young girl to mention— "You are Mr. Vinge, aren't you?"

"Yes, Ivar Vinge is my name."

"I am with the young lady you saw back there. My name is Kate Shaleen. I am engaged to travel with her and her father and spend a few months helping them to get settled in Canada, but I'm really going for the adventure. You see"—she laughed roguishly—"I'm really a schoolmarm, and we always think we ought to see a little of life before we settle down. We don't always do it, though."

Ivar did not know what to make of it, and before he could reply she had glanced at the shining river and was asking him, "Why do they call it the Red River, when it's really yellow?"

"They tell me it is red," said Ivar with extreme care, "down at La Grande Fourche, where the Red Lake River flows into this one. I have it marked on my map."

The girl laughed. "Have you never heard the true story of it, Mr. Vinge? An Indian brave once killed his sweetheart in Red Lake, and since then the water from it has always flowed like blood." Her expression changed to sober earnestness. "Do you believe that?"

Ivar felt silly and not a little annoyed. What right had even a schoolteacher to play upon his credulity? His eyes upon little Karsten, who was exploring a wild plum thicket, he replied

[47]

noncommittally, "Might be so. For children."

"Oh, but we must believe strange things, Mr. Vinge! We can afford to deny things that everyone else believes, but— Well, for instance"—she inclined her dark head with the coppery gleams in it toward the opposite shore—"there will be a great city over there one day, or maybe here where we are now. Strange things will happen among the people who will be born here. I believe in dreams and in fortune-telling and— no, of course not, I don't *believe* in them at all!" She laughed huskily, as if to herself, as if she were alone in this land she had never seen before. But then she got to her feet, and Ivar saw that she was taller than he had believed her to be. The low sun flashed across her hair, threading its darkness with unbelievable shades of gold and purple. It wasn't like hair at all, he thought in surprise, but more like some strange, unheard-of metal. He wondered what sensation a man would have running his hand over it. . . .

"It's a crazy river!" the girl said. "It runs north. A gypsy woman once told me that my fate was waiting beside a river that runs north. Should I believe that, do you think?"

"Ya—sure!" Ivar smiled, not to be singed this time. "So I believe things too!"

"It cannot be, and so—it *will* be!" She stood still, looking away from him into the dazzle of light and water. "That is why I have left my sister and brother and my father in St. Paul, and come away alone. I shall go back to them again, of course. But maybe we'll come—all of us—to this prairie. This is mine. I feel it—*here!*" She touched her breast, long, slender fingers spread, and did not look at Ivar.

A sound of renewed commotion came from the direction of Stafford's place, and Ivar started as if he had been rudely awakened from a dream.

"Karsten!" he called sharply to his son. "*Kom, du!*"

[48]

Why on God's green earth, he wondered, should he suddenly feel so relieved to get away from this girl who called herself Kate Shaleen, and who talked like one bewitched? He was glad to know that she was going to Canada, even though she threatened to come back some day. Oh, well, it was a strange land he had come to, and he might expect to meet strange people in it. Besides, there was surely room for everybody in a country where as yet there was almost nobody.

He hurried away, holding his son Karsten tightly by the hand.

III

HERE was the endless flat of the prairie and twilight brushing softly over it, while above the faint shine of the marsh water fireflies struck their brief, cool glow, and the upper air was swift with the dark wheeling of night hawks.

Beside the luggage on the wagon floor, the children slept, wrapped in a patchwork quilt. Magdali sat beside Ivar on the wagon seat, her lace-mittened hands clasping and unclasping as she gazed about her with spirited interest. The drowsy rhythm of the plodding oxen, the blurred and dreamful outline of their heavy wooden yoke, would have had upon a woman of a different nature a stilling effect after so long and arduous a day. But Magdali sat sharply alert to exclaim upon each new feature of the land as they neared their home.

Her energy, Ivar thought with a fond smile, was enough to put a good man to shame. She had told him of how, alone except for the willing but rather ignorant help of young Miss Shaleen, she had attended Mrs. Sondstrom at the birth of her little daughter in the shadow of a sumac bush, while the stage waited at a decent distance. She had told him in words that had made it all seem as nothing!

It was odd, Ivar reflected, that the Shaleen girl had said nothing about her own modest share in the event. She had taken no small part in it, apparently, as Magdali disclosed. She had swung the baby up by its feet, spanked it to its first yammer, and laid it flat on the ground while Magdali knotted a clean crochet thread about the navel cord at the proper distance and cut it. After that, Miss Shaleen wrapped the baby up in a sheet while Magdali looked after the mother. Then Magdali signaled to the men in the stagecoach, and after that Miss Shaleen seemed to be no part of the strange journey whatever. She sat looking dreamily out of the window until they reached Burbank.

"Look there, Ivar!" Magdali cried out now, pointing to a faint rise of land where trees darkened against the evening. "There would be a fine place for a homestead. Roald would like that, real good!"

The name of Roald Bratland, Magdali's bachelor brother, who, it appeared, intended to come to the Valley, made Ivar wince under his good-natured laugh. Wasn't Roald well enough off on his brother Karsten's farm in Wisconsin—in which he had a share? Of Roald's plan Ivar had had no inkling until Magdali's arrival. He suspected drily that she had kept it from him because she knew he could barely tolerate that monkey-spry, purse-tight brother of hers! With Roald's farming, however, Ivar had no quarrel—the man was shrewd and conscientious, and would no doubt make a good settler in this new country.

"We will have plenty time to look around," he said cheerfully. "The land, it will not run away, Magdi!"

"It will not run away, Ivar, but others will run here to take it, you will see," she said, lapsing into Norwegian and straightening her shoulders with an impatience that made him laugh again.

He put his arm about her with a sense almost of shyness: her firm, high breast yielded a little within the tight confinement of her basque.

"Let us not talk of land now, *kjaere*," he said in a low, stumbling voice. "See—over there by the willows—that is our house!"

There was still enough light for Magdali to discern the

[51]

shaggy silhouette of the stable and the log cabin thrust out from the sod house as from an anchorage of clay and grass.

While Ivar helped her down from the wagon, anxiously holding his breath for her first word, she stared beyond him with eyes transfixed and unflinching. Then she stood utterly still, one short-fingered hand pressing her bodice, and Ivar had a disconcerting recollection of the girl on the river bank, standing in an attitude similar but how essentially different! During those seconds Ivar felt numb and helpless; for now, through Magdali's eyes, he really saw the crude pathos of this structure he had called "home." The feverish days of toil he had put into its building counted for nothing now, while she stood as if stricken.

So suddenly then that Ivar jerked back with a start, she swung toward him, grasping his arm while her clear, decisive little laugh rang out. Twice before he had heard her laugh just that way. In the moonlit snow in Norway, when he had first had the audacity to kiss her and she had looked up at him and said, "Then we are promised, Ivar, and we shall be married and go to America!" Again, during the storm in mid-Atlantic, when he had been so anxious for her, and she had said, "Ivar, I would go on ten wedding journeys to get to America! It is the land of the future—but to be married first! I would not go just to live with brother Karsten and be *tante* to his children. I want many of my own—in America!" Their first, he knew, would be born in America. Magdali was already with child.

She laughed now. "It is *this* we have here, then, Ivar!" she said, in the old language. "Well, it might be less, and we shall make more of it. You have done well—do not be hurt if at first I seem surprised." She reached up and quickly kissed him. "Come, let us carry the children indoors first, and then the chests."

It wasn't quite as he had wanted it. He had wished that the children might be left to sleep for a moment while he and Magdali stepped together across the threshold of this, their first home apart from all others. But it seemed that the way of it must be otherwise, and now he strangely had no will in the matter, feeling only empty and foolish with an unreasonable disappointment.

"Wait till I get the lamp lit," he said. "The children may be dark-scared." He spoke in Norwegian, reflecting that tomorrow and from then on Magdali would insist on English. She wasn't so perfect herself, just yet, either!

He swung up the outer bolt of the cabin door, carefully struck a phosphorus match and held it so that it would not be wasted, and then lighted the kerosene lamp on the bare golden-oak table beside the door. Kerosene was too costly for every-day use, but on this special occasion he had hidden in a cupboard the clumsy and malodorous whale-oil lamp with its frowsy wick. As the clean flame sprang up into the shining lamp chimney, the shadowed room livened before his hasty glance. The red and blue flowers on the glass belly of the lamp were bright enough, but the brilliant tiger lilies Ivar had picked from the prairie grassland that morning and placed in a jug of water on the table looked sere and puckered. Still, Magdali would surely know that he had meant well!

Out of doors, he met her carrying the baby.

"No, no!" She waved him away, whispering, "I'll put her straight in bed. You get Karsten—he is waking. Then take the horsehair trunk that has the clean sheets in it, and I'll put them on the beds."

"I washed the blankets on the beds yesterday—" Ivar began.

"Sh, sh!"

Ivar walked thoughtfully to the wagon where his son was

dangling halfway over a wheel. He caught the boy up, felt really for the first time the sturdy heft of him, and laughed. "You and me, Karsten, we make good *jordbrugere*, hey? Good farmers!"

IV

THE thing about Magdali, Ivar marveled when late the next afternoon he came in from milking to a fine supper of partridge baked in cream, new potatoes, fresh *lefsa*, and fruit soup made of the wild plums and gooseberries that grew thick in the river timber, was the way she could get a thousand tasks done while a man for a moment had his back turned. The two windows of the log room fairly bristled with the starched white of muslin curtains edged with crocheted lace, and upon the square golden-oak table there was a red wool tapestry bordered in an old-country pattern of blue and green and yellow. A braided rag mat covered the middle of the floor, the oak planks of which were still not as smooth as Ivar had tried to plane them. There were Hardanger doilies and pillow covers, and snowy fringed spreads on the big walnut-framed bed and the children's trundle across the room. On one wall hung a lithograph of the Nativity, on another a wire holder a foot and a half square which supported rows of photographs of Magdali's relatives and his own, as well as one of Dwight Lyman Moody and one of Abraham Lincoln. Interspersed among these likenesses were little rosettes of bright ribbon, baubles from Christmas trees, and gilded pine cones. On the table lay an English and a Norwegian Bible, a Norwegian *salmebog*, and the *Fairy Tales* of Hans Christian Andersen. The high, narrow, cast-iron stove with its lower and upper shelves for cooking, and its ornately wrought back, gleamed from Magdali's polishing. The étagé stove was Magdali's great pride—a wedding present she had brought with her from the Old Country—and Ivar had not dared to tell her what it had cost him in freight charges to fetch it all the way here to the Valley. She would presently ask, of course, but he might as well put off the evil hour as long as possible.

The soddy behind the log room would be used, Magdali had decided, for her own work of washing and ironing, preparing meals, churning, candle-dipping, soap-making, spinning—when Ivar got himself some sheep for wool—as well as for everyday living, so that there would be a "best room" for Sundays and holidays. No matter how small the house, there must be a "best room." She would use her good stove in there for fancy cooking, since already she had got the knack of the clay-dobie oven and had not once fretted at its spit of heat. It would be a fine thing, she said, on the bitter days of winter to see the iron pot hanging from its cross-bar, dried-pea soup and smoked summer sausage simmering in it! She had brought firm lengths of summer sausage with her, swathed in cotton cloth with two ham loins she herself had cured and kept sweet in the cold-cellar at her brother Karsten's farm since the beginning of last winter. With the cow's milk—and what a delight the cow and the little heifer had been to Magdali!—the Vinges would want for nothing all this autumn and winter. Ivar's carrots and turnips were a stout pleasure to behold, and in the root cellar to one side of the stable they would keep for months on end.

All this flashed through Ivar's mind as he approached the front door that second evening, and then from the kitchen he heard Magdali cry out in English.

"Next time, Ivar, you come by the side door, in here! I told you this morning, we shall keep the other room for best. See, I have Karsten and Magdis playing outside where I can watch them."

Ivar came forward, sniffed at the food cooking, then smiled and put his arm about Magdali's calicoed slim waist.

"Next time," he said with mock solemnity, "I remember to come in *there*." He pointed, and while Magdali looked over her shoulder he tweaked the lobe of her ear and with a sudden rush of feeling gathered her into his arms.

"Such foolishness!" she cried, bridling rosily. "We are old married people, Ivar. Go away—get in the children—and I'll dish up."

He stepped outside again and met young Karsten, who came leaping about his legs. Ivar swung his boy up by both arms and held him on his shoulder. It was then that a sound smote his ears like the thin and long-drawn wail of some mythical monster in mortal agony.

The boy's eyes went wide, and Ivar's fancy livened with a curious thrill. He had heard of the half-breed drivers of the fur brigades that traveled from Canada to St. Paul, as many as a hundred carts at a time. It was said that on a still evening like this you could hear the strident rumor of them long before they became a reality to the eye.

It was something to stand and wonder at, especially when you had a son of your own who would one day remember it and would tell how his father had held him high on his shoulder while they both listened on a breathless evening in summer. The boy was gazing solemnly now, out across the ripe and golden flow of the prairie grass where the thin screech of the caravan was growing ever more loud and vibrant.

"That, my son," said Ivar at the child's look of wonder and near alarm, "is something you would not hear if it was in Norway you were born. It is the Red River cart brigade. It might be that it is them that soon must go forever! And it might be, if you try hard, you remember it when you are a grown man."

Ivar listened intently. The carriers were cutting across his land, to camp on his creek, perhaps. Magdali must see this. He would have time to eat supper, pen up the oxen and the cow,

[57]

and take his little family to the shallow broadening of the creek where the old three-rutted trail showed the fording place.

Magdali had come to the dooryard where little Magdis was busily burying her rag doll in a clay grave. She caught the child up and stared whitely at Ivar.

"Is it Indians?" she asked on a breath.

"No," Ivar laughed. "It is the fur brigade from Canada. It is something you must see, Magdi. When we've had supper we'll walk up the creek and meet them."

"If you go, you go alone," Magdali said. "I have no time to run after fur brigades. They sound more like a band of robbers, these cart men. Come now, let us eat!"

"I wanna see fur b'igades!" Karsten stormed suddenly, and in a firm tone Ivar replied, "You will. You'll go with papa."

Magdali's expression was blankly aloof, and though Ivar tried to re-establish the warmth of a few minutes ago, their first evening meal in the new home was marred by this exasperating petty difference that had come between them. They ate almost in silence, and when Karsten had piped the after-grace, Ivar took him by the hand and went outdoors. Magdali said nothing.

Dusk was already staining the land with violet when Ivar and his son seated themselves on a hummock above the little stream and waited for the caravan to arrive. The first unit had almost come to the creek's edge, but the shriek of those that followed seemed to Ivar to be making vocal the awesome loneliness of this prairie. It brought to mind those nights of his boyhood when, solitary, far up on the mountain at the *saeter* cabin during the summer grazing time, he had heard the raucous cry of herons over some mist-washed tarn.

"Look, papa!" Karsten shouted. "There is houses coming, an' elephants!"

Ivar gave a shuddering laugh as he clapped his hands to his

[58]

ears, then gathered the boy in his arms and stood up to watch the oncoming caravan. The units, eight or ten carts to a driver, were clearly discernible now, each animal tied to the cart in front, the driver riding alongside on horseback.

The first unit, led by a raw-boned ox, had come within hailing distance of Ivar, and he could see that the half-breed managing it had jet-black hair that hung to his shoulders. He wore moccasins and was equipped with a short whip secured to his wrist by a thong, a muzzle-loading shotgun slung across his back, a powder horn and shot bag at his waist. He was clad in coarse blue cloth belted gaudily with a sash of bright red flannel and glittering with polished brass buttons. On his wild-locked head was a small cap rakishly atilt. In a language unknown to Ivar, the man's shouts rang out harshly musical above the clamor of the vehicles. The brigade came to a halt.

Promptly a tall, spare-limbed white man astride a black horse crossed the creek. His sharp commands were those of a leader. Two other white men of lesser countenance, similarly mounted, came with him, both prodigiously armed with pistols in leather holsters.

It astonished Ivar to learn that his presence beside the hazel thicket on the creek bank was known, since nobody had glanced in his direction. But now the tall, light-haired leader dismounted and advanced toward him with a grave and courteous smile, removing his broad-brimmed hat and extending his hand.

"My name is Julian Fordyce," he announced.

Ivar took the man's hand. "I am Ivar Vinge."

"You have taken this land, sir?"

"It is mine," Ivar said.

"We have seen your plowed field and your house yonder," the stranger continued in precise English. "We do not wish to intrude, but we have been coming this way for a long time, and it has been our habit to stop here at the crossing for the night. We have done better than twenty miles today, the animals are dragging, and the men are hungry. If you have no objection—"

At the man's bow and the white smile of his teeth, Ivar said in surprise, "For why should I have objection? You are welcome!" He spoke slowly and carefully so that the *w* should not sound like a *v*. He felt himself in distinguished company. This stranger must be in his twenties still, and Ivar was reminded of the tweed-clothed, mannerly Englishmen who used to spend their holidays shooting ptarmigan in the mountains of Norway.

"Thank you," said the man. "I shall give the order to cross over and pitch camp." He turned and spoke quickly to one of his men. "This is your son, of course?" he added, looking down at Karsten.

"He is my son Karsten."

"Your wife is with you?"

"My wife is in the house," Ivar told him.

"If you have not yet had supper, perhaps you would join us," Julian Fordyce invited. "Our fare is rough, but—"

"Many thanks," said Ivar, smiling, "but I have had supper."

Little Karsten had wandered a few yards off and stood beside one of the carts, looking wonderingly up at the queerly dressed man with the bright buttons and the long black hair, who was pouring something from a bottle and rubbing it about the head and ears of the lead ox.

"Ze m'squeet," he said gravely, "she bite fierce. She mak blood, *voyez!*" He smiled down at Karsten. "You nice leetle feller, *oui?* You lak seet on my pony?"

To Karsten's delight, he found himself hoisted into the saddle, and the bridle rein placed in his chubby hands. The driver kept his arm about him while he urged the pony gently for-

[60]

ward five or six paces and the boy sat in blissful excitement.

"Armand is good with children," Fordyce said. "He has only fourteen of his own, to the best of his knowledge."

At that moment Ivar saw the flicker of Magdali's light-blue dress along the line of wagons. He heard his own name called shrilly, then Karsten's. Before he could move a step toward her, Magdali had seen the boy on the stocky little horse, had sprung forward and, her face blanched with anger, had seized the child and dragged him from the saddle, almost falling backward as she did so.

She was panting with fear and rage when Ivar and Julian Fordyce came up to her. But she had already turned upon Armand.

"You would dare—take hold of my boy!" she gasped. "You do not think he might fall off, such a small boy! Dirt, too, and sickness, maybe—"

"Magdali!" Reddening to the ears, Ivar grasped her arm and took the surprised and indignantly howling Karsten from her. "It was meant well—and it was fun for the boy." With helpless chagrin he saw the cool and sympathetic amusement on the face of Julian Fordyce.

"Madam, I am very sorry," Fordyce apologized, but Magdali did not look at him. She was flaring at Ivar.

"You do not know how to do with your own child? If you want to stay here, I will take Karsten home."

Anger mounted in a sudden burning to Ivar's eyes. "Take him, then. I will stay a little."

Magdali glanced in swift disapproval at the bizarrely clad drivers who had come up from their carts and were taking in the scene with jaunty interest. Then she seized Karsten by the hand and led him away through the long pale grass that flickered about her swaying skirts like brittle spears in the twilight.

To relieve the embarrassment which Ivar knew the stranger

[61]

must feel, he waved his hand toward the creek. "This place is yours when you come here," he said. "My wife, she does not understand."

"Thank you, Mr. Vinge," Fordyce replied gratefully, and set about giving orders.

The camp that grew before Ivar's eyes was a stirring spectacle he would remember if he lived to be a hundred. Almost before he could realize it, a dozen swarthy drivers were grouped about a roaring fire, each with a long stick tipped with steel upon which was impaled a dripping, hissing lump of meat that gave off a rank and oily aroma. From the great iron pot that nested in the embers, a smell of strange herbs assailed Ivar's nostrils—not unpleasant, but too foreign to be inviting. Ringed beyond the fire were the grotesque, top-heavy shadows of the carts with their precious freight of furs, and beyond them the sullen, sleepy-eyed oxen grazed and the sturdy ponies took their fill of the rich grass. Presently a plaintive *voyageur* ballad was begun, with a rhythmic swaying of the men's bodies as they sang. Incomprehensible as the words were to Ivar, the song was still one of wandering and homelessness that the heart could understand, and he was moved by the certainty that he was witnessing a thing that time would soon banish forever. As if they were already ghosts of a forgotten trail, the men did not even glance up to acknowledge Ivar's presence.

Julian Fordyce came back presently with two tin cups of steaming hot tea in his hands. "You will have tea with me, I hope. There's a spot of rum in it."

Ivar took the cup and sat down, savoring the hot liquid slowly and staring into the fire.

"Well, my friend, you have come at last," Julian Fordyce observed as he seated himself beside Ivar.

"Ya—I have come from *Wis*-consin," Ivar replied, conscious that his reply must seem irrelevant.

[62]

Fordyce laughed. "It doesn't matter where you come from," he said slowly. "I have been looking for you for a long time."

"For me?"

"Someone like you. I do not welcome you much, because I am a selfish man, Vinge, steeped in self-pity, and I had found a way of life that pleased me, and I wanted it to last."

"You are from England, I think," Ivar ventured.

"Yes. I might still be in England, except for an argument I had one evening with milord, my elder brother—and he sent me away on the next boat to Canada. It was the only kind thing he ever did for me, even though he didn't intend it as a kindness."

"Your brother, he is a lord?" Ivar said.

"Oh, quite! With a monocle and a paunch—and gout to come."

He tossed the dregs of his cup into the fire and called to one of his men near by to fill the cup again and top it with a measure of rum from the bottle that stood beside his effects on the ground where his blankets had already been spread. Ivar politely declined a second cup.

"You have it good, there in Canada?" Ivar asked.

The other mused for a while. "I have, indeed. The Company took me over and sent me north—to Norway House. There I met a girl with eyes blue-black as grapes on a vine, and hair like the mane of a wild horse. Slim and beautiful—half Scotch, half Cree. She died a few years ago, when my son Alec was born. Her Cree mother had put a curse on her for marrying an outcast Englishman. That's pride for you, my friend! But my son lives—tall, blue-eyed, but with his mother's beautifully savage hair. I was happy for a while at least, and that is more than my good brother will ever be, with his perpetually frost-bitten wife. Besides—I have my son!"

The handsome young fellow had spoken very much like a

[63]

written book, Ivar thought, a little tense from his effort to miss no part of his meaning.

"It is good to have a son," he said.

Fordyce seemed to catch himself up suddenly. "I am making myself tiresome. I talk this way sometimes when I am alone."

The sadness of the man's voice perplexed Ivar. "Sometimes a man talks better when he is alone," he said awkwardly. "Me, it would be better if I could speak so much as I understand."

Fordyce laughed and took a sip from his refilled cup. "I'd say you do extraordinarily well."

"My wife, she does much better," Ivar said. "She learned a little French, even. She went to *Dame Skolen*—lady's school—in Norway."

"How did you happen to come here?" Fordyce asked.

Ivar clasped his hands over his knees and looked into the fire. "My father has a farm near Bergen. It is my brother who will own the farm, because he is older. But one day, I think, he will not own it. The big owners get all." Certainly a man like Julian Fordyce would know about the struggles between the peasants and the moneyed men even in a little country like Norway! "My wife, Magdali, her father, he is a big owner. On Easter, we have skiing on our mountain, and Magdali come to our farm —from her father's farm down the valley. She is small and pretty, and she is two year older than me. But she cannot ski so good, so I show her, so we fall down together in the deep snow, in the moonlight, and all the mountains are blue and high far over. So—we get married and come to America."

"From a snow bank in Norway—to the banks of the Red River!" Fordyce laughed heartily. He took out his pipe. "Do you smoke?"

Ivar cleared his throat in embarrassment. "Tobacco is too much at the post, and I have no more left of the package I brought with me."

[64]

"Well—damme!" Fordyce hastily fished another pipe from his pocket and tossed his leather tobacco pouch into Ivar's hands. "Help yourself, my friend!"

Ivar packed the pipe and drew a flaming twig from the fire. He inhaled deeply of the pipe's sweetness and sat back in more supreme content than he had known for weeks. "You will come this way again?" he asked.

"For a while—but not for long. You are one of the first who will come to remove my hapless kind from the face of the earth," Fordyce observed very quietly.

"Re-move?"

"It is nothing against you," Fordyce said promptly. "I mean simply that we shall not be here in a few years. Next year— the year after—there will be a railroad—and there will be more men like you. *We* shall fade out like a sunset. My son and I—" He paused and drew slowly on his pipe. "We shall have to find our place farther north."

"*My* son and I—we shall be here," Ivar said. "I think might be I can grow wheat here. You know some—up north—that grows wheat?"

"They've been growing wheat in Assiniboia since the days of Lord Selkirk," said Fordyce with enthusiasm. "Of course you'll grow wheat. The river has slept for a long time in its sun, but now it is coming awake. You have stirred the soil with your plow, my friend. It will never be the same again. But come—I'll show you the carts!" He sprang to his feet and took Ivar's arm.

They paused before the first cart, upon which the dying light of the drivers' fire still played with erratic spurts. Ivar listened intently while Fordyce explained how the cart was made, almost entirely of oak, its two great wheels rising as high as the fenced body. He noted the width of the unshod felloes, and the huge hub indulged with a girdle of rawhide.

[65]

Wooden pins were the only fastenings. A cart, Fordyce declared, could handle as much as a thousand pounds, and when streams were too deep for fording the great wheels were lashed together and covered with rawhide to make a flat boat on which the cargo was loaded and ferried across. Pelts of mink and marten and fisher, of lynx and fox and wolverine, pressed into bales, were lashed down upon the sturdy wooden frames.

"And now," Fordyce said at last, "if you will come with me, I want to send a little gift to your wife."

From beneath a spread of canvas, the young Englishman drew forth two beautiful dusky skins that gleamed darkly in the firelight.

"These are beaver," he said. "Your wife may like them. I hope I may have the pleasure of meeting her again sometime."

Confusedly, Ivar tried to thank him and to protest in the same breath, but Fordyce grasped his hand. "Good night, sir, and good luck to you. I must have supper and then turn in. We move early."

He turned away, and Ivar stood alone, holding the furs in a bewilderment of disquietude and pleasure. And a strange warmth went with him as he paced slowly back toward home.

He found Magdali waiting for him, the children asleep in bed. He went to her where she sat beside the table and spread the two soft pelts before her, under the light from the lamp.

"These are your gift," he said, "from the man who sleeps tonight by the creek. His name is Julian Fordyce—and his brother is a lord—in England."

"So?" said Magdali, and arched her brows as she looked at the furs. "They are very nice. Perhaps too much pay, even, for the night he camps on our land. Maybe you told him so, Ivar?" She laughed and touched his cheek with a playful finger —and he had feared that when he came home she might not even speak to him! When would he ever really know his Magdali? "But you will learn, my Ivar," she went on, "you will learn we have land here—solid gold!"

"But he did not mean the furs as pay—and I would not ask—"

Magdali's eyes were on the pelts as she interrupted him. "Yes, a collar for you out of one, on your winter coat. The other for me—and Karsten may have it when he grows bigger. Or maybe for Roald when he comes to us."

For a moment Ivar was silent. Ever since Magdali had spoken of her brother's plan to come west, the thought of Roald Bratland had lain like a cold shadow across his mind and heart. Only during the past hour or so had that shadow lifted as he felt the glow of a new and strange friendship sweep through him.

"Sometimes I think it will not be good for us—that Roald should come here," he said gently. He had never spoken openly against Magdali's brother before.

Her eyes lifted sharply to his face. "Roald is my brother, Ivar," she reminded him. "He has been good to us."

Often Ivar had tried to say things that were somehow beyond any power of words to express, but it had always ended with Magdali laughing at him, while he felt sheepish and futile. The feeling came upon him now, even though she had not laughed at him.

He laid his hands over the soft fur upon the table. He did not want to speak of Roald Bratland just now. He did not want to think of him. He was thinking rather of all the wilderness springs and summers and deep winters in a far northern land from which these furs had come.

One other thought stole upon him, almost without his knowing. It was a memory, rather—the memory of a bright sweep of dark hair, golden-flecked in the sunlight, and of himself wondering what it would be like to lay his hand softly over it—as he was now laying his hand softly over the fur that shone under the light from the lamp.

And because he felt there was some hint of disloyalty even in cherishing such a memory, Ivar stooped and pressed his lips against his wife's sun-colored hair.

V

On a day in late October, when Ivar had finished backsetting the two acres on which he meant to experiment with his wheat next spring, Magdali's brother drove into the yard from the south trail.

Roald Bratland arrived in impressive style, erect upon the seat of a new green wagon, canvas-topped, and drawn by a pair of deep-chested, dapple-gray work horses. Ivar's feelings as he went forward to meet his brother-in-law were a mixture of amusement and irritation at the critical look Roald cast about him before he extended his hand.

"Well, you're here, then, safe and sound, Roald!" Ivar said cordially. "No trouble along the way?"

Roald was a cautious man. A word must be duly weighed and considered before it was allowed to pass his lips. While he hesitated over his reply, however, his eyes economically took in every feature of the place within view, for time was another commodity not to be trifled with.

"Yes—and no," he replied, judicially. "I bought this outfit in St. Paul. And I had a time of it, Ivar. But they found out they had somebody to deal with before I was through with them. It's a good team, and I had it at my own price, take it or leave it. I'm not so sure about the machinery, under the canvas there. I got it from a Dansker. Oh, ya!" He heaved a sigh. "It rained altogether seven and a half hours on the way. And down by Alexandria, somebody stole a ham while I slept, and the way I had to pay for meals at the stations was *bövelen!*" Characteristically, he had not yet got out of his wagon.

Roald never swore. He looked upon strong language as a kind of extravagance which might eventually impoverish him in some unpredictable way. But he had invented words for his own convenience, to be used as occasion demanded. Thus, *bövelen* was his blameless substitute for "the devil."

Magdali was coming across the yard from the house, the children skipping about her. Her white kerchief billowed out behind her head like a small sail in the brash October wind. Her step was buoyant and proud with the new life she carried, lightly still, within her strong, small body. Ivar felt an unabashed elation at sight of her, and said in a low voice to Roald, "Magdali is so again."

"It is not incredible," Roald muttered in Norwegian, with an approving nod as if in sufferance of the coming event.

"Hello, brother Roald!" Magdali greeted him with a smiling flutter. "Thank God you are safely here. And how is the world treating you, brother?"

Roald got down from his wagon. "I take the world as I find it, sister, and make what I can of it."

"And how did you leave Karsten—and Berta and the family?"

"The sun shines upon Karsten and his family," said Roald tersely. "He thought I went *galen* to sell out my share and come away. But Roald Bratland doesn't wait for apples to fall in his lap. The Lord spoke to Joshua!" With this somewhat enigmatic announcement, his narrowed eyes circled half the horizon.

"Well, the coffee is on," Magdali said briskly. "Come right in when you've unhitched. I have *römme-kolla* and syrup bread—your favorites, Roald. Did you remember to bring the *gjet-ost?* In a hundred miles here there isn't a goat, or I would have made some cheese myself."

"Ya, the cheese is in the wagon, and a crate with five hens

[70]

and a rooster too!"

"No!"

"Ya!" Roald's snuff-brown waistcoat spread above the throb of his own generosity, although less than an hour ago the memory of the two dollars he had parted with for the poultry had been gnawing at his heart, and he had had to comfort himself with the reflection that he loved a fresh egg as dearly as the next one.

When Magdali had gone back to the house, Ivar said anxiously, "I hope you remembered to bring my seed wheat, Roald."

"Ya, that I did. But it is a waste, I think. Everybody I ask along the way say it is a foolishness you think of, this wheat. The land is good only for hay and potatoes."

Ivar grinned. "My oats and barley came out not so bad, for a first crop. Thirty bushels oats each acre! I had to cut with the cradle and thresh with the flail, of course. I'll not raise much wheat till there is a threshing machine near—and a mill, might be. This next spring, I *see* just, how the wheat come up!"

Roald's cluck was skeptical. "Hay and cattle, and a little feed—that's all she's good for, Ivar. In the fall, drive the herd and haul the hay to Alexandria—the whole *spikilik* shebang! That way you make good money."

A great flock of wild ducks passed over just then, heading toward the marsh at the southern limit of Ivar's land.

"You have a plenty game," Roald observed with wary approval.

"More than enough," Ivar assured him. "Grouse and prairie chicken, and duck and goose and wild pigeon by the thousands, Roald. Passenger pigeons, same like we had in Wisconsin, but here there's more yet. People say they used to come over the land like thunder clouds. But south they have been slaughtered for profit—"

[71]

"What I ask about is deer and elk, and so," Roald broke in impatiently.

"Some—but the boats have sent them away from the river here. You must go a day's journey to be sure of venison. But it can be had. Only the buffalo are gone. One big fellow left his bones over there in the field two years ago, and went far into the Dakota territory."

Roald stared at him. "He went—without his bones, you say?"

"Ya, sure!" Ivar laughed. "It was his ghost that went."

"*Bövelen!*" said Roald, contemptuous of Ivar's attempt at humor.

"They still sell pemmican at the post in Georgetown. Makes good soup. You put a drop of holy water in it, and it keeps good for a year."

"*Holy* water?"

"That's what we called ours in Norway, Roald," Ivar said with mock gravity. "You don't remember, hey? Or maybe the Bratlands were brought up different as the Vinges!"

VI

ROALD proved in no hurry to locate his claim. "Marry in haste and repent at leisure"—how true when it came to taking up land! These were strong, bright autumn days for scouting about the country, sometimes behind his team, sometimes afoot with an old smooth-bore musket on his shoulder. Now and then he brought back a brace of partridge or a couple of fat Canada geese, and once when he was gone two days he returned with a five-point whitetail buck in his wagon.

He explored south and east. He visited the Sondstroms, snugly settled in their sod house on Buffalo River, where the baby girl Magdali had assisted into the world was fat as a potato dumpling. He had come upon the Endicotts, who had lived on their pre-empted quarter section for a year and a half and had secured title to their land. They lived in a bleak shanty with a lean-to stable in which were housed a cow you could see through like a picket fence, Roald reported, and a spavined horse. What farm machinery there was looked as if it had got tired out with sitting so long in one place and staring at the prairie that had scarcely been turned.

"They are the weak ones," Magdali observed. "In the end, someone else will take what they have now, and they will be left with nothing. It is the way of things. Doesn't the Bible say, 'To him that hath shall be given, and to him that hath not—'"

"Ya, it is so!" Roald exclaimed.

Ivar heard, but made no comment. He could make none. He could never tell Magdali what he felt was wrong about it.

Bad luck had dogged the Endicotts, of course. No sooner

[73]

had Charlie Endicott got the patent for his land, than he had the misfortune to break his leg while digging a well. His wife, a frail woman with lung trouble, had tried doing the farm work as well as looking after her husband and her three small children, but it had been too much for her. Roald had advised them to clear out of the country before winter set in, but the cool, clear autumn weather had brought a return of something like health to Mrs. Endicott, and she had begged her husband to stay until spring and try again. She wanted to see the pasque flowers blue once more on the wide and grassy prairie, she said. Roald had a knack of repeating almost word for word what others said in his hearing.

"Still and all," Magdali said as if she had been thinking to herself, "we can't let the poor things suffer. How far is it, Ivar —eleven miles, you said?"

"Ten and a half, sister," Roald put in.

"We shall go to them with some food," Magdali went on with her unfailing charity. "Sunday, perhaps, when we can leave Roald with the children. I couldn't take them, with sickness there."

Roald was content. He had looked the district over. He knew where the good land lay; he knew what he had come for. Nobody would disturb his equanimity before spring. He was a shrewd fellow.

Ivar had no fault to find, however, with the way Roald conducted himself about the house. Certainly not, when Roald was always up before any of them, getting the fire going, putting the kettle in place for coffee, heating the flat oak-cakes on a pan beside the embers. Certainly not, when Roald took Karsten on his knee on Sunday mornings and read passages from the Bible which made the boy listen and wonder, his fingers in his mouth! Roald was proud, too. He insisted on paying his two dollars every week for room and board. That was eight dollars a month!

Just the same, it was disquieting to see the man sitting by himself in the evenings, not speaking a word to anyone, his eyes narrowing and his brows knitting as he counted on his fingers, his lips moving with only a faintly audible whispering that always ceased abruptly when he found Ivar watching him.

He groomed his grays until they fairly shimmered that early Sunday morning of Ivar's and Magdali's visit to the Endicott place.

On the floor of the wagon were a sack of potatoes, carrots and turnips, a gallon can of milk, a jar of ground-cherry preserves, a two-pound crock of butter, and a white cotton cloth in which Magdali had wrapped a stack of crisp, thin *flat-bröd* —enough to last a small family a week. They drove southeast, almost directly into the path of the rising sun. Circled by the white prairie mist, the sun was a halo over the new earth.

"Just to think, Ivar," Magdali said, "in a year or two everybody for miles around will be up and on the way to church! I can hear, already, the bells ringing!"

But Magdali's eyes missed nothing of the features of the Endicott land where the trail crossed it a few miles east of Burbank. She saw its firm, good level, rising from the river bed, and the rich covering of growth the summer had given it, yellowing now under the late season. Her lips straightened with contempt for a man who had not had the enterprise to make the most of what was immediately under his nose. Such people had no right to be settlers in a new land.

She sat upright on the wagon seat and felt Ivar's troubled eyes upon her, but not even to him could she express her thoughts. He could not possibly see this opulent prairie as she saw it. Lovable as he was, there was much dreamy nonsense about him, else why had he refused to buy the comfortable farm next to her brother Karsten's, in Wisconsin? Oh, no, he had been looking in the paper and had been reading about the Red River Valley. Well, a woman must follow her husband —thus she had been taught by her own mother, who had said, while she stood watching Magdali packing her trunk to go to America, "That will no doubt prove to be your coffin, that!"

Coffin, indeed! Not for another fifty years, at least! Let them bicker over politics and entailments in her father's *stué* in Norway. This was America. But a quarter section of land would not be enough. As soon as Ivar secured his patent, the Vinges would set about acquiring as a tree claim the additional quarter section lying directly to the southward of their present holdings. Ivar would do the required amount of breaking each year, but Magdali herself would set out the saplings she would get from the government agent—white and black ash, a few poplars, some pine and spruce, and perhaps a red elm.

She was thinking about her trees, seeing them already in full-bodied foliage, when a pathetic huddle of buildings with only a scrubby clump of willows for a wind-break rose before her. Three children, a boy of about six and two younger girls, ragged, thin, and yet clean as Sunday, were rolling an old wagon wheel under the willows where Ivar stopped the horses. The children retreated at once, big-eyed and suspicious.

"The poor little ones!" Magdali exclaimed in Norwegian. "They look half starved. Why does the government allow such things?"

A gaunt-jawed, gravel-colored man in blue jeans came out of the house, and at his politely questioning look Ivar introduced himself and his wife, explaining that Magdali was the sister of Roald Bratland, who had been here a few days ago. An unmistakable moisture appeared in the man's brown eyes.

"You—are almost the first visitors we have had since we came here," he stammered. "When I saw you from the window

[76]

just now, I was sure I was clean gone at last!" He gave a meager, apologetic laugh. "My wife hasn't had another woman set foot in our house here. She kind of expected Mrs. Stafford, from Burbank, to come one of these days, but I guess she's busy as the rest of us. My wife has been sick, but she's feeling better now, and she'll be glad to see you. I hope you won't look too close at the way I've been keeping the house. It's hard for a man to know what's to do—and how to get it done."

Magdali gave him a reassuring murmur, and they followed Charlie Endicott, Ivar carrying the bushel basket into which he had piled the articles from the wagon.

Ardella Endicott sat beside the south window of the room, a clean white pillow behind her, a patchwork quilt thrown about her knees. At the sight of her visitors her eyes lighted to dark fires in her thin white face.

"How fortunate you are!" she exclaimed, as soon as they had been introduced. "You are among the first here—in a new empire of the world!"

Embarrassed by such melodramatic utterance, Magdali said hastily, "We brought you a few things we thought you might like, for we have more than we need. Maybe, Mr. Endicott, you should put the milk in a cool place."

"You are too kind, Mrs. Vinge," Ardella Endicott said. "Our cow has been dry since she lost her calf, and the children have had no milk. But Charles intends to take her up to George-town before spring, so perhaps—" She smiled and ran her blue-veined hand over a small book in her lap. "The spring. In this little book—by Mrs. Browning, you know—there are such lovely things about the spring. She lived for a while in a little place in England called Hope End, and yet—only hope kept her alive!"

Endicott had drawn up two rickety chairs for his guests and

excused himself while he stowed the contents of the basket in a sort of buttery built into one side of the shack.

Nearly two years here—no curtains on the windows, no mat on the floor, a bare pine table, three old chairs and a bench, a hair sofa with broken springs that one of the children slept on, no doubt, a sagging bed with a trundle showing beneath it, bedclothes ragged and thin, a rusty cook stove with broken lids —nearly two years here! That was what Magdali was thinking, Ivar knew unhappily. Such failure was immoral, no matter what the contributing circumstances.

"We have only parched barley coffee," Ardella Endicott said, "but with milk in it the taste isn't bad. Charles, put a pot on, will you, dear? And get the white cloth out of my trunk, and the flowered plates, and the red glass creamer and sugar bowl." She laughed gaily. "We must celebrate your coming. While I've been sick I've kept things out of the children's way. They'd make mud pies in my best dishes if they got hold of them!"

When the children came in and saw the feast of bread and butter and jam and milk on the table, their eyes stood out from their heads like glass marbles. Ivar had to turn away, a lump in his throat.

The Endicotts spoke little of themselves, except to say that Charlie had been a storekeeper in St. Paul before he had come here to take up land. He had brought some books on farming with him, but he had found it hard to apply the lessons they taught. Ardella had been a schoolteacher in the East before she came to St. Paul and married "dear Charles." It had been her idea that they should seek their fortune in the new country, but somehow . . .

The woman's gratitude, her wistful optimism, and her husband's resolute attempt to put the best possible face on his circumstances by discussing his plans for next year, were so

[78]

painful to Ivar that he drew a sigh of relief when Magdali said, just before noon, that they must really leave for home. They'd love to stay longer, but they had children of their own, and there was always so much to be done, even on a Sunday . . .

VII

THEY were pleasant weeks that followed, with the days growing shorter and the nights more cold. There were neighborly visits to the Sondstroms and charitable journeys to the Endicotts, with fried cakes and cheese, and woolen things for the children to wear; weekly trips to Burbank, with butter and eggs to trade for flour and coffee; and there were long nights together, with Magdali plying her needle while Ivar smoked his pipe and Roald sat by the stove, counting his fingers and whispering to himself. Now and then Magdali would speak up. "You will get some sheep in the spring, Ivar, or I shall walk to St. Cloud myself to get them, and have my baby on the way!" Or Roald: "The railroad will be here in the spring, and might be it will cross the river where I think." And sometimes Ivar dreamt to himself: "The deep snow will cover the land—and the spring sun will warm the air—and my wheat will come up green and high in the field!"

Shortly before Christmas, two letters came from the north, one for Ivar and the other for Magdali.

Ivar's letter was from Julian Fordyce. Julian had been far to the north, in the Lake Athabasca country, but on his return to Fort Garry he had attended a ball at the Governor's house, where he had met a Miss Shaleen, who had had the good fortune to journey northwest with Mrs. Vinge the previous summer. The meeting had prompted him to write and wish Ivar and his family a merry Christmas and prosperity in the coming year. Of himself Julian spoke briefly. For the sake of his growing son Alec, he had taken a clerk's desk with the Company, and had turned his back upon the trails he had traveled with so much pleasure for years. He hoped to meet Ivar again sometime, and perhaps become better acquainted with his family, though the future must remain uncertain for him now. And that was all.

Magdali's letter, in a script hair-fine and small, was from Kate Shaleen.

My dear Mrs. Vinge [she had written], I have often thought of you and have been on the point of writing many times since I came north. But a recent chance meeting with Mr. Julian Fordyce, of the Hudson Bay Company, brought you and your family and the Red River Valley so vividly to mind that I decided to write you at once.

My young lady has prevailed upon me to remain with her until spring, though I had intended to go south again long before this. I plan to return soon after navigation opens in the spring, and may seek a position as schoolmistress if any such position can be found. It would be nice to think that a school might be opened somewhere in the Valley, as my brother and sister have expressed their desire to come west and settle.

If fortune should place me anywhere within reach of you during the coming year, my first effort will be to find you. I shall never forget your cool courage, Mrs. Vinge, in that thrilling emergency in our stagecoach. I hope the baby is strong and hearty and a credit to its parents, who will be indebted to you beyond any human means to repay. You will, I am sure, become one of the great pioneer women in the Red River Valley.

Wishing you and your family every happiness in this Christmas season and during the year to come, I beg to remain,

Yours most sincerely,
KATE SHALEEN

"Well!" Magdali exclaimed, bright-eyed. "Isn't that sweet of her? If we only had a school ready for her when she comes!

She would make a good teacher, I think. She has the right spirit—you can see that, Ivar."

"Ya, if she isn't too young for a frontier school," Ivar replied with a disinterested glance at the letter that Magdali had read aloud.

Magdali raised her eyebrows. "Nonsense, Ivar. I was a mother at her age, I'm sure, though I don't know exactly how old she is." Her eyes twinkled as she looked at Ivar. "But you talked to her that day—by the river. What did you talk about? Perhaps you know how old she is."

"*Helvete*, no! How could I know?"

But he reddened angrily as he spoke, and turned away to shake off the irritation he felt at permitting himself to be teased by Magdali. There was more to it than that, he realized when he had time to think about it later. Some intuition warned him that Kate Shaleen would rue the day she ever took upon herself the responsibility of guiding one of Magdali's children along the paths of learning. He did not hold Magdali at fault. She was merely exacting, as a mother should be, especially where her offspring's education was concerned. There would be no place in her scheme of things for any such flights of fancy as the Shaleen girl had indulged in that afternoon when she had stood on the bank of the river and dreamed of the future. Kate Shaleen would be happier in charge of a school elsewhere.

On a calendar hanging above Roald's bunk in the kitchen, Magdali checked off the days remaining until Christmas—their first Christmas here in the Valley. The children's toys were already made and hidden away in the big chest: for Magdis a rag doll with black shoe-button eyes, yellow yarn hair, and a red-thread mouth—tucked in a tiny cradle complete with pillow and coverlet; for Karsten a sled that Ivar had made with painstaking care; and for each of the children a striped paper cone full of peppermint and horehound sticks and gum drops, from their Uncle Roald. Magdali had also made picture books out of an old copy of *Harper's Weekly* that had lain in the bottom of her trunk. On its pages she had pasted pictures cut from a *Children's Manual of Christian Behavior* which her brother Karsten's wife had given her just before her departure from Wisconsin.

One of the pictures struck Ivar as somewhat lurid. It depicted an incandescent cross atop a savage crag, toward which haloed tots in white robes struggled as though against great odds.

"Looks like a cold place, that, for little ones in their night-gowns," Ivar laughed.

Magdali retorted sharply, "Perhaps you can do better, then, to lead our little ones in the right way, in a place where we have no church."

"Oh, we'll have a church, Magdi, when they're old enough to read their catechism," he assured her. "We'll all live like gentlefolk here in a year or two."

Without knowing it, Ivar had hit upon something that had been at the center of Magdali's mind for many weeks.

"You are right, Ivar," she replied. "And so we must now get ready for it. We must bring together the ones who will help to make our life what it is to be. I've been thinking it would be nice to have the Sondstroms here for Christmas Day."

"There are others who might need it more," Ivar observed.

Magdali's small teeth worried at her lower lip and she said quickly, "It's a shame Mrs. Endicott isn't well enough to come. But I have made my old red wool petticoat into jackets for the little girls, and there's a piece-quilt we can spare. I'll have Roald drive down tomorrow, with fried cakes and some cottage cheese."

Ivar did not reply immediately. For once, he could see what Magdali was thinking, how she was already separating the sheep from the goats in this new country where he himself had fondly imagined there was neither high nor low among the few people they had come to know.

"Well, invite the Sondstroms," he said finally, and hid his smile behind a hand. "But both Pete and Ole like their *schnapps*, you know, and we'll have to find something to—"

"Ivar! Don't say such a thing. There shall be nothing like that in my house."

Ivar had the upper hand now. "Ole's wife doesn't think they are headed for the pit if they take a nip once in a while. And she made some of the best elderberry wine I ever tasted. After one *venlig* glass of it, the day I took over to them the seed potatoes, the sun was brighter for a whole hour!" He threw back his head and laughed.

Magdali's mouth latched stiffly. "Very well, Ivar. We shall have our Christmas without them."

But Ivar knew that would not be the end of it. Magdali would endure any hardship except that of having no one upon whom to bestow her hospitality.

He did not have long to wait. A few evenings later, when they were preparing to decorate the spruce tree that Roald had brought them that afternoon, Magdali said, "The things for the tree were not broken at all in my trunk, Ivar. The candles are whole, and I straightened the silver star for the top. The room will look real pretty, with the tree in it."

"Yes," Ivar replied, all innocence. "I swear there is not another room on the whole river as nice as ours will be, Magdi. It's a trick you have, to make so much of so little!" He looked blandly up at the ceiling. "And with that good fish soup of yours, with vinegar and onions in it—"

"I have decided to ask the Sondstroms, after all," Magdali put in suddenly. "We have a work to do here, Ivar. That is something you do not think about. I am thinking of the future."

"H-m-m!" Ivar thought he understood, but he was too tired after a day of cutting firewood in the timber to be concerned with Magdali's deviousness.

The house was made festive with fragrant spruce boughs interlaced above doorways and windows, with wild rose briars on which the berries still hung red, and with clusters of scarlet checkerberry and bittersweet to brighten the dark corners.

On *lille-Jul-aften*, the day before Christmas Eve, Magdali kept the family severely away from sampling the good things in preparation for the feast. Christmas Eve itself, of course, was a sort of prelude to the great day, with fish balls cooked in milk, and *römme-gröt*, that delicious cream pudding oozing globules of butter and sprinkled richly with cinnamon and sugar. Sugar was not for everyday—not at twenty-five cents a pound in Georgetown! Ivar's trading of milk, butter, and eggs twice a week at the post had to supply things more necessary than sugar. There would have to be a month of scrupulous saving after this extravagance, but it was well worth it, Ivar thought, watching the children's radiant eyes and his wife's happy industry. Food was really sacred to Magdali, though she would have been shocked had he put any such irreverent notion into words!

At dusk, on Christmas Eve, Ivar became concerned. "You have done enough, Magdi. Just now you must not overdo."

But Magdali retorted spiritedly, "One thing I can do that you can't do, Ivar—and that is carry a baby!"

Ivar grinned. "Well, if it comes to that, Magdi, I must have done what you—"

"Ivar! Get Roald and the children to light the candles on the tree in there. Then you go out and see if there's any grain left on the sheaf for the birds. It's going to snow tonight—I can smell it coming!"

"Ya—it's a little enough nose you have, but you make it

[85]

work for much, I think."

It was strange—but pleasant, too—to be alone for a while in the lead-blue twilight of this first Christmas Eve in his valley, Ivar thought as he stepped out of the house and stood under the sky, where loneliness stole like a ghost over the fields and the thinned, leafless murk of the woodland.

Of course it was no *valley*, as he had known valleys in the old country. That was the strange thing about it, because it drew as familiarly upon something within him as had the steep mountain pastures of his father's farm in Norway. He stood for a moment, suffused by the odd feeling that the loneliness was beckoning to him, that his real desire was to go far out there, to the north, where he might be enfolded by it. But he could never overtake it now—never! The day that Magdali and the children had come here, last summer, had marked its escape from him for all time. Though it might lurk just beyond his reach, embracing the earth as it had embraced him in his solitude, it would never again touch him with its chaste and inviolable whisper upon heart and brow.

He shivered a little—not from the cold. What kind of thinking was this, in a man who had everything to be grateful for? After supper, he and Magdali and the children and Roald would clasp hands and march around the candle-lit tree, singing *Glade Jul* and all the good old Christmas songs. Tomorrow the Sondstroms would come, Ole and Pete forewarned by Roald with respect to forbidden cheer, and Magdali would bloom in pride and joy at the happiness she was showering upon everyone in her house, this first Christmas in an all but empty land. . . .

In just such a triumphant manner the holiday did, indeed, pass for Magdali Vinge.

VIII

DESPITE the care Ivar had taken to chink well between the logs of his house, there were weeks in January and February when stove and fireplace had to be kept constantly stoked, or the cold raked one's very marrow. He was kept busy cutting and hauling firewood from the oak groves along the river.

On a trip to Georgetown he had traded a pot of Magdali's caraway cheese for seven pounds of fine wool fleece that gave Magdali enough to occupy her hands during the long evenings, carding and spinning and knitting, until the tearing winds of March wore the snowdrifts down into pocked hummocks, into rotting, yellowish shelves along the creek bank.

Roald Bratland drove his grays hither and yon as the days permitted, alert for any news that would bear a hint as to where the railroad, moving steadily westward, would ultimately cross the river. It was all very confusing. Even the advent of the motley crew of adventurers who had been darting about like grasshoppers for the past six months in the hope of staking claims on free land which they would shortly sell to the railroad company—even this harbinger of things to come failed to move the cautious Roald.

They had arrived, all right, and had pitched their tents at a point only three miles up the river, at a spot they had already named Lost Coulee—gamblers, dance hall promoters and their gaily bedizened company, speculators, traders, renegade evangelists—drifters who dreamed of sudden riches to be won overnight in the new country. As rumor shifted, the nondescript citizenry simply pulled up stakes and followed in a new direction. To make their plight more baffling, agents of the Puget Sound Land Company, an organization that included many railroad officials, went everywhere, diligently misleading speculators who were not of their select number. There was a watchful attitude of mutual mistrust even among the members of the "end of the track gang" themselves, so that a man rarely slept unless he left his wife or partner on guard to see that nobody decamped mysteriously during the night.

But Roald Bratland was not one to veer with every breeze. He moved about among the denizens of Lost Coulee, listened to every rumor, was alert to every new report, and came away to think it over quietly in his corner beside the kitchen fireplace. Not that he was altogether immune to the contagion of excitement that was everywhere about him when he journeyed forth. Now and then he literally hugged himself with joy that he had not rashly staked his claim as soon as he arrived last fall. He would have to make his decision sooner or later, of course, and the time was growing short, but Roald knew that. He would decide when the inner voice spoke with clarity and finality.

On an evening when there was an agitated quiver in his bandy legs as he skipped up and down the kitchen floor, Ivar knew that the voice had spoken.

"Now—tomorrow," Roald chortled, "I go three miles to the southwest, and there I will get me a homestead. There I will put down my stakes. No pre-emption for me! I will save my good money for something else. Oh, ya—three miles from here—three miles south—that will be just close enough to the railroad. Five, ten years from now, Ivar, think what that land will be worth! Not so I shall want to sell. Me, I am a farmer, no speculator. Ya, the Lord he has talked to Joshua today, you bet!"

Ivar sat silent, smoking his pipe and watching his brother-in-law's cavortings. There was something about all this glee that he vaguely disliked. It was as if this abundant northern earth were somehow being smirched by a small man's estimate of it in cloudy future dollars and cents. He glanced at Magdali. She blinked and straightened her lips.

"Don't be too sure about the crossing, brother," she said thoughtfully.

Roald pulled at his long, red-veined nose with a bony thumb and forefinger. "No, no—it can be no mistake this time!"

Magdali smiled. "We will wait a little longer, I think."

Roald's high cheekbones blanched with a moment's doubt. "But this man I talk to—he told me the chief engineer himself told him the crossing would be there—at the coulee. He has already a big tent-house, with poles and canvas, for a store. He will start to build with logs next week. He would not do *so*, if he wasn't sure?"

"Well." Magdali's smile was still patient. "When you hear the engineer himself say it, you will know it is true. Keep your ear to the ground for a little while longer." She pursed her lips down at the square of flannelette she was hemming, and said as if to herself, "If I had a sewing machine now—even one to work by hand—I could get these diapers done in half the time. It was silly of me to give most of Magdis's baby clothes to Karsten's wife. But how could I be sure of having another little one so soon? I am thankful for it, of course. Every child born into a family means that the Lord's prayer will be said one more time each day under one roof."

"Ya, it is so!" Roald observed devoutly.

"If we have a good crop next year," said Ivar, "you shall have your sewing machine, too."

Magdali folded the napkin in her square hands and gave Ivar an arch smile. "I have money enough for a sewing machine."

"*You* have it?" He stared at her.

"I have almost a hundred dollars—some from my father when we were married—and some from the Hardanger embroidery I did for the French family in Wisconsin. I have kept a nest egg, Ivar," she laughed. "But it is not going for a sewing machine. I am putting it together with Roald's—for land—so soon as we know where the crossing is really going to be."

Ivar sighed. "Have we not enough land, *kjaere?*"

Magdali was patience itself. "You will learn, my Ivar, what it means to own land. You will live and work on your land. But I shall take gold from mine without a plow. Either way, we do well. You shall see."

Ivar did not reply. Once again he found it impossible to say what was so sadly wrong in what she was thinking. But in the days that followed, even under the pressure of his work, he could not forget it.

IX

WHEN the frost was out of the ground to the proper depth, Ivar sowed his seed wheat, two venturesome acres of it, dropping it gently from his hands into the dark, shallow furrows, carefully harrowing the soil to give depth to the planting. He stopped short of actually saying a prayer over it, thinking with a whimsical grin that such an act would be an insult to the ground itself. He would let it be—he would let it be!

Of oats and barley he had ten more acres each this year. The going was easier since he had the use of Roald's implements, in return for which he would help his brother-in-law get started on his own quarter, wherever that would be. But there was the vegetable garden too, and the time had somehow to be found for its planting, with beets and beans to be added to last year's small variety. Magdali had grown heavy now, expecting her baby in late June, and Ivar forbade her working in the garden as much as she thought herself able.

Also, the river had opened with the spring, and now there were three boats besides the *International* plying between Abercrombie and Fort Garry. Ivar had taken a contract to supply wood for the furnaces of the new side-wheeler *Sheyenne*, hauling it from the timber north of his own land and piling it on the pier that he and Roald Bratland had built.

On a bright May day, Ivar called to his son in the yard. "Ho, Karsten! We're going to the river to cut wood for the *Sheyenne*. She will be coming from Canada tomorrow."

The boy gave a whoop of delight. There was nothing in all the world so joyous as a steamer day! The blast of the boat's whistle as she rounded the bend to Vinge's Landing sent shudders of rapture down to Karsten's toes, and the first glimpse of her blunt and gleaming snout and her mightily churning wheel made him feel curly and queer inside.

"When can I go for a ride on the boat?" the boy asked as they struck off toward the wooded river bank.

"Well, now," Ivar said, "we'll see. Maybe—"

Why not? The land agent had made his rounds only last week and had given a very flattering report on Ivar's progress. His patent would be forthcoming soon, but first he thought it best to secure his naturalization papers so that there would be no delay in the proceedings. He would have to be away for at least a week, but he could take the time off now more easily than he could later in the season. He could leave on the *Sheyenne* tomorrow, and take Karsten along. Magdali would object, of course.

But Ivar only laughed at her protests. "If I don't have Karsten with me, Magdi, who can tell what I may not do? There is life along the river these days. I hear stories—"

Magdali shrugged. The threat of that life did not impress her, she would have Ivar believe.

And so it was that on the afternoon of the next day, after the *Sheyenne* had taken on fuel at the landing, little Karsten, his hand clasped tightly in his father's, walked in round-eyed wonder up the oak gang plank to the deck of heaven itself. His mother stood on the shore, alternately waving her handkerchief and dabbing it at her eyes. Roald was with her.

"*Bövelen*, Magdali! They are not crossing the sea!"

"Who are you to talk?" Magdali retorted. "You have no children! This is the first time my boy has been away from my side. Ivar will get talking to someone and forget to watch Karsten—oh, I'm a fool to have let him go!"

"Great stars!" Roald muttered. "I'm glad I didn't marry that

[92]

Dena, back in the old country. Oh, ya—man is born to trouble, my sister!"

The *Sheyenne* was moving upstream, her great side wheels threshing up the yellow-green of the river into feathers of white, the sun radiant upon her pilot house, her proud smoke-stack, her sleek deck. Ivar stood at the railing with his hand on Karsten's shoulder, the gray telescope valise safely at his side. The boy was staring between the iron rods of the railing, his face too tense as he watched the water slip by.

"Come on, son," Ivar said. "We'll get dizzy in the head if we keep on looking over at the wheel. Let's see what's inside."

Captain Scott came along just then and laid a hand on Ivar's shoulder. "Got the big boy with you, eh?" He bent down and took Karsten's hand into his great paws. "Want to be a river man, young fellow?"

Karsten put his arms tightly about his father's legs and said nothing.

"Going to Lost Coulee for the ride?" the captain asked Ivar.

"Ho! I go all the way—as far as you go—and beyond that. I go to get my papers to make me an American!"

"Good! Well, I'm glad to have you along. There'll be a place at my table for you and the young man. Not many going out this time, but we'll be loaded coming back." He glanced along the deck as he spoke, to where a young woman stood at the railing, her eyes following the shore as the boat labored upstream. "Hi, there, Kitty Shaleen! I'm throwing you off at the next stop."

The young woman looked around, and Ivar's memory leaped to a hot day in August when a girl with brown hair stood beside the river and talked in a voice that was like music.

She smiled now and came along the deck, her eyes lighting with recognition as she saw Ivar standing beside the captain.

[93]

"Why, it's—you're Ivar Vinge!"

"You are right," Ivar said, and took her proffered hand. "And you are Miss Kate Shaleen."

She turned to Captain Scott. "We met last year, when I was on my way north. We saw the river together."

"Aye, the river has a way with it," Captain Scott observed with a faint burr. "I mind a young couple that came north with me last fall, the last trip of the year. They never saw one another till they got on—and they didn't wait a day after they got off before they were wed." He moved away. "Well, I've got my work to do. I'll leave you to do the talking, Kitty. But you haven't much time, mind."

He hurried away, and Ivar and Kate Shaleen were left together, alone except for little Karsten, who clung to the boat's rail and peered out at the churning wheel.

"Are you leaving the country, then?" Ivar asked.

"Oh, no! My brother and sister are waiting for me in the new town—Lost Coulee. I'll be getting off there in a few minutes." She smiled radiantly. "Didn't I tell you there would be a city here one of these days? There will be a school, too, and I'll be the teacher. Maybe your son will be one of my pupils."

She looked down at Karsten—at his starched and ruffled calico blouse, his neat tight pants fastened with two pearl buttons below the knee.

"Might be," Ivar conceded thoughtfully. "He grows very fast."

"But your wife—Mrs. Vinge—how is she?"

"She feels good. Her brother stays with us since last October. She will like to see you, that I know. Your letter at Christmas —she liked that too. I had one from Julian Fordyce at the same time."

"I saw him just before I left Fort Garry. He asked me to remember him to you."

"I knew him for just one night, but we smoked pipes and talked beside a fire."

"That's enough to make friends for a lifetime," Kate Shaleen assured him.

"Is he coming this way again?" Ivar asked.

"He doesn't think so—not with the carts, at least. But he speaks of coming south sometime, maybe to stay—unless he goes farther north."

"He will go farther north, I think. For a man like him—"

"I am sure of it," Kate Shaleen said. "He will never be happy anywhere else. We find our own places, don't we? I shall stay with my brother and sister here until I find a school." Her eyes shadowed as she added, "Our father died last winter, so there are just the three of us now. My brother Steve is bent on settling somewhere along the river, and my sister Delphy will go with him. They are with the 'end of the track gang' now." She smiled comically. "Are you landing at Lost Coulee?"

"No—we go on. I go out now—to become an American!"

"Well, good luck to you!"

There came a shrill, long-drawn-out whistle that seemed to make the very sky crack open above them, and Karsten leaped back and hugged his father's legs. Kate Shaleen laughed, then dropped to one knee and kissed the boy's curls.

"It frightens me too—every time," she admitted.

Around the next bend now, people would be thronging down to the shore, all shouting at once, Karsten thought. That was what Uncle Roald had told him.

He felt a little frightened by all the excitement and noise as the great boat heaved and throbbed and lurched to her moorings against the sluggish push of the current. The people crowded down to the end of the makeshift dock, and gaped up laughing as if they meant to take a bite out of the steamer's side! And what strange people they were—some in clothes that looked like rags, others dressed just like Sunday. There were ladies with bright red cheeks and black around their eyes, and loops and braids of hair under feathered and flowered hats that sloped like pancakes down over one eye so that they had to look up sideways. And there were men who wore wing collars and huge cravats with great jewels shining in them, and double-breasted waistcoats, and long-tailed coats. They wore their hats on one side too.

But Ivar had been watching Kate Shaleen as she hurried along the deck to where the gang plank was being run out. He thought he saw a woman wave to her as she stepped down toward the landing, but a moment later she was lost in the crowd of people who shoved each other about in their eagerness to get a better look at the boat.

The stay at Lost Coulee was very brief. In a few minutes the *Sheyenne* was on her way again, past Burbank, where there was still nothing more than the small huddle of Stafford's buildings, and then southward under a sky that had never been so pure a blue to Ivar's lifted eyes. He was in an exalted spirit as his gaze followed the sunlit river, past one capricious bend after another.

"I'm on my way now to be an American!" he addressed the river. "Just as American as you! Wait till I come back—you won't see any herring bones on my vest!"

Karsten took his fill of gazing at all the wonders on the boat, from the plush upholstered divans in the lounge to the fascinating mysteries of the pilot house. Captain Scott, who had time on his hands on the southward journey, spun a long and blood-curdling yarn for the boy about the Sioux massacre of '62, and while Ivar listened intently he hoped that Karsten would not improve upon the details when he breathlessly repeated the story to his mother.

But the most wonderful part of it all for Karsten was the invitation to sit on the bridge with the captain, on a white bench, and drink grape juice with a little vinegar and soda mixed in it to make it sizzle right up into your eyes. The captain added a little of something else to the other two drinks, and Ivar accepted his with a little feeling of guilt as he thought of Magdali.

Well, Magdali need never know.

X

Two days after Ivar's departure, Magdali resolved to satisfy her curiosity as to what was really going on down at Lost Coulee. Roald's protests when she revealed her purpose were sincere enough, but the broad streak of superstition in him was stronger than his fears for her safety. If a woman approaching *barsals-seng* felt an irresistible call to go somewhere, she must be humored, for she was certain to bring back good tidings—particularly if she went alone. The distance, after all, was only three miles, and the team of grays was easy to manage. For himself, with fat little Magdis helping him, he would weed the vegetable patch during his sister's absence.

He was on his hands and knees when he heard the sound of the wagon returning along the south trail, a full hour before he had expected it. He stood up and wiped a cold trickle of sweat from his brow.

"*Bövelen*, what a woman my sister is!"

In the yard, Magdali jumped down so blithely from the wagon before Roald could help her to alight, that the hair bristled upright on his head.

"Great mountains, woman!" he exclaimed in Norwegian. "What are you thinking of?"

"More than you would ever have the wit to think," she flashed back, and hurried past him into the house, to return a minute later with a leather pouch at which her fingers worked nimbly. She drew forth a packet of greenbacks and thrust them into Roald's hand.

"That's my money," she said excitedly. "You've still got

your own, haven't you?"

Roald could only gape, and nod helplessly.

"All right, then. Get up on that wagon and drive as fast as your beasts will take you—down to Endicott's. Go to Endicott himself, Roald. Offer him twenty-five dollars more than he paid for his pre-emption. That'll leave us both with something over. If he asks more, give it to him. He'll sell—I know it—because he didn't have enough out of his last year's crop for decent seed this spring. Give him anything—but don't come back here before you have bought his land."

"Ya, Magdali, but—"

"Stupid! Do I have to draw pictures for you? I heard the two chief engineers talking in Wendt's store an hour ago. The crossing will be at Burbank. So the railroad will go through Endicott's land, or very near it. Now—do you understand?"

Roald's lips emitted a thin whistle. "They said all this, in front of you?"

Magdali laughed and gave him an impatient push toward the wagon. "They didn't know I was listening, you numbskull! I went into the store and pretended I couldn't speak English. I just pointed to what I wanted, and I jabbered in Norwegian. Hurry, now, and be careful how you talk to Endicott—so he doesn't guess. Take him with you to Stafford and have him witness the transfer. It's a charity we're doing for the Endicotts, brother. You must think of that. Ivar said they want to get out right away, and it would take them longer before they could sell to the railroad. Now, go—you have no time to lose. Better not talk to anyone but Endicott until you get back here. When the news gets out, the whole gang down there will be making a stampede for Burbank. You'll see. There won't be a soul left there by this time tomorrow."

Roald hesitated still. "But if Endicott won't sell?"

"He'll sell. He's got to sell and take his wife back East with him. We're helping him—giving him real money—and a profit besides."

Roald felt dazed as he drove off, fumbling at the wad of bills he carried in a linen bag inside his undershirt. Now that he was alone, he was tempted to indulge in a stream of genuine profanity in gratitude for such a sister as his. But it occurred to him that the Lord might frown upon him for such a weakening of integrity. He had recourse to the one heartfelt word, *"Bövelen!"*

XI

THE encampment at Lost Coulee was in an uproar. That morning the news had exploded that Wendt the trader had moved out, lock, stock and barrel during the night, under cover of a thunderstorm that had kept everyone else within the crude shelter of dugout or tent. Men and women, wet and bedraggled, rushed about in a panic at the edge of the camp in search of wagon tracks to point the way the trader had gone. Tempers were short; there were accusations and counter-accusations. Someone else must have known about this, somebody was hand in glove with Wendt, to let him steal a march on the rest of them!

At the door of their tent on the outskirts of the camp, the Shaleens, Steve and Delphy, laughed at the scene of headlong confusion and rout.

Delphy drew herself up to her willowy height of five feet eight, and said in her lazy but musically clear voice, while she patted the crepe chignon cascading in ringlets from the back of her head, "It looks like we're on the move again, Steve! The Shaleens don't stay long in one place. Go and find Kate while I get things together and take the tent down."

Steve Shaleen stretched himself mightily in the bland sunlight. "Seems to me we'd do all right if we just stayed here. That's what I aim to do—somewhere if not here. I'm for settlin' down on a little piece of good land—and stayin' where I settle. I'm gettin' tired of this jumpin' round the country."

Delphy looked at him. "Settle down? On what? We've got to have something to live on before we can talk of settling down. And it looks to me like there's gold in that hump on the horizon three miles south of here, or I'm the mother of twins, which God forbid! Let's get on the move, Steve. With Jezebel gone lame on us, we'll be getting down there in the middle of next week, and by that time we might as well hit for Montana Territory. Find Kate."

Steve yawned and looked about him. "Where in hell is she?"

Delphy looked beyond him and saw her younger sister coming toward them out of the deep green of the river woods. Arms akimbo, the tall girl watched the slow and almost dreamlike approach of Kate, and a glow of affection suffused her dark eyes.

"She's the one should 'a' been an actress instead o' you, Delph," Steve said. "Just look at the walk of her! And her hair like dark gold wings in the sun!"

"Go on and laugh at me!" Delphy flared. "Just because I was with a medicine show for a summer—"

"I'm not laughin'," Steve protested. "You didn't do so bad in that side show in Chicago, before the gas flare set fire to one o' your seven veils."

Delphy laughed in spite of herself. "That was a bit of bad luck for all of us. I didn't tell you about the captain of a lake boat who was sitting out front that night. He was sweet on me and he would have married me, and we wouldn't be where we are today if he had. He wasn't bad looking, and he had money, but when the fire started he ran out as if all the devils from hell were after him—and I never saw him again."

"I don't figure that was bad luck at all," Steve declared. "A man afraid o' fire in any shape or form wouldn't be much good married to you, Delphy."

Kate came up to them, swinging her pink sunbonnet in one hand, her other hand clutching a bunch of spring flowers, violets, trillium, and wild columbine. Her long, heavy-lidded eyes, cloudily, darkly blue, looked with wonderment beyond her sister and brother to the feverish activity of the mushroom town, where from tents and jerry-built shelters men and women were hustling their belongings into wagons and carts as if a plague had suddenly struck.

"Moving again?" Kate inquired, her soft lips resigned in a smile. "And just when I thought we were here to stay! I found a nice spot for a school down there where the river bank is high. Just beyond where I caught the fish last night."

"It's a waste o' time, Katoot," Steve said sympathetically. "Might as well try to learn a pack o' coyotes how to add and subtract. These varmints don't want—"

"If you can add and subtract enough to see how many good legs Jezebel has left, get her and hitch up, for the love o' God!" Delphy said sharply. "If we don't get moving and find something we can make a living at, we'll be eating elm bark by the time the snow flies again. And me, I don't like elm bark. Sooner, I'd pitch in with Texas Brazell and help him run that dance hall of his. Come on, Kate, help me pack the junk and take down the wigwam."

Steve ambled off toward the mare that was tethered a short distance away, and Kate followed her sister into the tent.

"I don't like to hear you talk about going in with that Brazell, Delphy," Kate said as soon as they were at work. "I'll be getting to think you mean it. We'll get along somehow without that."

"Don't you worry your head about me, Kate," Delphy said, and began throwing the Shaleens' modest belongings into a humped and mildewed trunk. "I may never make a million, but I'll manage to turn up a dollar now and again when we need it, and I won't have to warm any man's bed for it, either."

"Delphy!"

"Whatever made you give that cashmere shawl to old Mrs.

Groman yesterday?" Delphy asked, by way of changing the subject.

"The poor woman needed a shawl. What made you give Mr. Groman that big slab of dried beef?" Kate countered, tossing an armful of cooking utensils into a box.

"That was food."

"Something we didn't need, I suppose." Kate laughed. "You're as much a Shaleen as any of us."

Delphy drew a heavy sigh and straightened back from the work she was doing. "The devil has put his black finger on the name of Shaleen! First, Ma dies of shock in the Sioux massacre in New Ulm. Then Pa loses everything he has when his blacksmith shop burns up in St. Paul—and *he* dies before he can get ready to come out here and take up land, the way he always wanted to. You want to teach school in a country where there isn't any school—and maybe half a dozen kids all told. Me thinking about acting on the stage, and the nearest I ever get to it is a side show in Chicago—and a fire put an end to that. And Steve, the lazy lump—"

"Steve isn't lazy, Delphy—not when he's doing something he likes," Kate put in.

"The Shaleens, ha-ha!" Delphy retorted. "We're a credit to the nation!"

"But we're starting out new, Delphy," Kate reminded her. "We can make it a name to be proud of yet."

"Yes—when 'Birnam wood do come to Dunsinane'!" Delphy observed. "Here—help me fold these blankets."

The Shaleen equipage was the last link in the hurrying chain of rickety carts and squealing wagons.

"Hurray!" Delphy shouted as they drove off. "Good-by, Bogusville!"

"Bogusville!" Steve said. "You've named it, Delph—and it'll

prob'ly stick for years to come. Still an' all, I felt a hand-hold o' the soil there, and I've a mind to go back to it. I will, too, if I ever get the guts to do what I want to. I never have done what I've wanted to. I'd 'a' gone to the war in '62, if it wasn't for Ma dyin' and—hell, this time I just want to see what comes up out o' this here ground!"

"We've got exactly thirty-four dollars and fourteen cents to our blessed names!" Delphy informed him. "And a precious little bit of canned stuff and flour. You can't start farming on that. We've got to get hold of a little money before we talk about anything else."

Kate's slim, long fingers twined tightly in her lap, her eyes gravely on distance, while Steve stopped Jezebel to permit a partridge hen to convoy her young brood across the grassy route.

"Well, we're here now, all three of us," said Steve, "and where we're goin' is like leaves before the wind!"

He shook the reins, and Jezebel plodded on. The trail debouched presently from a stand of flowering dogwood and yellow osier upon a scene of utmost confusion. The carts and wagons that had preceded the Shaleens were milling about on the river bank, jockeying for positions under trees or beside clumps of bushes, while their drivers shrieked at one another in good nature or ill. A few hundred yards back from the river stood the Burbank stage depot, and seated upon the log bench in front of it was Stafford, the agent, a broad smile on his face.

"Well, what do you want to do, girls?" Steve asked. "Wrastle with them fools, or make camp right where we are?"

Even as he spoke, a glossily mustached gentleman in a pea-green, tight-fitting jacket and checked vest heavily adorned with a fobbed and trinketed gold watch chain, came toward them out of the crowd. Delphy, observing him from the corner of her eye, burst into her rich mezzo-soprano—:

"When care comes and knocks at the door of his heart
Still the rascal don't oft trouble Ben;
He makes the unwelcome intruder depart
In haste and dismay does Ben, poor Ben—
He makes the unwelcome intruder depart
In haste and dismay does Ben, poor Ben!"

"Ain't he the stem-winder, though?" Steve observed, and nudged Kate in the ribs just as Texas Brazell took his last sauntering step toward them and smiled up at Delphy with a dazzle of gold teeth beneath the handsomely dangerous points of his mustache. His side-burns were symmetrically curled inward upon the flat bronze of his cheeks.

"And who is this you're calling an unwelcome intruder, Miss Shaleen?" he inquired jauntily.

"I wouldn't have to ask, if I was standin' right where you are," Steve said.

Brazell's black eyes narrowed menacingly, but Delphy pertly fluffed up her bustle on the too narrow seat. "Don't be offended at Steve, Mr. Brazell. He doesn't like anybody this morning."

"I can understand that, Miss Shaleen," Brazell said, "though your singing is a sign that you are on good terms with the world yourself."

"I wouldn't trust that for a sign, Mr. Brazell," Kate said with a laugh in her voice. "My sister often sings when she's in a bad mood—to get herself out of it."

"I was hoping she was getting ready for our grand opening concert tomorrow night," Brazell ventured.

"A concert, Mr. Brazell?" Delphy asked eagerly.

"We're putting up the big tent, Miss Shaleen. I have men at work clearing the ground already. If I could get you to sing a couple of songs, now, I'd feel we were getting off to a good start. I expect to have a place here as lively as anything they have in St. Paul. In fact, if you'd like to come in with me and

[106]

help me run it the way it ought to be run, you'd find it worth your while. We could make some real money here in the next few weeks. And I mean honest money, Miss Shaleen. There'll be a lot of people coming this way as soon as the word gets out about the crossing."

He waited for an answer, and Kate, listening intently, thought: Why, I believe the man has his eye on our Delphy! He has forgotten to twirl his watch chain.

"I'll think it over, Mr. Brazell," Delphy said with dignity.

"And I'm thinkin' we'd better get back to Bogusville," Steve said, as if he were talking to himself.

Brazell strutted a step or two, then became humble before Delphy's mocking eyes. "Think it over, then, Miss Shaleen," he urged. "I'll await your reply." He turned and walked slowly away.

Steve muttered something inaudible, then shook the reins along Jezebel's bony sides. "There's a cottonwood yonder that don't seem to belong to anyone in partic'lar. Jezebel, go to it!"

After a moment's silence, Delphy spoke. "It might work out all right—for a while, anyhow. There's going to be a town here—and a school, Kate—and the Lord knows what all! We might do worse. But if I do go in with him, he's going to change that green jacket of his to something that looks more like a coat. It's a fine color for a flag, that, but for a coat for a man—"

She cast a final glance in the direction in which Texas Brazell had gone.

XII

News of the headlong departure from the "new city" spread up and down the river with incredible speed. It traveled eastward and brought scores of men and women pouring into Burbank within a week, satisfied that at last the river crossing had been settled upon and the site of the city of the future fixed.

It was no longer news to Ivar Vinge, therefore, when the *International* nosed in to shore just before midnight, that the old stagecoach depot at Burbank had taken on the proportions of a young metropolis during his absence. But his first sight of the place was something to challenge belief. A trader from Georgetown, on his way home from Fort Abercrombie, was dumb with amazement as he stood at the rail beside Ivar and looked through the darkness at the flaming lights of fires and the gleam of torches that marked the spots where gaiety was rife. Inured though he was to the fickle flights and nimble shiftings of life on the frontier, he found it impossible to believe what he saw.

"Damn it, Vinge, the world has gone mad!" he declared.

"You are right!" Ivar said. "And maybe I have made a mistake. That farm of mine, now—it is too close to this. It is not what I came here for, when I left Wisconsin."

The *International*, of course, would not put in at Vinge's Landing, as the *Sheyenne* had. With a list of passengers that crowded every available inch of space on the decks, the captain was eager to get along without delay. But Ivar was not disturbed. He could spend the night with Stafford and find some way of reaching home in the morning. If it were not for the fact that he had Karsten with him, he would walk the distance tonight and think nothing of it.

Once ashore, however, Ivar learned with consternation that Stafford's little inn was already full to overflowing. People were even sleeping on the kitchen floor—at fifty cents a night!

"The way it is," Stafford explained miserably, "we make money now, or we don't make it at all. Me, I sleep out front, on my old bench, with a blanket around me. If it rains, I get under the bench. They drive in here, all hours of the night, wantin' to eat. I got to feed 'em, because the wife says she'll pull out and run her own show if I don't. So I sleep on a bench and dish out soup all night at half a dollar for a dipperful. If they want flapjacks, I get a dollar. You could have my half of the bed, Vinge, if my wife hadn't give it up to a woman who's payin' for it. You might go down to Texas Brazell's place, and see what they have. That's the big place down there where all the noise is comin' from. It'll cost you a dollar, and you won't get much sleep, but—"

"A dollar!" Ivar exclaimed. "Better I should sleep outside, but it looks like rain, maybe—and I have the boy here—"

"Tell you what you do, Vinge—" He broke off suddenly. "That name—Vinge! It's a hell of a name for anybody! Why don't you change it to something American?"

Ivar laughed. "My wife says we will change it some day— to Wing. Now I am American—"

"Wing? That's better. That's good! Smart wife you got there. Anyhow, look what you do. Go down the line there and get to see the Shaleen woman that's helpin' Brazell to run the place. If she knows you have a kid along, she'll find some way to put you up."

The Shaleen woman! Ivar was aghast. Well, nothing was unbelievable in this new country, it seemed.

He found Brazell just inside the entrance to the "hotel"—a

structure half log, half canvas, that looked as if it had been thrown together overnight. Brazell was rocking back and forth on the heels of his patent leather shoes, surveying the hilarious crowd that filled the place, his expression one of weary sadness.

When Ivar made his wants known, Brazell spoke to him without looking around. "Talk to Delphy about it, stranger. She's got the handling of that."

"Delphy? Where can I find her?" Ivar asked.

"Through that door," Brazell replied shortly, and nodded toward a rear exit.

Ivar found Delphy Shaleen in a small room, doing her best to instruct a fat young man in the art of beating waltz time on a bass drum.

"Heavens above and all the angels!" Delphy was shrieking as Ivar stepped behind her. "Do you think it's your paunch you're pounding? Make a noise! Listen—it's the *Memories Reverie Waltz*—the one they played in Washington, when President Grant—" She paused and looked over her shoulder. "Well, my friend, what do *you* want?"

"I want a place to sleep—for my boy and me."

Delphy Shaleen turned her full dark gaze upon Ivar, then looked at Karsten and frowned thoughtfully. "There isn't a rathole but someone's sleeping in it tonight," she said. "But that boy of yours ought to be in bed. Have you a blanket with you?"

"No," Ivar admitted.

"No—you expect the saints in heaven to provide for you! Like the rest of this wandering tribe that's crowding in on us!"

"I am not like them," Ivar protested lamely. "I am a farmer from six miles—"

"Never mind! My sister and I have a tent to ourselves, since my brother took to sleeping outdoors with Jezebel. Go down there—third tent on the right as you go out. You'll find two spare blankets in a corner. Unroll them and make a bed for yourself and the boy. We won't come near you much before daylight. By that time you ought to be ready to get out."

She gave him a warmly appraising look, and Ivar felt unspeakably foolish. He wanted to tell her that he knew her sister, but she was so tall and imposing in her orange poplin bustle and her tremendous coiffure built into a crimped false cataract at the back of her head, that he felt tongue-tied.

He put his hand into his pocket. "I must pay you something," he said haltingly.

"A dime, then—for luck!" Delphy said with an airy laugh that made him feel more ill at ease than ever. "Go on, now, and get that boy between the blankets. He's asleep on his feet."

With his telescope valise gripped in one nervously moist hand, Karsten's wrist in the other, Ivar strode away and found the tent Delphy had indicated. In the dim light he found the two blankets and spread them on the ground. A bunk stood along one side of the tent, and beside it a packing box with a bit of flowered cotton stuff tacked over it, a comb and a brush, a small hand mirror, and a box of rice powder. A rack of women's clothes was hooked into the canvas wall. There was something about the poor neatness of the place that made Ivar want to turn away. Whatever these Shaleens were—

"Pa!" Karsten said breathlessly. "You an' me can sleep in a tent! We can listen to the tree frogs, right down here!" He squatted in the corner, his ear pressed against the canvas wall, his eyes enormous from excitement.

Ivar hurried to undress him. He was a fine, tall boy now—he would be finer and taller than his father, Ivar knew, and was filled with pride. He tucked Karsten snugly in between the blankets, the boy murmuring that the tree frogs made a "bright green song." A bright green song! Ivar stared down at the flushed, heavy-eyed boy and wondered what Magdali would make of a remark like that.

Ivar himself had no desire to sleep. The journey, with its days of comparative idleness, had left him restless and eager for physical activity again. It would be good to get back to his fields where there was work for his hands. Days of talking with strangers who were on their way northward with high hopes in their hearts had filled him with a new excitement, and now the unaccustomed sounds from Brazell's place, close by, would probably keep him awake all night. He stepped out of the tent as soon as Karsten was asleep.

The "street" was alive with men wandering about aimlessly or standing in groups, their loud talk and laughter sounding strange in this place that had been so silent when Ivar had seen it last. The world—this little world beside the river, at least— *had* gone mad. There was no reason left in it. There was nothing left in it except the senseless scramble for land and the rush to be first to claim possession. And at the very center of this madness now stood Texas Brazell's. Ivar hesitated only a moment before the open doorway of the place, then stepped inside.

He stood and looked about him. Kerosene lamps hung bright as small suns on chains from poplar poles. Green-covered tables were surrounded by the oddest assortment of men Ivar had ever seen. A rough bar flanked one wall, and behind it glistened a row of bottles colored from palest amber to deepest red. Frontiersmen in overalls and plaid shirts, and suave individuals in broadcloth, leaned against the bar upon which sat two girls swinging their red French heels and coquetting their ruched silk skirts as they sang:

> *"I'm just a little violet,*
> *Lonesome in the dewy night . . ."*

while the men snorted and made a parody of the song that threw the girls into gales of laughter.

It was only after he had jostled his way through the raucous crowd that Ivar's eyes fell upon the one face he had been looking for. Kate Shaleen sat by herself in a canvas-walled alcove at the end of the bar. She appeared heedless of all that went on about her—the drinking, the gambling, the strident laughter, the occasional blare of an oath. Her eyes, the color of which he remembered was so strange and dark a blue, were wide and tranced-looking in a face that was, perhaps, too broad and irregular of feature for what was called beauty—Ivar could not tell. Her dark hair was not stylishly piled up and away from her face. It flowed against her cheeks and was carelessly looped at the back, and the lamp at the end of the bar struck a gleam out of it that was purplish red. With a certainty at once both chilling and warm, Ivar knew where he had seen that face first. It was in an art museum in Bergen, Norway, the only time he had ever visited the place. There had been an oil painting in a little niche, lighted from above, and a card beneath it —Madonna of the Vineyards. He knew nothing of painters, he could not recall the name of the man who had made the painting; and yet he knew that Kate Shaleen must have sat for the artist. A hundred years ago, perhaps, in a vineyard on a sunny slope of Spain? He felt an uncanny prickling of his skin.

Ivar pushed forward and stood before her. "So, it's *here* I find you?" he said.

She looked up quickly, the color flooding her cheeks. "Ivar Vinge! Yes—it isn't exactly what you expected, is it? I didn't expect it myself."

Ivar laughed. "Strange things happen in this world," he said. "Already we have met twice before—and there was something strange even in that."

"I told you I was coming here to meet my sister and brother," Kate reminded him. "My sister Delphy—"

"I have talked to her," Ivar said. "I have just put the boy to bed in her tent."

It was Kate's turn to laugh. "*Her* tent? It's mine, too."

"There was no place to sleep," Ivar explained. "The boat does not stop at our landing tonight, so I must stay here."

"You are welcome to it," Kate said. "But we never know what to expect of Delphy. Have you met Steve yet?"

"Steve?"

"My brother." She looked past Ivar at a young man who was standing near the end of the bar. "Steve!"

Steve Shaleen approached with an indolent ease, swinging his long, loose-jointed legs, and searched Ivar's face with his soot-black eyes.

"What's the trouble here?" he demanded.

"No trouble at all," Kate told him. "This is Ivar Vinge, the man I told you about." The two men shook hands. "Get Delphy over here, Steve."

Ivar's eyes followed Steve Shaleen as he threaded his way through the noisy crowd. It was a strange place to come upon Kate Shaleen, he thought to himself—and stranger still to find her a part of it, sitting here at a table that held stacks of silver dollars piled in a rack, and packets of greenbacks stowed away in a drawer that stood halfway open in front of her. He wanted to ask her about it, but his courage failed him. After all, it was no affair of his. Behind him, Kate was making change for the bartender.

A bright blond girl in a pink satin dress cut low in the bodice, with a black lace flounce on the shoulder, stood before Ivar and pouted her red lips up at him as she waved a black lace fan in his face.

"Run along, Imogene," Kate said coolly.

"Oo, finders keepers, eh, Miss Shaleen?" The girl gave a mere squeak of a laugh, flipped her fan edgeways to her up-tilted nose, and hoisted her elaborate, wreath-trimmed bustle with her other hand as she turned away.

What happened then came with such suddenness that Ivar felt dazed and unreal to himself. A large, dough-faced man, pock-marked and brutish, confronted him, his breath reeking of whisky.

"What's your name, stranger?" he demanded truculently.

Ivar tried to smile. "I am Ivar Vinge," he said.

"Vinge! The land hog, eh?"

"Mr. Unger," Kate said in a voice that was barely audible above the din, "please move along!"

Ivar turned and looked at her. She was sitting in her place, apparently unperturbed.

"I do not understand," he said, bewildered.

"Charlie Endicott did me a good turn once when I was down and out," Unger said. "He is my friend. Do you understand that?"

"I understand it," Ivar replied. "He is my friend too."

"A hell of a friend you are—to steal a man's land!" Unger shouted.

"I steal nobody's land," Ivar said. "I have my own farm, six miles north of here, and that's enough for me."

Unger thrust a huge fist under Ivar's nose, but Texas Brazell came suddenly out of the crowd and stepped between them. "Get outside, Unger," he ordered.

Unger's tremendous knuckles shot upward, and Ivar saw Brazell's feet leave the floor as he crashed backward across a table. Ivar knew what he must do, even with a hundred pairs of eyes upon him. He had never struck a man in his life, but now, as he clubbed his hand and swung a smashing blow that

[115]

landed between Unger's porcine eyes, he was filled with an exhilarated sensation that brought him close to nausea. Unger reeled backward, one of his feet in the air, recovered himself with the incredible agility of a cat, and before Ivar could move, planted his heavy boot squarely in the pit of Ivar's stomach. Ivar hurtled backward, striking the middle of his spine against the corner of the bar as he fell. For a second the pain blinded him, but he scrambled away from the bar, stretching his eyelids in an effort to collect his wits.

Above him, he saw Kate Shaleen standing at the end of the bar, one hand at her side, her fingers clutching something that gave off a dark, metallic gleam.

"Get out, Mr. Unger," she was saying. "Mr. Vinge had nothing to do with the Endicott land. He came in tonight on the—"

Delphy Shaleen appeared like a living tornado, sweeping the bystanders aside like so much chaff as she planted herself squarely in front of Unger. "Out you go, Unger! Put that gun away, Kate! Get back out of the way, Texas Brazell! I'll handle this." When Unger showed no disposition to move, she turned on him again. "I told you to get out! I don't speak twice to a tramp like you!"

She flew at him with both hands, so that Unger could do nothing but fling his great arms about him, retreating with a baffled grunt before he wheeled dizzily and rushed out, the crowd's laughter following him through the doorway.

The laughter fell away abruptly, however, as Delphy looked about her with eyes full of disdain. Hands on hips, she brought her gaze to bear finally upon Ivar.

"Well, if it isn't our star boarder! Who'd have thought you were out looking for—"

"Mr. Vinge had nothing to do with it," Kate put in.

"Mr. Vinge? Oh, I see. The man on the boat, eh? What

was all the ruckus about, anyhow?"

"I do not know," Ivar confessed.

"Unger accused him of stealing the Endicott land," Kate explained.

"All right, now, go on about your business!" Delphy said and waved her hand over the crowd. When they had dispersed, she looked at Ivar again. "The Endicott farm!" she said. "Sure —I heard something about that. Steve was telling me—a man by the name of Endicott sold out—east of here—for half of nothing, and took his wife and kids back to St. Paul. He left on the stage this morning."

The truth came slowly to Ivar, but the force of it left him stunned. "No—I do not believe it!" he said as if to himself.

"Listen, my friend," Delphy said, "you'd better get back and look after that boy of yours. This is no place for you anyhow."

"I am very sorry," Ivar said, standing awkwardly before her, hat in hand. "I didn't mean to—"

"Think nothing of it," Delphy said, her eyes laughing at him. "It's all in the night's work here. And the Shaleens look upon such things as fun. Now, get back to bed and stay there."

People stared at him as he went out, but while there was curiosity and even amusement in the eyes of some, he saw no animosity anywhere. He gave little thought, however, to what these strangers might think of him. With a mixture of baffled shame and anger—and a resentful gratitude for having come out of the affair as well as he had—he was wondering what Magdali would think when he told her of this night's events.

But even above that thought was another that would not let him rest until he had found out what he must know—from Magdali herself. He could not think of sleep now—he would not sleep before he learned the truth about the Endicott land, and whether Magdali had had any part in the matter. He managed to get Karsten into his clothes without waking him. Lifting the boy to his shoulders, he seized his telescope valise and started for the door of the tent when a shadow barred his way.

"Are you going?" Kate Shaleen asked.

"I do not want to sleep," Ivar replied.

"But you can't leave with your son, this time of night. Delphy made me come out to see that you were all right."

"We are all right," Ivar said. "But the boy and I—we're going home."

"Please," Kate pleaded. "We're sorry for what happened in there. You can't walk all that way—six miles, isn't it?—and carry Karsten and that heavy valise. If you'll wait until morning, Steve would take you home in the wagon."

"This is something you do not understand," Ivar told her. "It is nothing—what happened in there. It is something I must know—now. And so, I go now."

He heard Kate sigh. "You might leave your valise, then, and Steve will drive out with it in the morning. I'll look after it for you."

Ivar tried the weight of the valise in his hand. It would be heavier by the time he had carried it six miles over a trail that would be hard enough to travel through the darkness. Besides, Kate Shaleen had spoken as if she were asking a pledge of friendship, some token as proof that he bore her no ill will.

"It would be easier," he admitted. "But I can come for it myself."

"You are very stubborn, Ivar Vinge," Kate observed gently.

"That I do not know," Ivar replied. "But you—" He hesitated while he thought of the word he wanted. "You are very generous," he said carefully, and hunched Karsten higher on his shoulder as he stepped through the doorway of the tent.

XIII

ALL sign of rain had disappeared from the skies, and it was
easy to follow the trail under the starlight, once his eyes became accustomed to it. The way was dry, too, and the night
was cool, with a fresh breeze coming off the prairie laden with
the exciting smells of spring. Karsten's weight was no greater
than a man could bear without great effort, though how he
would be feeling about that at the end of six miles was another
matter. He gave it little thought. He could only think that
if he had not gone away, if he had kept his place at home, he
would not now be trying to blot out from his memory the
picture of Charlie Endicott as he had last seen him, harrowing
his field with tree branches to which he had hitched his
spavined horse. He would not be wondering about the ugly
haste with which Magdali had seized her advantage—with
Roald's help, of course—and had not even waited to ask his
advice about buying the Endicott land.

A sharp stab of pain in his spine reminded him again of
where the corner of the bar had struck him when he had re-
coiled from the blow of Unger's foot. He set Karsten, half
awake, upon the ground, and waited for the pain to pass before
going on again. Shame flowed over him there in the darkness
—shame and anger at his own carelessness in letting the man
take him unawares. He should have known what to expect.
Well, he would learn in time, no doubt. Wasn't Magdali always telling him that he had much to learn? She was right.
But she had had nothing like this in mind, he thought with dry
humor.

He was about to lift Karsten again when he realized that he had halted on the edge of the ground where once had stood the tent town they had called Lost Coulee. He cast his eyes about him in the dim starlight. The place was utterly deserted and lonely, with a desolateness that seemed deeper now because life had paused there for a brief space of time before moving farther up the river. He hoisted the boy to his shoulder again and hurried away.

An hour later he came to the single strand of wire that marked the border of his wheat field, the few acres he had broken when he was alone during his first days in the valley. He was home now, even though the house where Magdali lay asleep was still only a faint blur in the distance. Always, he knew, this one spot where he had set his hand to the plow and spoken the word to his ox team—always this would be home to him. Here in the years to come he would stand in a troubled hour, perhaps, and feel the soft flow of peace return to his mind and heart.

It was Roald who came to unbar the door.

"*Bövelen*, Ivar—where have you come from?"

"I come from Burbank—me and Karsten," Ivar told him in a civil voice. It was good to be back again, no matter what had brought him stumbling to the door with a streak of dawn already showing in the east.

He set Karsten down and struck a match. As the flame brightened on the wick, Magdali came from the inner room and stood in the doorway, a wrapper drawn about her. "Ivar —is something wrong? Is Karsten—"

"Karsten is as good as the last time you saw him," Ivar assured her. "And there is nothing wrong, Magdi, that can't be set right again if we go about it."

Magdali, unaware of his meaning, was on her knees, her arms about Karsten, who was still heavy with sleep. "My baby

—you're home again, with mama. Poor baby, he's sound asleep. Come, dear, mama will put you to bed."

She carried him away, and Ivar sat down wearily as Roald, still in his heavy winter underwear, seated himself on the edge of his bunk and blinked the sleep out of his eyes.

"You walked from Burbank, Ivar?"

"I did."

"And carried the boy?"

"That's nothing, when a man wants to get home."

"Ya—it is so, Ivar. We thought you would wait for the *Sheyenne*, maybe. But now—it is this way. Well, you are home! And you saw the new city—at Burbank?"

"I saw more than I liked," Ivar told him.

Roald gave a little sniff of a laugh. "Ya, like as not! But there will be people on the river now—a great plenty—and the city will grow. A smart man will do well to grow with it."

Magdali came back into the room and stood smiling down at Ivar. "I have my man back safe, then," she said, and came to stand beside him, laying her hand upon his head. "But you have walked all that way, Ivar—with Karsten—"

"And would do the same again, Magdi."

"Home is the best place, after all," she said cosily. "Next time, maybe you will not be in such a hurry to go away. But you do not ask me how I have been. You got your papers, I suppose?"

He nodded. His naturalization papers, of which he had been so proud, were of secondary importance just now.

"There is something else before I come to that," he said. "In Burbank they are saying that the Endicott land—"

"Ya—sure!" Roald put in quickly, his face beaming. "It is our land now, Ivar."

"Then it is true?"

"Of course, Ivar," Magdali said. "We gave him a good price

for it, too."

"As much as it was worth?" Ivar asked.

"More than it was worth to him," Roald answered. "He was glad to get what we offered him. And already we could sell it for a hundred dollars more—in one week, Ivar!"

"Charlie Endicott might have had a hundred dollars more, then, if he had waited a week?"

"Ivar," Magdali said in her quiet, cool voice, "he could have even more if he waited another year—until the railroad comes to the river. But he did not know that. And men like him cannot wait. We did him a charity when we paid him more than it cost him. Besides, we take the risk. And they have gone back to the city where they—"

"What did you want with more land?" Ivar demanded. "Already we have enough."

"You have said that before, Ivar. And I have told you what we want with it."

"I am a farmer," Ivar reminded her. "I own so much land now as I can bring to harvest at the end of a year. More I do not want. Can I not make you understand?"

Magdali laughed. "You need not think about this land, then, my Ivar. It is mine—and Roald's. We will hold it until—"

Ivar got quickly to his feet. "Magdali! Do you forget how it was in Norway?" He spoke in Norwegian now, because the words came more easily to match what he was thinking. "There was a day when men like me—men who loved the land—were up with the sun and at work as long as there was light to show them the way—and the days were long in that north country of ours. But they labored through the long days because they loved the land. Their hearts were in it. It was their life and they wanted no other. My father was such a man—and his father. But other men—they were men of the town—took the land from them that owned it, because it was

[122]

wealth. They did not work on it. They held it. One day all the land belonged to the few who had no love for it. Your father was such a man—and his father. But you married *me*. You came to America with me because we could not live and have our children work for the big landowners and have nothing for their labors. We left all that behind us. And thousands more will come, like us. Here we are free men. And now—already you and your brother would forget why we came. You would own more land than you can use. You would turn men away from their land so that the land can be yours to hold. It is a waste, Magdali, and it will bring destruction to us before we are done with it!"

He would have said more. He would have told her that already something had happened to their young dream, the dream that had turned their faces westward across the sea. But Magdali had stepped quickly away from him, her hand pressed to her heart, her face gone suddenly white in the lamplight. Roald was beside her at once, an arm about her shoulder.

"*Helvete!* You've said enough, Ivar!" he exclaimed as he looked down into his sister's face.

Ivar was mute, remembering that Magdali's time was not far off. He was frightened now as he saw her mouth twist, her white lips draw tight with pain. He went to her, all his tenderness returning, and drew her away from Roald.

"Come, Magdi—you must lie down," he said gently, and led her away to the inner room.

Three weeks later, in the middle of the night, Magdali gave birth to a daughter, with Mrs. Sondstrom attending.

"A girl!" Magdali cried petulantly, when she heard Mrs. Sondstrom's smiling announcement. "A girl—when what we need is sons!"

Ivar wanted to tell her that a girl could utter the Lord's

[123]

prayer under their roof quite as effectively as a boy, but he held his tongue. Magdali's piety, he thought with grim humor, was apparently based upon some kind of bargaining with the Almighty, in which she could not tolerate getting the short end of the deal.

He went out of the house and walked alone, heedless of direction, under the lonely stars. He knew then, as he had known on that night of his return home, that his feelings for Magdali could never be quite the same again.

XIV

To Roald Bratland, nothing was beyond belief. Had he possessed any fragment of the faculty to become amazed, that incredible summer of '71 would have brought about its complete destruction. In a valley seething with activity, where nights and days were filled with hurried comings and goings, where every man's heart was the dark center of mysterious designs upon which his lips had set their seal, Roald kept his own counsel and quietly put together the nicely fitted pieces of his own plan.

His sister Magdali alone baffled him. When others talked at random, she remained silent. In the midst of excitement she remained calm and collected. After that first protest upon learning that the child she had borne was not a son, she had not spoken of it again. Birth was an incident, nothing more, in this strange new land. Roald was convinced that Magdali would have looked upon death with the same detachment— an event of small moment in the inscrutable ways of the omnipotent God she professed to worship.

There was nothing mysterious about Ivar. His very simplicity was disarming. Roald often thought of the episode that had involved his brother-in-law with the profane establishment of Texas Brazell and the Shaleen woman. A less ingenuous man would have said nothing about it. Ivar must needs tell all. The affair, Roald knew, had outraged Magdali's sense of propriety, and yet she had continued to express a mystifying cordiality toward the Shaleens. It seemed almost as if she were determined to convince Ivar that she was as broad-minded as he in respect to the irregularities of life here on the frontier. And yet, there might be more to it than that. Magdali was a deep one.

But Fortune was smiling on Roald meantime. He had settled on a choice quarter section a mile eastward from the deserted site of Lost Coulee. He had acquired the beginning of a herd of Guernseys—cheap, too!—a three-year-old bull and four cows. And though he had planted late, the astounding soil was producing a crop of oats and barley such as he had not dared to dream of. From the looks of things at Ivar's place, it was producing good wheat too, by *oiens skalke!* Ivar would be coming to him one of these days to borrow his self-rake reaper, no doubt, because the wheat was there, plain as the nose on a preacher's face.

Oh, ya, it was a good country, where a man could lay his foundations for the years to come, when he might be a banker, a real-estate wizard, a politician of consequence, or maybe all three in one! He wondered if Steve Shaleen, who had taken land just west of his own and lived there now with his sister Kate, ever thought of that. Did they ever think of the future at all, those easy-going neighbors of his? Did it ever dawn upon them that the two soddies, their own and Roald's, standing there in clear view of each other, offered sound evidence that the country was filling up?

Well, it was pleasant to have neighbors, whoever they were. It was pleasant to saunter casually in upon them now and then with a bit of news. By such little ways you won confidence, even awe if the news was important. It was all very gratifying. Useful, too, if you had an eye to the future.

It was Roald who brought the tidings to Ivar and Magdali of the naming of the new city which had been building all summer beside the river where the railroad company had decided to put in the bridge. The young metropolis was to be called Moorhead, in honor of a director of the Northern Pacific.

There were rumors afoot, too, that the little hamlet of Centralia, across the river, was to be called Fargo, in recognition of Hilliard Fargo, of the Wells-Fargo Express Company.

"It is something to have a name, it seems," Roald mused aloud as he stood rocking to and fro, his hands clasped behind his back. "The name of Bratland, now, would have been a good name for a city. But Roald Bratland is not a Moorhead, nor yet a Fargo."

He glanced at Magdali, but her eyes were intent upon a bit of sewing, and her face told him nothing.

Roald was truly jubilant, however, when in December he came to announce that the steel had been laid as far as Moorhead and the first engine had reached the end of the line. A less hardy man would not have ventured through the bitter sleet of that night even with such thrilling news. But Roald Bratland held the elements in contempt.

The older Vinge children were in bed. Magdali was nursing the baby on a low basswood chair that Ivar had fashioned with skill before the fireplace during the lengthening evenings. Ivar himself was seated on his cobbler's bench, surrounded by shoes, patches of leather, and copper toe caps and nails. He had just fitted one of Karsten's stout boots on his last when Roald's seven thumps sounded on the door. Roald cherished a naïve faith in the occult powers of the mystical seven.

"Is the devil after you again, Roald, to be out on such a night as this?" Ivar greeted him while he divested himself of his frosted great coat in the light of the whale oil lamp.

Roald gave his nickering laugh. "Roald Bratland will have to be about in worse than this, if he is to make the most of the chances right under his nose," he remarked in Norwegian, hunching his shoulders and mincing to the fireplace, where he rubbed his hands briskly. Then he waited, as always, for the gratifying question as to what news he bore this time.

"It can't be," said Ivar wickedly, removing a shoe nail from his lips and inserting it in the hole he had made with his awl, "it really can't be, Roald, that the first engine has reached Moorhead today?"

The wind gone from his sails, Roald was becalmed with indignation. "So! You saw the celebration, with gun powder like the Fourth of July, and dancing round the bonfire right in the street? And you didn't stop in to my place!"

"Of course he wasn't there, Roald," Magdali put in testily. "He has enough to do here without going to celebrations. Anyhow, you know he never goes to that place except to trade, and then the children and I go along."

"Pete Sondstrom came by," Ivar explained, "on his way to Georgetown. He was at the celebration and told us all about it."

"So," said Roald. "But—might be he doesn't know all about it. There's more in Moorhead than Pete Sondstrom has the wit to see, Ivar." He smiled in broad satisfaction. "Did he tell you the squatters are moving across the river to Fargo-in-the-timber? Even Brazell has moved his dance hall and—"

"Isn't Moorhead good enough for Brazell?" Ivar asked.

"Well might you ask, Ivar!" Roald retorted. "Good enough, indeed! Might be it is *too* good. Have you thought of that? They have to pay a high price for the ground they stand on in Moorhead these days. You see what that means? That land we have—Magdali and me—it will be worth money now, you bet!"

It was the first time he had spoken of the Endicott land in Ivar's hearing since that memorable spring night when Ivar had come home from his journey to learn what had been done in his absence. Excitement had got a little the better of Roald, however. He looked to his sister for a word to reassure him and put him at ease.

But Magdali adjusted the baby at her breast with a delicate,

[128]

concealing tumult of her flannel dressing-sacque. "Shush-shoo, Solveig!" She began a low crooning as she rocked gently back and forth in her chair. "Hand me that blanket from the back of the chair over there, brother," she said in a voice that was barely audible. After a moment she got up deliberately with the sleeping baby in her arms. "Those who make money, Roald," she murmured as she crossed the room, "must first learn to be patient."

Roald gaped after her as she disappeared into the other room. Then he sank into the chair that Magdali had left and gazed in profound thought at the ceiling. "Ya, ya," he mused contentedly at last, "she is right, my sister. We must wait and hit when the iron is warm."

Magdali returned and prepared a bowl of hot sour milk with pepper and sugar, which she set before her brother. While he supped, she parceled a smoked Red River "salmon" for him to take home when he went. The facetious name the newcomers in the valley had given the humble gold-eye left it nevertheless a firm and tasty fish that appeared frequently on the settlers' table, since it was to be had for the taking.

"Are you going to the Sondstroms for Christmas, sister?" Roald asked, pausing with his spoon halfway to his mouth.

Magdali sighed. "They'll have such a houseful without us," she replied. "The Featherstones are to be there, and the Joseffy family. Those Joseffy children will probably eat ten times as much as ours. When I drove over to their place last week, with the milk and the potato cakes, the poor little things almost pulled my skirt off before I really got in the door. How does such a man as Joseffy think he can raise a family if he can't feed them? I don't know why such people come to a place like this."

Ivar could scarcely believe his ears. It wasn't so long ago that she had used almost the same words in speaking of the

Endicotts. Was she already wondering what would become of the Joseffy land when the struggle proved too much for its present tenants?

"Magdali," Ivar said, laying Karsten's boot aside, "Joseffy isn't Endicott. He is poor, but he will get along." There was an angry dryness about his lips as he spoke.

"I have no doubt, Ivar," Magdali said pleasantly. "But I'd hate to think we couldn't do better by our children than the Joseffys are doing by theirs. We were talking about Christmas, weren't we? I've been thinking—wouldn't it be nice if we spent Christmas here and asked Miss Kate and her brother over for the day? They will be alone, I expect, with their sister and Mr. Brazell busy all day in their saloon."

Her acid sweetness brought upon Ivar again the feeling of impotent fury he had experienced so often the past summer. He knew that she held Delphy in superior contempt, even though she never permitted an ungenerous word concerning her to escape her lips. At the same time she would never have entertained the idea of the Brazells—Texas and Delphy had been married in June—spending the day at the Vinge fireside.

On the other hand, her sharp awareness of Kate Shaleen was a thing so elemental that Ivar doubted whether Magdali herself knew what lay beneath it—a difference in spirit that was like the difference between the many-colored sea and a granite cliff. The sea, in time, would wear the cliff down, but the cliff continued to challenge the sea nevertheless. Magdali feared Kate Shaleen—even hated her, Ivar sometimes thought. Her unnatural amusement at his account of the little while he and young Karsten had spent in the shelter of the Shaleens' tent on that night in May had not deceived Ivar. Since Kate and Steve had settled on land so close to the Vinge farm, Magdali had often lamented her lack of time to visit them. "If I

[130]

was not so tied down with the children I could visit our neighbors more. Especially that nice Kate Shaleen, Ivar!" And she would twinkle at him in a way that set him almost beside himself.

"Ya, that would be good—to ask them for Christmas," Roald observed. "They are neighbors."

"Yes, though it wasn't of that I was thinking so much," Magdali replied. "I am looking farther ahead than this Christmas—or the next, for that matter. One day we must have a place of our own here—a town, I mean. Let them have their Moorhead and their Fargo. We shall need a church and a school for our children close by. And we must have a teacher if we have a school."

Ivar looked up suddenly. "You would not want Kate Shaleen for a teacher?"

Magdali's eyes widened as she shook her head ruefully toward Roald. "I can't understand what Ivar has against Miss Kate," she said in a plaintive voice.

"I have nothing against her," Ivar said. "It is you who will have something against her if you find she isn't teaching your children what you think they should learn."

"Dear me," Magdali smiled, "you seem to know a great deal about Miss Kate, don't you, Ivar?"

"Might be she will want to teach somewhere else," Roald put in quickly. "They talk of a church house and school together in Moorhead, by public subscription, and already they talk of a school in Fargo too. If it should be that she would want to be with her sister more, she would go to Fargo. It is what I hear only."

Roald's importance as a newsmonger having risen again, he got up from his chair, stretched himself, and went to warm his backside at the fire before starting for home. "Ya, it is yust so I thought in the first place," he said as if talking to himself. "We will wait till we hear more. Might be by January—"

"If you can say *January*, Roald," Magdali put in sharply, "you can say *just*. And don't lose your senses now, brother. Most of all, put no faith in that new town across the river. A place that's full of squatters can disappear overnight."

"You are right, Magdali," Roald declared, then chuckled to himself. "It is a foolish business, that squatting."

XV

It was the next afternoon, when Ivar was cutting firewood in the river timber, that he heard the crackle of a footstep on the frozen ground behind him and turned to see Kate Shaleen in her long, tightly buttoned, dark-blue coat and her red woolen hood, her hands tucked into a little round muff of sealskin.

Her shy smile came as she said, "I was walking along the river and heard the sound of your ax."

"It's cold weather to be walking in," Ivar said. He glanced toward the house, wondering if Magdali would be able to see Kate's red hood through the almost naked trees—and scowled at himself for the wondering.

"I get lonely at home," Kate said, "with Steve working from dawn to dark for the railroad."

"It isn't good to be alone, I know," Ivar admitted. "My wife has been thinking to visit you soon, but—well, the baby is getting her teeth, and there is plenty to do with three children in the house. She was talking about you last night. I think she would like to have you and your brother with us for Christmas dinner."

"Well—that's very kind of her. Mrs. Sondstrom asked us to go to her place, but there'll be so many. Anyhow, I told her I couldn't promise, because we might be going to Delphy's, over in Fargo. We're going there for Christmas Eve, but for Christmas Day—it would be nice to spend it with you and Mrs. Vinge. I know Steve will want to come."

Ivar looked once more toward the house. "You better come

with me up to the house for coffee. You can tell her then that you and Steve will be with us for Christmas."

"I'm not taking you away from your work?" She glanced at the pile of firewood.

"It is enough," Ivar said, laying his ax aside. "Tomorrow I come down with the ox and the stone boat and haul it up."

Kate Shaleen did not reply. Her eyes were fixed upon a red-crested downy woodpecker perched on the bole of an elm.

Ivar smiled. "He is my little friend. He comes every day when I am here."

"He wears the blood of spring on his head," Kate said—almost as if she were singing, Ivar thought, "and oh, may he live to see the spring again!"

"That is like a poem," Ivar remarked, and then felt somehow foolish for having said it. "We must go up to the house now," he added quickly, and started off.

Magdali had a freshly starched, ruffled apron over her dark wool dress when she greeted Kate Shaleen at the door. She had seen them coming up from the river, Ivar knew.

"So nice a surprise!" Magdali said warmly. "Come right here and sit by the fire. I have put the coffee on, and we'll have it in a minute. I was making it ready for my Ivar, anyhow. He must have his coffee when he comes in from the cold. Did he tell you I was going to your place one day soon to ask you here for Christmas?"

"Yes, Mrs. Vinge, he did," Kate told her, laying aside her hood and muff and unbuttoning her coat. "It is so thoughtful of you to ask us."

"Let me take your coat, Miss Kate," Magdali suggested brightly. "I'll just lay it on our bed in here. The baby is sleeping, or we'd go into the best room. A baby is always the boss, as you will find out when you have one of your own to care for. Ivar, see if Karsten and Magdis are coming into the house.

I let them go to the stable to look for eggs, though the hens aren't laying much these days."

"The children will know their way home," Ivar laughed, though he was guilty of a little stubborn perversity because of Magdali's manner.

He looked from the window, nevertheless, then wandered away to the corner of the room where he kept his pipe and tobacco.

Magdali served coffee from her copper coffeepot, and crisp little wafers sprinkled with cinnamon. Ivar sat apart with his pipe and cup of coffee, listening in stony and troubled silence while the women talked, wondering, too, why he should be troubled at all since they seemed to be getting on so amicably.

Magdali had contrived to bring the conversation to bear upon family history, to which Kate Shaleen was contributing ingenuously.

"My mother was Norwegian, from Stavanger," Kate was saying, "and my father was Irish, of course. They met first in New York, where my mother was a nursemaid with an English family. My father was a blacksmith when they married and came west to seek their fortune. I'm afraid father wasn't very lucky, poor man. He—"

"It was quite romantic, anyhow, for them both to want to come west," Magdali said. "Irish and Norwegian—I don't think I ever knew of a marriage between—"

"The Irish and the Norwegians have been married before, Magdali," Ivar spoke up. "Or do you forget your history?" He laughed as he took his pipe from his mouth. "One of my ancestors," he went on, careful to pronounce each word exactly, "beat the Irish and ran off with some of their princesses. He had help, I know. His name was Eric Bloody Axe, and some of the princesses they took back to Norway, and some to Iceland. Oh, yes, the Irish and the Norwegians have known

[135]

each other for a long time."

"Of course!" Magdali smiled indulgently. "And in a new country like this all kinds mix. Your pipe has gone out, Ivar." She took his pipe from him, scraped the bowl, and refilled it from the pouch. "A husband is as much care as a child," she said as she handed Ivar the pipe. "Have you done anything about finding a school yet, Miss Kate?"

"Very little, I'm afraid," Kate replied. "There isn't much I can do till they get a school. They're talking of having one in Fargo by spring and one in Moorhead too. I'd like to take the one in Fargo, where I'd be close to my sister."

"Yes, of course," Magdali said. "I wish we could have a school here—not so far away for the children, I mean."

Kate's eyes shone. "I wish we could have, too. Only today, walking along the river, I found a place that was made for a schoolhouse to stand in. But I suppose it will be a long time before anything like that will happen."

Magdali's eyes lifted toward the window. For a moment she gazed thoughtfully into distance, then said, "It may happen sooner than you think, Miss Kate. There are children in the district—we have a teacher ready to do the work—all we need is a school to put them in. I think it can be done. We must organize the district and petition the government. As soon as Christmas is out of the way, I'm going to see what can be done about it."

"That would be wonderful," Kate said. "I have almost promised to teach the school in Fargo when—"

"They haven't got their school in Fargo yet," Magdali reminded her, and added, "Nor yet in Moorhead."

"No, they haven't, of course, but—"

"It will be time enough to think of that when we must," Magdali said.

What could the woman be getting at now? Ivar wondered

as he got up and strode restlessly to the window.

"The children are coming," he announced.

"I think I hear Solveig waking," Magdali said, and bent an ear toward the other room. "It is time to nurse her again." She smiled at Kate Shaleen. "With a husband and three children, you have not time to wash your face."

"I must be going, before it gets too late," Kate said, and got up to put on her coat. "Thank you so much for the coffee and cakes."

"It was nothing," Magdali replied. "Then you'll bring your brother and spend Christmas with us, teacher?" She laughed. "See—I call you teacher already!"

"We'd love to come, Mrs. Vinge."

Karsten and little Magdis bounced into the house, Magdis proudly holding up one lone egg.

"Me find it!" she cried. "And me eat it! Kars'n don't get enny-never!"

Magdali shooshed the little girl and looked at her husband. "Hadn't you better go a little way with Miss Kate, Ivar? It gets dark so soon these days."

But Kate Shaleen was already at the door. "Oh, no! I wouldn't think of it. There will be starlight, and besides—I love winter nights!"

After supper that evening, the children in bed and a gentle quiet filling the fire-lit kitchen, Magdali said, "I'm so glad the Shaleens will come to us for Christmas, Ivar. Aren't you?"

"What you want, Magdi, is right with me. You have decided to have her for teacher, eh?"

Magdali was busy drawing a long thread through a needle. She spoke without looking at Ivar. "We must use what we have. Miss Kate is here beside us. It is my idea to get all I can for our children—for their future, Ivar. I am not like that fool Joseffy, who thinks the Lord will look after his children. The Lord will help them that know how to help themselves first."

Ivar looked at the clock. The fir-wood case was intricately carved and painted in the form of little dancing gnomes. It had been his father's wedding present to him and Magdali, and weeks of his father's scant leisure time had gone into its fashioning. Ivar saw vividly now that lonely mountain farmstead in Norway where his elder brother Christian might some day become the owner, unless the "barons" got the land first. The red painted hands of the clock stood at a quarter of nine. He must write again soon to his father, he thought, and it was a clear and simple thought, over others confused and troubling.

"I'll go and see to the animals, Magdali," he said, getting up.

"I'll have some hot cinnamon plum juice for you when you come in," said Magdali.

Ivar went out. In the full light of the moon that had risen in the past hour, he saw something that stiffened the hair on his head. This afternoon he thought he had seen a timber wolf skulking along the edge of the tree claim, but the light had been uncertain. Still, he had thought, tomorrow he must build a byre against one side of the stable to keep the sheep in at night, for the ewes would be lambing in May. Now he darted back to the house and seized his rifle from the wall in the kitchen.

He shot the wolf just within the fence of the sheep enclosure, where the moonlight revealed the animal's outlines, tense and harshly beautiful, an instant's frozen statue of darkness against the glitter of the frozen snow. With his pulse racing like a boy's, he walked to where it had fallen and stood for a moment looking down at the inert body, seeing the yellow eyes become glazed, the fangs exposed in a frustrated snarl. With the butt of his gun he rolled the beast over, and as he bent nearer an incoherent exclamation escaped his lips. It was a she-wolf, her dugs heavy with milk.

For a while Ivar could not move. Snug and confidently waiting in some cave would be the whelps of this gaunt killer who had set out to replenish her body that her young, in turn, might be replenished. As if the moonlight had entered his brain, a thought came to Ivar of such enormity that he could scarcely credit it with being his own. The Endicotts—perhaps the Joseffys—perhaps Kate Shaleen and her brother, even—and Magdali! Magdali and the fruit of her body that must be fed as she deemed wise and fit, though others perish in the process!

He looked vaguely about him at the sheep huddled in the lee of the straw stack near the stable. Then, without another glance at the dead she-wolf, he trod heavily away to his lamplit house and to Magdali and the children.

XVI

It was past the middle of February now, and for many weeks, even with Steve at home every night, Kate Shaleen had felt unaccountably alone. It was something she could not understand, for she had tasks enough to keep her from brooding.

She knew it was not because of Delphy's marriage to Texas Brazell last June, even though the event had marked the first real break in the little family group that had held together through heartbreak and tragedy for so many years. In fact, Kate had not been greatly astonished at the marriage. It was just like Delphy to fall in love with a small boy playing at being a highwayman. Beneath Brazell's theatrical swagger, there were virtues of loyalty, kindliness, and a certain rectitude which his environment had not quite crushed. He made no apology for his mode of living, but there was a deep loneliness within him, just the same; and that was what Delphy with her great heart had first seen beneath his absurd, villainous glitter. Delphy was happy, and Kate in her own loneliness was happy for her.

Texas Brazell's place had been doing a thriving business. The new town on the west side of the river had sprung up between sunrise and sunrise, its inhabitants lured by the bait of free land. Close by the "squatter town" was the imposing encampment of the railway engineers. The chief engineer and many of his attachés had brought their wives and families with them for the winter, and the activities of these people lent to the place all the brilliant commotion of an army post on the fringe of civilization. With Delphy at the helm, so highly moral was the tone of "Brazell's" that even the most critical of the settlers declared it did the community a service in providing clean and cheerful entertainment. The engineers and their wives considered it a gift from heaven.

Besides the dance hall and the saloon, all under one cover, there was a dining room which was no more than a raw poplar-paneled slot between the two main divisions of the bulky wood and canvas shelter. Here, over a roaring stove, Delphy cooked meals day and night and served them to the famished men who poured in from track or trail to sit down with robust enthusiasm at the bare pine-board table. Here, too, she ladled out like fare to the "swells" who came now and then from the engineers' encampment.

Delphy, too, had kept her eye on whatever the place had to offer in the way of entertainment. She had dismissed the girls, most of whom had gone to ply their trade in a place run by a competitor by the name of Steele. But she had added Luke Nisselbaum and his fiddle to Lambert's drum and Willie Bates's accordion with a result so harmonious that Delphy was ready to believe in magic. She had discovered Luke sitting in the wintry rain outside the tent soon after she and Texas had moved to the west side of the river, and though she had never been able to learn the origin of Luke himself, she believed that his music was conceived by angels. His bow could wheedle out of the strings heartbreak or hilarity, violent excitement or the mist of dreams.

No, her feeling of loneliness had nothing to do with Delphy, Kate thought as she trudged through the snow from the sod house to the coulee, the wooden water bucket swinging at her side. Only last Sunday Delphy and Texas had driven out by way of the river snow in a red and silver cutter, with bells tinkling on the harness of Cortez, the spirited bay gelding that Texas Brazell had presented to Delphy at Christmas. They had talked all afternoon about their plans for the future—how

Texas was putting money aside every week to provide for the school that would be started as soon as the frost was out of the ground in the spring—how Delphy was laying away a little every day for a purpose which she chose to keep a secret, although she declared it was not for the baby she expected by midsummer—how Steve was hoarding his meager earnings against the day when he could begin the serious business of putting his land to the test of growing things no other settler along the river had so much as dreamed of. It had been a wonderful afternoon, but Kate had gone to bed that night with a feeling that they were all doing something, planning something, while she was merely waiting.

Now against the razor edge of the wind she was on her way back from the coulee, plodding through the delicately tinted snow in the sunset. With one mittened hand she held up her cumbersome woolen skirts, with the other lugged the bucket of water from the spring in the gully bank. It was only an idea of hers, Steve said, that the spring water was sweeter than that of the well near the house. Perhaps so, but he had not heard its first timid whisper yesterday, as if it had listened to a porous, spreading sigh in the earth, a rumor of thaw after six weeks of icicled silence, and had ventured forth on glistening toe into the sun! But tonight it would be frozen again.

As she approached the soddy, the vague and rebellious emptiness of her heart gave way to a tender glow. She had helped Steve to build this, their first home on the prairie, and never would she forget the exultant pride with which it was completed. She had asked herself then: Those architects of ancient Rome and Greece who wrought their temples in marble, were they so much abler than she who, with the humblest stuff of earth had built a temple to earth itself, the temple of home? Even while she had flushed at the extravagance of her thought —as if somebody had been listening to it—she had set her lips stubbornly and added, "But it *is* so! These soddies on the prairie are shrines to a new and unspoiled earth, and we who build them must keep them beautiful and pure!"

There was one who must come near her meaning, she thought now, as she approached the soddy. Did he like music, that Ivar Vinge? If she ever got an organ again, would he bring his children to hear her play Handel's Largo, or maybe a Strauss waltz? She remembered him always as she had seen him standing beside the river—that day of their first meeting, when the sun was hot in an August sky—and that afternoon in the nakedly shining woods where the sun had been a sullen flame low in the west. How quickly he had turned away from her, on both occasions, as if in the fear that he would betray himself if he stayed!

And again Kate Shaleen knew what she wanted above everything else. Some day she would have her school here beside the river, even though she might have to spend a year or so teaching in the school that Texas Brazell was determined she should have in Fargo. That one thought was firm in her mind as her eyes lifted northwestward across the white sweep of prairie to the huddle of the Vinge farm against the ruddy dark glimmer of the brush.

That night, after supper—a supper of beans and side pork and blackstrap molasses and biscuits with wild gooseberry preserve set out on a red-checked cloth—Steve sat beside the dobie fireplace and read the paper he had brought with him from Moorhead. It was a Chicago paper, a week old, and Steve passed over the events in Washington where General Grant was urging something or other, and flicked the page to the advertisements.

"Listen to this, Kate—out of *Dreer's Garden Calendar*," he said, and began to read: " 'Trophy tomato seeds, introduced in 1870 at five dollars per twenty seeds, now selling for twenty-five cents per pack of one hundred.' That gives me an idea. I'll bet we can raise a crop of tomatoes on this land. Not that I liked the only one I ever tasted—remember, at Captain Falmer's place that time? It looked like a red apple, and I bit off a good half of it. Lord, what a sell! But them things are gettin' stylish. Maybe for twenty-five cents—oh, the hell with it! Even if they did come up, people round here would think we were tryin' to sell 'em poison."

Kate was half listening, her eye on an inner sheet of the paper which she had picked away from Steve. Mrs. Henry Wood had a new book out, *Bessy Rane*. Kate wondered if it would be as heart-searching as *East Lynne*. She sighed then, remembering that there was still no money in the house for such luxuries as new books. "Splendid Chromos" were advertised at half price. She wondered if "Asking a Blessing" would be much of a bargain at three dollars.

She turned the sheet and saw that there had been a "New Year Waltz" composed and arranged by Starr Halloway. Oh, if her old second-hand organ had not been burned with the blacksmith shop and the house! Her father had bought it for her when she was fifteen. The pang of loneliness came again. She winked quickly and read, "Heartburn same as water brash." And who didn't know that?

Steve was snoring in his chair.

"Better go to bed, Steve," Kate said gently.

Steve blinked impatiently and shook his head. "I got a notion about this land here," he said as if he had been wide awake and thinking all the while. "It's something that's got to be gentled, like a horse—and then let go, hell bent for leather! Maybe that's because I used to help pa shoe horses, and the smell o' the land was never far away." His voice became dreamy.

"I'll fix your bed, Steve."

"I've got waked up all of a sudden. I must've had a dream. I been thinkin'—we're here because we think it's a good place to be—and we think we're goin' to stay here, don't we? The way I see it—the Indians used to think this was a good place. They used to think it was pretty good back there where we came from in New Ulm. But they made a bargain with the gover'ment, and we got the land. When a few crooked officials went back on the bargain, the Sioux just naturally went on the war path and made us pay. We were the ones that paid for it, Kate—people like us who got themselves shot and scalped and burned out. Well, that leaves us square all round, doesn't it? But how do we know we won't be tricked out o' what we got, by the same crooks that tricked the Sioux—after we've plowed and planted, maybe, and dropped our sweat into the soil? I heard talk goin' round today that made me wonder. We think this is a new, free country. But there ain't much that's free— and we still got to figure on the old tricks. What I mean, Kate —we better not build our hopes too high, not yet a while. First thing we know, they'll be gettin' top-heavy."

Steve was past thirty now, seven years older than Kate, but he had always seemed younger to her before they had taken up this adventure in the Red River Valley. Of late, however, new and sharp facets had appeared in his nature, as in a stone turned about in the palm of the hand, under a brighter light.

"You may be right, Steve," Kate conceded doubtfully, "but there is something you're forgetting. I thought of it when I was helping you build this soddy. The northern Indians never built on the earth—they built on the wind. That's where we're different from them."

Steve shifted uncomfortably. "There you go, bustin' into poetry again! All I said was—"

"I know, Steve. We'll have people here who will want more than they need, just to show off their importance—people who will hustle and grab and stir up such a dust about them we won't be able to see the sun or the stars! America is beautiful, Steve, and it is people like us who must keep it so. Maybe, in a way, we are beautiful too. But we shall go back into the ground, and it will take a hundred years or more for the ground to yield our harvest."

Steve regarded her with embarrassed awe. "Jee-hovah!" he said, and began to get ready for bed.

Kate slept uneasily that night and wakened at dawn with a steel-colored blade of light thrusting through between the red-dyed burlap curtains of the small window that looked toward the east. She drew the blanket and the sheepskin cover close about her neck and shivered her body down into a knot upon the rustling straw mattress, while with one eye she looked around the corner of her calico-draped packing-box bureau to see if by any chance there was a spark left in the dobie fireplace. Of course there was none. She could see Steve's foot in its heavy wool sock sticking out from the bedclothes of his wall bunk, and in spite of the bitter cold she wanted to laugh because it struck her suddenly that she had never seen anything so soundly and utterly asleep as that foot.

Then, all at once, she knew that it had been some quite un-usual sound that had wakened her. She sat up instantly, clutching the throat frill of her flannel nightgown.

"Steve!" she called out, and groped down on the icy pine boards for her heavy felt house shoes. "Get up! I hear sleigh bells."

With shaking hands she threw on her old velveteen wrapper and her hooded cloak over that. While Steve confusedly un-tangled his red woolen underwear from the bed clothes, she sped to the door and looked out.

"Jee-rusalem! Kate!" Steve yelped. "Close the door. What in hell—who's coming at this time o'——"

"It's Texas Brazell," Kate said. "Oh, thank God, Delphy is with him! I was afraid—"

And then, before Steve had time to blink himself fully awake, Delphy and Texas were standing in the room, and Kate had her arms about her sister's heavy, quilt-swathed figure, while she stared at her from eyes wide with relief and amazement.

"Whatever brings you—" Kate's tears welled over, and Delphy with a shaky laugh dropped the quilt from her shoulders and sank into a chair.

"You two females get into bed till we warm this place up," Texas ordered. "Where's your kindling, Steve?"

Dressed as they were, Kate and Delphy crawled into Steve's bunk and lay there with chattering teeth while the men built a fire. Brazell's aquiline face was pinched blue with cold, yet fury flamed within him as he stood twisting his fingers before the roaring fire where Steve had piled logs with prodigal disregard for the limited supply of fuel he had stored against the winter's needs.

"Are you beginning to thaw out, Delph?" he asked with a glance of concern toward the bunk.

"I'm doing fine," Delphy said. "Go ahead and tell them what happened. The Shaleens are used to taking bumps."

"We never got used to takin' anything else," Steve growled. "What is it this time, Tex?"

"It's that damned Puget Sound outfit!" Texas replied. "They found out we were on Indian land over there, so—we're out, that's all. I might have been able to put up a fight, but I was selling liquor on a reserve, and even if I didn't know that, I'd have no chance against the government agents. It means—" He paused abruptly. "I'd better go and put Cortez in the stable before he freezes in his tracks. I can tell the rest later."

"You sit where you are and warm up," Steve said. "I'll look after Cortez." He hung the copper teakettle on the crane above the fire—the kettle that had once been his mother's, and the only thing of hers the Shaleens had saved from New Ulm, from

St. Paul, from all their various calamities. "Keep an eye on this, Tex. It'll be boilin', time I get back."

"I'll watch it, Steve," Kate said and swung her feet out of the bunk. "I'll have coffee ready for you when you come in."

She dressed quickly, while Texas dosed Delphy with hot water and a dram from the bottle he had brought with him. While Kate moved swiftly, preparing cornmeal mush, bacon, and coffee, she saw to her relief that the drink was having its effect upon her sister. The tight, bluish pallor over her cheekbones was giving way to a stinging red.

"You're looking better," Kate said. "I was struck all of a heap, thinking perhaps the baby—"

"It's a wonder we didn't scare you to death," Delphy mumbled from the bed clothes.

Steve came in, stamping his feet, and looked at the table. "I'll be glad when we get a cow," he said cheerfully. "I get so blame tired o' molasses on mush!"

While they ate, Texas bloomed into the narrative of what had happened. Before the Puget Sound Land Company could make their scrip locations, they were obliged to clear the land of its rapidly growing colony of squatters and settlers who had begun to feel secure and were looking forward to a blessed spring. Through their agents in St. Cloud, the company had discovered that the land was part of the Wahpeton and Sioux Reservation, and had obtained forthwith an order from Washington directed to the United States Marshal of Dakota for the removal of all trespassers in this area—and for the arrest of such of them as were trafficking in spiritous liquors. After the dispossession, the land company would negotiate at leisure with the government to its own satisfactory ends.

Late yesterday, Texas said, the settlement was agog over the arrival of a company of troops from Fort Abercrombie. But everybody had been given to understand that they had come to

[148]

quell a disturbance among the Indians on the Upper Sheyenne. By midnight, every squatter's tent and shanty was peacefully wrapped in slumber.

About four o'clock in the morning, however, Luke Nisselbaum had burst wildly in to where Texas and Delphy were sleeping, and announced that the river bank was being patrolled by guards and that sentinels were being stationed at every door in the settlement. While Luke was giving them his news, Texas and Delphy were dashing into their clothes. When they were dressed, Texas slipped his leather money pouch from beneath the mattress, grabbed a bottle from the bar, and quietly slashed a hole in the side of the tent away from the eyes of anyone who might be on watch. Delphy had seized a blanket from their bed, wrapped it around her, and crept through the opening in the tent wall. In the darkness, all three—Luke with his fiddle—had crawled on hands and knees through the stiff, snow-covered bushes that made a noise under them like the crack of doom, Delphy thought, before they reached the underground stable that housed Cortez.

Providentially, during these tense moments there had been an uproar close to the river where someone had discharged a gun. It was precisely the kind of diversion necessary to enable Texas and Luke to harness Cortez and put him into the shafts, and then they were off through a northwest glade of trees that gave them shelter to the bank of the river, a little more than a mile north of town. There they paused, and Luke removed the horse blanket with which he had carefully muted the bells. Already the sky was beginning to lighten with an iron pallor in the east.

Texas and Delphy insisted on Luke's going all the way with them, but Luke was bent on returning to Moorhead, where he had friends who would take him in until the trouble blew over. They drove off at last, leaving Luke standing in the frigid air

[149]

before dawn, his fiddle under his chin—playing a weird, un-earthly accompaniment to the sleigh bells.

"You should have seen him, Kate!" Delphy said, half laughing, half crying. "He was like something out of the Bible, standing there all alone in that queer blue light—but of course they didn't have fiddles or black caps with ear muffs in the Bible!"

"Well, there goes your school, Kate," Texas Brazell said, his voice heavy with regret. "It was the first thing I thought of as soon as I knew we had got away."

"It doesn't matter," Kate replied. "There will be other schools before long."

"If it was only summer, or if—" Texas twisted one end of his mustache to a needle point, and his dark, heavy-lashed eyes grew shy and embarrassed. Close to tears for his sake, Kate still wanted to laugh as she thought of how grandiosely sinister he had made himself out to be at Bogusville, much less than a year ago. "If Delphy wasn't in a delicate condition, we—"

"Have you got any money?" Steve asked practically.

Texas got up and took the leather pouch from an inner pocket of the fur-lined great coat he had left in a corner of the room. He came back and tossed the pouch on the table. "Delphy has some of her own tucked away, but that's special."

"How much is there?" Steve asked, nodding toward the pouch.

"Enough," Texas replied noncommittally. "If I can leave Delphy here, I'd like to spend a few days in Moorhead. I want to talk it over with the boys—Luke and Lambert and Willie Bates. We ought to be able to get together on something."

Steve sat for a moment in silence. He felt uneasy about Brazell's suggestion, but he decided to say nothing. "It's time I was getting to work," he said finally.

When he stepped from the house and made his way toward the stable where old Jezebel awaited him, the early morning landscape was made bleak by his anxiety for both Texas and Delphy. The broad white tide of the prairie looked as forbidding and impenetrable as if it were made of enamel, as if no plow could ever cleave the flush dark earth it covered. Above the little birch pole privy—a really ingenious affair with a seat made from the bleached collar bone of a moose—the sun stood now in a sky of colorless metal, flanked by sun dogs that would have teeth in them. Yes, the Shaleens certainly had a genius for cottoning to trouble!

Texas slept until noon in Steve's bunk, though he refused to remove more than his boots. Then, after a meal of partridge, thawed out from the rack beside the house and grilled over the fire with potatoes in their jackets, he kissed Delphy good-by and left for Moorhead.

He had been gone for five minutes, the sleigh-bell jingle fading, when Delphy, pale against the door they had closed upon the cold, looked at Kate and said:

"The money in my stocking is for you, Kate. You may as well take it now and put it away. I want you to have it—for an organ."

"Delphy!"

But Delphy put her hands out before her and started toward the bed. "I—I don't feel so—"

Then she collapsed in a senseless heap on the floor.

XVII

FROM HIS OWN soddy, Roald Bratland had seen Texas Brazell drive off toward town. The light of noonday was crisp and dazzling, but to Roald's eyes the fast-stepping Cortez hitched to the red and silver cutter bade fair to outshine anything under heaven.

His envious eyes had enjoyed a much closer scrutiny of the equipage last Sunday when the Brazells had driven out to visit Steve and Kate Shaleen. Careful to conceal his curiosity, he had walked over to spend a half-hour or so with the Shaleens. He had no need to ask how Texas Brazell had come by his prize. Pete Sondstrom had told him that it had changed hands a week before in the settlement of a gambling debt. They were still talking about it in town. Well, every man to his own way, Roald had observed sagely. In good time, doubtless, and in a way that would be somewhat more to his liking, Roald Bratland would become the envy of his neighbors.

But what had brought Texas Brazell to the Shaleen soddy in the middle of a week day? And away again at noon? Something out of the ordinary must be afoot. By midafternoon, Roald had harnessed his gray team and was on his way. He would make it the occasion for going to town for supplies, if need be.

He found Delphy Brazell in bed with all the blankets in the place wrapped about her. Kate had placed hot stones at her feet, had plied her with hot peppermint water and broth, and had rubbed her chest with liniment, and then applied a flour and mustard poultice.

"If I only had some hot goose-oil," Kate said, "but there wasn't enough on those wild geese last fall to make it worth saving. I'm so afraid—" She bit her lips.

Roald thought fast. He patted Kate's shoulder. "You must not be afraid. I go now and come back quick. All will be good!"

Ivar was at his workbench shaping a new yoke for the oxen when Roald arrived at the Vinge farm. The afternoon sun slanted in through the small soddy window and hung a burnished copper coin on each of the three bright copper kettles on the wall. Little Karsten stood watching with fascination the bold work of the drawknife upon the oak wood as his father patiently fashioned it to his designs. Magdis was busy in a corner washing the featureless face of her rag doll. Solveig slept in her cradle. Everything had been peace and contentment here until Roald came rushing in with his news.

"Sister Magdali," he said at once, "there is work for you to do at the Shaleen place. You must come quick. The woman is sick with might be lung fever in her brother's house."

Ivar set his drawknife aside and spoke with more calmness than he felt. "What woman, Roald?"

"Is it the one they call—Delphy?" Magdali asked, with a kind of fastidious hesitation before she uttered the name.

"Who else?" Roald replied impatiently. "She is alone there— with Miss Kate."

"Did they send for *me?*" Magdali asked.

"*Bövelen,* no!" Roald burst out. "I have come for you. Is that not enough?"

"It is enough, of course, brother," she assured him gently and got up from her chair, a polished look on her cool blue eyes. "I have never been at such a bedside, but—yes, it is my duty. I will get ready. Ivar, take the oil from the cupboard—and my onion medicine in the flask."

Ivar stared after her as she vanished into the other room, her

[153]

step vigorously light. When she reappeared, her head and shoulders were covered by a red and blue knitted shawl, her cloak buttoned securely at her throat. She carried her black string reticule, which seemed packed to capacity.

"There is the smoked mutton for your supper, Ivar," she said rapidly, "and the cabbage soup from last night. Put in more milk for the children. And there's barley soup on the stove—for the baby. I may not be back tonight. You, Roald, take the spare quilts out of the chest, there. Perhaps they have a chair I can sit in and rest a while."

"You think of staying the night?" Ivar asked.

"How can I know, Ivar?" Magdali glanced at Solveig, rosily asleep in her cradle, then knelt and gathered the other two children into her arms. "Take good care of papa, now, till mamma comes back," she coaxed, as Magdis began to whimper. "That's a big girl! Mamma has to go to make a sick person all well again. Next time papa goes to town you will get stripe candy—if you're good now."

Roald had brought the patchwork quilts from the chest in the other room. Magdali gave them a cursory glance and held them to her nose. "The sweet grass is still nice on them," she remarked, then with a sudden start, "Ivar—the assafoetida! I almost forgot it. There's no telling what the woman's trouble may be, after the place she and that husband of hers have been living in."

At last they were ready to go, and Magdali, after a quick look about the room, said, "The sugar-tit is in that blue bowl in the cupboard, Ivar, if Solveig cries too much with her teeth. If I do not come back tonight, Roald will come and tell you how it is there."

"That I will!" Roald promised.

"Good-by, Ivar," Magdali said.

"Good-by, then, *kjaere*," Ivar said, with a helpless feeling.

[154]

"Take care you don't catch something yourself. And come back as soon as you can."

He watched Roald's team disappear across the pink and violet shadows of the crested snowdrifts. Then he turned back indoors and gazed abstractedly about him. The baby Solveig still slept with a somewhat disdainful look upon her pretty face; Karsten was intently examining the knot in a smoothly shaved piece of oak; little Magdis, forgetful of her recent woe, was blackening her doll's face with soot from the bottom of an iron pot that hung before the fireplace so that she might wash it again.

It would soon be time to light the lamp and set about making supper for himself and the children, Ivar thought absently. He went to the window and stared out. Magdali, Magdali! Would her righteous kindness bring healing to the woman who lay sick there in the little soddy to the south? Would it ever bring true healing to anything?

But even while Ivar stood wondering at the window, Magdali was going about her task with all her wonted energy. She had persuaded Roald to remain with her to keep the fire going and the kettles full of hot water while she and Kate Shaleen attended to Delphy, dosing her with homemade remedies, rubbing her chest and back with hot oil, bundling her in blankets that had been hung before the fireplace.

By the time Steve Shaleen came home from work, Magdali was more than pleased with the results of her labors.

"She is in a good sweat now," she told Steve by way of quieting his alarm. "She will be all right, you will see. But she must stay in bed for a few days."

"I'll see to that," he vowed. "They can get along without me down at the camp for the rest of the season. I was thinkin' of layin' off anyhow."

[155]

They sat in to the supper Kate had prepared for them, and Steve held forth on the events of the night before that had routed the panic-stricken citizenry of the town across the river and sent them scurrying for shelter in the depth of a winter's night.

"It's a cryin' shame and an outrage!" Steve declared angrily. "Even the gover'ment has no right to—"

"Sh-h, Steve!" Kate cautioned him, with a glance toward the bed where Delphy had fallen asleep at last.

"It is too bad," Magdali observed sympathetically. "I am so sorry for the poor people who have no place to go. But wouldn't it have been better if they had found out—before they settled—"

"Who was there to tell them?" Steve demanded. "In a country where a man can walk a hundred miles in any direction and never find as much as a fence to bar his way, what makes a few acres there beside the river holy ground that no man dares to spend the night on it?"

Magdali smiled. "It is the way of things, even in a new land like ours. 'To him that hath shall be given, and to him that hath not shall be taken—' "

Kate's eyes were upon her brother, fearful of what she saw in his tight lips and the stubborn set of his chin. "I'm afraid we're disturbing Delphy," she said quickly and got up from the table.

For an hour then, Magdali gave her whole attention to making Delphy comfortable for the night. After a few final instructions to Kate, she looked toward Roald, who had been sitting back among the shadows in one corner of the room.

"It is time we were going, brother," she said. "I shall come again tomorrow and see if there is anything to be done. And Roald will go to town and tell Mr. Brazell about his—"

"I'll look to that myself," Steve said crisply.

In a few minutes Kate and Steve were alone with Delphy, who had fallen asleep again before Magdali and Roald had left.

"I don't like that woman," Steve said flatly as he drew his chair to the fireplace and began filling his pipe.

"How can you say that, Steve, after tonight!" Kate exclaimed.

"All right—all right. She did her 'bounden' duty. But it was an unlucky day for you, the day your ways crossed with hers!"

Suddenly there came to Kate the recollection of Magdali's holding Mrs. Sondstrom's newly born baby and whispering, "The poor little thing must live, anyway until a preacher can baptize her!" And Kate had wondered whether a sprinkling of water could be so very important, after all, to a God who sometimes let the flowers die for want of rain. The Vinges had taken their own baby Solveig into Moorhead one day when a Lutheran minister was there on a visit. The temperature had been forty degrees below zero, and Steve had remarked that the child had been saved from hell by an icicle!

"Oh, Steve!" Kate sighed. "We can't be hard on people, especially in a new country where we all need each other so much. Mrs. Vinge is a good woman. I sometimes think she is too nice to me to mean it. But that's her way. She spoke to me about the school, again, just before you came home. Now that the one we were hoping for in Fargo—"

"There'll be one in Moorhead, with the spring," Steve reminded her.

"Yes, I know. And I'll take it if I have the chance. But I'd like nothing half so much as to have my own school here in the country, where it would be more like having the beginnings of things all around me."

"There you go again! While you're dreamin' dreams, it'll be people like that Vinge woman and her bandy-legged brother that'll be gettin' where we'd like to be. They'll make a go of it. Not Ivar, perhaps. He's not like her. But that other two. They'll be walkin' over the likes of us, too, while they're at it."

Kate laughed. "Does it matter so much, Steve? We'll live on somehow, and we'll get more out of living than they ever dreamed of getting. You won't be able to change that, Steve. We're what we are, and nothing will ever make us different." The shadow of the future pressed down upon her suddenly, a palpable, breathing weight. "And maybe we'll have more than we think," she added.

"There's no way of tellin' about that," Steve agreed drily.

XVIII

It was remarkable how things shaped themselves toward the future, Ivar Vinge thought as he came to the end of the last furrow in the five grassy acres he had turned for next year's wheat.

Here he was, the owner of a sturdy chestnut team that he had bought for a hundred dollars from a horse trader in Moorhead more than a month ago. He had driven a good bargain with the trader, but he was already beginning to wonder if he had not been a little hasty in laying out so much money before he could tell what the season would bring. Since the disappearance of the snow in early spring, there had been no rain to speak of. Now, in June, the wind from the western plains drove its barren heat across the shrinking green of Ivar's young fields. Well, there was no way of guessing the seasons' moods.

He had got himself a hired man, too—Louie Spragg was scarcely more than a lad, of course, but he was diligent and biddable. Roald Bratland had shared in that arrangement. The boy would work on both farms, according to the need of each. His pay was only a few dollars above his keep, and since Roald had put little of his land under the plow, depending for the most part upon the wild hay as fodder for his growing herd, the scheme would work out well.

Louie was a lonely little soul who had little to say and preferred to spend his idle hours by himself in the stable where he had his sleeping quarters. He sang in a hypnotic monotone that charmed the oxen while he plowed. He also sang to the children, on the twilit doorstep after supper, eerie songs that were well-nigh meaningless to Ivar. They brought to mind the singing of those dusky travelers of the fur brigades two years ago. Where was Julian Fordyce now? Had he already faded into the past, having no place in the future that was already molding the life of this strange land?

Out of some old ticking, Magdali had made a good clean straw mattress for Louie Spragg, and there was a small chest for his clothing, with a piece of looking glass above it.

"Anybody working for us," she had said, "will get all the comforts we can afford to give."

Magdali had been busy, too, going about the district when she could, stirring up interest in the new school she would have them put up somewhere close by. She had visited the Shaleen place, where Kate was still caring for her sister Delphy, who had not yet fully recovered, it seemed, from her illness of the winter. But even there, things were beginning to take a recognizable form. Steve Shaleen had been experimenting with wheat, and had been a frequent visitor to the Vinge farm, drawing Ivar aside and talking about his work. Within the Shaleen soddy itself a wonderful thing had happened. Kate Shaleen had sent all the way to Chicago for an organ—a shining affair of polished oak, with carpet stuff on the foot pedals. Ivar had seen it himself and had heard Miss Kate play it—with all her fingers, he had reported to Magdali, not like her brother Karsten's wife, who used only one finger to pick out a tune.

Magdali's smile had been primly forebearing, as it had been at any mention of the Shaleens since the night she had first gone to see what she could do for Delphy. She had undoubtedly saved Delphy's life, Ivar admitted to himself, though he had never been able to understand why she had refused to accept the dress length of brown satin which Texas Brazell, out of his profound gratitude, had come to offer her as soon as his wife was on her feet again. Brazell, deeply wounded at her rejection of his gift, had driven furiously back to Moorhead and thrust it into the hands of the first cocotte he had seen in the street. Pete Sondstrom, gay beyond discretion from the *schnapps* he had imbibed in town, had come by and told Magdali the story. Ivar had enjoyed a ribald pleasure on hearing Pete's outrageous tale, but to Magdali it had been an insult she would not soon forget.

Ivar stooped and picked up a handful of the newly turned soil. It was good soil, black and rich and workable, but dry—very dry. He watched it trickle between his fingers and become dust in the hot wind. He was tired. He unhitched his team and led them down to the creek to drink. Great patches of sweat darkened their withers and flanks. A dozen greenish-brown grasshoppers nibbled greedily at the moist leather of the harness. There had been signs of grasshoppers in increasing numbers during the past month. Not enough to do any real harm here, although Pete Sondstrom over east said they had eaten the blossoms off his potato plants. Well, if it didn't rain soon, the grasshoppers wouldn't have much either.

He turned his team up from the creek, toward the house. It was then that he saw Roald Bratland's light trap standing in the dooryard, one of his big grays looking rather silly between the shafts.

Roald was sitting comfortably in the kitchen, drinking coffee and eating syrup bread. At an open window beside him, Magdali was carding wool. Ivar had only to sniff the fragrance in the room to know that she had used some of her jealously hoarded real coffee, not the parched barley sort that was for everyday consumption. Both brother and sister wore an air of beaming self-satisfaction.

Ivar perversely refrained from asking Roald what was up now. He took his time washing his face and hands at the tin basin on the bench beside the door. This feeling of being shut out from the communion of the Bratlands was particularly irksome today, in the dry heat.

"You can't guess what Roald did today," Magdali said at last, rising to pour Ivar a cup of her good coffee.

"Sold your calves to that fellow up the river?" Ivar asked.

"Ya—and got my own price for them too. We're in for a dry season, Ivar. No use keeping a big herd with the pasture land drying up every day." He wetted a spoonful of sugar in his coffee and coddled it between tongue and palate.

"Tell Ivar what you *really* did," Magdali urged.

"Ya—well, I sold the Endicott land to a speculator for three thousand dollars cash."

At Ivar's stare of astonishment, Magdali burst out laughing. "Do you think I was foolish, now, to get the land when I could?"

"Foolish?" Ivar echoed, still unable to believe what they had told him. "Then—you and Roald are rich!"

Roald deprecatingly pursed his lips. "Oh, no, not rich, Ivar. It will take time for that. But we have made a start. Money makes money. Tomorrow, Magdali and I will put our money into railroad bonds. There it will be safe till we know what to do with it."

"Yes," Ivar said slowly, "that is perhaps wise." It was not for him to say what was wise, it was not even in his place to speak of what belonged to Roald and Magdali. It was their money, to do with as they wished. For that matter, with the memory of the Endicotts still sore within him, he hated every dollar of it. "Well, you'll be getting yourself a wife one of these days now, Roald," he added by way of turning the talk aside.

"*Bövelen*—what would I do with a wife?" Roald exclaimed.

"She could milk your cows," Magdali suggested. "That Engebrigt girl—"

"Ya, I have seen her forth and back," said Roald, tugging at the high lapels of his worsted jacket. He would suffer the agonies of hell rather than be seen in town garbed like a farmer.

"She's broad in the rump," Ivar remarked, "but she has pretty yellow hair."

Magdali clucked reprovingly. "See what the children are doing down there near the pig pen, Ivar. Solveig was throwing stones at that brood sow again this morning. I wish that child had not learned to walk so early. She gets into everything, and she doesn't mind like the others. Sometimes I wonder if she is really my own child, the way she acts."

"Maybe she is a river elf," said Ivar in Norwegian. "She was the first of them born here, remember."

Magdali flashed him a strange glance. "Don't talk like that!" she said, and then, recovering to laughter, she added, "Get along with you! You are Solveig's father, anyhow!"

XIX

THINGS were shaping toward the future, too, in the town that had set its roots down at the spot where the railway company had decided to make the river crossing. Frame and log buildings had begun to take the place of the fly-by-night structures of the frontier. Men had arrived from the East who talked less now of moving on with the railroad into the plains that stretched endlessly westward from the river. It was as if a pause had come in that fantastic trek into the unknown, a brief halt beside the trail whose farther end shifted ever with the traveler's dreams, a breathing time in the headlong march toward the setting sun.

On this blistering day in summer, the dusty street that was the business center of Moorhead thronged with people who moved about briskly in spite of the heat. Rigs of every description stood at the hitching posts—spring wagons, buckboards, a few surreys and buggies. Flags and bunting bloomed everywhere, fluttering listlessly in every stray breath that moved in from the parched prairie. Ladies in straw bonnets that were too small to offer any shade minced self-consciously under frilled parasols and gathered up their dimity skirts to keep them clear of the dust. Dandies raised their hats, twirled their canes, and mopped their faces with huge kerchiefs as they strolled in and out of the crowded saloons. For this was the day toward which all eyes had turned for weeks. The bridge was completed, and the first locomotive to cross the Red River of the North stood on its shining rails, ready to make its brief historic journey.

No gayer crowd could be found anywhere along the dusty street than the one that had gathered in Texas Brazell's place. The large room with a bar that ran the full length of one side was fogged with smoke and redolent with the fumes of strong liquor. Men elbowed their way to a place within earshot of the overworked bartenders, or wedged themselves in at the small tables and shouted their orders above the ceaseless din. In one corner, Luke Nisselbaum sawed away on his fiddle to the accompaniment of Willie Bates's accordion.

It was not the sort of place that Delphy would have made of it, had she had anything to say in its fashioning. There was small pretense at serving meals beyond the free lunch that was stacked at one end of the long bar. The music was scarcely more than a wistful overtone to the clamor that filled the room, except on those nights when the customers were few and Luke Nisselbaum permitted himself to coax from the strings of his violin some of the heart-searching strains they held. No woman's face had been seen in the place since Texas Brazell opened its doors on a cold night less than two weeks after he had fled from Fargo. It was a man's place, and Texas had every reason to be proud of it.

Today, especially, he was the most genial of hosts. He moved about among his customers, attired in his best, the tips of his black mustache drawn to needle points above his smiling lips. No one could have suspected that beneath all that geniality lurked a gnawing anxiety that had been with him since early morning when he had sent the young doctor out to stay with Delphy through the ordeal which she was about to face. Time after time, since he had seen Delphy this morning, he had told himself that it was a natural thing, this business of giving birth to a baby. But he had kept Cortez harnessed to the light trap and had hired a boy to stand by the hitching post in front of the doorway and see that the horse was not frightened by the noisy celebration that filled the street. Texas was determined to lose no time when the tidings reached him from the little soddy three miles north of town, where Delphy lay under the watchful eyes of Kate Shaleen and young Doctor Mitchell. The doctor would come at once, Texas knew, and give him the news he was waiting for. There would be a round of drinks on the house, and Texas would be on his way as fast as Cortez would take him. Would it be a boy or a girl? It didn't matter. The only thing that mattered to Texas Brazell was that his Delphy should come safely through it all and be waiting for him with pride in her eyes.

But it was not the young doctor who brought the news. Texas was standing anxiously beside the open door of his saloon when he saw Steve Shaleen jerk old Jezebel to a stop and jump down from the ramshackle buckboard to the sidewalk. Yellowish froth stood on the mare's neck and withers.

Texas sprang from his doorway and caught Steve by the arm.

"What's wrong, Steve?"

"It's—it's Delphy, Tex. She's bad. Doc told me I'd better come in and get you."

Hatless, his face like frozen glass in the harsh sunlight, Texas Brazell leaped into the narrow seat behind Cortez and seized the reins. The horse lunged forward, turned in the middle of the street, and raced toward the railway crossing.

Steve watched the flimsy trap careening up the street, saw the locomotive start forward with a prodigious belch of smoke from its brass-trimmed stack, heard the shouts of warning as Cortez veered suddenly and reared backward from the black monster. He saw Texas Brazell stand up and lash out viciously with his whip. A moment later, he saw nothing, for horse and rig had hurtled across the track, the engine clanked to a halt, and the engineer was climbing down from his cab and hurrying

[166]

toward a motionless, strangely flat shape laid out beside the rails.

Steve closed his eyes and fought down the nausea that assailed him as he started running with the crowd that was already on its way to the railway crossing. When he stood at last and looked down upon the still form of Texas Brazell, one word only crossed his lips, a word spoken half devoutly, half profanely.

"Christ!" he muttered as the tears blinded him.

Just before dawn of the next day, Delphy Brazell gave birth to a baby girl whose name, she had insisted, would be Rose.

Then, when the sun was risen, Delphy's spirit went out to meet the spirit of him who had gone just a little before.

XX

THROUGH the twilight of the last Ice Age, the river had sculptured its patient course out of the glacial drift, out of the boulder clay; through numberless savage dawns its tributaries had flowed from the east and the west to join its northward flow, to cleave deeper into the precious silt left by the vast white ghost of the ice. The river had seen the slow and inexorable violence of change. The Indian and the buffalo, the French *voyageur* and the fearless little priest with his threadbare vestments, his hunger, and his silver cross; the dog sled, the travois, the stagecoach, the steamboat, the railway and its spears of steel flying westward into the sunset—all these things the river saw, perhaps with wonderment, but surely with unconcern. For the way of the river belonged to the river, and man's way was his own.

But the years brought those things to pass which left their trace upon the river, and upon the men who walked beside it. Thus in that gaunt and rainless season, while Ivar stood empty-eyed and looked upon his empty fields, the river shrank under the bitter heat of the sky, leaving on either side of it a margin of reasty mud like the blistered and rubbery hide of some uncouth animal. And when the great snows of the next winter melted and joined in the valley, the river shouldered up out of its banks in a glistening amber tide strangely brindled with light and shadow, and Ivar's westward-lying fields were engulfed so that his only plantings were to the east and southeast of his farmstead. While in one summer of prairie fires Roald Bratland herded his cattle far to the east for pasturage, in the next several of his calves were drowned before he and Louie Spragg could drive them to safety.

Ivar's own disappointments were braced by a passionate, profane rage that few others felt. While he stood and shook his fist at the bone-dry sky, or cursed the water stagnating on his fields, Magdali's calm refusal to acknowledge the calamities of nature sorely tried his temper. When his dream of golden acres of wheat vanished before the inimical spirit of the Valley, when weariness and a sense of futility all but stupefied him, Magdali's curious, scornful pride remained aloof, untouched. Had not a great railroad crossed the river the year before? Was it not even now pressing onward into the wild northern plains, toward the mountains and the sea? And think of the settlers pouring by hundreds into every corner of the country, out of England, out of Europe, lured by the promise of a paradise on earth awaiting them in America! Had Magdali not succeeded in her first project, looking toward the building of a community right here within sight of her own doorway? It had taken a lot of planning, a lot of work, to get the school she wanted; and Magdali had found it necessary to compromise a little before a site was finally chosen, but she had won her way through, and Kate Shaleen had begun her work on the first day of spring. Even the Almighty, seemingly bent upon destruction where many another was concerned with simple dreams, had come to Magdali's aid. God had removed Texas Brazell and his wife Delphy—a sad and shocking thing in itself, though it had relieved Magdali of the one embarrassment she felt in urging Miss Kate to take over the school when it was ready. For the greater part of a year, of course, Kate had given her whole thought to the care of the motherless baby that Delphy had left with her, but a benign Providence had sent Selma Engebrigt to become the wife of Steve Shaleen, so that Kate was free to take her place in the larger plan that was of Magdali's devising. The mysterious ways

[169]

of the Almighty never failed to awaken in Magdali's heart a kind of gratified excitement. Even the fact that she was expecting her fourth child soon was compensated for by her own certainty that this time it would be a son.

But in September of 1873 the westward advance of the railroad stopped as if the earth had fallen off into space beneath it. Not many of the settlers, dazed by what had happened, fully grasped the meaning of it. Financial panic—Jay Cooke and Company—were symbols written in air.

It was Roald Bratland, having heard the news in the crowded telegraph office in Moorhead, who saw the flame of ruin that surrounded those airy phrases. His knees weak as whey beneath him, he tottered out of the place and into his wagon, where he put the whip to his grays and headed them north toward the Vinge farm. All his shrewdness, his ambition, his hopes had in a trice fluttered out of his brain like heedless butterflies.

He was in sight of Ivar's tree claim—and even in his distraction he took note that the wet summer had not harmed the sturdy young grove—before it occurred to him that in her condition Magdali might not be strong enough to take the news he was bearing. But she would hear of it in a short time anyhow. Better have it over with at once, whatever the result!

He found Magdali in the kitchen, stirring a pot of dried peas and salt pork.

"Well, what news have you now?" she asked, putting the lid back on the pot and drying her hands on her apron.

"Where is Ivar?" Roald asked.

"He went to Georgetown this morning. He'll be back soon. But what is it you're keeping to yourself? Is it bad news this time?"

"Not so good that it mightn't be better," Roald replied cautiously. "The railway has stopped, Magdali."

"The railway has stopped? What are you talking about?"

"The bankers in the East have failed. The railroad cannot go on building without the bankers to pay the way. That much ought to be clear, even to you. But—our bonds, Magdali—they are paper now, nothing more. Our three thousand dollars—" His voice threatened to break. He sank heavily into a chair and all but collapsed forward against the table.

Magdali's face went pale. For a moment she said nothing. She stood and looked at him, her lips drawn thinly to a smile that had no mirth in it. "Are you a Bratland or a—a sheep!" she demanded angrily at last, and spoke in Norwegian. "Have you no legs of your own to stand on, or must I lend you mine? Take yourself home before Ivar gets here to see what a weakling you are. Or do you want to hear him laughing at us for our follies?"

Roald looked up at her, astonishment turning his face to a colorless mask. "Do you blame me now for what we have done?"

"For what *we* have done? Would you ever have the wit to do anything unless I showed you the way?"

"Ya, you call it wit—when we have lost the good money we had. If there is wit in that, I am glad you take me for a fool. *Helvete*, what a fool I was, indeed, when I listened to you!"

Magdali went and stood before him, her eyes ablaze. "*Halt kjaeften!* You will listen to me again. And you will do as I say. You have brought me bad news today. Our little has been lost, but—"

"Our little!" Roald whined.

"It is nothing when you think of what those bankers in the East have put into the building of the railroad. Do you think they will lose all now? They are not such fools. They will have even more—after all the little ones are out of the way. Will the steel rails rot on the ties? Will the engines stand and rust in the rain? Will the cities and towns die and all the farms go back to grass?"

"You are right, Magdali," Roald conceded, his eyes narrowing shrewdly. "But what are we to do about all that?"

"We must talk about what we shall do," Magdali replied. "We must talk quietly—and decide quickly. Then we must act before it is too late."

"I will listen while you talk," Roald said meekly.

Magdali talked and Roald listened. By the time Ivar drove into the yard and halted his team in front of the door, Roald was almost himself again.

Magdali met Ivar on the doorstep, her eyes sparkling up at him like blue trinkets. "You are safe home again, Ivar!" she said with a laugh as she looked close at his face. "And you have heard the news, I see."

"Yes," Ivar said. "They told it in Georgetown. I was afraid for you—"

Magdali reached up quickly to kiss him on the cheek. "That was nice of you, *kjaereste*. But the news may not be very bad, after all. I have just been telling Roald that his nose is too long for his eyes to see past it."

Ivar chuckled. "I have thought that before today. But you—"

"I have just made some fresh *lefsa*," Magdali interrupted. "We can have coffee before we talk." She became busy about the stove. "My poor Roald thinks I'm crazy, but in a few years he will be going around saying that it was his idea in the first place."

Ivar stared at her, bewildered.

"When our bonds are down to ten cents on the dollar," Roald moaned, pulling doubtfully at his nose, "she wants me to buy more of the same!"

Magdali calmly poured Ivar's coffee and set before him a

plate of rolled *lefsa* sprinkled with cinnamon and sugar. Then, retying her big, concealing white apron, she glanced at the carved clock on the shelf.

"Mercy me, Ivar, it's time already for you to get Karsten from the schoolhouse. Another year, and he'll be able to walk home by himself when the weather is good. I'll wrap some *lefsa* for you to take to the teacher. Her brother and Selma like it so much, too. And you might take a jar of pieplant preserves for Selma. I remember how it was with me when I was waiting for my first baby. A little taste of something different—"

Ivar rubbed his cheek and laughed softly to himself. For the life of him he could not tell whether Magdali's lively chatter was a reflection of what she really felt, or a veil to hide some deeper anxiety over the news Roald Bratland had brought. Ah, well, he had long since given up all hope of ever understanding her.

XXI

No such problems vexed the mind of Kate Shaleen as she counted the weeks of autumn and winter and held to a purpose as simple as that of the seasons themselves.

The schoolhouse was a little more than four miles southeast of the Vinge farm, and about the same distance northeast of the Shaleens'. It stood midway on the prairie trail between the Vinges' and the Sondstroms' over on Buffalo River. Looking due south from the small, square, log building, one could see the Joseffys' sod house and dugout stable, hunched and lonely on the bald prairie, with only a few wispy saplings like pencil strokes in the thin and distant air. East of the Joseffys, sheltered by trees along the Buffalo, lived the Engebrigts, a boisterous family of nine housed with merry good nature in three rooms of slab and clay. People had teased Selma Engebrigt before her marriage to Steve Shaleen, saying that he would never have got her except that she was tired of sleeping four in a bed. South again, between the Joseffys' and the Engebrigts', lay the homestead of Gimp and Pearl Featherstone, who boasted the only complete frame house in the district, a circumstance that surprised Gimp as much as it did everyone else, since it was said that he had not been aware of the roll of money in Pearl's stocking until the night he married her.

Kate Shaleen's first pupils numbered nine: Philip Groman, Karsten Vinge, the three Joseffys—Fritz, Anton, and Maria—and four Engebrigts—Lila, Gudrun, Sigurd, and Per. Kate was the frontier teacher, untrained and fortuitously hired, resolved to implant within the hearts and minds of her young charges

[174]

an idea of beauty, of gentleness and courage and a right way of living. Behind that resolve lay a feeling that never came really clear, but while her eyes dwelt upon the upturned faces in the square room, she thought that perhaps it was her queer old idea of *beginnings*, of a rooting of life, that stirred her so. Here were the awakenings of the struggle, the hope, the hate, and the love that would one day break in a flood through this long-slumbering northern valley of America. What, in the drift of the years, would they bring?

It was true, as Magdali Vinge soon was to discover, that Kate Shaleen did not impress sternly upon her youngsters the fact that two and two were bound to make four. But they learned to watch with rapture the free, swift arc cut darkly by a swallow against a bar of sundown, and to listen with awe to the variance in the song of the meadow lark, in the killdeer's plaintive cry. They may have gained only a vague notion of the Civil War's ugly shambles, but they knew the Gettysburg Address as they knew their prayers, and they were taught that Lincoln, too, had known what it was to stand and hear the infinite silence of a sunlit prairie, the stillness of the flowing grass. Flowers became people to them, dressed for a ball or a visit to the market; a cricket in the schoolroom wood box was a fiddler trying to get warm.

Upon her death, a young senator sent a great sheaf of dusky roses from Washington; but before that he had endowed a school for delinquent girls which Kate had founded in Minnesota and called Sunnyvale Hall. Upon her death, a young society woman in Chicago excused herself and withdrew from the company she had invited to tea in honor of the English nobleman she had chosen as a husband for her eighteen-year-old daughter—and went to her bedroom where she cried for an hour, remembering that she had once been little Lila Engebrigt. Karsten Wing—smoothly successful attorney in Minneapolis during the Boodle Mayor regime that ended in 1902 —heard of the death of Kate Shaleen and felt upon his cheek the touch of soft fingers wiping his tears away as they had done that day when young Fritz Joseffy had bloodied his nose in a fight at school. In England, Fritz Joseffy heard of Kate Shaleen's death, remembered his first lesson on the organ with Kate sitting at his shoulder—and played as he had never played before, in the salon of a well-known duchess, then rose, bowed strangely to the piano, and departed without a word.

These things came to be, but long after that summer of 1874, when Kate Shaleen gave a picnic for her pupils and their parents in a grove on the bank of the Red River of the North.

It was a Sunday, and everybody came, bringing hampers of food, dishes and coffeepots and tablecloths. They came in their ox-drawn wagons across the grassy trails from the north and the east and the south, and seated themselves in the solemn shade of the tall elms to listen to the sermon preached by the Reverend Clegg, the ardent young Presbyterian minister from Moorhead. Then, while the men sat about in their shirt sleeves and discussed their crops and livestock, and the children were occupied with their shrill games, the women spread the tablecloths on the ground, boiled coffee over the crackling fire, and set out the pickles and wild-fruit jellies, the molasses bread and the sugar cookies that were so rare a luxury.

Magdali Vinge had not come willingly. During the past eight months, since the birth of her son—yes, God had given her another son!—she had assumed the responsibility of having the minister at her house for divine service once a month, and the foregathering under her roof was a pleasure she jealously guarded. That he was not a Lutheran minister had troubled her at first, but the young man was earnest and deeply devout, and

[176]

Magdali had taken him to her heart at last. He had in a sense become her special agent for the spread of righteousness among the settlers in the district, who had gone too long without the spiritual guidance they needed. She had admitted to Ivar that the idea of a picnic was an excellent one, but during the week of preparation she could scarcely conceal her resentment that it had not originated with her instead of with Kate Shaleen.

When the jollity of the meal had subsided and the men sat back to smoke their pipes while the women cleared away the leavings, Ivar overheard Magdali pay Jensine Engebrigt an extravagant compliment on the new arrangement of her hair, which even a man could see was hideous. Kate Shaleen's hair, too, was dressed in the new mode, with a loose lock on the forehead; but on her it was carelessly becoming. Yet Magdali had not deigned to notice it. Ah, well, there was no reckoning with the minds of women!

A hot, high wind had risen from the west.

"We could do with a little rain," Steve Shaleen said, stretching himself on the ground beside Ivar, who sat with his back to a tree, smoking his pipe. "That garden truck of mine is burnin' up."

"Maybe rain would be good for your garden," Ivar said, smiling into the distance, "but this is pretty good for my wheat. Two weeks more, and it will be ready to cut. It will be a good crop, too."

"That's the hell of farmin'!" Steve observed. "One man wants one thing, and another wants something else."

"We make it work, just the same," Ivar said contentedly. "In the end we both have a little."

"We ought to get together more, though," Steve went on. "I was readin' in the paper yesterday about a book that tells how to test soil for what there ought to be in it for growin' this and that. Take your wheat, for instance. Wheat needs one

[177]

thing, but my onions need something else. It'd be a good book for the likes of us to have around the house. We could read it on winter nights when we sit warmin' our rear ends for the want of something better to do."

"I'd like to see a book like that," Ivar said.

"If I send for it, we could look it over and do a little experimentin' together, like, if you could get away from your family now and again."

"Ho, my family grows itself now," Ivar boasted.

Steve laughed. "That's one crop we don't have to worry about, rain or shine, eh, Ivar?"

"They come along—yours and mine," Ivar said, and glanced away to where Steve's wife Selma held her little Loren in her arms as she rocked back and forth to her own low crooning. A little beyond, Roald Bratland was standing over Magdali's strong eight-months-old Arne, who was on all fours, gazing raptly at the river.

"I keep tellin' Kate she ought to get herself a man and have a kid of her own," Steve said.

For a moment, Ivar could find no reply to that. What Steve had said was true, no doubt, even if his way of putting it was not altogether to Ivar's liking. He looked now to where Kate Shaleen was sitting in the shade of an elm, half a dozen children romping about her. He heard her call to little Rose Brazell, whom they called Rose Shaleen now, saw the child toddle on her plump two-year-old legs to fling herself across Kate's lap. Somehow, he had never imagined Kate Shaleen as married to anyone. He could think of no one who would be a fit mate to a girl so far removed in spirit from the very practical business of marriage.

Not that Ivar himself had always looked upon marriage as the merely useful expedient it had come to be in the last few years. There had been that moonlit night on the snow-covered

[178]

mountainside in Norway—and many nights and days afterward, when he had gone about in a dream world all his own. There had been those storm-tossed nights on the Atlantic when he had awakened to the incredible reality that Magdali was beside him. There had been other days and nights, some of them not so long ago, when the familiar heart-hunger had struck him like an obscure pain that would not be stilled. But Magdali had brought him to see the foolishness of that. Well, he had seen the purposes of Nature fulfilled, he had begotten sons and daughters, he would leave to them the heritage of flaming desire and its aftermath of bleak discovery.

But what of Kate Shaleen? Was she never to know either? All Ivar's strength of mind and body rose in protest.

"Find the man for her, then," he said sharply, and looked at Steve as he spoke. "It would be better so. We would lose a teacher but we—"

Steve jerked himself erect. "Let them look for another teacher, and the hell with it!" he exclaimed. His eyes widened suddenly as he stared toward the river road where a tall, lean individual with a long, melancholy face came shuffling toward the picnickers, mopping his brow with a huge bandanna. "Jee-rusalem! if there ain't old Fiddler Luke!"

Ivar saw Kate Shaleen get up and run to meet Luke Nisselbaum, who had halted, his fiddle under one arm, to survey the group before venturing closer. He saw the young minister leave his place beside Ole Sondstrom and his wife and walk toward the newcomer, his hand outstretched to welcome him. Then he saw Magdali snatch the baby Arne into her arms and retreat to the moving leaf shadows on the river bank.

"Your wife looks scared," Steve observed with a grin. "And little wonder! Luke is the nearest thing to a scarecrow in these parts. But the preacher don't scare easy. He likes music—out of hell or heaven. You can trust a man that likes music, Ivar,

[179]

even if he is a preacher."

Kate had led Luke to a knoll where the baskets were piled and was already plying him with sandwiches and coffee. Ivar was too busy with his own thoughts to give much heed to what Steve was saying, but when Luke Nisselbaum finally stood up and placed his violin beneath his chin, he leaned forward and touched Steve on the shoulder, a signal for silence.

"He is going to play," Ivar said.

Luke drew his bow, and it seemed that the trees above him paused in their rustling. It seemed that the hot wind died, and a cool, deep-sea greenness flowed over this glade in the woods where even the children sat large-eyed and still. Ivar had little knowledge of fine music, but he felt an aching fullness in his heart, a longing for something he had somewhere known and had forgotten—and yet had never known, would never know.

Luke played familiar tunes after that, hymns to which everybody sang, and comforting old pieces they all knew. Then, without warning, he burst into a wild cascade of music, a tumultuous rhythm that rocked and swayed and laughed in a kind of mad glory. It leaped upward and joined with the abandon of the wind in the trees. It sank and whispered shamelessly to the underbrush.

Magdali's face was shocked, and about Kate's mouth there was a troubled, withheld smile. But in the next instant, Steve and Selma, Pete Sondstrom and his sister-in-law Helga, the Featherstones and the four eldest Engebrigts were whirling about upon the grass in a hilarious and formless dance that brought shrieks of laughter from the participants and most of the onlookers.

The young minister, standing beside Ivar, leaned and said, " 'Man does not live by bread alone,' Mr. Vinge. We work too hard—all of us, every day of the week. This is the Sabbath, but the good Lord will find no fault with what we do here today. I think—" He paused, startled. "Your wife, over there—she is beckoning to you. Something appears to—"

Ivar hurried to Magdali's side and looked up to where she was pointing at the sky beyond the river. A darkly moving cloud bore toward them above the trees on the opposite shore. In a moment it became a solid mass of churning lead with ragged edges from which fragments shot downward, while from overhead came a sinister drone that smote beyond hearing to the very heart.

Luke's violin had fallen silent now, the dancers were rushing toward the river, their eyes fixed in terror upon the oncoming tide.

"That's grasshoppers!" Steve Shaleen bellowed. "Holy Judas, my vegetables! Let's get out of here. Kate—Selma!"

In the scrambling panic toward the wagons, the young minister was jostled aside, and Luke Nisselbaum came to stand beside him. He looked in mild wonderment, first up at the confused and crackling air, then down at the violin in his hands. A dozen insects had already settled upon the strings. He brushed them off, removed his coat and wrapped the violin securely within it.

The minister stared upward while the olive-green flight of death struck him in the face. "Dear Lord," he said softly, "give us now the strength we need!" Then he spoke to Luke. "I hope I may have the pleasure of your company back to town. My horse and cart are just over there beside the Vinges'."

Already in the wagon seat, Magdali was cowering as she drew her children about her. "It's God's judgment on a wicked people!" she murmured as Ivar got up beside her.

Leaving Magdali to take the children into the house, Ivar drove his frantic team into the stable and closed the doors. The cows and the oxen were running blindly about in the pasture, but he had no time to fetch them in. The sheep were huddled under the lee of a haystack beside the stable. In the farmyard, hogs and chickens were gorging themselves on the grasshoppers that had come down to devour everything in sight.

Magdali had already fastened the doors and the windows of the house. Leaving Karsten to look after the younger children, she gathered bed clothes, floor mats, cast-off garments, and piled them outside the door. There Ivar met her and together they staggered through the fiercely whirring drift of hideous brown and green that came endlessly on and on. Every square inch of earth was a crawling tapestry of small, savagely intent bodies. The vegetable garden was already flattened under their weight, and here and there the ground was pitted where the insects had ravaged carrots and turnips to their roots' ends.

They had thrown only a few covers over the vegetables when Ivar gave up in despair. The ravenous creatures were champing their way through the thick woolen blankets and the heavy mats. He ran his hand through his hair, and grasshoppers sprang out between his fingers.

"It is no good, Magdali!" he cried. "They're eating the blankets, too. Take them away. We must pull up everything we can."

They snatched the covers off and ran with them to the stable that was only a few yards away. When they came back, Ivar seized a fork that had been standing in the ground at the edge of the garden. Its handle had been gnawed so that it was rough to the touch.

"Bring a basket from the house," Ivar said, and began digging the carrots and turnips from the ground in a sightless rage.

Magdali went pale. Then she turned and hurried toward the house, barely able to keep her footing over the mass of dead and living insects.

[182]

Not once had Ivar dared to glance southward, beyond the stable, to where his ten acres of wheat stood ripening in the sunlight. On the trail homeward, he had seen what was happening to his oats and barley—those fields looked as if an enormous filthy paw had clapped down upon them. Scarcely a leaf had been visible in the stanch grove of the tree claim, but it had been hung from root to uttermost twig by a ghastly, crawling fruit.

Magdali came back and set the basket on the ground. "Do you know what's happening to your wheat—your good wheat, Ivar?" Her lips were a chalk line.

"Fill the basket!" Ivar ordered.

With a kind of low whimpering, Magdali went to work. When the basket was full, Ivar carried it to the stable, dumped the vegetables in a corner, closed the door securely and hurried back to the garden patch. When they had taken everything of worth from the ground, the sun was low, a soiled and vaguely distinguishable glow in the west. Ivar lifted the last basket of vegetables and paused to look at Magdali. Her face was streaked with dirt and perspiration, her blue gingham dress smeared and tattered.

"Get back to the house, Magdali!" His voice came harshly from his parched throat. "Wash your face and lie down for a while."

He went to the stable then, set his basket on the ground, and sank down, from sheer weariness of spirit, upon a pile of new hay that Louie Spragg had carried in that morning before going to Moorhead to spend the day. It was peaceful here at least, with the door closed, and the comforting sound of horses nuzzling the sweet smelling hay in their mangers. Presently he got up and went to the small window that looked southward to his field of wheat. It was easier, somehow, to face that total destruction of his dreams with no one beside him. He could

[183]

do nothing about it now. There was no way he could save a single golden head. Strangely enough, it was not so much of his own wheat he was thinking as he stood there at the small square of window. He was thinking of the tiny plot in one corner of the field which he had given Karsten to plant as his very own.

"Never mind, my son," he muttered aloud. "There will be another spring, and another planting. And you will help your father, because he needs you now."

When he first saw what looked like a plume of smoke rising from the edge of the field, he thought his eyes were deceiving him in the strange light shed from the setting sun. But a moment later he saw the solitary figure of Magdali darting about, half hidden in the weirdly tinted smoke clouds. He flung himself out of the stable and ran toward her, waving his arms and shouting, though he knew she could not hear him.

The wind was still coming strongly from the raddled sunset, heavy with an oddly acrid smell. Suddenly a flame leaped from the edge of the field and licked eastward over the swaying stalks of ripening wheat. Before it, the grasshoppers rose in sluggish clouds only to settle again a few yards farther on.

Ivar was gasping for breath when he overtook Magdali running with an armful of straw to where a kerosene can lay overturned on the ground.

"*Helvete*, Magdali! What madness is this?" he cried, seizing her arm.

She swung toward him in fierce scorn. "If *we* aren't going to have it, neither are *they!*"

Her foot shot out toward the kerosene can and sent it rolling toward the flaming straw. Ivar jerked her away from it, but she set her teeth as she fought to free herself.

"Let me go! Let me go!"

It was then that he saw the burn on the back of her left

hand. "Come away, Magdali," he pleaded. "There is nothing we can do here now."

She sprang at him, but he caught her by the shoulders and held her helpless. Struggling and stumbling, he dragged her by main force away from the burning field, back along the pasture, and into the yard in front of the stable. In all their years together nothing like this had ever happened between them. Ivar was aghast at the thought of the children witnessing any such violence. He opened the door of the stable and all but threw her inside.

The Norwegian epithet he hurled at her would have made Roald Bratland's hair stand on end, had he been within hearing, but Magdali smiled and said gently, "You might better pray, my Ivar!"

The soft uttering of his name only angered him the more. He lifted his hand threateningly as he stepped toward her. "Pray—on a day like this? I might better get drunk!"

Her eyes were bright with tears as she looked at him. "Sometimes, Ivar," she said haltingly, "you seem strange to me—as if we had never known each other. Don't you care for me now the way you did—at first? Or have you forgotten?"

He saw that her dress had been torn from her shoulder, exposing the soft curve of one breast. He felt the old thickening of his blood as she stood before him in the half-light of the closed stable. His body had known her many, many times, but there was a look in her eyes now such as he had never seen there before, the bold, unbridled look of a—yes, of a wanton, he thought suddenly, and was afraid. Had some madness smitten her during those hours of fighting against hopeless odds? He had read of such things happening to women who were forced to live on the nation's frontiers. Men, too, had lost their reason when the battle had turned against them.

"Magdali!" He put his arm about her, drew her toward him,

[185]

and hid his eyes against her hair. "You must not talk so. It isn't that I don't feel the same. And I haven't forgotten. It's just that you're different from me. You're the smart one, and I haven't always got the sense to see it."

She sighed in his embrace. "You are the strong one, my Ivar!" She gave a tender little laugh, reached up and kissed his mouth.

She held him so until she had drawn him down beside her on the new, sweet-smelling hay.

XXII

THROUGHOUT the Middle West in the months that followed, revival meetings were held in every community whether or not a preacher was there to give the authority of his cloth. For the locust plague had touched all hearts with a biblical significance.

The water in creeks and ponds was rust-colored from the foul leavings of the winged legions, and cattle turned away from the rancid taste of it until they were overcome by thirst. The flesh of barnyard poultry and wild game alike was so tainted that a man had to be well-nigh famished before he could swallow it. Fish from the river was likewise revolting, and a hen's egg, as Ivar observed when he ventured to try one, bore the flavor of a cast-off sock.

From Dakota Territory to Texas, the migration had stripped off every growing thing with the exception of the native grass, the leaves of certain mysteriously untempting trees, and the cane crops in the South. Through the heart of the new land, a swath had been cut, leaving a grim, drab scar from which people turned in fear and revulsion.

It was a time when individual citizens as well as the government unloosed purse strings and came to the aid of the pioneer. Clothing, food, and money poured into the Valley from the capital and other eastern cities; and Ivar, humbled beneath the paralyzing blow, was ready to accept the proffered help as the other farmers in the community were doing.

But Magdali, in disdain, would have none of it. "Whatever a Vinge might do," she said, "the Bratlands will never take char-

[187]

ity from any state or person. I'll write brother Karsten and ask him for a loan. Roald can take it with him and mail it tomorrow."

Then and there she sat down and wrote to her brother in Wisconsin. Roald, Ivar knew, was coming for supper. He would arrive any minute now. There would be endless talk— of the kind that would only infuriate Ivar if he listened to it. He would find something to do at the stable as soon as the meal was over.

He watched Magdali now out of the resigned gloom of his own defeat. At the window, young Karsten sat with a crayon and a smudged paper tablet, drawing butterflies. Magdis was in the dooryard, serenely at work on a mud pie. In a corner, little Solveig was busy with her own mysterious affairs, saying nothing. Ivar looked at Magdali's bandaged left hand, which he himself had dressed every day for the past week. The fine skin upon it would be forever marred in token of that dreadful day.

"Tell your brother," Ivar said dully, "that I'll pay him back every cent next year, with interest."

"He will expect it," Magdali said quietly.

"In the spring we'll burn the young 'hoppers and the eggs —on the ground," Ivar said. "That's what they're saying in town."

"See what Solveig is doing," Magdali said without looking up. "She has been quiet too long."

Ivar got up and stood over his little three-year-old daughter. In front of her was the pot of flour paste that Karsten had used in making a kite the day before. On the floor lay an open Bible, several pages of which had been pasted together. Ivar checked the words of reprimand that came suddenly to his lips, bent down quietly and took the child into his arms. Then he set the jar aside and closed the book—but not before he had observed that the pages pasted together were part of the Song of Solomon. Some day, he knew, Magdali would be shocked when she discovered the violation, but Ivar would meet that minor crisis when it came. He might even tear the pages out when Magdali was not around, and own up to it later. She had always been at a loss anyhow to understand why a place had been reserved in Holy Writ for anything so ambiguous as the Song of Solomon.

"Here comes *Bövelen!*" Karsten announced, looking from the window.

Magdali straightened. "Karsten! When did you start calling Uncle Roald that?" she demanded.

"Just now," Karsten replied innocently.

Magdali looked at Ivar, who was hiding a grin behind his hand. "Have you heard him calling his uncle—"

"No, no, Magdali!" Ivar assured her quickly.

"Never let me hear you say such a thing again, Karsten," Magdali warned the boy. "Shame on you!"

Ah, well, Ivar thought as he hoisted Solveig to his shoulder and went out to meet Roald Bratland, raising a family was a trial, however you looked at it. There would be much to contend with, no doubt, before they were old enough to take care of themselves.

XXIII

THE money from Magdali's brother came in August. Magdali spoke of it on the day the letter arrived, but made no mention of it thereafter, and Ivar betrayed no curiosity as to the amount she had received or where she kept it hidden during the days that followed. It was Bratland money.

On an afternoon in the first week in September, Ivar escaped from the house when he saw Roald's grays approaching along the trail from the south. He had no stomach for listening to Magdali and her brother discussing plans in which he himself no longer had any part. He had come to the point where he could not sit in the same room with them. It was not so bad when he was alone with Magdali. He had long since learned to avoid talking about things that irked her. Alone with Roald, too, he had a measure of peace. He could tolerate the presence of the bandy-legged gnome of a man for whom he held little more than contempt. Ivar could laugh at his cavortings. But sister and brother together represented something against which he had no defense.

There was a kind of solace in his acres, even in their desolation two months after ruin had descended upon them from the skies. The land was still waiting for him, biding its time until the seasons worked their healing magic and made them ready again for the labor of his hands.

He walked southward and paused at the corner where he had rested that summer night—so long, long ago!—to set Karsten down and ease the pain in his back before going on. Shame and anger had filled him that night at the thought of

[190]

letting a drunken stranger take him unawares. Shame and anger lay upon him now, but they were of a different sort. They were a dull ache that had grown with the years, that could not be dispelled by a brief moment's rest beside the way. And yet there was a strange comfort, meager though it was, in pausing here again on the edge of the field where he had first set his hand to the plow and given the word to his sturdy beasts. Here where he had turned his first sod—here was home to him.

Southward a little way stood the Shaleen soddy with the new frame addition Steve had given it soon after his marriage to Selma Engebrigt. He had seen little of the Shaleens since that Sunday afternoon of Kate's picnic. With a glance at the sun, he set off along the old river trail. There would be plenty of time for a brief visit before he went back home for supper.

Kate Shaleen met him while he was still some distance from the house.

"Oh, I'm so glad you came!" she said as she fell into step beside him. "Steve has been in a terrible mood for over a week."

"I'm a poor one to cure him of that," Ivar said.

"Just your coming will help. He hasn't left the house now for days."

"He's not sick?"

"Sick of everything!" Kate replied.

"I can understand that. It's a hard time for us all."

"But it won't last forever. There'll be better times ahead."

Ivar smiled. "Sure! Always the good times are ahead."

What a smile he had, Kate thought as they came to the door. "Isn't that where they should be?" she said, and stepped into the house. "Steve, here's Ivar Vinge to see you."

Steve Shaleen got up from his chair. "You were long enough gettin' here," he said to Ivar. "A man could have died a hundred times since I saw you last."

Ivar laughed. "A man dies once," he said.

"Not in this God-forsaken country! I've been fit for buryin' any day in the last month. But sit down, now that you're here. Selma is off somewhere with the kids, but she'll be back as soon as she thinks she can stand the sight of me again. Kate, open a bottle of that rhubarb wine and give us a drink. We may be takin' charity, but by God, we still have a drink in the cellar!"

Ivar had never seen Steve Shaleen so wrought up over anything. But in a moment the wine was poured from a cool bottle and the talk became easier as the men reviewed the havoc that had been worked in the countryside, the scanty stores they had been able to save from the plague of locusts, the preparations they were making for another year.

"I sent for that book I was tellin' you about," Steve said at last, when Ivar was ready to leave. "It'll give us something to do when the snow comes—maybe keep us from goin' plumb crazy before the winter's over. Kate, play us a tune before Ivar goes."

"What shall I play?"

"Let's hear that one you made yourself. She hasn't got the words for it yet," Steve explained to Ivar, "but there's music in it."

Kate felt the flame in her cheeks. "Really, Steve! There won't be any words to it. It's nothing but—a sort of a mood—like thinking when you are alone. I—"

"You got a name for it, haven't you?" Steve said.

Kate laughed, frowning and upset. "I told Selma I was going to call it 'O River, Remember,' but I—"

"You played it last week when the Joseffy boys came over. And you played it for old Fiddler Luke. Is it because Ivar is here you don't want to play it now?"

Almost angrily, Kate sat down at the organ. Then something took hold of her, and she put her hands to the white keys. To Ivar, listening, there came the slow and wandering gleam and darkness of the river, weaving their way into the lives of people and touching them softly with a dream of beauty. . . .

She turned from the organ at last and looked at Ivar standing near the doorway, his arms folded across the breast of his mended shirt. How neat the patches were, where Magdali had sewn them!

"I'm going a little way with you," she said suddenly, as Ivar turned toward the door. "Steve can nurse his grumps alone until Selma comes back."

Steve winked broadly at Ivar. "I'll feel better with the house to myself. Judas, Ivar, you're lucky you haven't got *two* women to hound you every day of your life!"

"One is enough!" Ivar declared as he started off, Kate beside him.

"I hope you won't mind my going along with you," she said as they took the trail that led eastward.

"Why should I mind that?"

"I wanted to tell you how glad I am that you came and talked with Steve. It was good for him."

"It was good for me," Ivar assured her. "Your music, too. I don't know how to say it, but I go home a different man now."

"You'll come and work with Steve when he gets his book from the city?"

"As often as I have the time. It will be a good thing, I think —for both of us."

Kate spoke then of the opening of school, a scant week away, and how she intended to have Steve put the organ in the schoolhouse a month before Christmas so that she could train the youngsters for the program she was planning for the last day of the fall term.

They had reached the place where the eastward trail crossed the one leading to town, when suddenly from the north, where the horizon was the indigo of some fabled sea, there came unbelievably the sound of many voices raised in a mighty chorus of song.

Ivar and Kate stood in amazement, shading their eyes away from the wild and prodigious glow in the west.

"There are oxen and covered carts," Kate said excitedly. "And there's a chain of men—and women, too—marching ahead of them. Why, look! They're all holding to a long rope, as if they're afraid of getting separated. Can you tell what they are singing?"

"It's an old Norwegian song," Ivar told her with an effort at steadiness. "It tells about how a man played his harp on a mountain and all his sorrow left him."

"What a beautiful melody!"

They waited until the strange caravan came within speaking distance, then Ivar went forward to meet the leader, a squat, powerful-looking man with tremendous shoulders, who uncovered his grizzled head and bowed deferentially as Ivar approached. Stillness fell at once upon the train behind him, the rough-clad men and women and half-grown youths stepping out of line to look at Ivar with courteous appraisal.

"Ve go Buffalo River," the leader announced laboriously. "Ve hear dere iss land on Buffalo. In Dakota it iss svamp. You *kanhende er Norsk?*"

"*Ja, det er jeg!*" Ivar said heartily, extending his hand.

They talked then in Norwegian, Ivar giving them directions as to where on the Buffalo River the best land was to be found. Upon learning that there were seven families in all, some with young children, he told them that there was a school within reach, and beckoned Kate to come and meet the strangers. The

[194]

leader gave his name as Jonas Holm; the two tall young men beside him were his son Einar and his son-in-law, Finn Langstad. The tall, raw-boned woman with a white cotton cloth over her black hair was Holm's wife.

Ivar offered the travelers campground for the night near his house, but the old man politely declined it—they must reach the Buffalo River before darkness set in. He trusted they would meet again, if it was God's will, and thanked Ivar for his welcome.

They picked up the long rope again at the head of the train, and the trek was resumed rhythmically eastward, the voices soaring anew as if in a paean of praise to the new land.

Tears stood in Kate's eyes. "It's like—like something out of the Bible," she said, her mouth trembling.

"They have been marching for many weeks," Ivar told her. "When they find a place that looks good to settle, they stretch the rope and hold it, so everybody will pray and believe it is where they will rest. They have done it many times, but cannot stay until all believe."

"But—they're coming here at the end of summer!"

"They have enough money with them for a year, Jonas Holm says, because they need so little."

"God help them!" Kate breathed, and looked away to where the line of covered wagons was already dwindling into the distance, looking for all the world like a pallid caterpillar creeping across the prairie.

In a moment she was gone, waving her hand to Ivar as she hurried homeward. Looking after her, Ivar felt again that disturbing conviction of having known her long before his lifetime began. The knowledge was unclouded by anything physical. Even the loveliness of her hair and eyes was remote from common life—as remote and lovely as the music he had listened to this afternoon. He had been unable to tell her how beautiful

that music had been. He would never know how to tell anyone about it. He knew only that defeat had dropped from
him like a faded cloak, and that desolation had lifted from the
land as he set his feet toward home.

He had gone less than a quarter of a mile when he met
Karsten, staring southeastward toward that amazing, unforgettable caravan. The boy had seen it, and had heard the
singing!

XXIV

WINTER and spring, and summer once more, and there was a patient wheeling of the year through different calls in the prairie wind, different hues on earth and sky, different fragrances from groves and fields that were resolved to live again. Nature was continuing, depleted but stubborn; and in the knowledge Kate Shaleen felt a surpassing joy, a certainty that good times for the settlers were not far distant.

With the children of Einar Holm and Finn Langstad, Knut Pederson and Johannes Stormo, the roll call in Kate's school had almost doubled. Marit and Olga Holm; Karen, Ingebjorg, and Lars Langstad; Ingolf Pederson; Harald and Bjorn Stormo —they had trooped in on the first day of school like young gypsies. Kate had hung the walls with cheerful lithographs donated by the young minister, Mr. Clegg. Poor Mr. Clegg! He had fancied himself in love with Kate. He had even asked her to marry him. Well, one didn't just *marry*. And so Mr. Clegg had felt the call elsewhere and taken his departure. For Magdali Vinge, at least, the loss had not proven intolerable. It had been more than made up in the arrival of the Lutheran pastor, Magnus Guldbrandson. Magdali had never quite trusted Mr. Clegg.

And then had come the long winter evenings, with Ivar and Steve at work testing the soil. How they had labored over the big words in Steve's book! A salt dissolving acid must be sent for—chlorohydric, was it?—in which to boil their samples of the soil. There had been much filtering and fussing and an endless searching of the book. Potash and soda, lime, magnesia, iron, phosphorus, and sulphur—Ivar's blue-gray eyes had kindled with new light as he used the words. To a bewildered Kate he had explained how they had placed a layer of subsoil in a box, covered it with top soil from which all growing power had been removed, and set it outside where it would freeze. In the spring, by another test, they hoped to discover how the subsoil replenished the top soil, proving that the marlite deposit . . . It had all been very mysterious and very wonderful!

In the spring there had been what Steve had jokingly called a "grasshopper bee." The farmers, with the help of men and boys from Moorhead and Georgetown, had burned the wild grass over half the county. Perhaps in reward for their efforts, Providence had spared the district from further ravages during the summer, although elsewhere the plague had been almost as destructive as before. Harvest had been bountiful, and even Steve Shaleen had been forced to admit that luck had been with him for once. He had dug vegetables from his garden that had been the wonder of everyone who saw them. Another couple of years like this one, and he wouldn't change places with the bishop.

Spring and summer and harvest, and now it was December again, with days that were blue and downily soft, with only a hint of wind now and then, and only a thin carpet of snow. For two weeks an April blandness had caressed the newly turned furrows where the farmers had completed their fall plowing and were ready for another spring. A few more trails were written now across the prairie, especially toward Buffalo River. If the land could be seen from a height, Kate Shaleen thought, it would look like the palm of a vast hand etched by the lines of life and heart and mind and fate.

Ever since the first of the month the Christmas program had been in preparation, with songs and recitations and tableaux.

The weather had held fine, but it was not to be trusted, as everyone knew. Magdali Vinge had protested that the entertainment should have been held earlier in the month. She had even disputed Kate's authority to keep the school open after the fifteenth of December. But for once Ivar had opposed her openly. Why not let the teacher run her school to suit herself? Magdali's response to that had staggered him. Perhaps Ivar would like to have Kate Shaleen run the whole community to suit herself. Perhaps, on his visits to the Shaleen place during the winter nights, he had discovered more than he had found in the book he had been raving about. Perhaps Kate had had reasons of her own for refusing to marry the young Presbyterian minister. . . .

But of all that, Kate Shaleen knew nothing. She had no way of knowing. The school had gone on, and now only three days were left before the afternoon of the Christmas program.

Kate looked at the oak-framed clock on the wall—a gift to the school from the county treasurer, who had expressed the hope that more teachers like Miss Shaleen would "bloom on the prairie." The clock said half-past two.

The day was bright and calm, and so mild that the big, pot-bellied, cast iron stove had been left with its morning fire still drowsing in it. The stove lengths of seasoned oak and poplar were piled against the cloak-closet wall, almost to the rafters, and just outside there was a neat cord or two that would not have to be touched till the new year. The men in the district always saw to it that there was plenty of wood for the school.

Kate rose to tap her desk bell. Heads came up gladly from books and slates. She had made it a rule to dismiss school early enough so that those living farthest away could reach home before darkness began to settle.

"We have time to sing the carols just once," Kate said, and waited for them to clear their desks and come to order before she took her place at the organ.

At the end of half an hour she paused abruptly in her playing and turned to look at the windows. Had the light changed, or was she just imagining things? It seemed as if a gray mask had come over the sky.

She left Fritz Joseffy to lead them in the singing of another carol, and then went quickly out of doors. The west was the color of boiling lead, with wreaths of sickly white. Not a dry twig rustled. Kate felt as though she stood in a vacuum, scarcely able to breathe.

She was about to go back into the schoolhouse again when she heard the rattle of a wagon coming from the east. A minute later, Carl Engebrigt tossed the single driving rein over the back of the white ox that was hitched to the wagon and leaped to the ground.

"Get my kids out, and all the others along the Buffalo!" he shouted. "I was going to town, but now I got to get back with the kids. We're in for something!"

"But what is it, Mr. Engebrigt?" Kate asked. "It doesn't look like snow—"

"It's snow all right, and plenty more. That's dust. She's going to be a black heller! Get the kids out."

Kate laid a hand on his arm. "Don't frighten them, Mr. Engebrigt. Remember—I'll have to stay with the others."

"Stay inside till somebody comes for you, then. You got wood to keep the stove going. Steve'll be over here as soon as—"

"We'll be all right," Kate assured him as they went into the schoolhouse. She would not tell him that Steve was in bed with a cold.

The children were huddled at the windows, gazing at the sooty murk that already filled half the western sky, from south to north. A thin whistling sounded about the eaves.

"Children, there's a snowstorm coming up," Kate said as they grouped about her. "Mr. Engebrigt will take all of you who live over on Buffalo River. The others will wait here with me. Lila and Marit, you help the little ones with their wraps. Hurry now! While they get ready, Ingolf, carry in some wood and pile it here beside the stove. Karsten and Philip will help you. Fritz, you light the lamp."

Though Carl Engebrigt knew that there was scarcely room in his small wagon for those who were going with him, the necessity of leaving the others appalled him. But Kate was reassuring, and in a moment the youngsters were climbing into the wagon. Only five children were left, Karsten Vinge, Philip Groman, the two Joseffy boys, and their little sister Maria. Thank heaven, Magdis Vinge had been kept at home today because of an ear ache. Kate closed the door and bolted it.

"I want to go home," little Maria Joseffy wailed suddenly, her dark eyes large and unwinking, her mouth crumpled.

Kate put her arms about her and drew her firmly away from the window. "You wouldn't want your papa to come out in this storm, would you, dear?" she chided brightly.

But her own words caught her heart in a net of terror as the wind under the eaves became a scream that brought the cold sweat to her brow. She sent up a formless prayer—let no one attempt to outrace this monstrous thing that had come down without warning out of a falsely tranquil west!

She took a sewing basket from a shelf and set little Maria to work sorting out the colored threads. The boys were lugging in wood from the cloak room, piling it well back from the stove. The snow was coming now, such snow as Kate had never seen before in her life. The shed that stood only a short distance from the schoolhouse had been blotted from sight. The windows rattled as if from a scattering of pebbles under the onslaught of the storm, and hissed under the freezing whips of the snow. Yet there was no danger, Kate told herself, so long as they remained in their snug shelter. There were even bits of food left over in the lunch boxes, and tea and coffee and cocoa on the shelf. But for anyone who might be out there . . .

Her feet seemed not to belong to her as they took her automatically to the organ in the corner. The binding on the hem of her long flounced skirt caught up chalk dust, bits of paper, dry chips of bark from the wood the boys had carried in. She was aware of nothing now except the look in Karsten's eyes when she had, at last, dared to meet them direct. If he had spoken, if he had given words to the terror in those eyes—but no, he had only gazed at her with mute and awful questioning.

"Let's try some of our songs again, boys," she said, fumbling at the organ stool. "Maria, move over here with your sewing, and you can sing too."

"But keep on the tune," Fritz Joseffy warned, "or I'll make you wash your ears!"

"I'm glad Magdis had to stay home today," Karsten said. "She can't sing no more'n a crow!"

They all laughed, a little giddy with the novelty of being shut in with the teacher.

"I had ear ache once and it busted and run all over the pillow," Maria related with pride. "I was *deef*, too, for a long time."

"Let's sing 'Silent Night,'" Philip Groman suggested.

Anton Joseffy snickered. "*Silent* Night! That's funny—ha, ha! *Howling* night would be more like it."

Kate pulled out the forte stop, placed her fingers on the keys, and raised her voice. The boys joined in, the sweet, shy soprano tones lifting with a valor that brought a hot mist to Kate's eyes.

And then, behind them, there came a tremendous thumping upon the door. Kate sprang up, but the boys were ahead of

[202]

her and had the bolt lifted, and Ivar Vinge stumbled over the threshold, slamming the door behind him.

"Ivar!" Kate stood rooted to the floor, staring at him, her hand at the high velvet collar of her dress.

A mantle of frozen snow covered Ivar from head to foot. He was throwing off his long, beaver-collared coat, his mittens, and his sheepskin cap. His face was almost purple, with white patches on nose and cheeks. Karsten had rushed at him, and he had pulled the boy close for a speechless instant, then thrust him gently away.

"A whole hour—to come four miles!" Ivar said. "I wonder what else they have in this country."

"Sit down!" Kate ran to him and caught his arm. "Karsten —rub his face with snow. I'll put coffee on to boil."

She hurried about while the four boys made a lark of plying Ivar's face with the crusted snow from his wraps. Now that his father was here, safe, Karsten was enjoying the exciting novelty of the storm.

"There, now!" Ivar said at last. "That's enough. You want to take my nose off? I must look to my horses. I'll get them into the shed."

He spoke as if venturing out into the storm, even to go three steps, was a simple thing. And it was a good fifty yards to the shed.

"But you can't go out—" Kate began.

"I came four miles—I can go to the shed. There is a rope here—it was left after Steve and I dug the well. We hung it in the cloak place."

"It won't be nearly long enough," Kate said.

"It was about fifty feet," Ivar said, and looked about the room. "There are the curtains on the windows—"

"And I have two stockings," Kate said, her cheeks glowing.

"With so much," Ivar grinned, "we should get somewheres."

"Have your coffee first," Kate urged, ready to take the pot from the stove as soon as it came to a boil. "Steve will be so worried—he's in bed with the grippe, or of course he would have been here. How does your face feel?"

"Just like a pin cushion."

"Aren't your feet frozen, Mr. Vinge?" Fritz Joseffy asked, eager for more excitement.

"Hah, it would take the North Pole to freeze feet so big!"

Kate handed him his coffee in a tin cup, and began measuring cocoa into a small kettle for the children. It would have to be made with water, but she could use enough sugar to make it drinkable. She went to the bucket that stood on a bench against the wall. There was a tiny mirror above it—Delphy's old mirror. It caught her eyes, and the resolute brightness in them frightened her. No need, surely, for all this courage! It wasn't as if they were on a sinking ship. . . .

It was past midnight.

The children, fed on what had been left in their lunch pails, were asleep under their coats, cuddled on the seats that Ivar had drawn close to the roaring stove. A half-hour ago, Kate had spread her own cloak on the floor beside the stove and had persuaded Ivar to lie down with his fur-collared coat over him and try to get a little sleep. There was no way of telling what he might be called upon to do as soon as another day dawned —if there should be any dawn at all.

He had fallen into a shallow and troubled slumber, his arms and legs jerking occasionally, his shiny, frost-bitten nose twitching in a way that made Kate laugh to herself in spite of the predicament that had overtaken them.

Her mind was strangely light and free. She remembered the first time she had met Ivar Vinge, on the bank of the river on a hot afternoon in August. She had felt then that he was a man alone. The same feeling had come to her many times during the years that had passed since then. She knew now, clearly, that he was not alone. He had a competent, pretty wife, and four handsome children. She, Kate Shaleen, was alone, and always would be. She felt it now, suddenly and starkly, at the very moment when the wind seemed to clutch the schoolhouse in a final, destructive embrace.

The groan of the timbers roused Ivar, and he sprang to his feet. But soon after, the wind sank to a slow, steady whine, while the cold grew and crept inward, mocking the red-hot sides of the big stove. A lassitude came over Kate that she fought against in vain.

"You sleep now," Ivar was saying. "I'll sit up. And don't you trouble about anything. The sun will be shining in the morning."

She stretched out on her cloak where Ivar had been lying, and he tucked his own coat about her. His quick, comforting steps as he moved about seeing to the children, the lamp, the stove, the windows and the door, were the steps a man should have, and a delicious drowsiness stole over her. In a half-dream she lived over again every precious moment of the afternoon and evening: the heroic singing of the children, Ivar's coming, the fun they all pretended to have knotting the rope together with the children's wool neck-comforts and the curtains and her own long gray knitted stockings which she had gone into the cloak room to take off! And then—the fastening of one end of the rope to Ivar's arm, and paying him out into the storm while she stood just within the door, hanging for dear life to the fringe of Maria Joseffy's scarf, while the four boys leaned against the door back of her to keep the wind from ripping it open. Finally, Ivar's return from the shed, with an interval when Kate was sure the crazy chain had broken a link somewhere! When he had heaved through the door at last, Kate could have wept. . . .

The snow came on, although the wind had fought itself out. The snow came on and on, a fine-spun web unlimited by any height or width of sky, any barricade of time. Kate slept.

When she wakened, cramped by her stays, she thought it must be sunrise, but the clock was ticking only half-past three. The lamp was turned low, and Ivar was hunched forward with his arms about his knees, on the opposite side of the stove. The five children still slept on the benches, Anton Joseffy with a gentle snore.

Kate tiptoed to the back of the stove and picked up her stockings that had been drying on a stool. She sat down on the stool, took off her high laced boots and put the stockings on. Her toes curled luxuriously in the warm wool. A good cup of tea, now, and what did it matter if she was to be an old maid forever? She had had this strange night, and she had known the sudden fierce grasp of the wind and its defeated quieting, and she knew in her heart that all who were under this roof would come safely home. She wanted no more—she asked for no more.

"I'll make some tea," Ivar said, "now you are awake."

Kate got up from the stool. "I'll make it."

"No, you warm your feet near the stove. This I will make, and you can laugh at it if you like."

She ought to be ashamed, she told herself, for sitting docilely by while he made the tea, but she wasn't. Years hence, she would remember that once she had been pampered, once she had stretched her feet out in woolen stockings toward a hot stove while a man she had no right even to think about made a cup of tea for her.

"The wind has gone down," Ivar told her, handing her a cup of the strong brew, "but it is snowing heavier. It was like this a few years ago in Wisconsin, I remember, but it was fine again by daylight."

"Your wife will be worrying," Kate said.

"She will worry, but her brother is with her. He came to talk about the railroad bonds they have—they think soon to change them for railroad land. That way they will have much land, for bonds that are worth little. I begin to think—" He rubbed his jaw and smiled. "I begin to think that Magdali and Roald will some day be the big people in the district."

Kate nodded, sipping her tea. "I am sure of it. Your children will have every advantage in the future."

Ivar's eyes moved fondly toward the bench where Karsten slept, one grubby hand shelled against his smooth cheek.

"There is a good boy," he said temperately. "He will be something some day. His mother thinks he spends too much time with drawing pictures. Arithmetic he lets go always to the last—and then he says his eyes hurt."

Kate was silent. She had known for some time that Magdali Vinge was sharply hostile to the work she was doing in the school.

"You may tell Mrs. Vinge," she said coolly after a moment, "that I shall see to it that Karsten's arithmetic is not neglected in the future."

Ivar laughed uncomfortably. "I am a clumsy fool to talk so. It is fine the way you help the boy. I do not think the way Magdali does, always. She is scared the boy will grow up to be a dreamer, and she thinks this is no country for any such." He smiled ruefully. "I do not know, but might be she is right."

Kate's laugh was softly proud. "She has never approved of how I do things here. She would like to see someone else teaching her children. She's probably blaming me right now for—for this."

"You did not bring the storm," Ivar said.

"No, but I kept the school open for a week longer than she

wanted. She will use this to prove that I am incompetent. It was my mistake. It might have been a pretty bad mistake. It —it may still be!" Her face sank suddenly forward in her hands.

Ivar sprang up in consternation. "You must not do that," he muttered wretchedly. "Don't—don't, Kate! You—it is not your fault." He put one hand on her dark hair and held it there as he bent over her.

The touch of his hand sent through her body a wild distress, as of chimes ringing silver terror in her heart. She lifted her eyes to his and saw in them her own ecstatic fright. Ivar let his hand fall, drew a harsh breath, and stepped away from her to stand beside the stove. Its iron paunch bore a red-hot nimbus. That central kernel of heat in this log schoolroom, with a white fury of cold outside, had somehow got into his brain. He felt dizzy. He felt as if Kate Shaleen were in his arms, her tender mouth beneath his own. He turned and looked at her, his hand raised to his forehead.

"We have talked too much," he said.

Kate got up, and with a white face moved across the room to the organ. Her fingers felt numb upon the keys, and she was scarcely aware of what she played. The music came so softly that with the hot ringing in his ears Ivar could barely hear it.

He stood in the aisle between the two rows of pine desks and benches, one hand clutching the back of a seat. What he felt or thought he had no way of knowing, beyond the fact that here, in this uncertain hour with the spectral legions of the snow coming on and on through the bitterly black and desolate emptiness of the night, something was passing from his life forever.

I

It SEEMED meant for evening sunlight, this sweet and forgotten place among the red willows, where the gravestones were humble and old. There was no trace left of the frame church that had stood here once, and had been struck by lightning and burned to the ground more than twenty years ago. The town council and the church board had disposed of the ruins before building the imposing brick church that overlooked the park. Wild blackberry brambles and chokecherry shrubs grew thick over the filled-in scar.

Traveling the level prairie lands of the West, the wheat lands, the river woods, the sliding yellow ribbon of the river itself and the woods again, and then the fields eastward to the bare immensity of the sky, the evening sunlight seemed to pause here among the willows and the headstones that were humble and old, and that asked for nothing more than this tender radiance at the end of day. There was no wind; the new leaves of the willows did not whisper; in a little while darkness would come, and dew would fall upon the young grass of the old mounds like tears from the summer stars above them. In time the mounds would be leveled, the stones and their granite names would crumble into a crumbling earth, and the stars would shrink in the timeless loom of their destiny.

Norma Shaleen walked with old Ivar Wing in the long, still grass between the graves. Each spear of grass stood sharp and individually gilded by the low sun, and Norma had the feeling that she was a trespasser in a place so curiously sentineled.

Over this feeling, however, she had been attentive to old

[211]

Ivar's account of each sleeper whose resting place they passed. For when Brill had been with her at his grandfather's farm last month, he had, with a frankly admitted superstition which she could not laugh down, refused to visit the old cemetery. "You were nine," he had said, "and I was fourteen when we were there last. Let's leave it at that, for the time being."

When she was nine and he was fourteen. Brill Wing, the blue-eyed lad with the dark swirl of hair and with legs too long for him, and Norma Shaleen, the skinny little girl, had stolen into the graveyard through a ghost-lit fog, a moon riding high and almost invisible above the mist. They had been scared stiff at the hop of a toad among the dank leaves, but Brill had got the use of his legs first and had left Norma behind him shrieking in terror. Oh, how chivalrous—and chattering!—he had been, running back to grab her by the hair and drag her through the picket gate that groaned like a lost soul!

Row after row were the names: Gromans, Engebrigts, Stormos; Helena Holm Shaleen, Norma's mother, whom she did not remember; and her father, Loren Shaleen, whom she had adored.

Old Ivar pointed with his cane to a simple slab of red granite about which stiff ribbon grass grew tall. It marked two mounds side by side, and the inscription was one that Norma remembered: "Stephen Lawrence Shaleen, Born April 9, 1841—Died November 16, 1918. Selma Engebrigt Shaleen, Born August 3, 1852—Died November 20, 1918. Back to the earth they loved."

"I was only four years old then," Norma said, "but I remember the terrible flu epidemic—wet sheets hanging around the house, smelling of carbolic acid. And sulphur burning on the stove."

"It was a terrible time." Ivar inclined his head for a moment, then walked slowly to a slender, gleaming white column that seemed to bear a faint pink luster from the high and profusely blooming wild rose bramble that clung lovingly about it. A swallow in flight was carved at its top, and beneath the pure intaglio appeared the name and dates: "Kate Shaleen, June 12, 1848—January 4, 1901." Nothing more. And yet all, Norma thought—all!

Old Ivar touched one of the full-blown roses with a trembling hand, and when he grasped the crook of his cane again his weathered knuckles stood out like pale barnacles.

"It's a beautiful monument," Norma said softly. "My uncle David told me about it once when I met him in New York, at an exhibition of his sculpture. Of course I had seen it here, but I was too young to appreciate it then. He told me that Kate wanted to be brought here. I used to think that was strange, because Aunt Maude told me that Kate had been bitterly disappointed over a school she had near here—in the old days."

The old man was silent for a long time, and Norma thought uneasily that she had made a mistake in touching upon that ancient story of her great-aunt's departure from the log school that had held her very heart. But she and Brill had argued so much about the origin of the conflict between her family and his that she longed now to know the truth of it.

"Yes," Ivar said at last, his face stern. "It was a cruel thing, that. But I had no say in it. After the great blizzard—they didn't call them blizzards until some years later, though—after that it was made out a man teacher was needed here, while the country was still so rough. Well, they got their man teacher."

Silence fell upon him again, so abruptly that Norma knew she could expect no more of the story from Ivar's lips, for the time being, at any rate. *They* got their man teacher, she thought with pity. Ah, the gallant defense of his dead wife's memory, the pride and courtly dignity of it!

[213]

At the upper end of the cemetery, in a recess almost woven over by wild grapevines, they came to a simple white cross, the gold tracing upon which was faded by the rains and winds of more than twenty years: "Louise Wing—February 7, 1901 —July 16, 1918."

"She was the one that was drowned, you know," Ivar said gently. "In the river. So young and pretty and tempersome she was. She should have married Tom Shaleen."

"But he was killed in France," Norma said.

"Yes, yes, of course. But she should have married him just the same, before he went over. And might have, too, if it wasn't for what happened between my son Karsten and your Aunt Rose."

Norma drew her breath, thinking of the terrible story of Karsten Wing and Rose Shaleen. Rose, because of the manner of her death, had not been given room here. . . .

"Brill has told me about Louise," she said.

"I suppose so. In those days we didn't speak of such things."

Norma stooped to touch the wild grapevine, and a slight faintness that she had felt briefly in the past day or two came over her again.

"And here," Ivar was saying, his voice oddly webbed over as if by silver filaments of memory that lived still in deep gentleness, "is my daughter Olina. She was my youngest, you know."

The white stone had chosen the form of an angel with half-folded, downward brooding and sheltering wings.

"My father and my Uncle David were both in love with Olina, weren't they?" Norma said.

"That is possible," the old man smiled. "But it was David she would have taken, if all had been different in those days. In the end she married Henry Cruse."

They had turned back and were walking toward the gate

now. Beside the grave of Stephen Shaleen, Ivar paused briefly.

"I am ninety-six years old, Norma," he said. "That's too old for any man. I'll be going soon, and I'll be put away here—near Steve somewhere. I have it written down. I'll not be laid out in that one north of town, where they put my wife and my son Arne. I wouldn't rest in any fancy place like that. But here—your grandfather and me—we were no account in the district, once it got going. We got on well enough to suit ourselves. Others took up what Steve and I started, and they made themselves rich men out of it. But we started it—the testing and the experimenting and all. Maybe we should have been bigger men than we were. Maybe we should have took a-hold, instead of letting it all get into the hands of the money grabbers. But how can a man look so far ahead? We can only see behind us. And maybe that's a good thing. But I'll lie here, somewhere near Steve Shaleen, when my time comes."

"What year was it," Norma asked quickly, brightly, winking fast against tears, "that the town was named after you? Eighty-one or eighty-three?"

His brown face crinkled under the white flow of his mustache and beard.

"That was in eighty-three—fifty-eight years ago this June. I was a young fellow then, not yet forty, and it was a great honor they paid me. But I wasn't the fool they took me for. It was my wife Magdali they had in mind when they named the town. It was my wife Magdali who changed the family name from Vinge. She and her brother Roald got the post office in—and the new school—and the church. The town would have been called Bratland if Roald had been able to get his way. But Magdali fought him on that. She would have it called Wing on account of the children. And she had her way there."

"You had a great deal of land here then, didn't you?"

"Not so much then—only two, three sections. There was more a few years before, but Magdali and Roald sold many thousands of acres to the bonanza farms. It was land they got for railroad bonds, and they made a big profit when they sold it. They were rich, the two of them." His faded eyes smiled without bitterness into the painted distance of the evening prairie. "They were rich—in money. They owned almost every stick and stone in the town. The bank, the mill, the hotel, the lumber yard—all of it! They got hold of most of the stock in a little branch railroad in the south part of the state, too, and money poured into their laps. And they both died before they could know that money is something that can be lost. They should have waited for what happened in twenty-nine. Maybe it would have done them no good. Some of my children and a lot of my grandchildren saw it happen. And little good it did them. Money in the soul is a heavy thing, my girl. A little in the pocket is a good thing. But I talk and talk. Might be—*maybe*—sometimes these days I let my tongue slip again—maybe you have heard all this before."

Norma caught his arm. "I'll never hear too much of it. Brill has told me as much as he could." She drew his arm close to her with a sudden surge of affection. "You're glad Brill and I are going to be married, aren't you?"

"Glad? Yes, I'm very glad. It will mean something that should never have been will have come to an end. It will mean a new beginning of something that is good."

Young Louie Spragg—there had been three Louie Spraggs in three generations—was waiting outside the gate in Ivar's old Ford. Norma looked back and saw shadows floating like palpable presences over the incurious mounds.

II

THE Wing place could scarcely be called a farm now, in the old prairie sense. Its small orchard fringed the town of Wing, and east of the orchard lay fields of alfalfa and clover, feed for the small herd of Guernseys that Ivar kept. There was an acre of vegetable garden flanking the fenced-in chicken yard where Wyandottes scratched in the sun and returned at twilight to their antiseptic roosts in white-washed shelters. There was a tractor, and only two work horses now. Rolf Nelson, a husky Swede, and young Louie Spragg ran the farm for old Ivar, while Louie's maiden aunt, Eudora, conducted the affairs of the big, echoing house, and tended chickens and garden with as much help from Ivar as she would tolerate.

Ivar's son Arne, after Magdali's death, had been responsible for reducing the home farm to a size not too unwieldy for the old man's management. His father was, after all, in his eighties at the time, but nothing could persuade him to move in anywhere with his kinsfolk. There were sixty acres left now of the original homestead—that was as much as Ivar wanted. It was an orderly place. Tourists driving by on the concrete highway were wont to pause and regard the old brick house, its gingerbread trim and cupola, with pleased surprise, remarking that "it gave to the Middle West a sense of settled age and dignity that reminded one of New England, though of course it was so different!"

The ancient collie, Hector, rose with a rheumatic wag of his tail as the Ford entered the driveway beneath the overarching elms. Norma and Ivar stepped down from the car, and

Hector forgot his years in a frenzy of joyous barks as he leaped about their legs.

"Maybe you'd better give him a bath tomorrow, Louie," Ivar suggested, "if it's warm like today. He's starting to smell old."

"I'll do that, Mr. Wing," Louie said, and drove the car on to the garage.

Eudora had kept supper waiting, and was a bit prim when Norma and Ivar entered by way of the kitchen, Hector at their heels. The cat that had belonged to Norma's Aunt Maude glowered at the dog, and Aunt Maude's canary sang his evening song in his cage before the window.

"There's ham and them new store potatoes, not even as good as our old ones," Eudora announced. "But I put parsley on 'em. And beets cooked in apple cider. And the Germans have just attacked the Russians on the radio!"

She swung about with the dish towel draped over her shoulder and peered into the oven.

"Russia!" Norma stared at Ivar.

He was looking down at old Hector, who had one paw appealingly lifted to shake hands. Ivar knelt and took the paw in his knotted fingers.

"It doesn't surprise me, Norma," he said. "Friendship has gone out of the world—friendship and honor and the strength of a man's word. But they will come back—they will come back!"

After supper, when they had listened to the latest startling news from the radio, Ivar asked Norma to play the piano.

"One of them, anyhow," the old man smiled.

Norma's own small grand, and the upright that had been in the house "since the beginning of time," as Brill said, stood side by side at one end of the big parlor. Great-aunt Kate's organ was in a corner at the other end.

[218]

Norma played a few simple things that were familiar to Ivar, and then suddenly the loneliness for Brill came over her again. But that was rudely erased by a return of the strange and watery squeamishness which she could no longer account for except in one way. Seated in his favorite easy-chair, Ivar saw her hand go to her forehead. His white brows bristled together, and his glance was sharp.

"You're tired, my girl," he said. "I don't see why you keep on with these piano pupils you've got coming out from town. You ought to take it easy till Brill comes back and the two of you get married."

Norma moved across the room and sank upon the sofa near the old man. "I want to keep busy, so that I won't have time to think too much about—well, about everything!"

"Ya, perhaps that is best," Ivar sighed. "So long as you do not overdo."

He peered at her from beneath the light of the modernistic floor lamp that had been a birthday gift from Ivar Gossman's wife—a lamp that shocked the eye in this turn-of-the-century room.

"I won't overdo it. You're so good—and it's so good to be here!"

Ivar got his pipe from the table, looking pleased at her words. She thought, *He wants to talk now. Dear soul, please talk, and bring Brill closer to me!*

"I am an old man, Norma," he said as he filled his pipe, "and it has taken me all my life to learn that what is to be will be. We cannot do much to change that. There was a time when I thought I would like to go back to Norway and look down the valley I used to know. That was forty years ago, the children were all grown up, and we were fixed comfortable here. But Magdali was busy with this and that, and we didn't—"

"Couldn't you have gone without her?" Norma asked softly.

His eyebrows lifted in humorous white curlicues. "A trip like that without Magdali? Not even to St. Paul. Oh, I took one once, on a river boat, when Karsten was a little boy. He went with me and we had to spend half the night with your great-aunts in their gambling place because there was no room anywhere else. Magdali never quite got over that. Then—" He fell silent, and Norma sensed his remote dreaming into the past and did not speak to urge him on. "Then—another time—I spent a night away from home. It wasn't of my planning. That was the night of the black blizzard. I spent the night with Kate Shaleen—in the log schoolhouse."

Norma's breath caught for a tense second before she asked, "Will you tell me the true story of that?"

Old Ivar turned his eyes slowly upon her, and they were amazingly clear and bright.

"That will be easy to tell," he said.

Norma uttered not a word while he talked with a simple vividness as if he were giving her an account of something that had happened yesterday. But her throat felt full and aching when he had finished his story.

"And so," he said finally, "there was nothing I could not tell to anyone. There was nothing to hide. But Magdali would have it otherwise. She was a righteous woman. She would have nothing more to do with Kate Shaleen." He laughed shortly. "And might be—except for her will for children, she would have no more to do with me. Kate resigned from her school. The next spring, her log school burned to the ground. It was a mystery, nobody ever knew how it came about. There was a new one built nearer our farm, and we had a man teacher, and I remember Magdali saying, 'Everything works out for the best.'"

That's where it all began, Norma thought. Not even to Brill had he ever told the whole story of that snowstorm when

Ivar and Kate and her small charges might well have per-ished in the log schoolhouse. Something had perished there, nevertheless—something that had no lawful right even to a name. . . .

"There were always reasons why Magdali couldn't take the trip this year, or the next," Ivar went on presently. "She was building a little empire, you see, here in this valley, beside this river, and Norway meant nothing to her any more. I thought it might be a good thing for the children to see what it was like over there." He hesitated, a little shyly, searching for the right words. "There was—there was poetry—and music—in the light on those fjords and mountains in the mid-summer night sun. In the people, too, who make so much out of the little they have. But Magdali didn't have time—and our children didn't have time—and our grandchildren didn't have time. Karsten was the only one who ever went to see it. Well, Solveig and her husband did make the trip to the North Cape once, but they were tourists. They didn't really see the—the poetry. They didn't hear the music. They didn't have time. Nobody in this country ever has time. I have often wondered what *time is*. It is a flowing stream—like the river itself. You cannot hold it long in your hands. You can drink from it when it's clean and fresh, but when it isn't you don't want to wash your hands in it. I thought our children might bring *time* back with them from the old country—something to put together with what we have here in this land. But—well, folks are different, of course. Magdali was different—or maybe I was different. It doesn't matter now."

He gazed through the smoke from his pipe, as if he was visioning the past.

"I hoped that Karsten would bring it back with him," he went on. "But that was not to be. When he went down with the *Titanic*—all that went with him. Magdali said it was God's will that spared us, because we would have gone down too if we had been with Karsten. Then came the war, and the family made more money, and Magdali was busy with board meetings of one kind or another, old as she was. She was a strange woman, Norma. I never *knew* her, and during those last years I scarcely saw her. I wondered afterward how she managed to find time to come home here to die."

He smiled reminiscently, without censure, Norma knew—with indeed a misty affection for the powerful little woman who had passed away peacefully, surrounded by the affluent families of Arne and Magdis, back in 1928. Olina, Karsten, Solveig—she had murmured their names at the last, in turn, as if they too had been there at her bedside. And to her serene last consciousness they *were* there, no doubt, her obedient children.

"But you might have gone to Norway in the last few years," Norma said as Ivar paused.

He smiled and nodded. "Yes, yes, that is so. I thought of it a month before the Germans went into Poland. There was a young captain on a Norwegian freighter—the grandson of an old friend of mine in Norway. He came here to see me, and we talked it over. We had a sort of plan about it, but before we got round to it Germany had old Norway by the throat!"

Had he spoken with vehemence or hatred, Norma would have found it easier to bear. But his gently ironic resignation, with his eyes half closed as he leaned forward on the cane he had picked up from beside his chair, brought the scalding tears to her eyes. It was as if he were looking down a long, mutilated vista of human deeds so inconceivable that his mind rejected them and withdrew to its own solitary peace.

"Damn them!" Norma whispered, her teeth clenched. She walked across the room and seized her handkerchief from a marble-topped table on which stood a hair fern in a fine old copper pot.

"Now, now," Ivar protested mildly. "I've been on a talking spree, haven't I? Everything comes and goes. This, too, will go over."

"And Brill, perhaps—with it," she said, her back turned toward him while she stared out at the serene night.

"Let us not think of that," old Ivar said, and added cryptically, "*You* are here—and so *we* are here, my girl!"

III

NORMA wondered about that speech, later in her room. Did the old man suspect—or even hope—what she herself had begun to fear? Yet—did she fear? No, she was proud, rather. Even if Alice should turn up unexpectedly to claim Brill again, she would still be proud. She would never be afraid!

This room had been Karsten Wing's when he was a youth, and later when he came home to the farm for refuge after worldly success and failure had bruised him, mind and soul. Brill had occupied it during his week here in May, while Norma had used what once had been Solveig's bedroom. When Brill had left this room last month, Norma had moved into it.

The cherry washstand with its set of brown flowered crockery basin, water pitcher, and soap dish still stood where it had been in young Karsten's time, although now there was a modern bathroom down the hall. Norma wondered if Ivar's grandchildren and great-grandchildren,—Wings, Gossmans, Tridds—had not been tempted sometimes to smuggle these things out and sell them for their value as American curios, if not quite antiques.

Dressed in her chenille bath robe, she took Brill's letters from her dressing table and read them all again.

"You are more than my love, you are all the loves before us through all those years. You and I will vindicate them, darling—Karsten and Rose, and all the others, the ill-starred ones. . . ."

Karsten and Rose. She stared at the photograph of Brill on her dresser, and strangely the clear eyes above the smart uniform seemed to become dissolved in her thought.

Karsten Wing had not fled when tragedy and disgrace had stabbed him to the heart. Because of old Ivar he had stayed on here in the Valley and fought his way back to a measure of success and honor. But his triumph had been a bitter stream in his blood. From what Aunt Maude and Brill had told her, Norma was sure that Karsten Wing had been content enough to be lost on that great ship in the north Atlantic, in 1912.

With a little shiver, she picked up another of Brill's letters, his latest one.

"*. . . so, my darling, after slaving on the opus during every hour I've had off duty, I think it reads pretty fair at last. I'm sending you a carbon copy. Hurry up with your criticisms, because I want to shoot it to Stevens in New York, pronto. Don't be too rough on the poor little thing . . .*"

But suddenly, now, the words ran together through the blur of her tears, and with the letter crushed against her face she huddled forward on the bed. The hot and rebellious longing for him which she could hold at bay during her working hours at the piano had leaped upon her again like some rending, animate thing. She strove for calm by summoning back the precious hours they had shared in the city and here at the farm before his orders had come through, taking him to San Diego. After a while she was able to sit up, smile across at his picture, and give him the nightly salute she had promised him.

Dear God, keep him, keep him for me, and for himself, and for all that the Wings and the Shaleens have missed—and for what they may some day mean for America—even yet!

She was putting the letters back in their drawer when the ringing of the telephone came from downstairs, a harsh, insistent alarm. Norma's hand caught at her throat. Only that day she had read of a training plane crashing out of the skies

[225]

in San Diego. She ran to the head of the stairs.

Eudora's sleepily grumbling voice brought her to a pause.

"San Diego calling Miss Norma Shaleen," the old woman announced, an excited quaver overcoming her peevishness.

Norma could scarcely hold the receiver.

"Yes? Oh, Brill, is that you?"

"Norma—is it you?"

"Who else? Darling—"

"How are you, sweet? What are you laughing at?"

"I'm not, Brill—I'm—yes, I am! I'm laughing. Your voice —it's so high and funny!"

"Cut it out, darling. There's nothing to cry about. Listen, I've got news for you. Michelson wired me today. You'll have his letter tomorrow."

"Michelson? Oh—what, Brill?"

"They finally traced Alice. This is blunt over the phone, kid, but it has to be. She escaped from France with a man she had been living with, and she was killed in an air raid in London."

"Oh, Brill, that's—that's terrible!"

"Lots of things are terrible these days, darling. I'm sorry it had to happen that way. I would have called you sooner, but I was busy upstairs."

"Upstairs? How high up, Brill?" She didn't know what she was saying now. Any words would do, no matter how meaningless, so long as she kept her voice going.

"Dearest," he went on soothingly. "I know how you feel. I feel even worse. But listen. I'm getting a week off next month. It might just happen that I'll be flying a special job up your way. I'll let you know ahead of time, of course, but I want you to get our marriage license and have everything set. Norma— are you there?"

"Yes, yes, darling! I'm here and I'm listening, and I'll have

[226]

everything ready. It's just—it's funny that you should be calling tonight—of all times—"

"What's the matter with tonight? Is anything wrong?"

She stared at the mouthpiece in an effort to steady the swimming room. "No, of course not! I—I was just so lonely for you tonight. Brill—if you fly a plane east—you'll be careful, won't you?"

"For Pete's sake, that's my job, isn't it? I'll be careful. I've got a date waiting for me, haven't I? Well, say hello to grandpappy. And—isn't a telephone a hell of a thing to talk over? Do you—still like me a little bit?"

"Oh, Brill!"

"Me, too. Smiling, sweet?"

"Smiling."

"Good night, loveliest Norma."

"Good night, my darling."

In her room again, after she had talked a little with old Ivar, who had wakened, Norma turned out her light and knelt beside the open window. Across the plushy darkness came the smell of clover fields in bloom.

Could there be any mistake about the news concerning Alice?

"Even so," she whispered fiercely, "I'll never regret anything, anything!"

BOOK TWO

Those Who Were Young Then—1888–1902

I

Karsten Wing was almost twenty-two, and home from the
state university to help with the harvesting of fourteen hundred acres of grain this summer.

He stretched out, long and thin, and yawned himself luxuriously awake to look down the length of the white crocheted
spread to the fancy brass convolutions and knobs that consti-
tuted the end of his bedstead. His feet stuck out from the immaculate fringe of his mother's handmade counterpane, and
he grinned at the size of them. Though they were well shaped
and large, they were none too clean. His mother's final admoni-
tion last night after supper had been that he should bathe in
the new tin tub that had a drain leading through a pipe right
down to the kitchen sink, thence through another pipe, and
so out to a ditch that debouched ultimately upon the hog wal-
low. But after that first day on the binder, under a sun as big
as the sky, and after the wonderful meal his mother and the
hired girls had put up for the men coming in from the fields,
he hadn't even glanced into the "bathroom" at the new tub,
a wonder painted green on the outside with pink roses rampant.

He had used it a number of times since his arrival home three
weeks ago, lugging buckets of water up from the reservoir of
the kitchen stove, although just before taking the train for
home he had scrubbed himself thoroughly with running hot
water, in his boarding house near the university. Mrs. Coombes
had heated the water for him especially, in the tank attached to
her kitchen range. Karsten had thought it best not to speak of
this to his mother, however, despite the fact that she was well

aware that such a thing as running hot water existed in the modern homes in the city. Magdali knew about such things. She laughed, even yet, when she thought of the time when Uncle Roald had come back from a "tonsorial parlor" in Grand Forks, where he had taken a bath in a tub "as white as a false tooth!" The cautious Roald had been suspicious of the contraption, and had got into it with his underwear on, in case of fire or some other unguessable emergency.

From the double windows of his room in the big white frame house, Karsten saw to his delight that he had wakened in time to catch the beginning of the broad prairie dawn—that sovereign color creeping up from the horizon, spikes of clean flame spreading and widening westward over a receding shore of sooty purple-bronze, over acres and acres of wheat. He leaped out of bed in the linen nightshirt his mother had made for him three years ago. The garment was too short at the wrists now, and it exposed his knees, that were like small half-skulls. He knelt beside one of the windows, pulled aside the stiffly starched lace curtain, and looked out.

From the southeast came a breeze with a freight of penetrating, dry sweetness gathered up out of the tremendous expanses of ripe grain. In the nearer pasture to the left of the big barn, the windmill, the corncribs, and the implement shed, bob-o-links and meadow larks were joyously heralding the dawn. Karsten held his breath while the fiery bubble of the sun flashed free of its pearly earth-haze moorings on the eastern crest. What a wonderful thing to behold—the filmy shadows, violet and stone-gray over the pasture land, gloomy gold over the wheat, like queer, insubstantial islands in flight to the safe darkness beyond the western rim of the world!

Karsten wondered suddenly if anyone in this house, save perhaps his little sister Olina, could see in those fleeing patches of color what he saw. His father might, but Ivar seemed to have grown more taciturn every time Karsten had come home for a vacation, as if he thought it quite unnecessary to attach fancy labels to such natural phenomena as sunup or sundown. It was a long time now since it had been decided that Karsten should practice law and forget his silly notions about painting.

Notions! On the night before he had left to enter the university, his mother had said, "We ought to be thankful Kate Shaleen resigned from the high school in Moorhead when she did, or Karsten would have had her for a teacher. She got his head full enough of *notions* in the country school, goodness knows! Do you remember the time, Karsten, when I caught you making a drawing of a *cobweb* in the barn?"

His mother had laughed, and his father had cleared his throat uncertainly.

Even after three years the incident had a stinging freshness. He winced now as he thought of the deception he had practiced all this last winter and spring, when he had gone with Miss Kate at least half a dozen times to art exhibits and concerts in the city. Once, even, they had gone to a stage play called *A Doll's House*, by a Norwegian whose name was Henrik Ibsen. This final adventure into new worlds was really in the nature of an escapade, because his mother had warned him repeatedly against the evils of the theater and everything connected with it. The theater was darkly synonymous with "painted women" and wine flowing red—or more sinisterly pale gold—and a shocking absence of morality.

Kate Shaleen had by no means lured him to these forbidden purlieus. She had been in the habit of coming to the city once a month to spend a week-end away from her arduous duties as head of Sunnyvale Hall, a school for delinquent girls that had been established a short distance south of the capital. When Karsten discovered that she intended to see the Ibsen play, he had daringly offered to be her escort. Kate had conscientiously reminded him that his parents would disapprove. *Parents*, she had said delicately, meaning his mother. To that Karsten had retorted that since he was going to be a lawyer it was high time for him to begin seeing what the world was really like. They had been having afternoon tea together in a little place close to the university, and Karsten had flushed at the glance she had given him. Was she still regretting his failure to stand against his family when he had yearned to become an artist? Well, he couldn't have done that. His mother had gently made it plain that there was no money for such "idle" schooling. She had been very reasonable about it. Hard-earned dollars were not to be thrown away without some assurance that they would return. Even the greatest artists had starved to death, and how could he be sure that his talent was sufficient to justify the expenditure of time and money? Drawing cobwebs! She had laughed soothingly and stroked her son's downy red cheek.

There had been no more to that. His mother, he was well aware, held the purse strings—she and his Uncle Roald. His father owned no more than his original three hundred and twenty acres of pre-empted land and timber claim, and the demands of the family were growing yearly. Karsten knew how hard his father had worked, was working, and could not in the face of that insist upon a career that might bring disappointment. Later, perhaps, when he had earned a right to it, he might try his wings into a flight of beauty—perhaps in ten years or so, if he met with any degree of success in his chosen profession.

It was with a kind of shaky bravado, then, that he accompanied Kate Shaleen to the theater that evening. But never would he forget the scenes and the people that lived heartwringingly before his eyes during those hours! To the rest of the audience it may have been make-believe, with gas lights

[234]

and a curtain that rolled down between the acts and proclaimed, "Halvorson's Livery—All Hours," "Peeker's Outfitting Shop, Gents Turned Out To Fit," "Come to Combley's For Cosmetics, Ladies! Powders. Perfumes de Style!" There was another curtain that swung down grandly in purple velvet to hide the first one, hitching only for a moment at the left side so that the word "Peek" appeared out of Peeker's advertisement, and sent a ripple of laughter through the house. But Karsten did not laugh. The play had been no make-believe. It had been life, tense and excruciating!

What a different world he was seeing now, at this moment of dawn, from the window at home! Miss Kate would have the right words for those colors, he thought.

The wakening sound of the house came to him. He saw a flotilla of leghorn hens advance as if in a stiff wind toward the chicken fence, where one of the two hired girls—Effie Strand—was tossing crumbs from a pan in her hands.

The house was really astir now. Even young Arne, who was fourteen and grumbled at having to rise so early during summer vacations, was stamping about in the attic room he had chosen for "privacy" just above Karsten's. The kitchen below was a clatter of pots and pans. Someone was shaking down the bed of coals in the big range, which even in the hottest weather was never permitted quite to die. A squealing giggle came clear above the clatter. That would be Gudrun Engebrigt, most likely, having her ample flank pinched by an extra hired man, who did not yet know that Mrs. Wing frowned upon any such levity among the hired help.

It would certainly not be his sister Magdis, Karsten reflected. Whether she was prim because she was homely, or homely because she was prim, had for some years been a vexed question. She was almost twenty now, and Karsten doubted that any young fellow had ever thought of casting sheep's eyes at her. Yet she wasn't really homely, either. She had the clear, blooming complexion of all the Wings. She was tall and strong, and she had dark hair that would have curled about her temples if she had not so mercilessly pasted it back into an unbecoming wad at the base of her skull. But her nostrils and her mouth were nipped in with an habitual disapproval of something or other, and her light-blue eyes held a stare of virginal suspicion. At fourteen, when she had had to stand in the row of the confirmation class for an hour of answering questions put by the minister, she had keeled over in a faint. One or two girls always managed to faint while being confirmed, of course, but Karsten did not really like his sister. Her reverence for work, inherited from her mother, might have been called a virtue if it had been even lightly tinctured with joy.

Karsten stepped back across the bare pine boards to the braided mat in front of the cherry washstand, and poured water from the large china pitcher into the matching wash basin. The toilet set was decorated with brown flowers of no known species. The brown-budded soap dish bore a cake of "Delight" soap. Karsten remembered well when his mother had made their soft soap from tallow drippings and leachings of wood ash—and a broth of rose petals that never quite disguised the sheep-and-lye smell.

He always felt a little embarrassed descending from his bedroom "all slicked up," to meet the hired men who had made their ablutions on the back porch after coming in from the bunkhouse. Louie Spragg, especially, who had been with the family since the frightful locust scourge of 1874, and was now married and living with his wife and small son in the old log house toward the river—Louie especially gave Karsten a crawling, unmanly feeling in the pit of his stomach. Not from anything that Louie did or said! To this day, whenever Karsten came home from school, Louie had been quick to draw him away from the greetings of the family, a whistle of some un-known song between his teeth, a song that cut back so deeply into Karsten's childhood that it was almost unbearable. It was as if Louie summoned forth from whatever realm they abode in now the spirits of Luke Nisselbaum with his fiddle, Lambert with his drum, and Willie Bates with his accordion. Where had they gone, those music-makers of a reckless frontier town? Kate Shaleen had made inquiries about Luke in letters she had written from her office, but she had learned only that he had "hopped a freight" one day and gone farther west, his fiddle case under his arm.

Whatever Karsten's emotions about washing "like a gentle-man" upstairs, his mother would have been indignant if he had come down and shared the tin basins with the seasonal em-ployees on the back porch. The men too, for that matter, would have thought it odd, knowing that Karsten could just as well have stayed away from the harvest fields if he had wanted to. The Wings—with the town half a mile away, and named after them—were among the richest families in the county. It was known that there was a commode in every bedroom in the house, with two hired girls to attend to them each day. Lest the extra help might think that he actually used the commode in his bedroom, Karsten always went directly out of the house and down the path to the small building dis-creetly festooned in wild cucumber vine, and then returned to wash his hands and face hastily again at one of the tin basins while the men lounged about waiting for breakfast.

This morning, when he had got into his shirt, overalls, and heavy boots, and had flattened his rough brown hair with wa-ter, he stepped out of his bedroom to find his sister Solveig standing at the window at the western end of the upper hall. She was still in her frilled nightgown, with paper curlers in her hair.

Solveig, seventeen now, should have been downstairs helping to set the long breakfast table and seeing to it that the mustache cups were in the right places. But there she stood, her
halo of red-gold hair bristling up above the curlers against the
still shadowy blue of the light from the west window. She suffered paper curlers because her hair was naturally too curly!
She had explained to Karsten that what she wanted was *smooth*
curls, and a *smooth* fringe about her face. To that end she was
content to lie in agony all night long. Karsten couldn't understand it. Neither could he understand her wishing to be more
lovely than she already was. With her gray-blue, heavy-lashed
eyes—like their father's, and like Karsten's—and with that
startling hair and milky skin and a red mouth that laughed
even when she cried, Solveig was so beautiful that it almost
hurt one to look at her.

But Karsten was the older brother. "Hey, Suvvy!" He
caught a paper curler and gave it a vigorous yank. "Who do
you think you are—the Lady of the Lake?"

Her eyes blazed with pain and rage. "I've got a right to
stand here if I like! Who do you think *you* are?"

"I'm not quite sure of that myself, yet," he shrugged. "But
ma might like to know what's keeping you, that's all. Not that
it's any of my business, dearie!"

She had turned her back on him, and with some curiosity
he looked beyond her stiffened shoulder, out at the buoyant
blue of the sky above the rich green ruching of river trees half
a mile away. What did she see out there? Near the creek, to
the right, with its windbreak of poplar and willow, stood the
old log house where Louie Spragg now lived with his family.
The sod room had long since been removed, and a timber wall
built up where the room had been shorn away, daylight flowing through now between the wall and the faint grassy heave
of the land. But to Karsten the soddy was still there, though

only a ghostly passage for the wind and the rain. Would Solveig be able to see it? No. Solveig lived entirely in her radiant body. Olina—the youngest, barely eleven—with her poet's eyes flecked green and gold like moss in sunlight, *she* would see it.

And there was Olina herself now, coming up barefoot from the river woods, her straight blond hair a cascade across her shoulders. With her was the collie Meg—named by Olina, after she had read and wept over *Little Women*—and Meg's litter of five puppies, who yapped about the girl's legs in fat and clumsy joy.

"Where has Olina been, so early in the morning?" Karsten asked, without expecting any reply.

"Down to see if the steamboat is in sight yet, I s'pose," said Solveig with a show of indifference. "And she hasn't braided her hair or put on her shoes. She'll get Hail Columbia, I bet!"

"You didn't send her, by any chance?" Karsten guessed shrewdly.

Solveig's face was averted, but he saw the tip of her ear turn the shade of a geranium petal.

So—that was it! He might have known. He *had* known, even if he had tried deliberately to close his eyes to what was going on.

Five years ago, a river boat southward bound had run aground off the old landing. It had been an event of some importance, and even Ivar had gone down and stood with the children, watching the big hulk heaving and straining in the clay, the muddy water boiling about her as the paddle wheel threshed forward and backward in an effort to dislodge the keel from the treacherous bar.

It had been a circus for the youngsters, but to Ivar it had brought a bright surprise that had left him almost speechless. When the captain of the unfortunate steamboat came ashore in a dingy to get a better perspective on his craft's predicament, Julian Fordyce had been with him, and Julian's dark-haired, handsome young son.

"Well, it's an ill wind that doesn't blow some good, what?" Fordyce had laughed, wringing Ivar's hand. "I'm on my way to St. Paul, on business, and I shouldn't have had time to stop over to see you if Fate hadn't stepped in and made the arrangements. This is my son Alec. Shake hands with Mr. Vinge, son."

"It's *Wing* now," Ivar grinned self-consciously.

While the two men talked, Karsten had edged his way forward and done his best to talk with Alec Fordyce. Magdis had hung back, but Solveig entertained no such scruples. She said little, and Alec's responses were monosyllables, for the most part. Karsten, in fact, soon became aware that he alone was doing all the talking. Solveig and Alec Fordyce were staring at each other out of unfathomable eyes, apparently unconscious of anyone's existence but their own. The visit had been necessarily brief. The dingy put off in a few minutes, the steamer was finally released and on its laborious way upstream. On the deck, Fordyce and his son stood waving until they were out of sight beyond a bend in the river. And for long minutes afterward, Solveig had stood gazing in the direction the steamer had taken, deaf to Karsten's urging that it was time to go home.

Two years later, young Alec Fordyce had appeared at the farm—alone. He had got a temporary job on one of the river boats, after his father's death. Julian had made one more trip up into his beloved Far North country, and had been lost there. . . . Karsten had been somewhere in the fields and had not seen Alec that time, but Solveig's trance-like detachment had lasted for days afterward. Nor had that been the end of it, as Karsten was to discover to his amazement during the several years that followed. Alec was on the river; and Solveig, having recourse to her own devices—and Alec's help, no doubt—

knew when his boat was due to pass the landing, going or coming. Less than two weeks ago, she had slipped away from the house after supper and had not come in again until well after ten.

Karsten leaned close to her shoulder now. "Take a little advice from me, Sis," he said kindly, "and don't meet Alec Fordyce on the river bank in the evening again!"

She flared about at him. "What do you mean—"

"Tut, tut! I wouldn't make a scene if I were you. If it hadn't been for me, mother would have caught you last time. She was out looking for you, and I told her you and Marit Holm had walked over to Gimp Featherstone's soda parlor for a root beer. All she said was that it was a mistake to let Gimp open the place in town and keep kids out of bed all hours. Next time you may not be so lucky."

"That was two weeks ago!" Solveig cried angrily. "Why didn't you tell me?"

"Well, it wasn't exactly my business. And I had other things to think about. Besides, you always raise Cain when anybody tries to interfere with you. How'd I know Alec Fordyce meant anything special to you? A roustabout on a river boat—and one of the last of them, at that! *Omnia mutantur!*"

"If you want to swear, why not do it in your own language?" Solveig quivered.

"I wasn't swearing. I was just saying that all things change. You'd better take Latin this fall and get Alec off your mind."

"Alec's a gentleman." Solveig's red lips straightened defiantly. "He's had to make his own living, but he's going to get on in the world."

"Listen here," Karsten said with severe quiet, "Alec Fordyce's father used to come through our land with his Hudson Bay freighters. You know that, but *I* remember it. He told pa that he was married to a squaw. What does that make Alec?"

Solveig had gone white. "You're a dirty snob, Karsten Wing! I know all about Alec's mother. She was half Scotch and half Cree. And she was beautiful. What do you think you're made of? You're scared stiff of mother, but I'm not. And if I have to wait fifty years for Alec to come and take me away, I'll wait! And you can put that in your pipe and smoke it!'

Karsten whistled incredulously. A fast pacer, this sister of his! He hadn't dreamed that she had—but she was so young, so impressionable, and that fiery-eyed, handsome, dashing river adventurer—why, damn it, they were both crazy! In another year or two there wouldn't be a boat left on the river. What would they do about it then? Karsten pulled himself together suddenly. Solveig might just—yes, she might!

A heavy tread sounded on the stairs from below. Behind them, their father spoke sharply.

"What's all this racket about? Magdis has called you to breakfast twice. You—in your nightgown, Solveig! Are you sick?"

The annoyance on his brown, weather-coursed face changed to anxiety. Solveig stood with stiff dignity, and in spite of his consternation Karsten wanted to laugh, because two of her curlers had come undone and her bright hair was standing up like devil's horns on either side of her head.

"No, I'm not sick," she said coolly, and Karsten saw the glint of her set teeth. "I just don't feel like going downstairs yet."

"Well—" Ivar scratched his head helplessly. He never knew where he was with these daughters of his. But Magdali would be short with Solveig when the girl finally did appear below.

"I'm afraid your mother will—" he began.

"Tell her I've got a headache," said Solveig laconically. "I have, too, now," she added, casting a meaningful glance at her brother.

"Come on, pa," Karsten said. "Leave her alone. Maybe she thinks she's in love!" He favored Solveig with a sarcastic grin and put his hand on his father's shoulder as they walked together down the stairway.

"Girls I never could figure out," Ivar observed lugubriously. "That one—she never did seem to belong to the family, and she's getting more funny all the time!" He sighed. "You start on the southwest quarter today, Karsten. Then you can lay off half an hour if you feel like it and go for a swim. It ain't quite fair for you to work all day and read your books half the night, too." He spoke with a brusque timidity that stirred within Karsten the deep affection he had always felt for his father—the more so because yesterday Ivar had made a surprising admission. Reaping had begun on the east fields first, the crop having matured there earlier; but yesterday Ivar had said that it would please him to have his son work on the south and west fields, where the land was really Ivar's, not the property of Magdali and Roald Bratland.

"The work doesn't hurt me," Karsten replied haltingly. "It feels good to be outside after so long—"

"You take that field, anyhow."

There was a scuffling of chairs in the dining room, where the harvest help and the family were taking their places. The stout-footed hired girls tramped to and fro in the kitchen, whence streamed almost visibly the enticing aroma of bacon and eggs, fried potatoes, flapjacks and coffee, and freshly baked apple pie. Karsten's mouth watered. Lord, how good to be home, even if—well, even if Solveig tried to ruin breakfast for him with her silly notions about Alec Fordyce.

The table—covered simply with blue and white sprigged oilcloth while there were so many to be fed at it—had been extended to include all its extra boards, and was ten feet long. Ivar sat at one end with Karsten beside him, Magdali and Magdis at the other end; Arne and the four extra hands were ranged along one side, while the other provided places for the two regular hired men, Jake and Rusty, and Solveig, Olina, and the two hired girls. Gudrun and Effie could scarcely be said to be "seated" at the table, for so rapidly did the platters have to be refilled that the girls, rather massive birds though they were, took their nourishment on the wing between dining room and kitchen. In one respect only did Magdali imply a difference between her daughters and the hired girls—the Wing women worked equally as hard as Gudrun Engebrigt and Effie Strand, but they did not wait on table. It was a simple distinction, and one that Magdali had brought with her from her father's *gard* in the old country. It bore no taint of empty elegance. Magdali merely sought to imbue her daughters early with a sense of dignity in their station in life. It had its effect upon the extra hands too. This was no slap-dash household where they might with impunity make free with the hired girls. Gudrun and Effie knew their place, and that place was not larking in the lee of some twilit haystack.

Everybody at the table was quiet at last, Magdali gave the signal to her husband, a modest smile that carried above the piping hot dishes augmented by jellies and pickles, mesas of bread and mountains of butter—and Ivar bowed his head and said grace. He had never quite got over the feeling that saying grace in English was somewhat of an affectation.

"For what we are about to receive, O Lord, make us truly thankful. Amen."

From beneath lowered lids, Karsten caught his little sister Olina gazing at him instead of sitting with reverently bowed head. What was the matter with her?

Severely flicking his eyes away from Olina, he saw in an unnatural brightness the whole interior of the dining room. Its wall paper was a medallion design of yellow and green, freckled with gilt. A calendar adorned the wall at one end, the other three walls bearing framed pictures: "The Stag at Bay" and two Currier and Ives prints, "The Day of Rest" and "Home for Thanksgiving."

The lamp at this hour was drawn nearly flush with the ceiling, and the fringe of red and white beads on its shade glittered almost baudily—as was its right, Karsten thought, since Ivar had bought the lamp for thirty-five cents at an auction in Moorhead, only to learn later that it had originally graced "a house" on one of the side streets in town. Magdali had been kept in ignorance of that, however. But Karsten had been old enough to share the joke, his father chuckling while he told it.

On the golden-oak sideboard reposed Magdali's polished copper pots and kettles, a cut-glass fruit dish, and a handpainted sugar bowl and creamer that Magdis had won at a church raffle. There was the old carved wooden clock on its narrow shelf, above a ball-fringed doily. The linoleum on the floor testified to the affluence of the Wings even farther than did the flowered Brussels carpet in the parlor.

Suddenly and unaccountably, Karsten felt lonely for the unpretentious soddy kitchen he had known when he was a boy. But breakfast was in full swing. Magdali prided herself upon setting the best table in the district, and it delighted her that the men always ate a meal as if it might be their last on earth. Karsten's appetite needed no goading. It rose to meet the challenge.

Magdali surveyed her table in a nettled mood. Solveig's place, beside Olina's, was empty, and Olina's hair looked as if it had been braided in uncombed haste.

"Why isn't Solveig down to breakfast, Olina?" Magdali asked. Since she had begun to get stout, she always spoke slowly and gently when she was out of patience, lest she lose her breath and her dignity with it.

[245]

Olina, who shared Solveig's bedroom, replied in a sing-song voice, her eyes on her plate while she dallied with pancake and syrup.

"Oh, she stubbed her toe when she got out of bed. I left my copy book on the floor—and I had a thistle pressed in it—a purple thistle. I guess she stuck her toe on it."

That a child of hers should be given to pointless fibbing had baffled Magdali ever since this youngest had been able to talk. But perhaps it was God's punishment being visited upon her, Magdali Wing. That year—1877—when the land business took her far and wide with Roald so that she could not afford to think of her own physical state—who would ever have thought that the Lord would reward her struggle by letting Roald's horses bolt at a stroke of lightning, so that she had been thrown into a ditch and had given birth to Olina a full month before her time? After Olina, there could be no more children. It was sinful, Magdali knew, but she sometimes looked upon her youngest child as a changeling, or—much worse!—as a stroke of lightning, for wasn't Olina's straight pale hair the color of lightning?

From the smooth, governed look on his mother's face, Karsten knew that she would deal with Olina later, discord of any kind being absolutely unthinkable at the table. But why had the kid invented that story in defense of her sister? Did she know something more about Solveig and that fellow Fordyce than Karsten himself knew? Olina must have been abroad searching for the elves she still secretly believed in, long before Solveig was out of bed. Karsten's brows knit, and his second helping of bacon and cakes seemed to have lost its taste.

Up and down the table the talk was about the harvest prospects in the valley, the steady growth of the village of Wing, and the likelihood of its soon being on a branch of the railroad that rumor had already built and put in operation from the south. Jim Jewel, a great, raw-boned, talkative fellow from St. Paul, whom Ivar had hired only two days ago, had already made himself acquainted in Wing, and was proud of working for the folks for whom the town had been named. Karsten could see his mother's good humor being restored by the compliments he was paying her openly. Perhaps she would forget about Olina, after all!

"They tell me, Mrs. Wing," said Jim expansively, "that you and your brother, the banker, was in with the first ones in the county to start the fight against the railroad rates in '84. I call that pretty spunky of a woman, ha, ha! And you got what you wanted too, by cracky! If it hadn't of been for you, the legislature wouldn't of passed that law regulatin' the damn' hogs of railroads and given us the board of warehouse commissioners. No, siree! Oh, I heard how *you* wrastled for it too, Mr. Wing; but when the women get their hands in the fur sure begins to fly. Seems to me they ought to put up a monument to you, ma'am, smack in the center of that town!"

Under the circumstances, Magdali was obliged to ignore Jim's breezy "damn." Above the starched white bib of her apron her face glowed with pleasure at the hired man's tribute. And she deserved the tribute! How many meetings had she not helped organize, working week after week to stir up the agitation that finally forced a drastic reduction in the prohibitive freight rates!

For that matter, there never would have been a town of Wing, had it not been for Magdali's shrewdness in years gone by. Roald had helped, of course, though there were times when she would have fared better without him. Poor, dear, shortsighted Ivar, with his maddening way of cherishing the small and the humble, would have thwarted her if he could. There had been the exchange of railroad bonds for land, the subsequent sale of the land to the bonanza farms at a pretty profit, and the timely buying out of settlers who "couldn't make a go of it"—a feeble excuse for shiftlessness! Then there had been the platting of the new town, the sale of lots when the time was ripe, and finally Roald's establishing of the Farmers' Security Bank. Magdali couldn't help feeling sorry for Ivar, who had been rather dazed by all that she had done. Well, she had told him years ago, during the bitterly hard times, exactly what she intended should come to pass.

And now Jim Jewel was suggesting a monument. Utterly ridiculous, of course. Monuments were for people who had died.

"The town itself is a monument to mamma," said Magdis, then blushed crimson at her own loquacity as she fixed her eyes upon her plate.

"So it is, daughter, so it is!"' Ivar agreed hastily to cover her confusion.

Magdali laughed, rosy and young-looking. "You'll have me so vain you won't be able to stand me! We all worked hard for what we finally got. Gudrun, this coffeepot is empty."

Olina, who had again fastened the deep-pool shine of her eyes upon Karsten, said dreamily, "Rose Shaleen came home yesterday."

"Well, what of it?" Karsten replied. "I didn't even know she was away."

"She has been visiting her Aunt Kate for a whole week," Olina was saying over her glass of milk. "David told me yesterday."

Karsten hated himself for the feeling of discomfort he suffered at any reference to Kate Shaleen in his mother's hearing. There had been something deep-rooted in her antagonism toward Miss Kate, he knew, though he had never been able to understand what it was.

"And where did you see David Shaleen, Olina?" Magdali

asked pleasantly.

"I was watching a turtle laying eggs down by the river, and David came along in his boat. We both watched, and we didn't say a word. It laid fifteen eggs—"

"As big as goose eggs, I'll bet!" Arne remarked from across the table.

"Don't tease your sister," Ivar reproved him.

"I'm not teasing her," Arne replied. "And I'm not believing her, either. You can't believe—"

"Arne!" Magdali said gently, and shifted her attention at once to Jim Jewel. "You haven't met the Shaleens yet, have you, Mr. Jewel?"

It was her custom to call the new hands by their surnames until several days of work had proven them satisfactory. It was always easier to dismiss a man while he still retained some degree of anonymity.

"I've heard of 'em, ma'am."

"They're not really farmers." Magdali smiled tolerantly and sipped her coffee daintily. "They came here soon after we did, but they haven't bettered themselves much in the time they've been here."

"They have three children," Ivar remarked with a twinkle.

"Four, really," Magdali said. "The one they call Rose is a niece, of course. Her name was Brazell, but they call her Rose Shaleen. Her father was a—a gambler, in the early days—quite a picturesque character. He was killed in a runaway, the day before Rose was born."

"You almost were too, weren't you, mamma, before I was born?" Olina intoned absently.

Magdali's bright, even color changed to abrupt patches. Her eyes became points of steel fixing her youngest daughter, and Karsten was aghast. What wouldn't Olina say next!

"I was speaking, Olina," Magdali said quietly, and turned

[249]

again to Jim Jewel. "Steve Shaleen has always been easy-going, and I'm afraid his children are just like him. They don't want more land, because it would mean too much work and responsibility."

Ivar cleared his throat. "You forget, Magdali, that it was Steve who experimented with fife seed—"

"And you started on blue stem," Magdali interrupted. "I'm not forgetting, Ivar. You both did good work with your funny little bottles and things. But Steve is like a sailor that's satisfied with a little lake to sail on. Do you think his children will be satisfied with as little?"

"Well, now, Magdali," Ivar said slowly, "they don't want much, any of them. Loren, the oldest—he's fifteen now—is like his father. He's already trying out sugar beets and some new kind of corn over there, Steve tells me. The county agent comes in once in a while and talks with Steve."

Yes, Karsten thought, the county agent used to come here too, in the early '80's, when his father was experimenting with blue stem wheat, planting a berry in each separate finger-hole and studiously watching it sprout and grow, keeping a note of each plant's performance, generation after generation. Then had come the sowing of the seed from the most vital plants, in a small, fenced-in plot at a distance from the other fields, and finally the product of the enclosure used as seed on freshly turned soil where no other wheat had ever been grown. Karsten knew that his father and Steve Shaleen were dreaming of a strain that would be immune to rust. The trouble was that, while Steve would have plenty of time to experiment, Ivar had become a slave to the vast family holdings and would never again know the pleasure of watching the evolution of a single grain of wheat—for rust resistance or anything else.

"Loren is going to have the farm," Olina sang out. "But David is going to be an artist. He says Karsten should have

[250]

been an artist. Rose has a picture that Karsten painted two years ago—when the creek was flooded. He left it on the bank, and Rose took it and kept it."

Karsten had colored painfully. "She wouldn't know any better," he muttered.

"Rose Shaleen—is growing on seventeen," Olina chanted.

"You've done a good deal of talking this morning, Olina," said Magdali. "Are we all through with breakfast?"

She looked once around the table, then got up from her chair.

II

It was midafternoon, and the blistering heat, like an invisible puppeteer, kept the white air dancing in long, dizzying waves. The rhythmic clatter of the binder through the sigh of the ripe grain—a bronze, brittle sound, Karsten had always thought —and the oily sliding of the harness along the sweat-patched flanks of the horses, had brought him to a stupor of half-sleep. Hawks wheeled above the freshly stripped swath behind the binder, in fierce search of small creatures left unsheltered. Karsten's nostrils burned from the hot, mealy smell of the wheat, and his blue denim shirt felt like sandpaper where the sweat had dried against his skin.

At the corner of the field nearest the river woods, he thought of the jug of raspberry vinegar he had buried in leaf mold and moss to keep it cool. There was a gate in the fence here and, jumping down from the binder, he led the horses through it to the shade of the trees. Then he unearthed the jug and carried it through the dim coolness of the woods to the steep river bank.

The river moved in tawny languor under the blaze of the sun. There was no sign of life anywhere. Even the birds were mute, and the leaves on the trees that arched toward the water hung spent, like panting tongues. Karsten stripped rapidly and waded in, and for the first minute or two the slow current gliding against him seemed blessedly cool. But the scorched air soon dispelled the illusion, and he hurried out again and pulled his overalls up over his glistening wet body. He was stooping to draw on his boots when the rowboat rounded the tree-curtained bend.

"Golly!" he whistled. "I just made it!"

For the one person in the rowboat was a girl. Now he clawed up the bank as fast as he could and settled himself with his jug of raspberry vinegar under a clump of dwarf shad. He lay back, tilted the jug up to his lips, and heaved a contented sigh.

Wasn't it something, after all, to have the mysterious, challenging thing called life before you, and to know that in another year or so you would come to grips with it on your own? He would never have been any good at painting—he knew that now as he thought of the visits he had made to the gallery in the city, with Miss Kate. Why, he could slave for a thousand years and never approach the kind of thing he had seen there —Corot and Millet, Rembrandt and Frans Hals! He might feel as darkly, as brightly, as vehemently the truth of beauty as they had felt it; but never would he be able to express it. There were already too many artists who had got "half there." Why add another clumsy stroke to all the mediocrity in the world?

He gazed up through the leisurely green of the trees and intoned aloud, " 'A book of verses underneath a bough, A jug of wine, a loaf of bread—and Thou—' "

At once an uncomfortable tingling passed over his skin. He was acutely aware that someone had been within earshot and had heard his silly incantation there by himself. He sat bolt upright and glanced about him through the underbrush.

She stood eight or ten feet to his left, toward the river bank. She was long and thin and brown as an Indian, in a blue-figured calico dress too tight in the bosom and too short in the skirt. Her red-brown hair was carelessly caught up behind her ears in a blue ribbon knotted on top of her head. She was staring at him with eyes bluer than the first rainy evening of spring, and her lips curved red and open in wonderment.

[253]

Karsten was annoyed. She had deliberately anchored her boat upstream and stolen upon him here!

"Hello, Rose!" he said with a dignified frown. "Doing a little snooping on your own, eh? I suppose you think I'm crazy, or something, spouting off poetry all by myself."

With a curiously flowing motion, Rose Shaleen seated herself only a step nearer than she had been at his first sight of her. She drew her skirt about her bare, sunburned legs and tied the string of her canvas shoe.

"That was from the *Rubaiyat of Omar Khayyam*," she said musingly. "Aunt Kate gave me the book for my birthday. Is that the kind of thing they teach you at the university?"

Karsten reddened. "Well, not exactly. But we're supposed to do a certain amount of outside reading during vacation, and I happened to hit on it." He looked down at his jug and laughed shortly. "Here—have a swig of raspberry. It's mother's—strictly non-alcoholic!"

She got up with the sudden grace of a blue and amber fountain rising. The last time he had seen her—Christmas, wasn't it, at the Engebrigts' sleigh party?—she had been a gawky, blushing kid. But now—good Lord, it was almost a sacrilege to think it, but she hauntingly resembled her aunt, Miss Kate!

"Thank you," she said gravely, after she had swallowed a considerable draught from the jug. The golden, backward curve of her throat while she held the jug aloft had captured Karsten's eyes so that he was still staring at her when she spoke. "Don't you want me here?"

"*Want* you? Why—" He was too taken aback to know just what he had meant to say. "I don't want you or *not* want you. You're a free agent, to come or go as you please, aren't you?"

"Agent?"

Young girls, what unenlightened bores they were! Still, she had known about Omar Khayyam. "I mean—your soul is your own, more or less, isn't it?"

Rose Shaleen leaned back against the trunk of a tree. "No—it isn't."

"No? What do you mean by that?"

"It's yours."

Karsten jerked up as if he had been stung by a bee. "What in blazes are you talking about?" he demanded. "I said your *soul!* What did you think I said?"

"I know what you said. You said—*soul.*"

He was completely dumfounded. What was the girl driving at? He scarcely knew her. The young Shaleen fry had hitherto been quite beneath his notice. But all at once he was conscious only of the wide-eyed and rapt attention she was giving to his naked arms and chest. Only then did he remember that his shirt and socks were still lying beside him in the grass. The hot blood rose to his temples. He forced himself to laugh.

"Well, Rosie, you—so you think you have a soul!"

"My name is Rose, not Rosie," she replied in such a gentle way that now, strangely, it was he who seemed young and callow.

"All right—*Rose.*" His amused concession did not ring quite true, even to himself. "But what makes you think your soul belongs to me?"

He waited for her to speak. He waited so long under her unfathomable blue gaze that the sensation of prickly heat came over him again, and with it a muffled ringing in his ears. Could anything be crazier? The girl looked—well, the way she was considering him, she looked absolutely *indecent!* No, that wasn't the word. She looked—he had to swallow hard against the constriction in his throat.

"You've never taken any notice of me," Rose Shaleen said at last. "But I've thought about you—all the time. Aunt Kate gave me some drawings you made when she was your teacher.

[255]

And I've got the painting you threw away once, near your creek. I have it hidden in my bureau drawer, under the nightgown Aunt Kate gave me."

That clumsy painting—the one Olina had mentioned at breakfast—reposing now under Rose Shaleen's nightgown! It was too ridiculous. And more ridiculous that a burning film should suddenly settle upon his eyes, so that the girl became magnified and wavering there, against the tree.

"Well, that's—that's nice of you, of course," he stammered. "But those things aren't worth keeping."

"They're all I have. I could never do anything like that. I can't even play the organ very well, though I've tried. And I can't write poems, even though I hear them in the wind sometimes at night before I fall asleep. But I think I could help you paint pictures, Karsten. I mean, I would just be there—and you would paint them."

Karsten could scarcely breathe. This slim-legged girl with her dwelling, beautiful eyes was speaking the truth. He knew it now, suddenly. All she would have to do was just *be there*, and a man would follow his cruel and patient star, his destiny, implacable and passionate and wondrous bright! He wanted in that instant to cry, to hide, to get away from her—and his rage at her came near to overwhelming him. His mouth twisted as he got awkwardly to his feet, his shirt and his socks in his hands.

"I've got work to do," he said sternly. "I've got to get back to the field. You'd better get back home, Rose."

"All right, I'll go," she said in that voice of hers that reminded him so much, too much, of Miss Kate's. "You'll be cutting at your farthest south corner tomorrow afternoon, won't you? There's a strawberry patch on the other side of your fence—in the pasture."

"I know," he said gruffly. "What of it?"

[256]

"I'll be there."

And before he could say another word she had glided away through the trees like something fashioned out of a wild, improbable dream.

III

THE moonlight clove his room from the southeast, slowly moving across it and in its sweep creating one fantastic shadow after another. He had lain awake for hours.

Damn the girl, he half sobbed into his pillow, bringing back so relentlessly the longings for things that would never be!

Tonight, at the supper table, his mother had said, "Now that we have our big boy with only another year at law school, we can start planning our brick house. Brick is the sensible thing—cooler in summer and warmer in winter—and more lasting. With a good furnace in it. I was talking to Jepson the other day, and he says it would be easy to rebuild this house with brick, because it was well made to start with. Mr. Gossman, the big potato grower south of the railroad, has a brick house. That reminds me, Magdis, Mr. Gossman was asking about you this afternoon, in Wing. He remembers you from the ice cream social on the church lawn, on the Fourth of July. He said your cake was the best there."

Magdis blushed like a red cabbage, while Arne grinned knowingly and the hired girls checked a titter.

So the future was being planned for Magdis, too. Not that Karsten cared much about that. If it hadn't been for Rose Shaleen today, he might even have felt proud there at the table when his mother's reference to him had implied a meed of praise. But Rose Shaleen had been there in his consciousness like a wild flame, to spoil it all!

He wouldn't see her again! If he did, he would lose no time in putting her in her place. Young upstart! From Steve down

—except for Miss Kate—the Shaleens were all queer: Rose, Loren, David, and Maude. Only last fall, before he had gone back to the university, Karsten had seen the three of Steve's children on their way to school, ambling along although it was long after nine o'clock. It had taken them quite a while, they explained seriously, to force a snake to disgorge a pretty little deer mouse, and after that another while before they were able to revive the mouse so that it scuttered away. No, they had not killed the snake. Loren had carried it by the tail to a safe distance from the scene of the conflict and had let it go.

His mother was right, of course. The Shaleens were a shiftless lot—misty dreamers and loafers. They had finally got themselves a frame house, but it had not been painted since they had given it its first inadequate coat. Their fences were always in need of repair, and even the flower garden, though things grew luxuriantly there, had no order to it at all. Selma, Steve's wife, who had been such a brisk Swedish girl before her marriage, would rather sit now and laugh with the children around a bonfire of autumn leaves than do her housecleaning for the winter. The Shaleens seldom went to church. They slept late on Sunday mornings, and then little Maude or Rose would play the organ that Miss Kate had left with them, while the others sang. If they had sung only hymns it wouldn't have been so bad, but people who had dropped in for a Sunday visit told how they sang lusty ballads that were a far cry from anything you might expect on a Sunday afternoon. Even the Joseffys, who were good Catholics, often joined them in their sabbath revels, and Fritz would play for them if he happened to be home from the conservatory of music in the city. Miss Kate had told Karsten that Fritz had a touch of real genius. . . .

A faint wind drifted in on the moonlight, carrying the fragrance of newly stacked hay from the meadow land where the old swamp used to be. Karsten remembered the brown, mysterious water of that swamp, the queer water bugs that used to people it, the golden fists of cow-lilies shining on its surface, the stout brown plush of the cattails with redwinged blackbirds swaying and fluting atop them, and the blue dragonflies, magically for an instant fixed in space on iridescent wings and then suddenly darting erratically this way and that as if they were sewing stitches in the air. But the swamp had been drained to make more land. . . .

Oh, it was a lie, all this he had been telling himself about the Shaleens! It was an echo only of his mother's beliefs. He was a coward and a liar in his own heart. With a sense of abysmal despair, he turned over face down and clutched his pillow in both hands. He could no longer tolerate the moonlight and the sweet smell of the hay streaming in from the south, and he knew why all too clearly. Those night things came to him from the direction of Rose Shaleen, sleeping so young under a roof that needed shingling. She was probably no more aware of the moon than she was of the havoc she had this day wrought in Karsten's innermost soul. Soul—she had had the brazenness to speak of a soul! Well, he had no place in his life for hers. He would tell her so tomorrow.

Rose Shaleen, growing on seventeen!

That silly rhyme of Olina's! Girls were noodleheads—unless they happened to be born like Miss Kate. Rose Shaleen had no right to look so much like her. Rose—Rose Shaleen. . . .

Yes, tomorrow he would tell her.

IV

OLINA was wide awake. She had fought off sleep, and had seen the moon lift itself above the trees, and there was a smile on it —and that meant good luck for somebody!

She had Solveig's note to Alec Fordyce pinned fast to her apron pocket, and she knew exactly at what hour tomorrow afternoon she must be under the big elm toward the river from the strawberry patch. The apron was hanging, securely hidden, in the closet. Solveig wouldn't be able to meet Alec until later, because at supper tonight mamma had told her that she would have to help with the churning tomorrow afternoon. That meant mamma suspected something. Olina quaked deliciously at the thought.

Solveig was sleeping soundly. But of course she had had to work hard all day, while Olina was having fun with David Shaleen—and mamma knew nothing about it. They had dug up buffalo bones in the pasture and made an altar of them— David had called it An Altar to the Sun—and they had knelt and said a prayer there to the buffalo gone so long ago. And they had crossed their hearts and spit over a white stone, and had sworn they would never tell. Then David, who was thirteen, had clawed up some moist earth and made a head that was Uncle Roald's, with its drooping nose and funny little eyes, and Olina had doubled up in laughter. Loren had come along and had been mad because he hadn't helped to build the altar. But Loren was quiet and funny, not like his brother David at all.

Tomorrow—she might meet David again—when she went

[261]

to the river with Solveig's note for Alec. She was wide awake —awake—and the moon had David's dark, impish smile and —and then—

Like jumping over a stick, it was day!

That morning, Olina was scrupulous about every task set to her. She almost overdid it. She even cut out the cookies for her mother, something she hated because she couldn't bear the touch of flour.

"What's come over you this morning?" her mother asked. "Is there a thunderstorm in the offing?"

During storms, Olina was always meek and helpful about the house, thinking to propitiate the angry gods.

Only once during the morning did she run afoul of her older sister Magdis. Magdis was swatting flies on a closed window where the screen had been taken off to be repaired. She struck twice at a fly before she realized that it was on the outside of the pane, and Olina howled with laughter. Magdis, near-sighted, turned upon her angrily, but she took to her heels and sought out Solveig in the cool of the milk house. The hired girls were both with Solveig, scouring the separator and the cream cans, so that Olina could only pat her apron pocket significantly before strolling out to inspect the blackberries that were ripening along the creek bank.

"It isn't as hot today as it was yesterday, is it, mamma?" she said to her mother early that afternoon.

"Dear me, child, it's hotter!" Magdali replied, taking the golden loaves from the oven and setting them on the table for buttering. Her mind was occupied with the problem of choosing a pattern for Magdis's new challis dress. The material was white, with a dainty little pink and green flower design. Sleeves were getting fuller at the shoulders, bustles were modified now, but guimpes and frilled skirt fronts were fancier than ever. Puffed sleeves, of modest elbow length, and a yoke just revealing the collar bone, would be the thing, Magdali decided. The yoke edged with pink velvet ribbon, and a velvet bow cunningly fashioned at the waist, into which Magdis could tuck the chantilly lace handkerchief her Uncle Roald had given her last Christmas. With the petticoats and ruffled drawers, it would take her and Magdis a good week of their spare time to complete the outfit. The Sunday following next, then, would be the earliest occasion on which they could plan to entertain George Gossman. Magdali worried briefly about the croquet set—Olina had left it out in the rain so often that the colored bands looked far from bright. But perhaps Karsten would find time to paint them back to life with those tubes of paint he must still have around somewhere.

She was glad she had bought Magdis the pointed white kid slippers that reduced the size of her feet. She sighed. Now that it was no longer considered immodest to display an ankle accidentally, she herself was too old to care about it. Good gracious, she was in her middle forties, two years older than Ivar! She certainly didn't feel it—far from it! A bit heavier, perhaps, from childbearing, but not a thread of gray in her hair. She wondered if she shouldn't have bought Magdis that switch at Pruden's Emporium. Twenty inches long, and only two dollars and fifty cents. Magdis's hair was thick, but it came far short of her waist. Still, the switch hadn't been quite dark enough. One thing she was determined upon—she would wheedle Magdis into cutting a fringe and letting her hair curl in its natural way. Where any daughter of hers had got such strait-laced notions Magdali simply could not figure out!

The girl liked George Gossman—her gloomy blushes at the mention of his name proved that—but wouldn't you think that natural instinct would prompt her to gloss her feathers a bit for his sake? Magdali sighed again and thought of Solveig. There was one! She couldn't pass a mirror without exchanging the time of day with her reflection. And altogether too pretty for her own good. In a year or two she could have her pick of the county—of the state, if she took the trouble to get around a little. Already, every man who saw her stopped and gaped, but Solveig merely pursed her lips and looked down her nose at them all. Or did she—at them all? Lately—but no! Magdali denied any special luminousness in her daughter's eyes. In the fall she would be going back to complete her schooling in Moorhead. Olina might be more of a problem. Only eleven, of course, so there was no telling how she would turn out. But she was as slippery as moonlight.

What was the child standing there for now, twining one thin leg about the other? She looked as if she never ate.

"Are you hungry, Olina? Get yourself some jam and—"

"No, mamma. I think I ought to take cold buttermilk down to Karsten this afternoon, don't you? He's working in the south field, and that's nearer the sun, isn't it?"

Magdali smiled and quickly patted Olina's cheek. The child was really kind and thoughtful, in spite of her queer, moony ways.

"Wait till I'm through with the bread, and I'll fix you an ice cup to take to him, with some buttermilk."

Olina breathed in panic. An ice cup was an awful thing to carry—a bowl lined with flannel and a chunk of ice in it, with a dish to cover it. The flannel kept the ice from melting. She wished furiously that the Wings had never owned such a thing as an ice house. If she had to carry the cup and the can of buttermilk she might not get to the big elm in time to meet Alec Fordyce. Solveig would be wild!

"Karsten doesn't like ice in his buttermilk, mamma," she said quietly.

"Nonsense! You just don't want to carry it. What must I do to put a stop to your fibbing? Run along and get the flannel piece out of the cupboard, and I'll bring the ice from the chest. You can stop at the milk house and see if the girls have any fresh buttermilk yet. Karsten likes it right out of the churn."

Anguish possessed Olina. What did she care about Karsten and his buttermilk? She would dump it. No—her mother would be sure to find out if she did. She would have to run and pretend to Karsten that she had dropped the bowl, ice and all.

"And remind him to put green leaves in his hat," her mother was saying. "I told him, but he's so absent-minded. It's a wonder he didn't get sunstroke yesterday. He looked as if he had, when he came in for supper last night. I'll make some oatmeal water again tonight for the men to take out with them in the morning. There's nothing better against sunstroke. That's something you might try to remember, Olina."

Olina gripped the flannel-fringed bowl her mother gave her, and sped out of the house. She touched her deep apron pocket in her flight. Outside the milk house, she set her burden on a bench.

"Solveig," she said in her thin little voice, "mamma wants me to take buttermilk down to Karsten. Is there some fresh?"

Solveig's nostrils quivered. "Why didn't you—it must be after three o'clock. Karsten was expecting his buttermilk at half past three."

"I know, Solveig," Olina whispered, gathering up her apron. "But I'll run. Give me the can of buttermilk, quick."

Solveig gave it to her. "If you're late, you don't get those lace gloves of mine, remember!"

Olina raced away, past the ice house, glancing aside as she hurried along the edge of the pig pen. There they were, the big, shiny black sows with their greedy litters like stuffed black socks! She had seen a sow grunt over and take the head off a little one, only last year. Someone had come and carried her indoors, where she had been so sick that her mother, feeling her fever, had sent for the doctor. Now she stood back from the fence and threw the lump of ice straight at a snorting proud sow. The sow lumbered to her feet, shook her head, and glared from her mean yellow eyes.

Once across the wire fence and into the stubble, Olina could handily trip over something and drop the bowl with its cover and its piece of flannel. She achieved the feat neatly, almost convincing herself, then loped like a deer toward the southern stretch where Karsten was at work on the binder.

Her brother looked so big and brown as she panted up at him and held out the can of buttermilk. Karsten was handsome, that's what he was! And he had a white shirt on today—his Sunday shirt, really. He had changed after dinner, and Olina had wondered about it, thinking that Rose Shaleen ought to see him with the collar rolled back so gracefully.

"I got this for you specially, right out of the churn," she gasped. "But I stumbled and dropped the ice mamma fixed for you in the flannel, and it melted before I could find it. Mamma said for you to put leaves in your hat, Karsten. You tell her I remembered to tell you, won't you? Please!"

"Sure, I'll tell her. But what's the matter, kid? You didn't have to run like that in the heat, did you?"

"Mamma thought you might get sunstroke." She backed away, almost hearing the rustle of the big elm where Alec Fordyce must be waiting, wondering what had happened.

Karsten smiled down at her. "I'll put leaves in my hat. And I'll not say a word about the ice. You're off to meet Dave Shaleen, aren't you?" He chuckled sympathetically. "Well, let me tell you something. Young Dave is an imp of Satan. He can make a wood carving look like something, and he can draw—but he's an imp of Satan, just the same, and you'd better look out!"

He watched her streaking toward the woods, her pale braids tossing over her shoulders.

Olina found Alec Fordyce lying on his back beneath the big elm. A straw sailor hat covered his eyes, and his thumbs were hooked patiently in the armholes of his green and yellow striped vest. He had on new buttoned shoes of light brown, with high bumps on the toes. Oh, he was so fashionable, so thrillingly tall stretched out like that! David would be short, but then—he was David!

"Well!" Alec was sitting up, tossing aside his straw hat. "So it's you, *mon enfant!*" His deep eyes crinkled warmly and he glanced beyond Olina at the empty field. "Where's Solveig?"

"She couldn't come," Olina quavered tearfully. "She had to churn. But here's a letter. She said for you to tell me if you can meet her here tonight."

Alec's thin, aquiline face darkened with disappointment. His hands trembled as they clutched the note. While he read it, his expression changed from happy light to morose shade and then back again, so that to Olina, breathlessly watching him, he did not seem to be part Indian at all. Indians were supposed to show no feelings.

"Damn it!" he exclaimed, folding the letter tenderly and tucking it into his vest pocket beside his watch fob, which was a glittering affair of burnt leather stamped in gold. "The boat leaves at midnight. I've got to be on deck at eleven. Listen, youngster—you tell Solveig that I'll hire a rig and be out here at eight sharp. That'll give us a couple of hours anyhow."

In the heat, Olina shivered. "You—you're not going to elope?"

Alec laughed bitterly. "Not this time! I've got to have money to do that. But I'll do it some day, by God!"

Olina quaked wonderfully at the oath. "Solveig wouldn't care if you had money or not," she ventured.

"She doesn't know the world—and she doesn't know how beautiful she is. I'd be afraid, unless I had enough to take care of her right." He got up from the ground and stretched his long arms above his head. "Well, you better get going, Olina. Tell Solveig eight sharp, eh? When I get some real mazuma, I'll set you up."

Whether that was a threat or a promise, Olina could not be sure, but it was thrilling anyhow.

V

KARSTEN unhitched his team from the binder and drove them through the gap in the fence. Leaving them to graze in the shade alongside the stretch of wild pasture, he walked back to the fence, assumed a loftily condescending expression, and let his eyes drift idly across the flowing, rough grass.

His preparations went for nothing, however. The figure he had confidently expected to see was not there. His pulse quickened with chagrin and anger at himself—and something more, which he hated to acknowledge. But there it was—disappointment! Changing into a white shirt, like a damned fool, and marching nonchalantly out of the house under the astonished gaze of his mother and the girls, as if a white shirt in the middle of the day were nothing out of the ordinary! Luckily his father and the other men had not been around.

He was turning away to walk back to his horses when he heard a soft laugh above and behind him. He glanced over his shoulder and saw Rose Shaleen almost hidden high aloft among the dense branches of a gnarled old oak tree.

Karsten took off his wide straw hat and wiped his forehead.

"I thought you were going to pick strawberries," he flung up at her. "Or was it acorns?"

With the swift agility of a boy, she scrambled down branch after branch and finally swung herself to the ground. Then, rubbing her hands on her hips, she smiled at Karsten.

"I waited to see if you'd come," she said artlessly. "I wasn't going near the patch if you stayed away."

His expression became very indulgent. "Nonsense! Where's

[269]

your pail? I'll help you for half an hour, then I'll have to get back to work. Aren't there any strawberries nearer your own place?"

"Of course. Mamma and the kids are picking in our field this afternoon."

Rose had always called Selma and Steve Shaleen "mamma" and "pa," and to Karsten it still sounded queer. She picked up the tin lard pail she had left under the tree and started toward the fence. Karsten followed, but before he could hold the wire up for her, she had crawled under it, quick as a lizard, while he caught a glimpse of her long, thin brown legs.

A few yards from the fence, where the trees cast a lacy shade, there was a slight hollow in the grass, and here Rose sat down with her pail. The sweetly acid, sunny smell of the wild strawberries was hot on the motionless air. The red clusters were knotted so densely through the grass that Karsten stepped warily before he found a place to seat himself. But Rose had not hesitated. Already there was berry juice all over her brown ankles.

"I always hull as I go along," she said. "Here—I'll put the pail between us."

Her fingers flashed through the twinkling grass like bright minnows through water. She was so amazingly deft at snapping the lush red drops off the stems without bruising them that for moments Karsten merely sat and stared at her. Then, when she glanced up at him, he went to work, promising himself that ten minutes of this would be plenty. After that, he would tell Rose plainly that she must forget all that nonsense about his being an artist. He would warn her not to plant such notions about him in the mind of Olina, moreover. The kid was likely to say almost anything when the family was around. He would make everything plain to Rose, in as few words as were necessary. Then he would go back to the field and get on with his

[270]

work. He should be there now, for that matter.

Supposing his mother should happen to come down this way? The thought clamped chillingly on the small of his spine. Picking strawberries with Rose Shaleen in the middle of a work day! His father, if he came by, might be mildly surprised, and then sit down and eat the berries himself. But his mother—!

"A penny for your thoughts, Karsten!" Rose said suddenly. "You look as if somebody just walked over your grave."

Karsten grinned mechanically. "I felt a little shiver just now. I guess I got too hot, there on the binder. It's funny how you can shiver when it's so hot."

Her widely spaced eyes fastened upon him with a look of alarm. Then, before he knew what she was about, Rose had leaped up and seated herself close beside him, her thin, bare arms tightly wound about his shoulders, the warmth of her firm, lissom body tingling electrically against his own.

"Come over, close to me!" she commanded. "A chill like that is dangerous. Pa got one once, and it went to his kidneys. Here —let me rub your back. Mamma says that's the thing to do, if there's anybody around to do it."

Karsten never did learn whether the chill was a genuinely physical one or not. And now, in a wildly rhapsodic instant, he did not care. There rushed over him such a wave of un- dreamt ecstasy that it might have been the burning blue of the sky itself inundating his body. He muttered incoherently as he swept Rose into his arms and buried his face against the burnished softness of her throat. The warm pulse beating within it was like the pulse of deep and flowing summer. Kar- sten swayed backward into the redolent grass, still clasping Rose hard against him.

For seconds they lay inert, their breasts striving one against the other in the rapid rise and fall of their breathing. Then with supple swiftness Rose twisted about, lifted herself on one

[271]

elbow, and thrust her head into the grass. The next moment, Karsten was looking into her laughing, sunlit eyes, and her mouth was close above his with a cluster of blood-red strawberries held between her teeth.

He caught her by the shoulders, gave a laughing cry, and pulled her lovely mouth with the strawberries down to his own. The sweet wild fruit was crushed between their meeting lips.

Joined blood of the sun and the earth, the sweet wild fruit in strange guise must have swung its crimson globes above the darkly breathing soil out of the riddle of ages before the beginning of known time.

Karsten thrust her head back from him with hands that felt numb. "Rose!" he said. "Rose Shaleen!"

Her dark blue eyes, above him, glistened as if shot through with silver rain. "Karsten—kiss me—like that—again!"

Her arms were about his neck, the sun-smell of berries and ripe grass and shimmering air were all in Rose Shaleen's arms —those things were all Rose Shaleen. He drew her mouth to his own, to his eyes and his cheeks, and the feel of it was like dewy silk. Then all at once the terror came over him again, but more strongly now. He straightened up in angry fear, ran his hands through his hair, and stared at her.

"We're—we're crazy, Rose!" he managed to say.

"No, Karsten," she said coolly. "This is the way it should be for us."

"But—we must wait—we've got to think this out. We can't—"

"I've thought it out. I love you, Karsten."

He got dizzily to his feet, lifting her with both hands and holding her before him. "Listen—meet me here, will you—tonight? I've got to get back to the field now. But—meet me here—about nine o'clock."

"Say you love me!" Her voice was soft, her eyes mistily dark.

"Lord in heaven, yes, Rose! I adore you!" He was almost sobbing as he caught her off her feet into his arms again. "You're —oh, you're not human! You're something out of the ground, out of the sky. I don't know. I don't know anything—except that I love you like— I don't know!"

She clung to him with a long and blissful tremor. The air had grown cool and still about them, and Karsten looked at the sky where a feathery soft gray obscured the sun.

"Listen, will you?" He shook her gently, and she raised her face to him, cupped in her slim hands. "If it doesn't rain to-night, I'll meet you near the fence in your north hay field. Not here—it's too far for you, back and forth. Can you get away about nine?"

"Yes," she said, her eyes shining. "I'll meet you—anywhere. Oh, Karsten, I'm going to take care of you. I'm going to make you what you want to be. I'm not too young. I'm old in ways you don't know. Anyhow, next year, when you're through the university—I'll be old enough then, won't I? Tell me, Karsten—can I have you then, for always?"

She was so fluently slim and yet so strong in his arms. As he kissed her again, he heard a far-away rumble of thunder. He set Rose back on her feet and picked up the lard pail, only a quarter full of berries, and handed it to her.

"Here," he said. "You'd better run unless you want to get soaked. There's a shower coming up. And remember—your north fence, about nine."

She was yards away from him before he was aware that she had really moved. When she turned to wave at him, her eyes seemed to hold all of the blue-clouded sunlight.

VI

OLINA crouched in the willows beside the creek. For more than half an hour—ever since she had left the supper table, in fact—she had been waiting to see Solveig come out and walk lazily toward the river. It had taken all the courage she could muster to venture out alone with the threat of thunder still in the air. There had been a few vicious flares of lightning just before supper and a few ear-splitting crashes that shook the house with terrifying suddenness. There had been a few splots of rain, but not enough to lift the blanket of heat that had lain for days over the land. Now, crouching among the willows, Olina was more apprehensive than ever.

It was not for herself alone she feared as she waited breathlessly for Solveig to appear. The hired men were in the bunk-house, dressing for a Saturday night in town. From the back porch came the voices of the hired girls, clear as thrown crockery. What if Solveig didn't come? What if something should happen at the last minute, so that Alec would be left waiting down by the river until it was too late and he would have to go away without Solveig seeing him at all? Worse still, if a storm should come up suddenly and Solveig should—

Olina settled herself deeper in the willow shade, for now her big brother Karsten had come out of the house and was peering up at the western sky. What, she wondered, did he have to worry about? Much of the cutting was done. A tornado might rip the shocks off, but they had had only one tornado in Olina's memory, and that was after the threshing was all done and the grain safely stored in the elevator at Wing. Karsten's hair was combed and damped down as if he meant to go somewhere.

[274]

Suddenly the screen door of the back porch slammed, and Solveig curvetted out, in a white lawn dress with ruffles at the ankles and a light blue *faille* cape over her shoulders.

"Where do you think you're going?" Karsten asked Solveig.

"Where do *you* think?"

"There's a storm coming up, in case you haven't noticed."

"Let it come."

Karsten gave her a shrewd look. "You'd better lick it down there before mother sees you. If she wasn't working on that dress for Magdis, you wouldn't have got out of the house!"

"And where do you think *you're* going, my dear brother?" Solveig queried. They were walking straight toward where Olina was hiding among the willows. "You wouldn't be going down the line in Moorhead with the hired men?"

Solveig waltzed away, her nose toward the billowing black threat of the sky, but Karsten came on, his face aflame with insult. Olina had only a vague idea of what Solveig meant by "going down the line"—gambling and drinking, perhaps, and ladies with paint on their faces, feathers and jewels in their hair, and with short, swishing, sparkling dresses and lace stockings. From the talk of the older girls she had got a hint of such things, and to her it had all sounded like a circus. Still, Karsten's face was angry as he looked after Solveig.

Suddenly his eyes found Olina's hiding place and he stopped in his tracks.

"What are you doing out here?" he demanded. "Good Lord, is the whole family going crazy? Mother has been looking for you. Come out of that and get into the house."

"Where are you going?" Olina dared to ask.

"Nowhere—if it rains. Come on, now—get into the house."

Olina leaned back on her pointed elbows and looked up at him. "That's the difference between you and Solveig," she said.

[275]

Karsten frowned at her. What did *she* know—about anything? That elfish quality, though, was not to be trusted. In another age she would have been burned at the stake for witchcraft, he thought, child though she was.

There was a sharp thrust of lightning, and boulders of thunder rolled from clouds so close, it seemed, that one might reach up and touch them. Olina hardened her little arms against the earth. Fear paralyzed her so that she could not move. And yet, somehow she must get up. She must follow Solveig and see that nothing happened to her.

Green-blue lightning suddenly tore the creek open, and the crash of thunder left Olina flat and limp on the ground. Karsten sprang forward to pick her up, but she fought him off fiercely with her small fists.

"What's wrong with you?" he demanded in consternation, turning his face away from her clawing hands as he caught her up unceremoniously and strode off toward the house. When he set her on her feet in the kitchen, she shook for a moment, then burst into hysterical tears.

"Olina!" He knelt beside her and put his arms about her childish middle. "Do you want to bring everybody in the house here? Tell me what's wrong. Aren't you my best sister?"

She flung herself upon his shoulder. "I wanted to follow Solveig," she whispered desolately. "Something might happen—"

"Listen——you can't follow Solveig—not in a storm like this." He glanced at the window, a square of sullen greenish-gray now, with the rain athwart it in blown sheets. Damn it, an all-night downpour, most likely! But Olina, at least, was letting up. Her sobs grew muffled against his shoulder.

"I'll tell you what, kid—you can help me paint those croquet balls. I'll get out my old paints, and you lug the set out of the closet. We'll do them here in the kitchen." He patted her shoulder affectionately. "Don't you worry about Solveig. She'll come back, all right."

Half-assured, Olina went to get the croquet set, while Karsten hurried upstairs to dig his old paint tubes out of a box in his room. No use in dwelling with sentimental irony on this! If it distracted Olina for an hour—or until perhaps the rain did cease—it would occupy him as well. He would have to do something—

From the small room opposite the parlor, came the whir of the sewing machine. The door was slightly open, and as Karsten started upstairs he could see his mother and Magdis surrounded by billows of ruffles and ribbons. Magdis stood in her petticoat, like a glum statue, while her mother prepared for some fitting. The girl's corsets—the "Iron Maiden," Karsten had called them once when he saw them being aired on the clothesline—almost reached her armpits, forcing her full bosom up near her collar bone, and pinching her in at the waist so that her face was like mottled red granite from her effort to breathe. Her obvious distress filled Karsten with renewed joy in the thought of Rose Shaleen, so that he whistled a bar of "Oh, Susannah" as he leaped up the stairs two at a time.

His mother called him as he came down a few minutes later with his paints. He looked into the room—which Magdali used as an office when she wasn't sewing—and Magdis primly wrapped a dressing sacque about her.

"Didn't you tell Olina to come here?" his mother asked.

"You wanted the croquet set painted, and she's going to help me. Can't you get along without her?"

"I suppose we can," Magdali sighed. She looked tired, Karsten thought, and a pang of guilt smote him as he thought of Solveig—and then of himself and Rose Shaleen. He was in love with Rose—hopelessly and irrevocably—but this feeling of divided loyalty—

[277]

"Try not to mess up the floor, Karsten," his mother said. "It has just been scrubbed. And when Solveig comes in with the Holm girls, see that they wash things up afterwards. I don't mind them making candy, but they always leave such a mess. Last time Effie stepped in a sticky pan they left under the sink and almost sprained her ankle. I hope she got to town before the rain started. I warned her against going out, but my warnings don't seem to mean much to her. See that she changes her clothes when she comes in, if she got wet."

So that was Solveig's ruse, Karsten smiled as he went down the hall to the kitchen. And of course she would be ready with some explanation as to why she had not met the Holm girls! Well, if she was as daffy as that about a river roustabout, more power to her. A reluctant sympathy for Solveig came over him now. Maybe young Fordyce wasn't such a bad fellow, after all. Anyhow, where did the Wings get the idea that ordinary people weren't good enough for them?

The rain was still drumming loudly, although the thunder was lessening toward the east. That meant there would be a steady drizzle until midnight at least, Karsten thought despairingly. Rose Shaleen would certainly not leave the house on a night like this. Or would she? He was of half a mind to go and see. The meadow was midway between the Shaleen house and the Wings'. It would mean a three mile ride back and forth on Arne's saddle horse. Karsten glanced into the dining room where Arne was playing Old Maid with the two hired girls. It was the only card game their mother permitted in the house. Arne had a smirk on his chubby face. Although he could always beat Effie Strand and Gudrun Engebrigt at any game they chose, they were none the less willing to play with him whenever they had an opportunity. The girls were about the same age as Solveig and Magdis. Arne was not yet fifteen, but he had already made a show of using Karsten's razor, and his manner with the hired girls was swaggeringly assured.

Karsten saw Effie's pink hand reach down and stroke Arne's thigh. At the same time, Gudrun looked across the table and smiled fruitily at him. Karsten suppressed a laugh and went on into the kitchen. His young brother would certainly be busy for the rest of the evening. There would be no trouble about taking Arne's horse out for a couple of hours if the rain let up.

In the kitchen, Olina had the croquet balls and the mallets spread out on newspapers on the floor. She was crouching down, peering at the columns of advertisements.

She began to read aloud. " '*Pinafore, Pinafore!* Almost everybody has it. All the words, wit and music, with libretto, complete for one dollar.' I wish we had an organ, Karsten. The Shaleens have always had one, and they're not as rich as us."

"It's too dark in here," Karsten said. "I'll light the lamp."

" 'Mexican Mustang Liniment,' " Olina continued to read at random. " 'Agents wanted for Back from the Mouth of Hell, by one who has been there.' " Olina shuddered exquisitely. " 'Rise and Fall of the Mustache, by the Burlington Hawkeye Humorist.' " She giggled. "Imagine, Karsten! Have you read that?"

He was relieved to hear her laughing. In a few minutes, perhaps, he could trust her to finish the painting alone.

"Those things were advertised when I was your age," he said, feeling old. "But you're right, Olina. We ought to have an organ. Or a piano, rather."

"A *piano!*"

Fritz Joseffy had played a piano in the opera house in Moorhead last year, and everybody had gone to hear him. He was a little older than Karsten, and although his father was not well off, he had been sent away to the conservatory to learn music. That was because Miss Kate Shaleen, Rose's aunt, had said he was gifted. The whole Wing family had gone to the concert, all dressed in their best clothes. The new surrey with the fringed top had been used for the occasion, and Olina remembered that her mother had worn her bengaline dress with the lace fichu. It was in the paper, too, that the Wings had been among those who had attended the concert. Olina would never forget it. Fritz Joseffy had looked like a dusty dark toad, but he had made colors and singing things spill all through the air. And once she had seen Karsten rummaging about for his handkerchief—and then rubbing his new celluloid cuff across his nose when he thought nobody was looking.

She gazed up at Karsten now while he adjusted the wick in the lamp and said again, "A piano?"

"Why not?" Karsten replied. "We've got all the newfangled binders and mowers and hay tedders and sweep rakes and feed grinders and manure spreaders—and the whole shebang! Why shouldn't we have a piano?"

The explosiveness of his own voice shocked him. Declaiming for little Olina! He must get hold of himself.

It was still raining. From the dining room came Arne's raucous laugh, and the silly whimper of one of the girls, who must have ended up by being the "old maid" this time. The sewing machine still hummed in the room where his mother and Magdis were at work.

Squatting on the floor beside his sister, Karsten recalled the time he had bought these tubes of paint in the city two years ago, with money that had been sent him for shoes and shirts. When he had come home and his mother had helped him unpack, she had looked at the tubes and patted him affectionately on the shoulder. "It's all right, Karsten," she had said, "even if it is foolish. So long as your marks in school are good. Far better, anyhow, than playing cards and drinking, like college boys do, I hear."

He would never forget how his very scalp had seemed to jerk from the sting of that compliment. But that was two years ago, and since then he had used the paints only furtively. And now—the seductive, Circe colors were being used to brighten the bands around croquet balls, so that Magdis and George Gossman might get better acquainted on the lawn a week from tomorrow.

"These paints weren't meant for a job like this, exactly," he said to Olina, "but it'll probably stay on for a few games anyhow. Put a little more oil in that ocher, kid."

"I don't think ocher *sounds* yellow," Olina observed, squeezing the tube. "And *lake* is certainly a silly word for crimson. I like the smell of paints, don't you? Do artists ever get painter's colic, Karsten?"

"Not from paint. From starvation." He watched Olina trace a faded band with fresh yellow color and turned his ear toward the door. It had almost stopped raining. "Do you think you can finish this job yourself, kid?" he asked lightly. "I was thinking I might step out and look at—"

There was a sound of horse's hoofs and the wheels of a buggy in the yard. That would be his father coming home from his visit with Uncle Roald in Wing, Karsten thought. He had gone in to talk over some important business while Magdali was busy with her sewing. Karsten knew how his father hated acting as Magdali's agent, especially when the business involved sitting in with Roald for an evening.

One incident Karsten always recalled with delight. A few years ago, when Roald Bratland's banking business was less imposing than it was now, he had caught Roald sitting one bitter afternoon in the Christmas holidays with his wool-socked feet toasting on the apron of the cast iron stove that took up a disproportionate amount of space in the modest office. How Roald had started up and pulled on his boots, before he saw

[281]

that his visitor was only his nephew Karsten! A moment later, Karsten had picked up from the floor a newspaper in which Roald had pencil-bracketed an advertisement stating: "Widow in good circumstances will marry healthy man of any age, so long as single."

There was a tramp of feet in the back porch, and the kitchen door opened. Ivar came in, and behind him—Roald Bratland.

Roald was clad in a fancy plaid mackintosh with a shoulder cape, and on his head was an oilskin hat shaped like a coal scuttle. His raiment in latter years had kept pace with his growing importance as a citizen in the community. Gone were the wool socks of other days; silk hose now graced his thin ankles, regardless of the season; and if he suffered in consequence, nobody ever heard of it. His scarfs, his flowered four-in-hands, his knitted wristlets and gaiters, his congress shoes, and his sleeping apparel—pajamas instead of nightshirts—were the marvel of the town's citizenry. Roald's housekeeper, old Mrs. Trimcobb, who had been with him ever since he sold his farm to Magdali and moved into a cottage in Wing, kept the curious ones informed concerning such articles as were beyond the public gaze. Roald could not resist advertisements that suggested improvement of his person. On his washstand he kept both liquid and powder dentifrices, a Doctor Scott's "electric" hair brush that was guaranteed to forestall baldness and gray hair, and a can of rice powder with a "masculine scent."

Roald disenveloped himself from his mackintosh and greeted Karsten heartily—as though he had not seen him but two days before.

"Well, well, my boy! You spend Saturday night at home, eh, instead of bamboozling around with the boys? It is better so! And little Olina! What do you do there? Painting croquet balls, eh?" He leaned down and patted her head, and Olina

[282]

withdrew delicately to set a red-banded ball on the paper to dry.

Karsten glanced at his father, who was hanging his weather-proof on a hook near the door. The furrows in his brown cheeks still glistened from the rain. It was clear that Roald was bursting with news of some sort. Karsten couldn't remember when he had learned to read the signs in his uncle's face. The news this time was obviously good.

"Well, what's news on the Rialto, Uncle Roald?" he asked. It would be best to humor the old fellow—and get rid of him as soon as possible.

"Good news, my boy, good news!" Roald beamed. "I just been telling Ivar—he made his mistake when he did not take those first mortgages on improved farms in the valley three years ago, like we did. Eight per cent on his money! Your mother and me—we get our eight per cent, you bet! And now, what do you think, Karsten? Today the good news comes. We get our railroad branch—and so much for the right of way through our land that if I am a drinking man I almost drink my hair tonic! The railroad comes right through Wing! What do you think of that, Karsten?"

Ivar had taken his pipe from its place on the shelf beside the door and was filling it from his tobacco pouch with a preoccupied expression.

"What do I think?" Karsten replied without looking up at his uncle. "It makes me think of something one of our professors said to the class about a month ago. There's nothing easier than making a lot of money, if you're not hampered by too much brains."

Roald began an asthmatic laugh that brought on one of the coughing spells with which he had been afflicted for some time.

Olina, stretched face downward, began reading shrilly from a page of the newspaper spread on the floor. " 'The Only Lung

Pad—Absolutely cures consumption, asthma, bronchitis, and all diseases of the throat and lungs and chest. Detroit, Michigan.' You ought to send for one of them, Uncle Roald. You cough all the time."

"Run in and tell your mother we're here, child," Ivar said quickly, a smile lighting his eyes.

Roald took from his vest pocket a small tortoise-shell case, from which he extracted a cubeb. "I have not been so much troubled since I smoke these here," he said.

But Karsten noticed that his uncle's eyes were upon the page of newspaper from which Olina had been reading. Before he left, another neat clipping would be added to the collection in his burnt-leather wallet.

"Where is Solveig?" Ivar asked suddenly.

Olina, who had risen slowly from the floor to do her father's bidding, abruptly flung her arms about his neck and kissed him tempestuously on the cheek.

"What's this—what's this?" Ivar demanded with mock gruffness.

Olina was his pet, the heart of his heart, the more so because of Magdali's unspoken yet manifest bitterness toward the conditions resulting from her birth. But since Magdali had set herself at the helm, Ivar had grown shy even with his own children. They all knew that it was their mother's dexterity that had already provided them with so much of the world's goods, and would provide more. Recently Ivar had seen a photograph of Queen Victoria and her consort, Prince Albert, taken a few years before the latter's death. It had occurred to him that he had something in common with that hapless, dreamy fellow— a sort of hired man whose chief assets were his suspender straps.

"What do you want now, Olina?" Ivar asked.

"I don't want anything," she said. "But—Solveig—"

"Go on in and tell mother that Uncle Roald is here," Karsten

[284]

interrupted sharply, and Olina, with an aware, frightened look at her brother, left the kitchen.

"I will tell Magdali the news myself," said Roald, starting off with his jaunty, capering step. "We must talk together."

"Better knock before you go in," Karsten called after him. "Magdis is probably standing in her pants."

"Where *is* Solveig?" Ivar asked when Roald had gone.

Karsten put the finishing touch to a green ball and set it carefully in a row with the others, out of the way under a window shelf.

"That old freight boat is on its way back north," he said reluctantly.

"Young Fordyce, eh?" A smile, half tender, half regretful, crinkled about Ivar's eyes. "When I think of how his father went—on that last trip that he did not need to take, but the wild north country called to him, and he went through the ice with his dogs and sled and all—well, that was the way Julian would like to go! Now young Alec is after Solveig, eh?"

"Uncle Roald shouldn't hear anything about it," said Karsten. "And mother would worry if—"

Ivar nodded. "Yes, it's best to say nothing." He sighed. "Solveig will go her way anyhow. Like the river goes."

His eyes were resting on Karsten, but he scarcely saw his son. He saw Julian Fordyce, the erect, clear-eyed Englishman, the Red River cart train, the stolid oxen, the swarthy *bois brûlés* singing as they sat about their campfires. And he saw Magdali hurrying from the encampment in anger and fear, little Karsten's hand clasped in hers.

"Alec is a good boy," he said, and his voice sounded a stubborn note.

Karsten glanced from the window. It had stopped raining, but the sky was a surly black, and the wet chill of the night reached depressingly into the kitchen, where the range fire was low. There could be no chance now of finding Rose Shaleen at the hayfield. If it weren't for Roald's presence, he'd tell the family at once that he would bring Rose here to the house tomorrow. They might draw their own conclusions from that. But Roald had such a detestable way of gloating over news of any sort!

Voices were mingling in the dining room. Magdali was reminding Olina that it was Saturday night; she must carry hot water upstairs for her bath—and be sure to clean the tub afterward.

Ivar looked at Karsten with a wry smile and told him that Roald had further news. He was fixing up a law office above the bank, and had even found a lawyer who was ready to begin practicing as soon as the place was furnished.

"A middle-aged fellow with money, but not very good health," Ivar explained. "He came from St. Paul. Roald has it all set with him to take you into partnership next year. He wants a young man like you. It mightn't be a bad place for you to start, Karsten, right in our own town."

Karsten frowned. "I'd just as soon see the man before Roald starts cooking up anything for me. What's his name?"

"William Cole. His wife and daughter are staying with him at the hotel in Moorhead. That's where Roald met him. He's been there about a week, looking around for a place to settle in the valley. He was in Wing yesterday and he likes the look of the town. His daughter is about twenty—a pretty girl, Roald says."

"Sounds like a good bet for Uncle Roald," Karsten observed indifferently. "He ought to marry her."

Arne and the hired girls came into the kitchen to finish their card game. Ivar joined Magdali and Roald at the dining room table, where one of their lengthy business conferences would ensue. Ivar would sit for a few minutes to please Magdali, then he would go upstairs to bed.

"Come in here with us, Karsten," Roald called out benevolently, as if he were about to present a small boy with a surprise package. "I have something to tell you."

Karsten clicked his teeth. "In a minute," he said. "I'm going outside for a look at the weather."

Somewhere up there, beyond the tattered darkness, rode the same moon that had haunted his room last night. It couldn't have been only twenty-four hours ago! He walked toward the creek—aimlessly—and the smell of the rain-drenched land under its mask of cloud assailed him with an unbearable, brooding sweetness. Distantly, from the south, from somewhere in the river timber, a whippoorwill chanted his infinitely lonesome requiem. From the south—from Rose Shaleen!

Karsten sat on the overhanging stone at the creek's brink, so memorable out of his boyhood's fancy. He would have to think things out, clearly and courageously. There was no need of skulking about—surely he was old enough to know his own mind and to have the right to express it as he felt necessary!

That any diplomacy should be used in gradually bringing the family to a knowledge of his feeling for Rose was a painful and humiliating thought. If she were a complete stranger, it would have been easier. But she had lived since her birth only a few miles away, and Karsten doubted that she had been in the Wing house half a dozen times. That, despite the fact that Rose and Solveig were almost the same age and had gone to school together! Gently but firmly Magdali had discouraged any intimacy with what she deplored as "that hopeless Shaleen tribe."

She believed that Steve Shaleen had gypsy blood in his veins, although it was known that his mother was soundly Norwegian. But the Shaleen children never looked thoroughly scrubbed, and it was clear that Selma had degenerated as a

[287]

housekeeper since her marriage to Steve. Oh, things were *clean* enough, but there was always a topsy-turvy look to the house, as if a playful tornado had just blown through it.

And then there was the old, strange legend about Kate Shaleen—not a legend, even, but something vague and troubling, like a dream that would never come clear. Even more serious, of course, was the vivid romance of Delphy Shaleen, Rose's mother. Karsten mulled all these things over and then shivered as once again the whippoorwill's call came to him, more remote now, fainter and more forlorn.

Tears smarted in his eyes, and in shame he sprang to his feet. A man, he told himself severely, would make sure first of all that it wasn't some midsummer madness, a kind of sublime sunstroke, that had overwhelmed him, before he called it love!

Bracing his shoulders, he strode back into the house, where Roald and Magdali sat alone beneath the bead-fringed hanging lamp that had once shed its light in a Moorhead "parlor" above a saloon.

VII

Even with the ever-looming cloud of a two-hour church service in the offing, Sunday morning in summer usually had a pure, quiet brightness, a vast and empty listening warmth, Karsten reflected as he washed his hands and face at the brown-flowered basin in his room.

Today, the amiable spread of the sun was maddening beyond words. Karsten felt like shaking his fist out of the window at it, but instead he picked up his razor and began carefully to shave his upper lip, although there was little need of it, since he had shaved hopefully after supper last night.

His door opened softly an inch or two, and it was Olina's small voice that asked, "Can I come in?"

"If you aren't crippled," Karsten replied, grateful that it was only his little sister. His mother might have looked in to ask how he had "slept on" Uncle Roald's suggestion of the night before—that he should meet the lawyer, William Cole, and commit himself to a partnership with him next year, after his graduation from law school.

Olina's pale hair hung about her shoulders, and beneath her nightdress her bare pink toes shrimped up from the cool floor. She bounced into Karsten's bed, nested the blankets about her, and exclaimed sociably, "Oh, it's so nice and cool this morning, after yesterday!"

"Yea-um," said Karsten, almost dislocating his jaw to get at an elusive whisker. "Why aren't you dressed, infant? It's time you were ready for breakfast."

"I don't want to eat—before I go to church. I'm going to be

a nun, Karsten."

"We haven't got nuns in the Lutheran Church."

"I know. And mamma thinks the Catholics are heathens, because they worship the Virgin Mary. Maybe—are there any Jew nuns, Karsten? What are Jews, anyhow?"

"Well, they're people," Karsten replied. He had seen a few —there was Goldfarb, the gentle-eyed and generous pawnbroker, to whom some of the boys at the university took their watches every month. He himself had never been forced into such straits. To him Jews seemed rather imaginary, biblical and remote. "And I don't think there are any Jewish nuns. I've never heard of any." He wiped his face tenderly, leaned forward to inspect it, and added, "What did you really come in here for, Olina?"

Olina drew a deep breath. "Solveig said I could tell you, even if you're not nice to her. She likes you, Karsten, honest she does! She doesn't like Magdis and Arne, but she—"

Karsten tossed his towel on the rack. "Come on, now, what are you getting at? Are you making something up again?"

"No, cross my heart and hope to die! Alec Fordyce is going to the South Seas—to get pearls—and then he's coming back to get Solveig. He's going to sail on a schooner from San Francisco next month. And perhaps it will be a year or more before Solveig will see him again!"

Karsten looked his astonishment. Pearl fishing! And all at once a languorous, sapphire sea dazzled his eyes, and palm trees waving slowly, voluptuous fronds in the immense and gorgeous wonder of a tropical sunset, and coral reefs and glittering strands, hibiscus flowers and gold-skinned, graceful, joyous natives—a paradise for a painter! He stared at Olina and felt a tight shrinking about his heart.

"Doesn't Solveig want to go along with him?" he asked dully. Rose Shaleen would want to go!

"Only men are allowed on the schooner," Olina informed him. "She'll wait for him, though, if it takes forever. That's what she says. Oh, it must be wonderful to be in love like that! I think perhaps I'm in love with David, even if his mother does have to make him wash his neck. How can you tell, Karsten?"

He was busy getting the elastic band of his blue and white dotted tie fastened about his upstanding wing collar.

"How can you tell what?" His image reddened in the glass.

"If you're in love or not. I read a book that Solveig borrowed from Marit Holm last spring. Mamma didn't know she had it. It was called *East Lynne* and a lady by the name of Mrs. Henry Wood wrote it. It made me cry something terrible, Karsten. Lady Isabel Vane thought she was in love with a serpent, Captain Francis Levison, and eloped with him. And then she discovered—alas, too late!—that she was in love with her own married husband, Archibald Car—"

"You're too young to read that sort of thing," Karsten interrupted. "And you're too young to talk about being in love with anyone. Go and get dressed."

Olina threw the bed clothes aside. "Alec is going to send letters to the livery man in Moorhead, and Solveig will get them when she goes to town."

"I see. You'd better tell her to burn them, so mother doesn't get hold of them."

In blue serge trousers and light crash jacket, Karsten took his new straw sailor with the blue and white striped band out of the closet. The hat at a rakish angle, he surveyed himself critically in the mirror. If there were only a remote chance of Rose Shaleen's being at church! Perhaps he had too much pomade on his hair. He removed his hat to peer intently at the glossy wave reflected by the glass.

"You're a real dude," Olina said admiringly. "Perhaps mamma won't let you wear that cream-colored jacket to

[291]

church, though."

Karsten had already thought of that, but he decided to risk it. He selected a white silk handkerchief from the box Magdis had given him for Christmas—an elaborate example of her skill at woodburning, with his name in a scroll beneath the head of Pocohontas. He took his bamboo swagger stick from its hiding place on top of a window frame, where he kept it safe from the vandal hands of his brother Arne, who had jeeringly said it looked like half a fish-pole, and had once chased Effie Strand all around the yard with it.

Olina had crawled out of bed and was standing at the window. "I saw Rose Shaleen walking on the other side of our creek this morning," she said dreamily. "Before anybody was up."

A qualm struck Karsten in the small of the back. "Rose Shaleen? What are you talking about?"

"I did. I was kneeling in front of our window, and it was just coming light, and the willows were sort of silver purple, and the dew was like silver spiders on the grass, and I saw Rose Shaleen walking slow toward the river, and not looking at our house at all!"

Karsten felt wildly that he must be dreaming. Rose—walking at dawn three miles from home, boldly beside the Wings' creek! What if someone else had seen her? His mother, for instance, who was always up and about even before the hired girls. Her first thought would be that Rose wasn't quite *right* —she suspected the Shaleens were slightly deranged, anyhow.

What the devil did Rose mean by risking everything in such a way? On the chance of seeing *him*, of course! A perverse rapture fired him so that it was all he could do to speak.

"I wouldn't mention that to anybody, if I were you," he said with an air of carelessness. "It sounds kind of queer to me."

Olina turned from the window, humming "Listen to the

Mocking Bird" and thinking of the orguinette she had seen advertised for eight dollars. All you had to do was pump the pedals and turn a crank, and there on perforated sheet music was a four-piece orchestra!

VIII

THE CLANS of Holms and Langstads and Pedersons and Stormos streamed into the little white frame church. Their original number had been added to by marriages over the years, but today Karsten saw them in a strange clarity as they had appeared so long ago, when he stood on the prairie and saw a chain of people and oxen and covered wagons coming out of the evening, out of "farthest north," the people singing to the grand loneliness of a new earth and sky their brave and wistful songs of an old land.

He must have paused, involuntarily, for now his father touched him on the arm. "Roald is beckoning to us," Ivar said. "We better wait for him."

Roald! Karsten beheld him with a start of irritation, as always. His uncle was not only a pillar of the church. He was practically the foundation, since the Wing and Bratland money had gone into the building of it. And today—well! He was arrayed in his Prince Albert, with everything to match.

"Karsten," he said as he came up with them, "I heard this morning there's somebody else trying to get William Cole—in Crookston. We must act quick. We don't get such a man here every Friday!"

"Go ahead and act, then," Karsten said. "I'm not standing in your way."

" Yes, but Karsten—like I told you—he wants a young fellow to go in with him. I have been thinking. I could bring him out today—for coffee—about four o'clock. That way you can see him and maybe talk to him."

Karsten thought quickly. Four o'clock. He had made up his mind to see Rose Shaleen, somehow or other, this afternoon. All right—he would bring Rose to the house with him. Fate had a way of deciding things, after all.

"I don't see any reason why you shouldn't," he said to his uncle. "I'll talk to him. You'd better say something to mother about it, though."

"Ya, sure!" Roald replied warmly and put an arm about Karsten's shoulders. "We better go in now. We're the last."

"If you are there in time to pass the collection plate," Ivar said, straightening a grin, "it'll be time enough."

Church, and home in the surrey, and fricasséed chicken for dinner, and before long it was three o'clock, with the sky a lofty blue.

Karsten had bolted the meal, which Pastor Flatta had gustibly shared, and had taken Arne's filly and ridden over to the Shaleens'. Steve had come out of the house, taken drily amused note of Karsten's riding breeches and striped silk shirt, and had finally admitted that Rose had strolled off north, just after dinner, toward the hayfield.

It was there that Karsten found her, at the north edge of the Shaleen cutting, sitting with her back against a haystack, a book in her hands. She threw the book aside and flashed up into his arms.

"I knew you'd come," she said softly against his mouth. "We missed last night."

He held her away from him. "You weren't here—"

She smiled as she nodded her head. "Until it must have been past midnight."

"You shouldn't have come out in that storm, Rose."

"You don't know me very well yet. I love storms and things." She laughed and added shyly, "And then do you know what I did?"

[295]

"Something just as crazy, I'll bet."

" I got up before daylight and planted a red rose bush, earth and all, that I took from our garden. I planted it on the other side of your creek. I didn't intend to tell you anything about it until maybe you found it there yourself. But—you'd never find it! And besides—I have to tell you everything, Karsten."

Karsten choked a bit while his arms tightened about her. But he smiled down at her. "I would have found it—sometime," he told her. "It was a beautiful thing to do. Just like you, my —my darling!"

He kissed her again, under the tall, still blue of the summer sky. Then they sat down against the clovery fragrance of the haystack, upon which Arne's filly Beulah was by this time gorging herself.

"Look, Rose," Karsten said at once, "I can't stay here more than a few minutes. Uncle Roald is bringing some old duffer of a lawyer to the house for coffee at four o'clock. They want me to go into partnership with him—Cole, his name is—next year, after I graduate. So—I've got to be at the house to meet him."

"Oh, Karsten, I—can't you—"

"Listen—you're coming with me. I won't have to talk to him long, and then we'll go and find that rose bush you planted."

"You mean—I'm going to your house with you?"

"Why not?"

Rose was thoughtful for a moment. "This old gingham is so faded! I ought to go back and put on my—"

"You're beautiful just the way you are," he stoutly insisted, and wound a loose tendril of her burnished hair about his finger.

"I've got a blue organdy that Aunt Kate gave me—it comes right down to my ankles—and a new pair of blue kid slippers, with curved heels and—"

"Save them all for another time."

"How soon do we have to go?"

Karsten took from his shirt pocket the stem-winding gold watch his mother had given him. The back was chased in a dove and olive branch design, and engraved within the cover were the words, "To my son Karsten Wing, Christmas 1885, from his loving mother." He frowned as he looked at the time.

"If we start now, we can just make it. Wear your new dress next Sunday, Rose." In sackcloth, he thought proudly, she would outshine any girl he knew, with the exception, perhaps, of his sister Solveig.

"All right," she faltered, and then suddenly laughed her exciting, throaty laugh. She threw her arms about his neck and nipped the lobe of his ear with her white, not quite even teeth.

The playful impulse roused in Karsten a sudden turmoil, and scarcely aware of what he did he thrust her back roughly against the hay and kissed her as he had never done before. She was not laughing now. There were tears on her cheeks, saltily sweet against his lips. She said nothing, and in the silence Karsten could hear his own heart thudding. Shaken by a confused fear of himself, he listened with an abrupt keenness and heard something else—the sound of his watch ticking.

"We'll have to hurry, Rose," he said in distraction.

When he lifted her to her feet, she stood back from him and looked straight into his eyes.

"Karsten—do you want to go into partnership with this lawyer?"

He laughed at her. "How am I to know, darling, until I've seen him and talked it over? I won't have to make up my mind today, anyhow."

"You want to make a lot of money, don't you?"

"It takes a lot of money to live the way we're going to live," he told her gravely, and tried to take her hands. But she clasped them behind her and continued to stare at him solemnly.

"I couldn't bear it if you gave up everything else just for—for money," Rose said. "Maybe I wouldn't even want to marry you, Karsten."

He started with disbelief. A love like theirs—unlike anything that had ever happened before—surely it was proof against any circumstances!

"What would I be giving up?" he asked her.

"People who make a lot of money give up—everything," Rose said. "You'd give up your painting?"

He laughed uneasily. What would she think if she knew he had spent most of last evening squeezing the colors from his precious tubes—to paint croquet balls!

"You don't know what you're talking about, Rose," he told her in a voice of gentle understanding. "I'd never be a great painter. If you could see some of the work in—"

"I don't care about that," Rose declared. "I want you to be a lawyer—because that's what you want to be. And I want you to be a *great* lawyer some day. But there's something else. Even if you never could be a great painter—if you only kept on trying—"

"All right," Karsten said lightly, "I'll go on smearing up good canvas with good paint till you'll wish I had never been born. Come on, now, we've got to hustle."

He picked her book up from the ground. "*Ramona*," he said, glancing at the title. "I read it a few years ago. Do you like it?"

"It's beautiful. I'm reading it over again. Do you remember? Ramona married Felipe after Alessandro died, but she never forgot Alessandro. He was her only real love."

"Yes, I remember." Even to Rose he could not confess that he had come close to weeping over the fate of the heroine. "I have some books you'd like, I think. There's one—" He hesi-

[298]

tated, wondering if his suggestion would not be improper, to a girl so young. "It's called *The Scarlet Letter*. It—"

"Oh, I've read it! Aunt Kate has it. It was very sad, but I don't know how Hester Prynne could have loved such a weak coward as Arthur Dimmesdale, do you?"

Karsten laughed and remarked learnedly, "It's supposed to be a great study in psychology. Here, let me help you up."

Rose was so slight as she perched in front of him on the saddle, it seemed that she was almost without substance. And yet, how strong she was in her embraces, like a slender, tough young vine! He buried his face in the sweetness of her hair for a moment, and then turned Beulah toward home.

Only now did a brief misgiving stalk through his mind. Perhaps he had been hasty. Perhaps this was the wrong day to bring Rose home with him for the first time. There would be such a stir in the house over the visit of a stranger from the city that perhaps nobody would even notice that Rose had come in with him. On the other hand, there might be a certain advantage in that. With the issue confused, so to speak, Rose would have a chance to put herself at ease before the eyes of the family were pinned on her in amazement.

He cut across the hayfield toward the county road, a straight north-running ribbon of slate-colored earth still rutted and miry from last night's rain.

Rose looked down where the wild grass had been cut close for hay. "Look, Karsten—you can still see the old Red River cart trail, where the halfbreeds, with loads of furs from Canada—"

He could see her face, and it seemed to him that her eyes were veiled with wonder, as if in some way the fabulous past of this rich, tamed prairie looked out of them. A mysterious thrill smote through Karsten.

"I saw them once," he said. "It's my earliest memory, just

about, and it's more like a dream than anything else. If my father hadn't kept talking to me about them, I'd probably have forgotten them. But I remember. They had long black hair, and jackets with brass buttons. The leader was an Englishman. I'll tell you more about him one of these days." Rose could surely be trusted to share Solveig's secret, he thought.

Just within the gate, they were met by Louie Spragg. Rose slid from the saddle with a radiant greeting for Louie. Karsten glanced beyond them to the carriage yard across the square of lawn, and saw his uncle's folding-top buggy standing in the shade of the driving shed. He looked at his watch—it was ten minutes past four. Well, what of it? There were millions of William Coles in the world, but only one Rose Shaleen!

"I just put your uncle's horse in the barn, Karsten," Louie said. "He come with a dried-up old codger looks like a good sneeze 'd blow him away. But he's got a fancy daughter, though."

"He brought his wife and daughter?"

"No wife. Just his daughter and a pug dog she calls Punkins. She left her parasol for me to fix. 'Please, mister man,' she says, 'can you make this catch stay?' So I took it and righted it after I got the horse in the barn. You better take it into the house to her. I left it settin' over there along of that tree."

Karsten looked at Rose and saw flight in her wide eyes. He grasped her hand and drew her with him as he went to pick up the sunshade. Rose stared at the frothy lace thing.

"Please, Karsten," she said in an anguished voice, "let me go home. She's a swell, and I'm not dressed up to meet—"

But Karsten glowered and started across the lawn with her at once. The flower beds were trim and bright in their girdles of river clam shells and whitewashed stones. The porch was empty, but of course the parlor would be used for these special guests. Karsten kept one firm hand on Rose's arm, while the

[300]

other gripped the nonsensical parasol.

The double doors were open from the hall into the parlor, and voices emerged with a hushed, important sound. But that sacred room always subdued any voice, as if a funeral were afoot over the flowered Brussels carpet, in the midst of ponderously carved walnut and horsehair furniture, marble-topped, claw-foot tables and red-velvet window drapes. A more hideous room Karsten could not imagine, yet it was his mother's pride.

"Your hair is all right," Karsten muttered, seeing Rose brush it back with nervous hands. "Come on and let's get introduced."

As he spoke, he saw on the opposite side of the parlor a girl whose hair was modishly high-coifed and fringed. Her dress of fine white lawn, close-bodiced over her pouting breast, was draped up at the hem and held by small bunches of flowers that looked like forget-me-nots. She sat well on the edge of the sofa so as not to disarrange the sweep of her bustle, which was modernly high and not too protruding. At her feet lay a fawn-colored pug dog, his hide rippling with fat, his soot-black snout boredly reposing between his paws.

As Karsten paused in the doorway, the girl leaned forward and craned her neck expectantly toward him, but Roald was already on his feet, prancing forth to meet him.

"Well, Karsten! You are here. Come, my boy, you must meet our good friends—" His jaw fell as he saw Rose. "And Rose! Solveig is around somewheres—outdoors, I think—"

"I want Rose to meet Mr. Cole," Karsten interrupted, his eyes darkening. If he hadn't caught a glimpse of his father as Roald spoke, he might have turned on his heel and gone out of the house. But Ivar looked so awkward and bewildered, sitting with Arne beside the only open window.

Roald blinked, but recovered himself with alacrity. "Yes,

[301]

yes, sure! Come, then!"

But Karsten marched past him, Rose's hand tight in his own, and presented himself before Miss Cole.

"Permit me to return your parasol, Miss Cole," he said politely. "It has been repaired. I am Karsten Wing—and this is Miss Rose Shaleen."

Miss Cole accepted the parasol, fluttered thick, black lashes, and smiled from Karsten to Rose as if in delighted surprise.

"Oh, thank you so much!" she laughed. "I'm afraid I was a nuisance, but the catch wouldn't work." She set the parasol aside and looked at Rose. "You've been out walking? I wanted to go walking today and look for wild flowers. But I had to put on this stuffy dress and come a-visiting with father! Just a dutiful daughter—" She broke off with a gay laugh. "Here comes father now, with Mr. Bratland." She glanced at Karsten. "Be careful! Father is a sly old fox, though he looks so harmless. You sit down here with me, Miss Shaleen. Men's talk is so stupid, don't you think?"

To Karsten's grateful astonishment, Rose sat down on the sofa beside Miss Cole. Her face was composed now, quite unreadable, and the flashes of bright color on her cheekbones only heightened her beauty, so fresh and wild beside the powdered prettiness of Miss Cole.

Karsten bowed with an awkward jerk and turned to meet Roald and the lawyer. Beyond them he saw his mother and Magdis busy with the coffee and cake trays that had just been brought in by the hired girls and placed on one of the marble-topped tables. Arne and Olina were there, too, and his father stood alone now, looking blankly out of the window. Of Solveig there was no sign.

While he was being introduced to Mr. Cole, Karsten was acutely aware that his mother had seen Rose and that she was fortifying her facial expression against any betrayal of her feelings. But the feelings were unmistakably there, in the faint tensing about her nostrils, in the briskness of her manner.

William Cole was an emaciated, sallow-faced man, almost totally bald. His features, with a little more flesh, would have been good, but the candle-colored skin seemed to be all there was over cheekbones and long blade of jaw. His flowing black mustache was incongruously luxuriant, his large, dark eyes lighted with sensitive intelligence. When at last Karsten was able to fix his attention upon the man, he felt a spontaneous liking for him. He had charm and humor, and a dry kind of gentleness, as if he had seen a great deal of humanity, yet was more ready to pity than to censure.

"It doesn't matter," Mr. Cole was saying with his tolerant smile, "whether Cleveland is re-elected or we get Benjamin Harrison. Harrison is a weak man—weak enough to be used as a mere figurehead. Maybe, by the end of another four years we'll be able to find a stronger man. But we're in for a bad time of it in Washington, mark my words. Whether it's Democrats or Republicans or the new Farm and Labor Party, we shall see political patronage that will make the 'star routes' graft look piffling. Such things run in cycles, and the nineties are due for dirty politics such as we've never seen before. There isn't any doubt of that in my mind. The farmer will have to fight corporations of every sort, from the bankers to the manufacturers of hayracks. Are you interested in politics, Karsten?"

Hearing Mr. Cole address him thus made Karsten fumble clumsily for a thoughtful response, and out of the tail of his eye he saw Uncle Roald looking on, bland as a custard.

"I'm not ambitious to become president, Mr. Cole," he said, "but I'm interested in what you've just said. I hope you're wrong. Daniel Webster said in his *Remarks on Agriculture*, 'When tillage begins, other arts follow. The farmers therefore

[303]

are the founders of human civilization.' I should think the corporations would know that and be careful how they deal with the farmers."

He felt rather proud of himself and thought, *That should set old Bövelen back on his behind!*

William Cole's eyes had lighted with pleasure. "Very good," he said, "very good, indeed! You have been doing your reading, I see. Young people nowadays seem to find no time for serious reading. My daughter Edna rarely opens a book, and when she does—"

"She is very pretty," Roald interrupted archly.

"They tell me so," William Cole conceded with a smile. "Who is that charming young creature sitting beside her?"

"A neighbor's girl," Roald said with his little cough.

"Rose Shaleen," Karsten added stubbornly.

"Rose Shaleen," William Cole repeated slowly, as if he were savoring each syllable of the name.

But now Magdali was urging them all to take chairs for coffee. He went to the table and returned in a moment with three empty cups to stand before the two girls on the sofa. Edna Cole was holding Rose's right hand, palm upward, in both of her own.

"You are of a very sensitive nature," Edna was saying. "And that goes with what I have just told you about looking out for enemies. I see a cross here—in your life line—" She glanced up in a transfixed way, as out of deep absorption, and saw Karsten looking down at her. "Oh, gracious—"

"We're going to have coffee," he said shortly. "If you don't mind, I'll draw a chair and sit with you two girls."

He did not really look at Rose until he was seated near her, his cup and saucer on his knee. Then it seemed to him that her face looked strangely unfamiliar, small and pointed, her mouth drawn in, the pupils of her eyes dilated. She almost smiled

[304]

back at him, but glanced down instead at her open right palm. Karsten shrugged and grinned, with an inward seething. Such nonsense! Rose ought to know better than to take palmistry seriously!

Effie Strand was there immediately with the coffee pot, Olina demurely in her wake with cream and sugar on a copper tray. Olina's hair was tightly braided, a blue ribbon bow on each braid, and her forehead shone like a peeled onion. Effie steamed past to the men on the other side of the room, but Olina lingered, after Karsten and Rose had taken cream and Edna Cole had taken both cream and sugar.

Edna lifted her cup daintily, little finger curved out, and smiled at Olina. "Did anybody ever tell you that you are a pretty little girl?" she asked.

"I am not pretty," said Olina. "I'm beautiful, like Rose. That's what David says."

Amused, Edna said, "And who is David?"

"He is my brother," Rose told her, looking down at her cup. "He is only thirteen. You shouldn't listen to what he says, Olina."

And for no reason that Karsten could gather, Olina moved thin-leggedly on her way, humming to herself the tune he had heard her humming early this morning, but with a difference that did not escape Karsten's ear. This morning she had hummed it dreamily, as if her mind had been on something else. Now it sounded saucy, almost impertinent—"*Listen to the Mocking Bird!*"

"Oh, how I wish I had sisters and brothers," Edna sighed, and looked wistfully at Karsten. "It's truly *tragic* to be an only child. It's—it's *criminal* of parents to have one lonely child in the home. Miss Shaleen, I suppose you have lots of brothers and sisters besides this—this young David Olina spoke of?"

[305]

Rose lifted her head, startled and confused for a moment, then laughed apologetically, her teeth against her lower lip.

"Oh—I—David is really my cousin. They're all my cousins. Their father is my uncle, and I have their name, because I was brought up in the family."

"Oh," Edna said, hesitating delicately, "I'm so sorry. I didn't understand." She broke off a morsel of cake.

"Rose's right name is Brazell," Karsten explained, somehow disliking himself for it. "Her parents both died when she was a baby, and her uncle adopted her. Her story is quite romantic, Miss Cole."

What a false note that was, he thought miserably. As if there were any need for explaining Rose and her existence to a tricked-up doll like Edna Cole! But in this parlor you had to make some sort of conversation. You couldn't just get up and leave. Still, why couldn't you? He felt his mother's eyes upon him from the other side of the room, where she was seated with Roald and Mr. Cole and Magdis.

His father and Arne were together again, drinking their coffee near the open window—discussing some farm work, no doubt, since Arne bore an expression of mature importance on his round face. Olina had skipped out with the hired girls, and Solveig had not yet come in. Karsten felt desolately alone, as if even Rose herself were no longer here.

"You *must* tell me all about it some day, my dear," Edna Cole was exclaiming to Rose, "now that I'm to be a neighbor of yours—in Wing." She laid a soft hand on Rose's arm. "*Wing!* Isn't it a thrilling name for a town? It has such a *lift* to it. And to think that it was named after your family, Karsten! Oh, dear—I didn't mean to—" She laughed in pretty confusion. "Please don't think I'm in the habit of calling gentlemen by their first names so—"

"Why shouldn't you?" Karsten asked with stiff politeness.

"Won't you have some more coffee, Miss—Edna?"

Edna's laugh pirouetted forth. "There, now—I call that real gallantry, don't you, Miss Shaleen? He calls me Edna because I accidentally called him Karsten. No, thank you, I daren't have a second cup. Mamma says it muddies the complexion."

"You'll have some more, Karsten," Rose said, and before he could protest she had taken his cup and moved with her slim, young-animal grace across the room to the coffee table. Her blue gingham skirt, though longer than the one she wore yesterday, did not properly reach her ankles, and following Edna Cole's eyes Karsten saw that Rose's petticoat showed a half inch beneath the hem of her skirt. Again he hated himself for flinching at so slight a flaw in the object of his love.

"It will be wonderful living in the country!" Edna remarked with a sparkle. "One can go about dressed just as one likes, can't one?"

Karsten glanced at her suspiciously. He was not used to girls and their ways, but he couldn't help feeling that Edna's observation was a bit too guileless.

"You'll be living in Wing," he said. "That isn't exactly the country, even if it is only a village."

Rose came back with the coffee. She leaned across Edna to hand it to Karsten, and a drop splashed over on Edna's immaculate dress.

"Oh—! I'm awfully sorry, Miss Cole!" Rose gasped. "I'll get sour milk and salt—"

"Why, it's nothing!" Edna declared. "It'll wash out. You sit right down here and finish your cake. I must ask your mother, Karsten, if she prepares her coffee with egg. It's so nice and clear. That's one thing mamma can't make at all—coffee. I suppose it's because she's English, poor dear. But she does have a wonderful knack with tea. Of course, I can't do

[307]

one or the other, yet." She drew a comical face. "At boarding school they teach you everything except what you ought to know, it seems, but one of these days I'm going to learn how to cook." Her voice had reached a gay, high pitch as she glanced across the room at Karsten's mother, who was deep in conversation with Roald and Mr. Cole.

Karsten saw his mother smile and get up, and heard the faint whisper of her violet surah silk gown with its lace fichu fastened now by a cameo pin instead of the old tinkling Norwegian ornament he remembered. It came to him sharply then that his mother had gradually discarded every vestige of her immigrant past, while his father was still—well, what *was* his father? Surely an American now, but with the best, the most vigorous and honest and spiritually simple qualities of the old land giving something to the new. He looked at Ivar, near the window, and it struck him that his father wasn't really listening to Arne at all.

"Are you young folks getting acquainted?" Magdali beamed. "We old ones have so much to talk about that's serious!" Then, as if she had just seen Rose Shaleen for the first time, she exclaimed brightly, "And Rose! How you are growing, child! Dear me, I don't know when we saw any of you people last. Is everybody well at home?"

"Yes, thank you, Mrs. Wing, we are all well," said Rose earnestly. "That is, except pa. He's troubled with the rheumatism when it rains, and we have to rub him with—"

"The Shaleens are our neighbors to the south," Magdali explained comfortably to Edna. "But you know, when we work as hard as we do, you don't have much time for neighboring. I overheard you speaking about coffee." Her corsets squeaked a little as she bent to pat Edna's knee. "One of the first things a wife must know is how to make good coffee. A cup of coffee will always put a man back in good humor if he's cranky. Karsten, bring Miss Cole some of my rainbow cake. She hasn't tried it yet, and it is very good, if I do say so myself!"

Karsten fetched the cake plate and held it before the two girls, smiling down anxiously into Rose Shaleen's eyes. How to get out of this room at once was the question uppermost in his mind. Rose could certainly be no more uncomfortable here than he was himself. He tried to convey that thought to her by a look. She shook her head at the cake plate, but the quick gladness that lighted her face cheered him. She had read his meaning.

"Oh, but the pieces are so big, Mrs. Wing!" Edna protested as she took one. "Karsten, you'll help me eat it, won't you?" Daintily she laid half the piece on Karsten's plate.

"I suppose you and your mother will be busy this next week getting settled in Wing," Magdali said to Edna. "Those rooms I mentioned to your father, over the hardware store, are nice and clean, even if they are small. They would do until you build, later. And I hope you *will* feel like building, my dear!"

"Oh, thank you, I'm sure we're going to love it here!" said Edna, fluttering her lashes at Karsten. "Everybody is so friendly—and—" Pathetically she spread out her hands. "I was simply terrified—leaving all my friends in the city. I thought I'd die of loneliness. But you're all so kind, and I'm not a bit afraid now!"

"We'll have to see that you meet all the nice young people," Magdali assured her warmly. "Karsten, next Sunday Mr. Gossman is coming over—wouldn't it be nice to have a few of our young friends in so that Edna can meet them? You and Solveig and Magdis could invite—where *is* Solveig, anyhow?"

She caught her frown into an indulgent smile. "I shouldn't wonder if she's out somewhere watching for Einar Flatta to ride by."

"Einar Flatta?" Karsten inquired.

"You didn't know your sisters were growing up, did you?" she said, and turned to Edna Cole. "Einar is the nephew of our Pastor Flatta. He's a nice boy—going into the ministry —and I *think* he and Solveig are becoming interested in each other." Magdali could be quite coy on occasion.

"We'll go and find her," Karsten said, and put his hand out to Rose.

His mother's face became completely expressionless. Over her eyes came a frosty blue film that might be blinding her to something she did not want to see.

But Karsten got up and hurried away with Rose. They spoke scarcely a word until they had crossed the little footbridge to the other side of the creek. The three red roses in full bloom on the bush had drooped, but the young buds were already opening, firm and delicately flushed. Karsten reached down and touched one. Then, with a reckless disregard for anyone who might be looking, he put his arm about Rose Shaleen and drew her vehemently to him.

"It'll have to be watered every day," he said.

"If you want to keep it."

"What do you mean by that? Why shouldn't I want to keep it?"

Rose walked to the bank under the willows and sat down. Her eyes were fixed thoughtfully on the opposite side of the twinkling ribbon of water.

"I planted the bush on this side so your mother wouldn't see it and take it away."

"Rose!" He sat down beside her and took her hands hard into his own. "Look at me!"

[310]

Slowly her eyes turned toward him, and although they smiled, the lashes were winged back with tears. She drew her hands away.

"She thinks I am not good enough for you," she murmured, and began to pluck at a tuft of grass. "She'll never, never let us—"

"She'll have nothing to say about it!" Karsten cried. "Nobody will have anything to say about it—except us. Mother doesn't even know yet. I haven't had a chance to tell her. You just feel hurt because she treated you like a—a kid, in there. She doesn't realize that you're grown up. And then, we had company and she had to pay attention to them, or she'd have—"

"Company—that's it!" Rose laughed and nibbled at a stem of grass she had pulled up.

"Be fair, Rose!" Karsten begged. "What else could she do? The Coles are strangers to us, and mother had to—"

"They won't be strangers very long," Rose interrupted. "*She's* the one your mother wants for you, already."

"Oh, for God's sake!" he exploded. "Now you *are* being a kid! Worse than Olina. Do you think I'm such a spineless boob? And if you *do* think so, how can you—"

"I don't think you are, Karsten." Rose covered her face with both hands and choked back a sob. "Oh, I *don't* think you are! But—but I know—"

His arms were suddenly about her. Let them look from the house across there if they had a mind to! Let the world look on, for all he cared. Soon they would all know, anyhow!

"Rose, my little Rose," he whispered against her cheek. "Trust me, won't you? Everything is going to be all right. Nobody is ever going to come between us—nobody, do you hear? Come on, smile at me!" With thumb and forefinger he lifted her chin.

Her smile fluttered on her lips as he kissed her.

"You'd better go back to the house now," she whispered. "I mean—for Mr. Cole's sake, you really must, Karsten."

"All right." He tilted her face in his hands again and kissed her. A dark mist had suddenly come over his eyes, in which she seemed to float tensely pale and unreal. "You won't come back in with me?"

"No, I'm going home now. I'll go this way, down to the river."

He could not have held her. She was gone like a bright leaf in the wind, westward through the trees to the river.

IX

THERE was a border of pink-blossomed bleeding hearts just under the porch rail, and Olina sat in the shade of a snowball bush, where the lawn was soft and fine and untrodden. She was playing mumbly peg all by herself. It was Arne's knife she had, a fine, pearl-handled one he had got for Christmas from Uncle Roald. He prized it highly, but Olina had had the good fortune to catch him kissing Effie Strand in the barn this morning, and had laughed out loud because Effie looked so silly being kissed with an apron full of eggs in front of her.

Olina had meant no harm by laughing—she simply couldn't help it. But Arne had whirled around, red in the face, and had said, "If you tell ma, I'll stick your head in the rain barrel!" Olina, above tale-bearing, had felt insulted. For that reason more than any other, she had hinted that the loan of his pearl-handled knife for the day might compensate for her silence. Her own pocket knife was a clumsy affair. With Arne's she could practice, and perhaps beat David Shaleen even on the back-hand double-toss next time she met him at the river. Only once had she been able to win from him, and that was when his thumb was wrapped up from an embedded fishhook.

Now and then, after a successful toss of the knife, she glanced across the sunny green haze of the lawn to where her sister Magdis was playing croquet with Mr. George Gossman. They both looked grimly red in the heat. It was too soon after dinner for even such light exercise, but Magdis had been prompted by her mother to suggest it, because in another hour or two there would be more company, and then perhaps

Magdis and George would not have a chance to be alone together.

Olina thought Magdis looked funny with her hair done in a fringe—sort of like the screen door with the fly strips at the top of it—and her sailor hat, in spite of its pin, seemed about to take off from her head any minute. Magdis had won the first game from Mr. Gossman with unsmiling, furious effort, knocking the ball "over into the cabbages" whenever she got the chance, but always mindful not to expose her ankle in raising her foot to her own ball for the murderous stroke.

Nearing the end of the second game now, Mr. Gossman took a long shot at the red ball lying in position before the "basket" on the way home. It was a hit, but—wonder of wonders!—both the red and the green ball went through the difficult arch. Then Olina beheld something that was really worth looking at.

George Gossman caught Magdis's hand so that her mallet fell to the ground. Then he swept his straw hat from his head and bowed low, so that for a moment Olina was sure he was going to kiss Magdis's finger tips.

"I take that for a good sign, Miss Magdis," he said. "Together we go through thick or thin!"

Then he laughed, and Magdis shyly nestled her chin toward her bosom. "Mr. Gossman, I—"

"You know I went to the New Orleans Exposition three years ago," he went on. "There's already talk of another one —the World's Fair—in Chicago. If you would just say the word, Magdis, we could go to it together."

World's Fair—in Chicago! In 1893 Olina was to remember with wonderment what George Gossman had said that day. For in 1893 Olina was sixteen, and David Shaleen was at the Columbian Exposition gazing upon the marvels that were there, and sending her postcards full of exclamation points.

But now Olina made herself small and flat under the snow-ball bush, and listened hard for Magdis's reply to George Gossman.

"Are you—proposing marriage, Mr. Gossman?" asked Magdis.

Her profile, under the brim of her hat, looked almost as if she had suffered an insult. Olina wanted to laugh. What else *would* he be proposing? What had all the sewing and embroidery been for, if not for the young potato baron, Mr. George Gossman?

"Won't you call me George, Magdis?" Mr. Gossman pleaded, both hands clasping hers now. "I am offering you my heart and hand."

Olina could scarcely contain herself. Hadn't he given Magdis *both* hands at once? But she found herself embarrassed by the glad and frenzied look that covered her sister's face just then. She glanced between the snowball bush and the porch and found a quick way of departure. She would have to find Solveig and tell her that Magdis was going to marry George Gossman!

X

THE engagement of Magdis Wing to Mr. George Gossman was to be announced on the following Sunday afternoon. With joyful vigor, Magdali began at once planning the occasion—a festive one to which thirty or more guests were to be invited. It would be a lawn party, with chicken salad, potato salad, sandwiches, relishes and pickles and jellies, strawberry ice cream, and pink lemonade.

On Monday evening, Magdali was busy at her desk in the corner of the sewing room which she humorously called her office, a sacred nook the children had been forbidden to approach. When Olina was seven she had received a sound spanking for exploring the contents of drawers and cubby holes of the "secretary" and leaving her mother's records in gay confusion.

Now, in the nine-o'clock starlight, when she was thought to be innocently asleep, Olina was perched in the low crotch of the weeping willow just outside the sewing room, where she could observe comfortably the changing expressions on her mother's face while she made out the list of guests for the engagement party and wrote the invitations in lavender ink on gold-bordered cards. The window was wide open, and Olina would certainly get Hail Columbia if she should be caught spying upon her mother. But a person who didn't know his face was being watched could be so funny! Frowning—pursing the lips—raising the eyebrows—smiling in relief at some fresh thought—Olina found herself aping her mother unconsciously until she stuck the pen nib into her mouth by mistake and jerked back so indignantly that Olina almost lost her hold upon the branch from which she had been leaning for a closer look.

She was reluctantly preparing to get down from the tree when Karsten strode into the sewing room. And what a look he had on *his* face! As if he were in fetters and about to be burned at the stake!

Magdali smiled and said, "Well, Karsten, what is it? I'm so busy getting out these invitations—"

"I'll only be a minute," Karsten blurted out. "I just wanted to know if you were inviting Rose to the party next Sunday."

"Rose? Oh, the little Brazell girl—"

"Shaleen," Karsten corrected, with a flash in his eye that delighted Olina. She leaned over as far as she dared.

"Well, whatever!" Magdali laughed indulgently. "If the child would enjoy the party, I see no reason why we shouldn't invite her. I hadn't thought of it. But if she does come, I hope she'll hitch up her petticoat and have her hair tidy." Magdali's eyes twinkled with cool curiosity. "What made you think of asking her? I might have put Selma on my list, but she hasn't been feeling well, and I'm afraid she'll lose this baby she's expecting any minute—it's so long since the last one was born. I'm sure they'll understand why they haven't been asked. But if you'll ask Rose—we must be neighborly!"

Olina was thrilled at the pallor of Karsten, which was that of Hamlet, Prince of Denmark, in the play by William Shakespeare.

"Neighborly!" he cried. "I'm going to marry Rose Shaleen, mother, and I thought next Sunday would be a good time to announce it."

Olina's ears rang so that she missed her mother's gasp of astonishment. But she did not miss the flying back of her eyelids, the swift clutching of her breast with a plump, short-fingered hand. And yet—immediately, there was a composed smiling, a tender shake of the head.

"You children," said Magdali, "will be the death of me, with your surprises! First Magdis, and now you, Karsten. Rose is a very pretty girl, son, but she's only sixteen. Hadn't you both better wait a while before you announce your engagement? Have you told your father about it?"

"Yes," Karsten replied at once. "He thinks it's fine. He's going to talk to you about it."

"I see. Well, I'll say no more until we have talked it over, your father and I."

"Is it all right, then, for me to ask Rose to the party?"

Magdali nodded. "Certainly, Karsten."

"You don't need to be afraid of how she'll be dressed. She has a new blue dress her aunt gave her, and shoes—"

"Her Aunt Kate?"

"Yes, and she looks beautiful in it. She had it on when I went over there last night."

"Oh, so that's where you were!" Magdali smiled. "Out courting. The Coles dropped in before George left, and they were so disappointed that you weren't home. But I told you about that this morning, didn't I? Dear me!" She sighed. "I'm all of a heap with your news. I think—maybe you could get Rose to come over and have coffee with me—say, Wednesday afternoon, Karsten. After all, I scarcely know the child. I'd like to talk with her before next Sunday, if she'll come."

"I'll tell her, mother. And I know she'll come."

Karsten's eyes held a radiance that was painful to Olina, though she could not have told exactly why. And suddenly she decided that she had spied long enough. Tomorrow she would send a message by David, whom she had promised to meet on the river bank where they were delicately removing the bones of a huge carp they had found rotting in the warm sun. David was going to make drawings of the skeleton when it was ready. The message would be to Rose, of course, and it would say, "Have your hair combed and your petticoat up before you come here on Wednesday. Karsten showed me your rose bush. It's doing fine!"

XI

ON WEDNESDAY afternoon, Olina lay cheek by jowl with the water drain on the south corner of the porch eaves, where the Virginia creeper tendriled up with its live, fresh hold on the shingles. She could not see much, but she was hidden by the overhanging elm, and she could hear every word from the porch below, where Rose Shaleen was visiting with her mother over coffee and angel food cake. Solveig had gone off to town, ostensibly to help Magdis purchase material for her trousseau, but actually to see if a letter had come from Alec Fordyce, as Olina well knew. If her mother knew that, while she was talking to Rose!

"Marriage is a serious thing, my dear," she heard her mother say. "Are you sure you and Karsten know each other well enough to live together for the rest of your lives?"

"We have known each other as long as I can remember, Mrs. Wing," Rose said.

"Yes, of course, my dear. But that isn't quite what I mean. We change as we grow older—especially at your age—yours and Karsten's, I mean. Later, perhaps, when you've both lived a little longer and seen more—"

"That won't change us, Mrs. Wing," Rose said quickly. "Nothing can change us. I've always been with him, even when he has been away—and even when he didn't know it. But now that he knows, we'll be together—always—even if we're never married."

"I'm afraid I don't quite understand, Rose."

"It's—it's something—in here, that tells me. I've got to be

[320]

with him, because I've got to help him be what he wants to be."

"But he wants to be a lawyer. He'll be one in another year. I don't quite see how you—"

"It isn't only being a lawyer that matters," Rose put in. "I can help him, even at that. But it's something else—it's something I can't tell you about, I guess."

"I see." Magdali's voice was ineffably gentle, with a little sigh in it. "Something that only you and Karsten understand, naturally." She paused for a moment, but Rose remained silent. "Now, my child, what I'm going to say will make you very unhappy for a while. You must know, too, that I would be the last person in the world to cause you any unhappiness. But when you are really grown up and married to the right man, you'll thank me."

"What—what do you mean, Mrs. Wing?"

Olina could barely hear Rose Shaleen's voice. It sounded like the very ghost of terror.

"If you really love Karsten, Rose, you will not marry him. He is very young, and he thinks he's in love with you. He doesn't know his own mind yet. It hurts me to say this, my dear, but when he is older he'll look back and wonder at himself for ever thinking that you and he could be married. You both think you are very much in love now. But love of that kind soon fades. There must be something more. You see, Rose, your people and his are so different. I know my son so well! He's very proud, Rose. He's a real Bratland—and the Bratlands have always been proud of their blood. It has come down from the old kings of Norway. So, you see, if Karsten—"

"But he called me a princess! And there were Irish kings—"

"Yes, yes, my dear child! I suppose everybody could find a king or queen in his family if he went back far enough. I

[321]

didn't mean to make so much of that. It's just that—oh, I have a present for you! I almost forgot about it."

Olina heard her mother move, and would have given anything to see Rose's face when she beheld the gift. For Olina knew what it was. She had been in town with her mother yesterday when she bought the dress length of red silk.

But Rose seemed to be taking no heed of it. Her voice came on stilts when she said, "Do you mean that my father and mother aren't good enough for Karsten, Mrs. Wing? My real father and mother, in heaven?"

There was a long, dreadful silence, and Olina began to shake and feel dizzy.

"Please, Rose. Try to understand. I didn't know your father well, of course. But I nursed your poor mother through a very serious illness, as you probably know. We have been neighbors for years. We stood by each other when times were much harder than they are now. We have understood each other. But Karsten is going to have an important place in life. He will have enemies who will do their best to hurt him. People can be very cruel. That's why he must have a wife nobody can point a finger at because of anything in the past. It would be unfair to him—and to you. I am only trying to be kind, my dear."

"I understand, Mrs. Wing," Rose said. "I understand—everything!"

"I'm sure you do, Rose. We must try to be very sensible, even if it breaks our hearts to give up what we want." She sighed deeply. "You must come to Magdis's party on Sunday, of course. Now—open your package, my dear, and see if you don't think you can make a pretty dress out of the—"

"I—I'd better go home now," Rose said.

Olina heard no rustle of paper, but she heard the slam of the screen door below as Rose Shaleen took flight. A moment later she saw Rose hurrying toward the creek. She saw her pause on the little foot-bridge and look at the package in her hands as if she were wondering how it had got there. For one breathless moment Olina was sure she was going to throw it into the creek without even opening it. But in the next, Rose was running along the other side of the creek, toward the fringe of river woods, her dark, coppery hair streaming behind her.

Karsten was harvesting in the north field, and Olina saw him leap down from his binder. He had seen Rose. But now, astonishment whipped Olina's breath clear out of her. For above Rose Shaleen's head sailed a scarlet banner of silk that signaled gaily up at the wide blue sky—then caught in the branches of a tree, where it hung limp in the hot, still air.

Olina found Solveig behind the house, gathering up the bed linen and towels that had been spread on the grass to bleach. There she gave her thin-breathed account of her mother's smooth cruelty to Rose Shaleen, talking until the tears finally choked her voice.

"Crying about it isn't going to help anybody," Solveig said, putting an arm about the little girl's shoulders and gazing off toward the river. "If Karsten and Rose can't fight their own battles, you can't do it for them. I'd like to see anybody try to come between me and Alec!"

"Suvvy! You're really going away with Alec when he comes for you?"

"If I have to wait a lifetime!"

"I'll miss you terribly," Olina said. "I'll even miss you when you go back to school in Moorhead this fall."

"I'm not looking forward to that with any pleasure. I s'pose I'll have to live with Magdis and George Gossman. I'd rather live in a cellar. Not that I give a darn! All I'm doing

[323]

now is waiting. Come on, help me get these things in. They've got to be ironed before supper." As she spoke, she looked up and saw Karsten and his father coming across the barnyard. In the north field, Karsten's team had been left standing unattended. "Take these in to the kitchen," she said quickly, and gave Olina a half dozen sheets and pillow cases. "Then go upstairs and find my side combs. I don't know where I left them."

"You haven't lost them?" Olina cried in alarm. "You promised I could have them when you go away."

"Go and look for them!" Solveig ordered, hastily gathering an armful of towels from the grass.

Solveig was in the hall when Karsten stormed into the sewing room and demanded in almost sobbing fury what his mother had done to Rose Shaleen. Then she saw her father go into the room where Magdali, unruffled, was mildly and frankly telling Karsten that she had acted only in the best interests of both her son and Rose. For the first time in her life, Solveig heard her father's voice blare out like thunder.

"You've had your way again, wife!" he roared, and struck the roll top desk with his fist so that the windows rattled. "The harm is done, but mark you my words—you will live to regret what you did today. Come out, Karsten, before I forget myself!"

Solveig breathed hard back against the shadowed wall as they came out together, Ivar's arm about Karsten and Karsten straighter than his father, though his face was twisted and white.

XII

DURING the weeks that followed, Solveig watched Karsten covertly, feeling pity for him but something of contempt too. Pity and contempt were never far apart in Solveig's nature. Karsten was trying to see Rose, she knew, but Rose kept herself indoors, stifling her misery under her pride even in the presence of her own family. Solveig herself made at least one attempt to talk to her when she came upon her pumping water in the Shaleen yard, but Rose's eyes blazed with tears, and the cry she gave filled Solveig with uncomprehending terror. If she loved Karsten so much, why on earth didn't she just take him away? It was plain that he didn't have the gumption to take *her* away!

"Leave me alone, Solveig!" Rose implored her. "Just—leave me alone!"

She ran into the house then, the water from the bucket splashing down upon her scuffed shoes. A few days later, David told Olina that Rose had gone to live with her Aunt Kate.

The days passed, and the pall of Karsten's silence in the house seemed to descend even upon the hired girls and the extra threshing crew that had come for the end of the harvest. Only Magdali seemed oblivious of it, cheerfully going about her plans for Magdis's wedding.

The ceremony was held in the church, in August. The day, fortunately, was cool, or Magdis, Solveig felt sure, would have burst out of her stays, her white moiré wedding gown, veil and all. The church was thronged, but no Shaleen was present. People understood, of course—Selma had lost her baby only a week before, and had all but lost her own life in the ordeal.

Magdis's two-weeks' honeymoon in Chicago and Niagara Falls was secretly amusing to Solveig. Wherever she and Alec went for their honeymoon, it would at least be somewhere more exciting than that!

And then it was September, and Solveig was living in the Gossmans' brick house in Moorhead and attending the Young Ladies' Seminary, spending her week-ends at home. There was at least one consolation in the arrangement—she was closer to Jake's livery stable, where she could inquire every day for letters from Alec, and drop her own letters into the post office, addressed in care of the San Francisco shipping company whose name Alec had given her. Soon, she knew with aching patience, there would come long months when she would not hear from him, when she could only have faith for the safe return of the little schooner adventuring through the magical Ceylon seas.

The first week of Solveig's "durance vile," as she called it, in the Gossman house was especially tedious because Magdis never tired of showing off her new possessions to her visitors. Bureaus, chiffoniers, china cupboards, what-nots, linen and silver and carpets—even the canopy of lace and net above the vast brass bed that dominated the master bedroom—all these things Magdis displayed with fresh enthusiasm whenever her friends came to see her.

On an evening when Magdis and her husband had invited a houseful of the town's "best" people to a whist drive, Solveig sat alone in her room, her books unopened before her on the table. She had just read once more the four letters she had received from Alec Fordyce, the last one describing the snug little schooner *Cassandra*, upon which he was about to embark, the ship's motley crew, the stalwart Swedish captain, and Alec's five partners on the expedition that was to return at the end of another year laden with priceless plunder from the sea. How thrillingly he had described them all, even to the native Malayan who had been educated by missionaries and had made a small fortune in pearls from an earlier expedition! Solveig read the letter over and over, her wild fancy following Alec over billowing seas, braving with him every peril her imagination could invent, facing death itself so that they might be together at last—anywhere in the world!

She glanced aside at her untouched books. There were no perils here, no hazards for the sake of love. She had learned the meaning of *amo, amas, amat*, but it was not from these words she had learned the meaning of love. Did Karsten, with all his lofty advice to her to brush up on her Latin, have any idea of its meaning? Only three days ago he had come here to her room and thrown a box containing what was left of his paints on Solveig's table, as if to rid himself of the last reminder of his precious hours with Rose Shaleen. Renunciation, that was it—and yet not quite, Solveig thought. Why hadn't he thrown them in the river, beyond all hope of their being recovered? Why had he never more than half done anything, always halting somewhere short of completeness? He was to go back to law school in the middle of this month to begin his final year. Would he see Rose again? How could he tolerate living at home, now that Rose had gone to the city?—unless it was because of their father, Solveig thought suddenly. Ivar had been almost as deeply affected as Karsten, she knew, and it was only recently that the polite strain between him and Steve Shaleen had shown any signs of easing.

The hilarity in the Gossmans' parlor below was mounting, George's booming laugh riding the crest. Solveig got up from her table and stood before the window. Across the misty, starless dark came the smell of autumn leaves, like spiced quills to the senses. Somewhere, Alec Fordyce breathed the air of adventure, salty, reckless, alien. Somewhere at this very moment he was listening to the slap of waves against his wind-borne craft—while she heard only the laughter of Magdis's fashionable guests at their game of whist downstairs.

She moved back to the dresser and looked at herself in the mirror. Her eyes were big, with no rest in them—only a perverse rebelliousness that even she herself only vaguely understood. She took out the box of rice powder she had hidden under her petticoats in the dresser. From her closet she brought Karsten's paints and picked a tube of scarlet color for her cheeks. A half dozen charred matches furnished black for her eyelids. The "fancy ladies" she had seen in the North Bridge district provided the model. When she was done with her face, she stood back from the mirror and gasped in unholy delight.

Her clothes, she realized, were too sedate and schoolgirlish by far. Long, gored skirts, shirtwaists with collars starched to the ears, and prim velvet bows. Her new fall coat was cut princess fashion, slim at the waist, navy blue with black frogs running down the front—rather natty, it was true, but it needed a dash of something. Her round, blue velvet hat, and the black dotted veil she had bought with the little spending money her father had given her the day he left her here at the Gossmans'—that had dash! But the coat? The sable furs that George Gossman had given Magdis—Magdis would not be going out of the house tonight, with her party in full swing—reposed in the closet of the master bedroom down the hall. It was a simple matter—

But not so simple a matter to creep down the back stairs, unheard, and out into the darkness of the back yard. Especially when she had no very clear sense of why she was doing it at all! The gas light on the street corner seemed miles away, and far beyond that the North Bridge district. Spears of fright pierced her as she stepped into the street and did her best to simulate an "air."

It was a dozen blocks or more to the district by the round-about route she chose, but at last the street lights shone before her, netted in river mist, the filmy ghost of rain that did not fall. The street itself was silent, only a lighted window here and there pointing its sinister suggestion through the enveloping fog. Somewhere a door opened briefly to spill a moment's high-pitched laughter into the street, then closed sharply as if upon a secret unwittingly betrayed. Directly in front of Solveig, a woman stepped from a doorway, drew her black cape about her thin shoulders, and swept her spangled gown up from about her ankles. She looked at Solveig.

"Just come to town, huh?"

Solveig swallowed, in triumph and fright. When she did not reply, the woman went her way. Solveig proceeded at a studied, ambling walk down the street. And then, just ahead of her, two tall young men rounded the corner. Here, then, was the moment to which she had been looking forward with inner trembling. She was about to be accosted. She paused abruptly. One of the young men had halted and was lifting his face to the foggy nimbus of the street light, as if he were looking for the moon, and his face was as pale as the fog—and he was her brother Karsten. Solveig clung back against the dark wall of a building that fronted the street.

"What are you looking at?" Karsten's companion demanded impatiently, and Solveig recognized his voice. He was Hugh Allen, a boy from town who was attending the university with Karsten. "Come on—I know the ropes here. Look—there's one waiting for us down the street."

Solveig dug her nails into her palms to check the scream

in her throat.

"I don't know," she heard Karsten say dully. "I got a queer feeling all of a sudden. As if—I don't know. You'd better go on by yourself, Hugh. I'm going back."

Solveig took a parting grip on the dark wall, picked up her skirts and ran.

In her room, she threw herself across her bed and moaned, "Oh, Alec, Alec, hurry home to me!" His was the real adventure—hers the make-believe, which she had never intended to be anything more.

Perhaps had she known that night that before another autumn brightened the Valley, she would learn that the schooner *Cassandra*, homeward bound, had been wrecked during a typhoon in the South Pacific, her high young heart might have been crushed—to mend again and accept what lesser romance life had still to offer. But in the twelve-month, her ardent spirit shaped itself to a votive passion of waiting—a passion never to be dimmed although it was almost a decade before the marooned survivors of the *Cassandra* were rescued from their tropical island and brought safely to their home shores. . . .

XIII

AND in that decade, Olina Wing became twenty-one.

For two months, since last June when she had been graduated from the Normal School in Moorhead, Olina had thought frequently of the importance of being twenty-one. But on this August evening, in 1898, her coming to maturity—how suddenly it had happened!—held a particular significance for her, because the conversation of the distinguished guest in the Wing parlor that evening had touched upon the controversial matter of woman suffrage. The guest, a congressman who owed his seat in Washington chiefly to the political zeal of George Gossman, had entertained George and Magdis at dinner in town. Afterward, the three had come out to the farm so that the congressman might pay his respects to the "greatest little woman of the county." Magdali had beamed under the compliment, and George Gossman had applauded it with a hearty "Hear, hear!"

The congressman, it seemed, had recently read an article by Miss Kate Shaleen, in which she appeared to be on the side of "these brick-throwing females in London!" What was the world coming to?

Kate Shaleen! Olina, sitting near the hall door, had flushed and glanced quickly at her mother. Then, to her astonishment, Magdali had said, smiling at the congressman:

"The time will come, my friend, when you will not laugh at the women's vote. My daughter Olina, here, is now trained for a teacher. If she is fit to teach the young, she is fit to have a voice in deciding who will run our government. We are no

[331]

longer cave dwellers. In two more years we enter the twentieth century. Please God, it will be the Women's Century!"

Twentieth Century! The phrase had rung a strange little cool bell somewhere deep within Olina, and she had glanced across the room at her father sitting somewhat apart from the others, as she herself sat. He looked suddenly old and lonely, with his big hands spread on the crocheted doilies that covered the arms of the red velvet chair. She knew he was longing for his pipe back in the small sitting room of the big brick house that had never seemed to belong to him since it had been remodeled from the old frame structure.

At a glance from Magdis, George Gossman hastily changed the subject to the peace terms that had been offered to Spain.

"Yes," said the congressman confidently, "the protocol will no doubt be signed. And we'll get Puerto Rico and the Philippines."

"Do we want them?" Ivar asked mildly.

The congressman looked puzzled and drew a cigar from his pocket by way of covering his embarrassment.

"I'm sure you gentlemen would like to go to the back parlor now for cigars," Magdali said with a graciousness that wholly concealed her aversion to tobacco smoke in her drawing room. She rose, smiling her dismissal of them, and her plump figure was very straight in its modish sapphire satin gown with the leg-o'-mutton sleeves and the passementerie trimmings. Magdali was fifty-five, but she looked years younger than Ivar, who was fifty-three.

Olina had been glad to escape upstairs then and leave her mother and Magdis to discuss the possible danger involved in giving orange juice to little Ivar Gossman, as the new-fangled doctor in Wing had prescribed. Magdis had not only blossomed during her ten years of marriage, but had, as Solveig rather coarsely put it, borne fruit on every limb, since she had

[332]

four children, two boys and two girls. Her husband, whom Karsten called "the potato baron," was one of the richest men in the Valley. Upon her able guiding of her eldest daughter's destiny, Magdali Wing might well congratulate herself. She had seen her son Karsten, too, safely married to Edna Cole four years ago, and although she was somewhat disturbed that as yet Edna had presented her with no grandchild, she had reason to be happy over Karsten's success as a lawyer in Minneapolis. It had been a near thing, that—Karsten's puppy love for Rose Shaleen!

These reflections went through Olina's mind as she sat combing her long, pale hair before the dresser mirror in the bedroom she still shared with Solveig. Poor Karsten! And poor Rose, who had come home from her work in Kate Shaleen's refuge for girls that summer of Karsten's marriage—and a few weeks later had suddenly become the wife of Gideon Gaffley, the young cashier in the bank at Wing. Olina had cried so hard over Rose and Karsten when she was eleven that she could not remember having really cried again until David Shaleen went away to study sculpture in Chicago in 1893, when she was sixteen and he was a couple of years older. It was his Aunt Kate who had made it possible for him to go, and he had come home for only a brief visit since then. That was two years ago, before he went to Paris on a scholarship he had won in Chicago.

But he had written her such wonderful letters about his life in Montmartre, a life that seemed to be a veritable prism of experience, with all the miraculous, pure colors heightened by the ever-lurking shadow of defeat and failure. That young artist friend of his who had been found strangled by his flowing tie in a freezing garret—but David would never be lost in one of those shadows! He was David Shaleen, and he would shortly return to his own country where he would be a suc-

[333]

cessful sculptor, and he would marry Olina Wing, no matter what her mother thought of the Shaleens!

Olina swung her hair over her shoulder and made a long braid of it. Solveig should be coming home soon. She was—as far as anyone knew—at Arne's house in town. Arne, too, had been a fulfillment of his mother's hopes. He was working in the bank with his Uncle Roald, and had recently been married to Cecily Brill, a society belle from St. Cloud. Young as he was—just twenty-five now—he saw his political career bright ahead of him, and in his ambitions his mother rejoiced. Under the astute guidance of George Gossman, he was being led along a path that one day, with a little luck, might easily bring him to Washington. Oh, yes, one way or another, and in spite of dangerous hazards, the Wing family would one day come to the place that Magdali had resolved should be theirs!

Olina picked up the bottle of perfume David had sent her from Paris last Christmas, and touched the stopper to the ruffled yoke of her muslin nightgown. Her mother had been amusedly tolerant of the gift—as she had been of David's letters, which she generously did not insist on reading. "In Paris," she had said, "among those artists, he will soon forget a simple little country girl like you, Olina. You might give the perfume to one of the hired girls—but if you'd rather keep it for a souvenir, I can see no harm in that. You must not put it on your clothes, of course. Ladies don't use perfume. A sachet envelope or a little toilet water—but French perfume, never!" Was it possible that her mother didn't know that she loved David?

She dropped some of the perfume down between her small, firm breasts, and watched the white skin spring out in goose flesh from the pleasant, sharp chill of it. The fragrance rose, exotic and tantalizing, Fleurs d'Amour—flowers of love,

[334]

David had written. What would he think to see her skin rise like this? she wondered, and was not ashamed. Husbands never looked upon the naked bodies of their wives—but sculptors had to see the bodies of women. It was like being a doctor, David had told her on his three-days' visit two years ago. And she must not be afraid, as his wife, to sit as a model for him. She would be Diana, or Daphne, or a nereid rising silvery from the sea.

The tall grandfather's clock in the hall downstairs struck ten. The Gossmans and their congressman friend were bidding good night to her father and mother. And where was Solveig, at ten o'clock? Olina stared at herself in the glass, saw her slim little mermaid-eyed face, and saw terror there again—as she had seen it so many times in the nine years since Solveig had got the news of Alec Fordyce's ship being lost at sea. Never had Solveig had that look—never! No, Solveig had just become queer and fixed and more aloof from the family than she had ever been before.

Olina thought back now upon that day in autumn, nine years ago, when Solveig had come in and thrown a letter down on the table in front of her parents and said, "You can read that—both of you. It's from a friend of Alec's, in San Francisco. Alec's boat is lost, but I know Alec is still alive —I know it!—and I'll go on waiting for him." She had turned to her mother then. "So don't try to boss me into marrying any rich dude in the Valley. I'll live here, but I'll do as I please until Alec comes for me!"

Magdali had gone very pale, but Olina had seen the grave quirk of a smile about her father's lips.

"Yes, Solveig," he had said carefully, "you will live here, of course. Where else, my girl? You will do as you please, too, I think. And maybe—yes, I believe it—Julian Fordyce's son *will* come back!"

[335]

To the twelve-year-old Olina, there had been something eerie, something unforgettable, in that moment. Her father's face had held a strange light. Her mother had shrunk back in a dry, defeated way, as if it was all beyond her understanding, beyond her power to comprehend. And afterward, no matter how odd Solveig's conduct became, her mother had always been ready with some offhand excuse for her daughter's doings.

When Solveig, the beauty of the family, had at once proceeded to make herself as unattractive as possible, pasting her curly hair back into a knob more severe than any Magdis had worn before her marriage, her mother had explained to neighbors that Solveig had become interested in missionary work. There was some truth in that, of course, for Solveig had been reading everything she could find about the South Seas and cannibals, and there were several years when she had thought seriously of joining some mission—just on the chance. . . .

But when she took to wearing overalls and raising her own small herd of Swiss cattle, Magdali was secretly relieved. It was scarcely a ladylike interest, but it was at least a healthful one that would take Solveig farther away from her unbelievable loyalty to a man who was nothing more now than a memory. Solveig took no part in Christmas gatherings or community celebrations of any kind. Men—important, moneyed men—saw her loveliness and heard her soft, insolent voice, and wanted to know more of her, but Solveig kept herself from them. And because she was the first of the Wing children born in the Valley, her mother held her in a kind of superstitious awe that was akin to fear, clinging meanwhile to the hope that Solveig would somehow free herself of her strange obsession.

"The child will grow out of this nonsense," Magdali would

[336]

say, her crochet hook stabbing at the linen thread, on evenings when Solveig had gone off riding somewhere on her horse.

"Perhaps, Magdali," Ivar would reply. "Let her grow."

And he would puff on his pipe in a way that had always sent through Olina's heart a glow of hope for Solveig and Alec.

Solveig and Alec, Karsten and Rose, herself and David! And still Magdali Wing refused to recognize the answer of three of her children to the call of vagabond blood. What Magdali hated and feared, she simply convinced herself did not exist. It was for that reason, no doubt, that she showed no apprehensive curiosity concerning David's letters.

Olina was about to take the packet of letters out of their locked drawer again when she heard a sound on the back stairs. That would be Solveig now, because the hired girls were in bed.

There was a light step in the hall, and Solveig came into the room. She was clad in her gray riding habit, full skirt and jacket, with a white stock at her throat, the only feminine costume she ever affected except such modest attire as she wore to church. She threw her leather gauntlets on the bed and laughed with a happy sob in her throat.

"You haven't been just to Arne's tonight, have you?" Olina whispered excitedly.

"Not much, kiddo!"

Solveig knelt beside Olina's chair, flung her arms about her and burst into a storm of tears.

"Suvvy, for goodness sake—"

Solveig straightened back, gasping. "Don't stop me! I've wanted to do this for years. Now—I'm doing it—when there's no need. He's alive, Lina, he's alive!"

"Suvvy, I can't bear it! Is Alec—"

"He's alive—in Vancouver, in British Columbia. There was a telegram for me at Jake's—addressed to me, in care of Jake, so even if Jake—wait!" She fumbled at her jacket pocket and drew out the crumpled sheet of paper. "Listen, Lina! 'Solveig,'" she read shakily, "'I'm alive and well rescued by tramp freighter arrived here today telegraph me Apperson Hotel Vancouver if already married wish you all the happiness in the world Alec.'" The words jangled over her rapid breath and she sat back and looked up at Olina. "I sent him a telegram and told him I was waiting for him. Oh, Lina, he—he ought to be able to come for me in a week, anyhow! How am I going to live for a whole week now!"

Olina laughed. "You'll live all right, Suvvy."

"But nobody must know, Lina—nobody but you and pa. Oh, I don't care—let them all know! I'm not afraid of anybody or anything now. Alec is coming for me—after nine years!" Tears sprang to her eyes again.

"I'm so glad for you, Suvvy," Olina said softly. "But perhaps we'd better not say anything about it—to anyone. Let's have a little time to think. You know what this will do to mamma."

"What do I care? She hates me—and she has hated the very thought of Alec all these years. She thought she'd marry me off the way she did Magdis and Karsten and Arne—and the way she'll do with you, if you aren't careful."

"I know," Olina said. "But she's proud—and she has something fine in her. If we are as strong as she is we'll get what we want out of life. It may not be what she would want for us, but it may be better. Remember, Suvvy, we didn't get all our good points from pa."

Solveig got up from the floor and flung her jacket aside. "All right, it doesn't matter now. I'd like to tell pa, though. He'll help us—and he likes Alec."

"Tell him tomorrow," Olina whispered, scarcely knowing what she said. Alec Fordyce had returned, and oh, yes, David Shaleen would return! Things were coming right for the Wings—even though Karsten's loss was forever. Or was it? Olina felt the premonitory dread about him that she had felt so often of late.

"Now," Solveig was saying, "we must go to bed, little Lina. And oh, what dreams I'll have tonight!"

XIV

AT THE breakfast table the next morning, Magdali announced that she had decided to go to the Twin Cities with Magdis for a few days. She had some business matters that required her attention, and certain household furniture to purchase, the mail order catalogue's description of which she did not trust. She and Magdis had talked it over last night. They would take the afternoon train and might be gone for a week, since the Lutheran Synod was meeting in St. Paul, and they had received a special invitation from Pastor Gavle to attend the conference.

After breakfast Solveig whispered to Olina, "We'll not tell pa until tonight—or maybe for a couple of days. He might think he ought to tell mamma, and that would simply raise the dickens!"

All that morning, Olina helped her mother prepare for the journey to the cities, and by her own nervously eager industry she was reminded of the times in her childhood when a thunderstorm threatened and she stayed close to Magdali, begging for socks to mend or potatoes to peel. But along with her guilty knowledge of Solveig's plans, she was now troubled by a strange pity for her mother. For it was likely that before Magdali returned from her trip, Solveig would be gone with Alec, to the ends of the earth perhaps, but certainly to no respectable haven where their children would be brought up in security.

Their children! That was a thought to turn Olina's imagination upside down. Alec's mother had been half Cree. His and Solveig's children might be throwbacks—Olina had picked up the word somewhere—and turn out to be entirely Indian! That would certainly be romantic, but what would Magdali think of it?

In the early afternoon Ivar hitched the team to the surrey and drove Magdali to Moorhead. Solveig went along, but Olina feigned a headache. It would be too much to see her mother bid good-by to Solveig, and to know that the farewell might mean forever, though Magdali would be unaware of it.

When they had gone, Olina tried to untrouble her mind by looking over three or four teaching offers she had received from school superintendents in the Valley since her graduation from Normal School. They were flattering offers, and between the lines she could read the hint that a daughter of the Wings would be very desirable as a teacher if she could see her way clear to accept the position. She laughed unsteadily as she recalled something that David had written in his last letter. ". . . and although I am proud that you have graduated with such good marks, and am sure you will be a 'good influence' on the young, I am hoping that your good influence will be on our own young. . . ."

Olina blushed, then took the letter from the drawer and pressed it to her lips. It was almost, though not quite, as delicious as David's farewell kiss to her on the river bank before he went to Paris two years ago.

"You won't forget, Lina," he had said then, "that you and I made an altar to the sun out of buffalo bones when we were kids. You have a lovely, small body—like a dryad's. I want to immortalize it in marble, Lina. You wouldn't be afraid to sit for me, would you?"

And she had leaned with sweet courage against his breast, and had whispered that she would not be afraid—of anything, anything!

[341]

It was almost dark when Solveig came back with her father from Moorhead. She immediately took Olina's hand and drew her upstairs, where she closed the door of their room and pulled a telegram from her pocket.

"Alec will be here before the end of the week," she breathed. "We'll be married right away and go to Canada. To —to the Yukon territory! He has enough to take us up there and he wants to go to the gold fields. Lina—imagine—putting all that into a telegram!"

"Have you told pa?" Olina asked, shaking with excitement.

"No. If he knew, mamma would blame him for not telling her. I'm not going to say a thing about it till Alec comes." Solveig hugged her sister with inarticulate joy. "Oh, I won't be able to sleep or eat or think about anything except—"

"You'll have plenty to do," Olina pointed out practically, although her heart was fluttering almost as if she herself were the central figure in this mad romance. "We'll have to sew you some underwear and night dresses. Would you dare to have a silk night dress, or d'you suppose Alec would think that was fast?"

Solveig laughed giddily and threw herself back on the bed, gazing with wide eyes at the ceiling. Since last night, it seemed to Olina, she had become so ripely beautiful that it made one ache to look at her. Yet she was twenty-seven years old—an old maid, by all usual reckoning.

"Fast? Do you think he's going to blush every time I take my hair down? Oh, darling, you don't know! A silk night dress! I'll have silk stockings some day—not that I wouldn't go barefoot to be with Alec. Still—it might be sort of cold up there in the Yukon. It must be near the North Pole, isn't it? Let's get your atlas out and see exactly where it is."

XV

IVAR listened to the dark drumming of the rain on the windows of the small sitting room where he sat in the lamplight, in his favorite rocking chair, trying to keep his attention on the rather boastful newspaper account of the peace terms the United States had offered Spain. He sighed. It had been a farcical war. But men had lost their lives in it none the less.

He felt old tonight, old and tired and of little use in the world—and he knew why. It was because of Solveig's vivid activity in the past few days, and Olina's mysterious tenseness whenever the telephone rang—Magdali had had the instrument installed a few months ago, and Ivar could never answer the two-long-two-short signal without a sense of being in the presence of the supernatural. Something was afoot, he knew, and his daughters had not confided in him. Oh, well, they had brought their secrets to him when he was able to help them in their little troubles. They were grown now. They could get along without his help. But all this frantic sewing, their quick silences—what could it mean? He laid his paper aside and reached for his pipe on the table. For the first time in years he felt a loneliness for Magdali, not as she was now, but as she had been when they were both young. Now even she had no need of him. She least of all, he sometimes felt. Magdali was a little principality all by herself here in what he used to call "my Valley."

A sound of carriage wheels smote through the rain on the gravel driveway at the side of the house. Ivar got to his feet, listening. Then, from Solveig's and Olina's room upstairs came a great hurrying, a swift rush of voices that sounded over-wrought as the two girls flew down the stairs into the hall and threw open the front door.

Could it be David Shaleen—or even Alec Fordyce? Ivar wondered. It might be either, though how it could be Alec —he smiled gloomily to himself. All these years he had been a silent conspirator with Solveig. He had talked with Olina about David too, guarding her secret as if it were something beyond price. And now he, the willing conspirator, was not being admitted into the conspiracy! Well, what had he been able to do, after all, for his son Karsten, married now to that selfish flibbertigibbet, Edna Cole? Was it any wonder his daughters had no faith in him?

Minutes passed, with remote sounds from the front parlor. Then Ivar heaved his shoulders as against a weight and strode into the hall, where there was a renewed commotion of young and rapturous voices.

"Pa!"

Solveig sped to him, threw her arms about his neck, and mixed unintelligible words with laughing and crying, while over her head he stared into the dark, thin, and gravely smiling face of Alec Fordyce. His first thought was that the boy looked older. Then he noticed that he was dressed in well-made, quietly fashioned clothes.

Alec came forward at once, his hand extended. Ivar clasped it without a word, for speech had suddenly left him.

"It's good to see you again, sir," Alec said with a strange formality. "I thought Solveig would have told you, but—"

"I knew he was coming, pa," Solveig broke in, her voice confused with willfulness and regret. "I wanted to tell you, but I didn't want to worry you—and I didn't want mamma to know before Alec got here. Oh, surely you know why I didn't say anything about it, don't you? We're going to be married right away, pa!"

Ivar nodded with a dry smile and patted Solveig's hand where it lay on his arm. Then his eyes sharpened critically toward Alec Fordyce.

"You're like your father—Julian," he said. The words came haltingly, but there was warm approval in them.

"Thank you, sir," Alec replied, his white teeth flashing in a smile.

"Well," said Ivar, feeling somehow embarrassed, "why do we all stand here? Come in and sit down, Alec. You'll have a story to tell, I expect."

"But, pa!" Olina spoke up hurriedly for the first time. "They want to be married tonight—in Moorhead."

"Tonight?" A foreboding thought of Magdali struck sharply across Ivar's mind.

"We have the license," Solveig said. "We want you and Lina to come with us, then Alec can tell us all about it at the wedding supper. We're going to stay in Moorhead tonight and take the train in the morning—for Canada."

Ivar laid a hand heavily upon the stairway newel post. "Yes —it is better so, perhaps," he said after a little thought. "You have waited a long time—a long time. It is too bad your mother—"

There were tears in Solveig's eyes as she came to him again and put her arms about him. "It can't be any other way, pa," she said. "I know she'll never forgive me, but I can't help that. She wouldn't have forgiven me anyhow, even if I had waited. I don't want to leave you like this, but after I go you'll still have Olina." She turned quickly to her sister. "Tell pa *your* news, Lina."

The blood sprang to Olina's cheeks. "I had a letter from David today," she confessed. "He has landed in New York and is coming west. He's going to spend a day with his Aunt

[345]

Kate on the way, and then he's coming home."

"You mustn't let mamma stop her from seeing David," Solveig said. "She has as much right to be happy as I have."

A sense of reckless detachment possessed Ivar all at once. Why should Magdali be permitted to interfere with the romance of little Olina, his youngest born, the heart of his heart, whom Magdali had resented for years because she must forever be the youngest? Solveig's naming of Kate Shaleen, too, had turned back sharply numbered pages in Ivar's memory.

"David will be welcome in my house as long as I am here," he declared.

It was a speech that should not have been rewarded by a burst of tears from Olina, who turned and fled up the stairs. Solveig, following her, looked back over her shoulder.

"Get ready, pa," she said. "I'm all packed. We'll be down in a minute."

XVI

It was late August, and the autumn scent of loneliness already hovered over the river woods where Olina and David Shaleen had been sitting for the past half-hour while the sun reddened down deep in the west.

"So that's the way it is, small Olina," David said with stern force as he tucked her close against his stocky shoulder. "I've waited around here a whole week longer than I intended to. Clark's studio in New York won't be vacant forever, and I've got to get back there and grab it before somebody else moves in. Doctor Miller tells me your mother has recuperated very well. You say she's feeling fine. Let's go right now and tell her we're going to be married."

His eyes, black brown like his father Steve's, lighted his blunt-featured, ruddy face with impatience. Even his dark shock of hair seemed to bristle vehemently, and a delicious weakness overcame Olina as he crushed her against him and kissed her.

"See?" he laughed triumphantly. "You're mere putty in my hands, darling, and you don't give a damn for what your mother thinks!"

"Oh, David," Olina struggled to say, "it's only two weeks since she had that—that stroke—"

"There's something I've got to tell you," David said stubbornly. "Your mother didn't have a stroke."

"But David—"

"Just a minute. She's your mother and all that, but I can't forget what she did to Karsten and Rose. I had an idea from the very beginning that she threw a first-class fit when she heard about Solveig sneaking out on her. You told me yourself that she went to the kitchen and literally washed her hands of Solveig after she read her good-by note. She had time for that dramatic little stunt before you had to call the doctor for her. She put on a show for your father's benefit, because he had aided and abetted Solveig—"

"But Doctor Miller—"

"I went to see Doc Miller," David said. "He told me it wasn't a real stroke. Does that convince you? Go and ask him yourself."

"Oh, no, David. I can't believe it! I was there when it happened. She was really sick—with a fever—and her pulse was so fast I could hardly count it, that first night. Pa and I were afraid she'd die before—"

"All right, sweetheart. Have it your way. You know what you're doing, of course. I've got to leave here in a week and get to work. I can't go on loafing like this. Those two commissions I told you about are haunting my dreams. They'll make fine studies—the rich old lady and her grandchild—and I'll make enough money out of them for you and me to live on for a whole year. Think of that! In a year I can finish off a half dozen themes I've had in mind—with you to work for."

"Themes," Olina repeated, her voice rapt.

"Themes in marble," David said with simple assurance. "That's how I think of them." He took her slim hands into his own that were so hard and square and impatiently alive. "The point is, my little Olina, I've got to get back and you've got to come with me. Shall we go up to the house together—now—and tell your mother, and get that part of it over with? Or shall we speak to your father first? Whatever you say, *cherie!*"

She looked at David's unruly mouth, his dark, gypsy glow

[348]

ing eyes, and thought—*Themes in marble!* "No," she said suddenly, and kissed him, then flashed to her feet. "You wait here. I'll go and tell mother. Pa knows about us now, and I won't have him worry any more about us kids. You sit here till I come back." Then she dropped again to her knees, an extraordinarily disembodied feeling overcoming her, as if she had already left him and this was only her spirit clinging to him. "David!" she cried out. "I love you! Hold me a minute."

"Lina!" he muttered in alarm, his arms tight about her. "You don't have to go back to the house at all, you know, if you don't want to. Come away with me now—just the way you are—"

But with pale determination she released herself, stood for an instant before him, and said, "Wait here!" then sped off through the woods to the clearing.

Magdali sat in the rocking chair in her bedroom, wearing an embroidered blue satin dressing sacque which Magdis had brought her when she became ill two weeks ago. A patchwork quilt lay over her knees, a hassock beneath her wool-slippered feet. The lamp was lighted on the table beside her, the shades drawn against the sunset. She laid aside the newspaper she had been reading when Olina entered the room, and smiled as she removed her glasses.

"Well, dear, you've been gone a long time. Aren't you just about ready for supper?"

"I've been down to the river," Olina said, brightening her voice as she took a chair near the table. "How do you feel, mamma?"

"I feel ashamed of myself!" Magdali laughed. "I should have gone down to supper *last* night, but Gudrun keeps on pampering me with tea and things on trays. First thing you know, I'll get to like it. I think I'll go down tonight and eat with you. I'll be up and about tomorrow. Have you seen your father?"

"Pa is still out at the barn. I saw him just now, when I was coming in. Mamma—" Olina took a hard swallow and dwelt for an encouraging moment on the healthy glow of her mother's face. "I didn't tell you before, because I was afraid of upsetting you. But—David has been home for nearly two weeks." A clammy moisture broke out in her palms as she saw the hard lines set about her mother's mouth.

"Well, dear," Magdali said softly, "there's nothing upsetting about that, surely."

"Oh—you know what I'm going to say!" Olina cried, clutching at her throat. "I can see you're already set against it."

"Olina!" Magdali leaned forward, plucking at the quilt on her knees. "What are you trying to tell me?"

"Mamma, I love David. I've loved him all my life. I want to marry him and go with him to New York. He has to go back to work right away—this week. He wanted to come and talk to you himself—with me—but I told him I'd come alone, because you must know, mamma, how it is and—" Her voice was a rushing jumble that she herself seemed to hear as an echo when it stopped abruptly.

For at that moment, she sprang from her place to catch her mother as she collapsed over the arm of her chair, her eyes closed, her face like chalk with veinings of red.

The doctor had come and gone, and Ivar said in the hall downstairs, "You'd better go up to your mother now, Olina. She's asking for you." His arms were crossed before him, and he did not look at Olina as he spoke.

Her feet, so light and narrow, were like lead as she climbed the stairs. Would David, she wondered distantly, be waiting for her still in the river woods? It was over an hour since she had left him.

Magdali was in her bed again, a curved rubber bag filled with ice at the back of her neck. Her eyes were open and glassily bright.

"Mamma," Olina whispered, seating herself on the edge of the bed, "I didn't mean to do this to you! I thought you were well again—"

"This is not the first time," Magdali smiled vaguely. "When you were born, you almost—but that wasn't your fault, either. Now—it is you who must live, Olina. You are young and I—" Tears began streaming down her cheeks, and Olina sat rigid in terror. "I have done my best for my children," Magdali went on, her voice trembling. "I can do no more now. I have trusted you, Olina. I would not believe you would throw your life away now—after all that has been done for you—marrying a man who has been living in Paris—spending his days among naked models—drinking and becoming godless in that city of iniquity. I had a brother once—your Uncle Jorgen, Olina—who left Norway and went to Paris and was never heard of again. We never spoke of him. And now—you—my little girl—my Olina—the only one left to me—" The voice ceased, and Olina clutched her mother's hand with frantic contrition and began rubbing the wrist where the pulse was racing again.

"Mamma!" she whispered desperately.

"It will kill me, Olina!"

"No, no, mamma. I—I won't go. I won't leave you. I'll stay here—with you!"

A fluttering smile touched Magdali's lips, her eyes half opened, and then she sighed wearily.

[351]

"There will be another—a better man for you, Olina," she murmured, and drew her hand away. "Go now—and take care of your father. I'll try to sleep a little."

Olina stumbled blindly through the dark woods, calling David's name. No watery ember of sunset was left on the river, and she could not lift her head to see the new stars. It seemed to her that the river itself was gone—and David with it.

But he was there, and he caught her in his strong, angrily loving arms. "Lina! I thought you'd never—" He touched her face with his finger tips. "You're crying! What happened?"

"I shouldn't have come back, David! I should have left you then—and just remembered how sweet—"

"Be still a moment!" David ordered, his voice unsteady. "You're talking wild. Sit down and tell me what happened."

"I can't—I don't dare!" She pressed away from him, her hands to her wet cheeks, but he caught her again and urged her gently down beside him on the ground. Dimly she saw his face in the tree-broken starlight, and through her broken sentences she let him know what had occurred in her mother's bedroom.

"So you see, David," she added with infinite effort, "it will be at least a year before we can think of being together. When she has really got over thinking about Solveig—"

"What I see," David Shaleen flung out violently, "is that she has done it again. Your mother, Olina, is a—a female vampire—a ruthless—"

"David!" Olina cried in horror.

"Do you know what your mother can do to you in a year? And teaching? I want you the way you are now—not the way you'll be after another year away from me!

You've got to come with me now—tonight—not a year from now."

Olina stiffened against the tremor that passed through her. "It would kill mamma!" she said. "I know it would. I almost caused her death once, and I can't—"

"*Her* death!" David snorted. "She'll live forever—and trample on everybody forever! She'll kill *you!*"

Olina drew herself close to him in the darkness. "We can wait—just one more year."

"I won't wait. I've dreamed about that nymph's body of yours till I can't stand it. I love you—and I want you. I've got to have you!"

"Oh, David, David! I love you so!" She pressed her lips to his ear and whispered, "If you want me, David, you can have me—*now*—all of me! I'm not afraid."

He moved away from her slowly and got to his feet without speaking. For a long time he strode up and down, twigs and dried grasses crackling under his feet. Finally he swung about, seized Olina's hands and lifted her from the ground.

"There's something you may not understand," he said hoarsely. "But I'm going to tell you just the same. It would have been easy to take you just now—how easy, my God, you'll never know! I have had women I didn't want—and thought nothing of it afterward. They meant less than nothing to me—except, perhaps, for one insane moment while I was with them. When they left me, I was ashamed. I wouldn't do that to you—nor to *myself*. Your mother has always thought the Shaleens were not fit to walk on. Whether she's right or wrong doesn't matter, but we've still got something left that's clean and decent—and we're going to keep it, by God! Now, go home and tell her that, if you like. Anyhow— go home!"

Olina's teeth almost bit through her under lip. She was

[353]

aware of stretching up on her toes to her full height there in the darkness.

"I'll go."

It was somebody else, not herself, who was running almost sightless through the timber and into the clearing again, with her name ringing after her, just once, from David Shaleen's lips. It was somebody else. . . .

And somebody else, too, who rode in the buggy to Wing the next day and bought medicine for her mother, and met Ella Sondstrom on the street.

"Oh, I went to the barn dance last night with David Shaleen!" Ella exclaimed. "And how *he* has changed since he went away! The way he talked!" Ella was blushing furiously now. "Though you can't tell with *him*, of course, how much he means by it!"

"I'm sure he meant plenty," Olina said coolly. "I'm sorry, Ella, but I have to hurry home with this medicine for mother."

"Oh, is she bad again?" Ella asked anxiously, but Olina was already down the street.

And there she met David himself coming out of Gimp Featherstone's soda parlor. Her eyes widened blankly up at him, through him, and far, far away.

"Lina!" He caught her arm in a hurtful grip.

She made her smile dazzling. "Ella has just told me you were at the dance with her last night."

David laughed. "Ella's a big, handsome girl. With no clothes on, she'd look like a Juno. She didn't tell you I kissed her?"

"You couldn't wait a year for a little nymph," Olina said, "so you had to kiss a Juno!"

He leaned toward her, his face twisting in miserable doubt. "Listen, Olina—you know darn well I didn't kiss her! How could I—"

"Let go of my arm, please."

He dropped his hand, and Olina, her trembling fingers tight about her mother's medicine, walked straight and white down the sunlit street of the town of Wing.

On the day before the opening of Olina's school, in September, she walked through the old south pasture with Sir Galahad, who was a son of long-gone Meg. His name was "Sir" for short. Even he was getting along in years now, and spent most of his time about the house and barn. Occasionally he took a walk in the fields with Ivar if the weather was fine, or dug into a gopher hole with a melancholy backward look now and then in mute admission that his old time frenzy was no more.

Olina had not been at the river woods since David left— the day after she had seen him in Wing. She would probably never go there again, she thought desolately. And what directed her footsteps to the small pasture which was to be plowed up for sugar beets next year, she did not know. Perhaps—yes, perhaps to say good-by to it, too! For it was here that she and David had gathered buffalo bones and built an altar to the sun. . .

She hesitated as she saw a lone figure cutting across the pasture from the south. It was Loren Shaleen, carrying an implement of some kind over his shoulder. Oh, yes, he had come and borrowed a posthole auger from her father a few nights ago. She remembered how shy he had been in her presence, especially when he had spoken lamely of a letter he had had from David, in New York. David was at work again, and sent his regards to "everybody."

Loren's hair was a lighter brown than David's, his eyes bluish like his sister Maude's. He was tall and thin, a little stooped already from hard work. But he had a warm, very young smile, and as he paused to greet her Olina felt her throat tighten sorely. David's brother—who had always been left out of their games when they were children!

"Out for a walk, Olina?" he said cheerfully.

"I felt kind of shut up in the house," Olina said.

"It's a nice day for it. I'm just taking this auger back to your dad. Got to get a new one myself one o' these days. You're going to leave us, I hear."

"Tomorrow, Loren."

"Be away till Christmas, I expect."

"Except for a few days at Thanksgiving."

"Olina." Loren reddened as he leaned awkwardly forward on the auger. "You won't mind if I talk to you a little?"

His voice had a startling urgency.

"Why, no, Loren, of course not. But if it's about David—"

"It's not about David," he blurted out. "He's my brother and I'm proud of him—but he's an awful damn fool, or he'd never have gone away without you!" His eyes were wistful with an intolerable, blue anxiety as they met hers. "Or maybe I'm the fool. I always stepped aside whenever he showed up. I wasn't smart, like him. But you must have known, all the time, that I cared just as much for you as Dave ever did. Maybe more, because he can't think about anything except turning stone into something God never intended it to be. I would never have talked to you like this if he hadn't gone off the way he did. But he told me all about it, and I'm free to talk now as I want to. Olina—you and I—we're here, on the land. It's our place, this. Do you think—I mean to say—would it be hard for you to think about me a little, Olina? Not just now, of course, but later on, when—"

"Oh, Loren!" Olina began brokenly. "You've always been so good—so kind. I can't think of anything now. I'm going away to teach—and forget everything. I—"

[356]

Her eyes, filling, moved from him, and then she saw what the old collie, Sir Galahad, was about. The dog had burrowed deep into a gopher hole and had come up with a bleached bone. The sun struck dully upon it where it lay on the up-flung earth. Olina stared unbelievingly and Loren's eyes followed her gaze.

She turned with trembling lips and looked at him. "No, Loren," she said softly. "Don't ever think about me again, that way. Whenever I see you, I'll think of David. It will always be so. And I must forget him. Please try to understand, Loren—there's nobody in the world better than you."

Olina called Sir Galahad and began walking without direction through the pasture, away from Loren Shaleen.

XVII

KARSTEN WING, now in his thirty-sixth year, sat alone in the library of the home that had been his since he and his wife Edna moved to Minneapolis, almost eight years ago. On the large table before him lay the journal in which he had for the past three or four years entered items that seemed important from time to time. Tonight he was making his final entry.

He had not decided yet what form the entry would take. So far he had written nothing of a personal nature in those revealing pages. With a painstaking accuracy he had set down only the story of a corrupt civic regime that had become a national scandal and had only recently been broken by a supreme court of enquiry. But a man cannot write such a record and keep himself wholly out of it, particularly when he has had a part in the events he is recording. He had never been proud of his alliance with the city's "Boodle Mayor." There were times when he had been ashamed of it. But he had been ambitious, and he had come to his present unenviable position by easy stages in a very simple process.

He could see those stages clearly now. He had never been able to forget what William Cole had done for him during the short time they had worked together. Under the guidance of that shrewd old attorney, Karsten Wing had developed more legalistic agility than he could have achieved in ten years of practice by himself. He had thought to repay at least a part of his debt of gratitude by marrying the old man's shallow, vain, and flirtatious daughter just a few months before her father's death. That it was a loveless marriage had not seemed important at the time. He had given all his love to Rose Shaleen. He had come to feel that a man must eventually marry some woman as anchorage, even though he had lost the one he wanted. Edna was pretty and physically attractive, and William Cole had made no secret of his wishes.

But a debt, even a debt of gratitude, may not be so easily discharged. When, upon the death of her father, Edna came into a modest fortune, Karsten began to feel the insidious toils draw more tightly about him. He might have torn himself free in that first month following William Cole's death, he might have turned his back upon the false beginnings of his career and struck out afresh with what young courage he possessed. But his mother had thwarted him in that. With a gentleness and an understanding that left him helpless to oppose her, she had shown him where lay the path of duty and had sent him forth resolved to follow it to the end. With Magdali's blessing, then, he had left the little town of Wing. Edna had never cared for "the country" anyhow. The greater opportunities were in the city—where all her friends were.

Success had come with amazing swiftness. It had come to many another who was not loath to mortgage some part of his eternal soul to the men who held the keys to the city's treasury. Edna's demands had increased with the years—sables, imported evening frocks, jewels, a brougham with matched blacks and a coachman in livery, and finally a hazardous contraption that was popularly known as a horseless carriage, which Edna drove at the dizzy speed of twenty miles an hour, complete with goggles and gauntlets, veil and duster, and looking like a woman from Mars! It had come as no surprise to him when, the end of her extravagant living in sight, she had left him and begun action for divorce. He could have found grounds for such action himself if he had wished, but he had placed no barrier in her way. That chapter of his life was closed, and he could feel nothing but relief.

He looked at the book lying open on his table, the page on the left only partly filled with the latest paragraph he had written there more than a week before, the opposite page blank, awaiting his final scrawl. Within those pages was evidence of political malfeasance—from the activities of the lowest madam of the dives to those of the highest administrative official. There was evidence of flagrant cases he himself had argued in court to a satisfactory dismissal of charges—and for fees that had more than compensated him for the services he had rendered. Why had he kept a record of such things? Ah, the perverse self-grueling! Far better, perhaps, if he had never set down a word of it. And yet, now that it was done, he knew he would never destroy what he had written—even though it condemned him equally with all the other malefactors he had named. For the first time in his life he had brought to an end something he had begun. The record was complete. He had only to write *finis* and close the covers.

That other story—the record of the heart—would never know any such completeness. Its parts would never be blended into any pattern. His love for his father, the awe with which his mother had always inspired him, his envy of Solveig, his devotion to Olina, and his disdain for Magdis and Arne that equaled though it did not surpass the contempt he felt for himself—these were threads that would remain forever raveled, frayed at the ends, loose and dangling on a crippled loom. What had happened to them all? Those who were young—then! Solveig, the proud, the insolent—roaming the northern wilds with her adventure-loving husband—already on her way back now, and planning to buy a hotel in New York! Magdis, clinging to her mother's skirts, fainting away at her confirmation, hiding her ankles demurely when she set her foot atop a croquet ball—how had her potato potentate husband managed to get her to bed with him at all? Or did even she sometimes waken in the night, troubled with a vague regret? Arne, kissing the hired girls in the barn, his face looking for all the world like one of his mother's gold-banded dinner plates the last time Karsten had seen him—selling real estate now and seeing himself mayor of Wing one day, or even congressman if George Gossman lived long enough! And little Olina, cowering at the approach of thunder, breaking her young heart over Dave Shaleen—and marrying Henry Cruse at last, a rich railroad man twice her age, after Dave had wed the sturdy Ella Sondstrom! Poor little Olina! She had come close to dying from pneumonia four years ago and had never been strong since then, but she was expecting to present her solicitous husband with a son and heir before the year was ended. Even Rose Shaleen, sunlight and shadow, laughter and tears, her very name a singing in the heart—married now to that limp-handed creature, Gideon Gaffley, who had become vice-president of Roald Bratland's bank! What a mad fabric, as if the weaver had grown weary of drawing the threads together only to see them slip from his none too agile fingers!

If time had only stood still back there somewhere—with the fur-laden carts coming down out of the North—with the steamboats laboring against the yellow surge of the river in flood—with the snowy trail leading to the little log schoolhouse that had become a sanctuary because of the woman who waited there in patience—with golden fields and busy hands and the smell of ripe strawberries in hot summer grass! If somewhere they could have paused in their headlong rush of living and given thought to where they were going—

Suddenly Karsten Wing felt a thousand years old. Loneliness such as he had never known in all his life before possessed him. He wanted his father—the father who had drawn him into his arms on a summer evening when the ox-carts came laden to the ford, who had borne him aloft on his shoulders through the night, at the end of their long journey on the river, who had given him a dole of his precious wheat to plant in ground he could call his own, who had risked his own life in a blinding winter storm to bring him safely home—the father whose very nearness had warmed him, whose voice had calmed him when he was afraid, whose spirit had embraced him when they stood together in the silence and listened to the flight of wild fowl overhead.

There were tears in Karsten's eyes as he closed the journal and thrust it aside. From a drawer he took a sheet of clean white paper and spread it on the table before him. He dipped his pen and began to write slowly, thoughtfully:

> *Laurel Hill,*
> *Minneapolis,*
> *June 4, 1902.*

DEAR FATHER,

There have been many times in my life when I have felt the need of talking with you, but never before has that need been so great as it is at this very moment. What I have to say will, I know, prove painful to you. It is even more painful to me to write it. But there are things that must be told, and you are the one friend I have in all the world to whom I feel I can tell them without veiling the truth or making excuses.

I have been sitting here at my library table all evening—alone. For eight years, as you must have known, I have been alone in this house I have called "home." Tonight I am alone in *fact*. Edna has left me and has already started suit for divorce. I mention that in passing. I shall say more about it later. I feel no loss, no bitterness, no regret—only a blessed relief.

It is of something else I would write you tonight. Mother has often spoken with pride of my success since I came here to the city. I have always wondered whether you did not see a little deeper than she—understand a little more clearly what has been going on during all the years since I left you. Did you know that it is possible for a man in his mid-thirties to have come to the end of his career, with nothing but wreckage to show for his efforts? I am not referring now to Edna. I am thinking rather of the dream that must have been yours the day you held my hand and helped me take my first proud steps across the floor of Uncle Karsten's kitchen in Wisconsin. I have no recollection of that, of course. But I do remember that day in August when you led me down from the stage depot and gave me my first sight of the river. The years have dimmed the memory of it, but it is there. What were your thoughts that day? Did they outrun the sluggish current to the river's end?

Beside me, as I write, lies the journal in which I have recorded the details of some of the—

The jangling of his telephone startled him. With his hand on the receiver, he paused while his heart beat steadied a little before he answered the call. The voice that finally reached him there in the dead stillness of the library was the voice of Ivar Wing.

"That is you, Karsten?"

"Yes, father. I was just—"

"I have bad news for you, my son. Can you hear me?"

"Yes, yes, father! What is it?"

"Yesterday we took Olina to the hospital. And tonight—" The voice faltered and broke.

"Olina is dead?" Karsten said. It was scarcely a question. He *knew*.

"She was not strong. The baby came too soon—and Olina just went to sleep when Doctor Miller gave her something for the pain. Our little Olina is gone."

For a moment Karsten clung to the telephone, unable to speak. At last he said, "You would like me to come home?"

"Ya, Karsten—if you are not too busy—if you can come home now, we would like that. We would feel a little better."

"I'll leave on the morning train," Karsten promised. "Can you meet me at Moorhead?"

"I'll be there to meet you," his father said.

Karsten would have said something more, but the connection was broken abruptly. He set the receiver gently back in its place and turned away. Little Lina! He closed his eyes and saw her—running breathless toward him across a sun-steeped field, bringing him a pail of buttermilk fresh from the churn.

XVIII

THEY had come together out of the house, Ivar and his son, that first night after Karsten's arrival from the city. All afternoon, Karsten had marveled at his mother's brave spirit, her calm strength under the cruel blow that had been dealt her by Olina's untimely death.

"God knows best," she had said when he came into the living room and put his arms about her. She had seen the tears in his eyes and had drawn him close to her. "Whom the Lord loveth he chasteneth, Karsten."

To her questions concerning his work in the city he had given only evasive answers. He had already told his father as much as he had time for on their drive home from the railway station. But when supper was over, all the arrangements for Olina's funeral having been completed, Magdali had wanted to know why Karsten had not brought Edna home with him.

"I should think she would want to be with you. She knows Olina was your favorite sister."

Karsten had told her then. There was no evading the truth any longer. And his mother had listened, almost in complete silence, while he spoke of Edna and of his own utter failure in a career that had begun with such promise. When he was through, Magdali had got up from her chair and gone majestically off to her room and closed the door.

They had come together out of the house then, Karsten and his father, and had sat on the garden seat in the shadows at the farthest end of the lawn. They were silent for a long time, aware only of the light in the window of Magdali's room.

"It has been too much for her, I'm afraid," Ivar whispered at last.

"I suppose so," Karsten admitted desperately, "but what was I to do? If I had waited until after—"

"Yes, yes, I know," Ivar sighed. "She would have blamed you for that. It is hard to know what to do sometimes."

Karsten lit a cigarette and tossed the burning match away. It fell upon the neatly trimmed lawn where it lay for an instant, a bright pool of green light in the dewy grass, before the tiny flame died.

"The trouble is," he said impatiently, "that we have always protected mother. All of us—except Solveig, perhaps. It's time she was told the truth—about herself and about what she has done to the rest of us."

"The time is past for that, my son," Ivar said. "She isn't a young woman now. What you say may be true enough. Your mother was too much for us all. She was always the strong one. But we must not forget—we had to have strong ones here when she came to the valley."

"I often think of that too," Karsten said. "But we needed something besides strength. If Olina had married Dave Shaleen—or if I had married Rose—"

He paused as though the girl's name alone had been too much for him to utter, and Ivar cast him a sharp, uneasy glance.

"You still think of Rose. I have hoped you might have forgotten, perhaps. You told me so little, that time your mother and I visited you and Edna in the city."

"I couldn't talk about it—even to you, father."

Ivar laid his hand on his son's shoulder. "I can understand that, Karsten."

"If she had only been willing to see me—if she had let me

[366]

speak to her again!" Karsten went on. "I tried to see her when I went back to school again that fall, but it was Miss Kate who met me and talked to me. She was all sympathy, of course, but—" He broke off with a harshly caught laugh. "But it might as well have been sympathy for somebody who was dead. She told me Rose was ill, and I must forget her—as Rose must forget me. She did her best to show me that we would never be happy, with mother's opposition. She seemed to know more about it than I did, and I went away without seeing Rose. I wrote her, but my letters came back—unopened."

Karsten dropped his half-smoked cigarette and ground it under his heel.

"I didn't see her until that summer after Edna and I were married. Rose was home on a visit, you remember. Edna had met her at some woman's affair in town. I don't think she ever suspected there had been anything between Rose and me. But she found Rose fascinating—and she was always a great hand at collecting 'fascinating' people. Anyhow, she invited Rose to the boating party she was giving that week, and Rose came —more out of pride than anything else, I suppose. I'll never forget how tall and cool she looked in her blue and white boating costume, and her hair done in the latest curly bang. She shook hands with me and smiled as if we were meeting for the first time, and wished me happiness in my marriage."

Karsten fumbled in his pocket for another cigarette.

"Then when the rowboats and canoes began pushing away from the pier," he continued, "I saw that Rose was in a canoe with Gid Gaffley, and I had a wild impulse to jump in and pull her out of it. And that was only a month after my marriage to Edna! He was cashier in Roald's bank then. I always thought him a weak sister, but I must have been mistaken, because he has done all right for himself since he married Rose—that same summer. If she had married some healthy, hard-working

[367]

farmer, but Gid Gaffley—with that limp, sandy hair of his, and eyes that always reminded me of fish scales—I couldn't understand it! I tell you I went through hell for a while, before I left and started a new life in the city. A new life!"

His voice had been a monotone until it ended in that one explosive phrase, and Ivar patted his arm in awkward, diffident warning, and nodded toward the lighted window. Karsten's lips twisted sardonically as he lighted his cigarette.

"Funny they haven't got themselves a flock of kids by now, isn't it?" he said indifferently.

"The sap doesn't run very strong in Gideon's veins," Ivar replied drily.

"I don't think I ever told you that Edna refused to have a child," Karsten said.

"No. I have wondered, of course. Your mother has talked about it too."

Karsten's laugh was bitter. "She was afraid it might spoil her beautiful figure. Besides, she had her precious Punkins to look after."

"Punkins? Oh, you mean—"

"Yes, that damned dog of hers! I didn't think I'd ever tell anybody about that," Karsten confessed. "But maybe you'll get a laugh out of it, and God knows it's time we got a laugh out of something! I wouldn't have believed I could ever hate anything the way I hated that dog. He slept in her bed—he ate at the table with her—he went everywhere she went. She used to give him birthday parties—and Christmas parties—with presents and everything. I got to the place where I couldn't think of anything except how I could poison the little brute without her knowing how it happened. When he died about three months ago, at the ripe age of eighteen, Edna just about lost her mind—and I went into my library and literally thanked God! But that wasn't the end of it. She actually had the damned

[368]

thing stuffed and mounted, and set it on the floor beside the bed, where she could talk to it last thing at night and first thing in the morning. I came home one evening about three weeks ago, after a hard day in court, and found her spraying it with something to protect it from moths. I guess I must have lost my head. I picked the thing up and tore it limb from limb, while Edna stood there screaming at the top of her lungs. Then I threw it out of the window and went out for a long walk to cool off. When I came back, Edna had the doctor looking after her. The next day she packed her bags and left the house—with what she could find of her poor Punkins. She has been living with her cousin Jane ever since."

Ivar had been chuckling to himself, rocking back and forth in the way he had been doing of late when anything amused him. Now he became serious again. "But what do you think of doing, Karsten? Will you go back to the city again and start over?"

"No—I can't go back. I'll have to go and settle up my affairs, of course. That'll take a few days. After that—I don't know."

"You wouldn't think of coming here—to Wing?"

"I'd rather get away somewhere where nobody knows a thing about me. I feel—I feel dirty, after all that business I did for the crooks who hired me to clear them in the courts. I'll tell you more about that when we have a chance to go over it. But I've got a little money. Perhaps I'll go west somewhere. The war with Spain has opened up the Philippines—there ought to be a spot for a young lawyer out there. I have a friend in Washington, Joe Lury, who might be able to do something for me in that direction. I don't know."

"I wish you could stay with us—open an office in Wing, perhaps, so we'd be together more."

"I'd rather not think of anything for a while," Karsten said.

"Ya—well, stay with us here on the farm till you can think

of something," Ivar said. "It will do you good. And Solveig will be coming soon."

"I'm not going to skip out overnight," Karsten assured him. "It'll be great to see Suvvy again."

The light in Magdali's window went out as he spoke. Ivar got up from the bench and stretched his long arms above his head.

"We'd better go in," he suggested. "Tomorrow will be a hard day for all of us."

XIX

Two days later, Karsten and Ivar stood on the station platform at Wing and waited for the train coming in from the north. It was a fine, gentle afternoon. The chestnut team, in their tasseled fly-nets, and the fringe-topped surrey were standing in the shade of the box elders below the platform.

"I think you'd better tell Solveig about—about Olina," Ivar said haltingly. "I think I must be getting old."

Karsten took his father's arm and looked away along the shining rails. "It was better for Olina to go the way she did than be an invalid for the rest of her life. But I'll break the news to Solveig." He looked back toward the town. "What's keeping Arne? The train is due now."

He wasn't thinking so much of Arne just then—nor of Magdis, who had decided to stay home with her mother rather than come to the station to meet Solveig. He was remembering how his mother had stood frozen in her black taffeta yesterday after Solveig's telegram was read to them over the telephone.

"I have no daughter by the name of Solveig Fordyce," Magdali had declared, frigidly calm.

Ivar had looked at her, his eyes still red from weeping beside Olina's grave only a few hours before. "I have a daughter by that name, Magdali. And I have a son-in-law by the name of Alec Fordyce. I will get them the best room I can find in the hotel at Wing. They will stay there as long as they like."

He had walked out of the house then, to the big barn, and Magdali had turned upon Karsten with a blanched chill over the fine red veins in her cheeks.

[371]

"It isn't enough that my eldest son is a failure in his marriage and his career, and that my youngest child dies before she can become a happy mother! A daughter who has been a disgrace to me and to our name must return—brazenly—at the same time, bringing with her the money she has made in God knows what corruption and vice!"

"I have never thought of gold mining as a vice," Karsten observed quietly, "though it may be, for all I know."

"What about the gambling place they had in Dawson City?" Magdali reminded him. "But that has nothing to do with me. She ceased to be my daughter when she turned her back upon me and left the home I had made for her. And now your father turns *his* back—and walks out of the house as if I didn't exist! Does he show any feeling for me? My toil is forgotten, my usefulness is over. I might better have gone to the grave with her who almost cost me my life the day I bore her!"

Karsten was astonished. "Do you know what you're saying, mother?" he asked her. "Or are you just being dramatic?"

"They shall not enter my house while I'm here to prevent it," his mother announced.

Something broke inside Karsten's mind. "Very well, God damn it, they won't come within sight of it!"

His mother's face went white. "Karsten—how dare you speak to me like that!"

Karsten checked his anger as he faced her. "All right, forget that I said it. I'm trying to tell you, mother, that Solveig was the only one of us who had the guts to choose her own life and live it in her own way. It might have been better for some of the rest of us if we had done what she did. I wouldn't be crawling back home now like a beaten pup—and Olina wouldn't be—"

"God forgive you, Karsten!" Magdali said, her voice breaking. She recovered herself immediately, however. "You will

[372]

live to see whether she did right, my boy. Why is she running away now from the life she has been living since the day she left me? Why has she never had a child of her own to that—that half-breed she married? Is she still too proud of her own blood to mix it with—"

"Mother, for God's sake!" Karsten interrupted her. "Can't you let them decide even that for themselves?"

"As you and Edna decided it, I suppose? And what came of that?" Scornfully Magdali sailed with a rustle of black taffeta out of the room and up the stairway, leaving Karsten to gaze after her as he dug his tightly clenched fists into his pockets.

He was standing there when Magdis appeared from the kitchen, where she had gone upon hearing the news that Solveig would arrive the next afternoon. She paused in the doorway and looked at her brother.

"You ought to be ashamed of yourself, talking to mother like that! After all she has gone through to help you, she certainly deserves something more than being cursed at."

Futile rage enveloped Karsten. "Christ almighty, you—you thing!" he flung at her, and went out to look for his father.

The train was in sight now, its whistle shrieking, and along the street Arne was racing toward the station, his head bare, his coat tails flapping behind him as he ran.

Down the platform, Karsten saw Alec Fordyce step from one of the rear coaches, a telescope valise in one hand. With his other hand he reached up to help Solveig.

"Great day!" Arne exclaimed. "Look at her, pa! She'd stop an eight-day clock!"

Karsten had to agree that Solveig was a vision. Her cream lace dress was princess style with a tremendous foamy flounce on the skirt, and the picture hat on her elaborate pompadour was as big as a parasol and decked with roses the size of dinner plates. But the flamboyant clothes were as nothing compared to the physical radiance of Solveig herself. She was in the full bloom of her loveliness, opulent of breast and hip, and unblushingly aware of both if the design of her gown were to be taken as any evidence. Just as well, Karsten thought as he went forward with Ivar and Arne, that Magdali was not there to see her.

"Pa!" Solveig cried joyously, embracing her father. "And Arne! Oh, isn't this wonderful! And Karsten, you great handsome thing. We didn't expect to see you till we got to Minneapolis. How did you get here?"

Karsten evaded her question and turned to greet Alec Fordyce. It was years since their last meeting, and Karsten had only a blurred recollection of him as a somewhat quixotic and romantically intense young man. But Alec had matured into a solid and quite prepossessing figure, and his protective solicitude toward Solveig might well have given her mother something to think about.

"You're both looking fine," Karsten said. "And quite civilized!" He laughed. "I half expected you to come in driving a string of malemutes."

Solveig looked about her. "Where are the others?"

"Magdis is at home with her mother," Ivar said with slow deliberation. "We might as well tell you, Solveig. We have a room for you and Alec at the hotel. We'll take you over there in the surrey."

A hard flush struck across Alec's face, but Solveig's eyes were flames in her sudden pallor.

"I intended to stay at a hotel, myself," Alec began, "but I thought—"

"Hush, Alec!" Solveig commanded. "I knew mother would never forgive me. I was quite prepared for it. Let's go to the hotel. Magdis and Olina can come to see me there."

Arne drew back, but Ivar and Karsten exchanged glances.

"We'll go over to the hotel, Solveig," Karsten said, "and then I'll tell you about little Olina."

Solveig clutched his arm. Her voice went high and thin as she cried, "Olina's dead! Karsten—tell me!"

He nodded bitterly. "We buried her yesterday. It happened so quickly, Suvvy. She was expecting a baby, but with the lung trouble she had after her pneumonia—she just went all of a sudden."

For an instant Solveig stood immobile and white. Then, turning to Alec, she said, "If our baby is a girl, we'll call her Olina."

XX

Solveig and her husband spent two days in Wing.

They had been two strange days, Karsten thought as he stood on the station platform again and watched the train disappear. His father had sat in the hotel room throughout the forenoon of that second day, and would have waited with Karsten to see the train leave, but Solveig had begged him to go home and avoid the sharp pain of a last-minute parting, with bystanders looking on. He had consented readily enough, though Karsten knew he would be standing by himself somewhere in one of his fields to watch the train steaming southward and bearing Solveig away from him—this time, perhaps, forever. *We meet to part again, but bear no assurance of another meeting.* Solveig had been almost gay. She and Alec would live in New York until their child—expected at Christmas— was old enough to travel around the world with them. No mere "grand tour" of Europe for the Fordyces! After that, they would settle down in New York, in the hotel business, Solveig said comfortably, since both she and Alec had discovered in the Yukon how to make people happy sleeping or eating. But before the end of this year, they would send for Ivar to visit them and his new grandchild, in New York. Ivar listened, smiled, as if he knew in his heart that something would come in the way of his going to the great city to behold a little grand-daughter who was to be called Olina.

"Ya—sure!" Ivar had said heartily. "You let your old pa know when the little one comes. And—I am glad you married Julian's son, Solveig. Julian was my first friend here on the prairie. God bless you both!"

Solveig had burst into tears then, but even that she did with grace, Karsten thought with bleak envy. No matter what tragedy she might encounter in life, she would never meet it clumsily, as he had done.

Magdali had remained obdurate, of course, as if some sacred duty to herself and to her God held her to a path from which she could not turn aside. Magdis had spent an hour with them in Solveig's room last night and had been studiedly cordial, though she declined to drink the wine that Alec had provided for the occasion. Today, she had told them over the telephone, she could not leave her red-brick house in Moorhead, because one of her children was suffering from an upset stomach. Arne had been with them last night, showing off insufferably, all but trotting out his bank book to convince Solveig and her husband that a man could make a go of it without risking his neck in a Yukon gold rush. Real estate, right here in the Red River Valley, that was the ticket! Even Roald Bratland had put in his appearance, resplendent in a fresh linen suit and flaming tie, and had pranced about on his brittle shanks, his little eyes leering at Solveig as he clucked to himself over his own hidden thoughts. He had taken his wine, too, with a zest and a smacking of his thin lips that had made Karsten wonder whether the old boy was quite as abstemious as he professed.

But that was all over now. The train had gone, and Solveig's perfume still lingered with Karsten like a long farewell of something intangible. He had ridden into town on young Louie Spragg's saddle horse, so that he would be free to go home later in case his father did not care to stay. He cast one last glance down the railway tracks.

"So long, Suvvy!" he said with a catch in his throat, then turned from the station platform and saw Rose Shaleen standing under the tree where he had tethered his horse.

Within him a little fist seemed to clench—and stay there—like a hard knot. He drew a swimmer's breath and stepped down from the platform.

Rose Shaleen—no, Rose Gaffley, Gideon Gaffley's wife—wore a dress of green china silk, with short, puffed sleeves. Her elbows were pointed, and her throat was a soft, moist hollow above the sharp V of her collar bone. There was a questioning and a wonderful dignity in the shadowed blue of her eyes—eyes too large now for her face.

"Rose," he began, "I—" And stopped there.

"You don't *have* to speak to me, Karsten," she said swiftly. "I thought I'd get down in time to say good-by to Solveig, but the train left before I got here."

"You knew she was in town?"

"Roald Bratland told Gideon. I saw her for a little while this morning—at the hotel."

"She didn't tell me she had seen you."

"I asked her not to."

"Why?"

Something of the old wild-rose tint flowed into her cheeks. "I didn't want you to think that I—expected to see you."

"Why should I think that?" His voice was leaden. "You're happily married—to one of the important men in town. Why should you want to see *me?*"

"You're still Karsten Wing," she said meditatively. "You'll always be Karsten Wing."

He laughed. "Sure—the guy that got out of that mess in Minneapolis by the skin of his teeth. The guy whose wife is suing him for divorce!"

"No."

Karsten glared at her and was about to get up into the saddle, then realized that he was being rude. He reached for the bridle rein, and said with ponderous courtesy, "It's warm. Would you like to walk over to Gimp Featherstone's with me and have an ice cream frappé?"

"Thank you," Rose said. "That would be nice. And I know Gimp and Pearl would like to see you again."

Karsten led his horse as he walked beside Rose, past the lumber yard and across the open area behind the blacksmith shop where four men were pitching horseshoes while several boys squatted on the ground and watched them. The pungent, ironish black smell of the smithy filled the still sunlight, and the clang of horseshoes striking the stakes at intervals seemed to make the hot air wince.

Glances were cast at Rose and Karsten as they passed, and two of the men raised their hands to their hats. The other two were bareheaded. One of the boys placed a blade of grass between his cupped hands and produced a piercing whistle.

Karsten involuntarily put his fingers to his collar to loosen it from the abrupt heat at his throat. "Am I supposed to know those fellows?" he asked Rose. "Or are they just the town loafers?"

"Not exactly. You used to know one of them—Lars Langstad's son. He works on the railroad, and he comes into the bank to cash his pay check twice a month."

Lars Langstad's son! Karsten remembered the evening, years ago, when he had stood on the sunset prairie and watched the chain of settlers coming down the trail, singing—out of "farthest north," as he had thought of it then. The memory brought an indefinable hurt within him as he turned his head for another look at the men.

They had come to Main Street where, two blocks down, across from Stacy's Emporium, stood Gimp Featherstone's Ice Cream Parlor. Gimp was a year or two older than Ivar Wing, but he was spry as a cricket and had been doing what he called a "flushing business" ever since he had persuaded Pearl to sell their homestead to Magdali Wing. Magdali had sold the land for many times what she had paid Gimp for it, but he was content. Farming wasn't his meat, anyhow.

Pearl paused midway in the act of concocting a banana split, wiped her hands on her apron, and leaned across the counter to shake hands with Karsten. There were tears in her eyes. Gimp strutted over from one of the round, flower-painted tables where he had served a group of young people with tall glasses of soda drinks, and seized Karsten by the shoulders.

"Man, oh, man!" he shouted with all of his wizened frame. "Welcome home, big feller! You're a sight for sore eyes, that's what you are! Ain't he, Rose? Ain't he, Pearl? Yes, sir!"

"You're not looking so bad yourself, Gimp," Karsten laughed. "And I hear you're doing a rushing business."

"We're doin' fine. Couldn't be better. Tell you what, young feller, you sit right down an' let me make up one o' these here fandangled sundaes that'll stick to your ribs! Pearl, dish out the tutti-frutti with peak nuts an' whipped cream an' marshino cherries! This is on the house, Karsten. 'Tain't every day we see one of our pioneer boys come back home. No, sir! Hope you're here to stay, this time."

They sat down at one of the small tables, and Karsten felt clammily idiotic. But Rose said quietly, "Don't chew your lips that way, Karsten. Gimp is doing his best to make you feel at home. And he really means it when he says he hopes you'll stay. He and Pearl have more than an ice cream parlor here. They have thirty years' worth of friends, and a lot of them are pretty well off. You could do a lot worse than open a law office right here in your own town."

Pearl and Gimp both came to set with a triumphant flourish the ornate dishes of ice cream before Karsten and Rose.

"Gosh," Karsten grinned up at the beaming couple, "I never ran into anything like this in the city! You ought to move down there and show 'em, Gimp."

"Might, an' might not," said Gimp. "We like it here, eh, Pearl? Took me a while to gentle her," he added with a wink at Karsten, "but I got her thinkin' like me now."

Karsten smiled at Pearl, then looked back at Gimp. "I'll bet you're not putting much over on Pearl."

Pearl sniffed. "Let him think so, if it makes him feel any better for it. And let him go down to the city if he has a mind to —just so he don't figure on comin' back. I'll make a go of it."

When Karsten and Rose went out into the street again, they stood beside the hitching post where Karsten had left his horse.

"This has been very pleasant, Rose," he told her. "And maybe that isn't such a bad idea of yours about opening an office here in town. I'm going to think it over. I've been playing with the idea of going out to the Philippines, but I don't know."

Rose brought her slim hand up to the green silk of her breast. "Karsten—don't stay here. Go to the Philippines."

He looked hard into her eyes. "You've changed your mind, all of a sudden," he said. "I thought you were trying to tell me—"

"I've been with you less than an hour," Rose said, and stroked the horse's nose as she spoke. "It's all I can stand, Karsten. I—I thought I was strong, but I'm not. You must go away."

He reached out toward the slim wrist close to the horse's muzzle, then withdrew his hand with a muttered oath. "Rose —I must see you again—right away. We've got to talk things over. Can't we meet somewhere—"

"No, no, Karsten—please!"

"I'll be down at our old landing on the river—tonight about nine o'clock. Nobody goes near the place now. There'll be moonlight."

Her face gathered into sudden fear, and then as suddenly

lighted with a defiant smile that banished the fear.

"Yes, Karsten," she said. "Gideon is in Grand Forks. I'll meet you at your landing. But let me tell you this—if Gideon and I had had any children, I wouldn't see you again—ever!"

"I understand, Rose. But—well, the old landing—at nine, then. I'll be there before you are—waiting."

She turned from him and walked slim and tall up Main Street, in the town of Wing, and Karsten got into the saddle just as the boy who had shrilled through the grass blade in the blacksmith's yard came around the corner whistling "A Bicycle Built for Two."

Karsten rode slowly home.

The hired girls had laid supper for himself and his father only, his mother having kept to her room with an attack of what the doctor called "migraine." The big house seemed to be all rooms and nothing else.

Over the cold cuts and fried potatoes, Karsten had a mad impulse to say to his father, "I'm meeting Rose Shaleen tonight, down at our old landing, and I don't give a damn who knows it! She's still Rose Shaleen—she never belonged to Gideon Gaffley!" But that would have been outrageous.

His father was talking, weighing his words in the manner he had now, and Karsten pinned his attention to what he was saying.

"While you were gone today, your mother talked on the telephone to three big men in the Valley who could start you out fresh in your law work right here, if you wanted to, Karsten."

"They must have been big men," Karsten observed acidly.

"Well, yes, I suppose they are. She's going to have Louie drive her to Moorhead tomorrow, so she can call on them. I thought it was rather soon after—after the funeral, I mean—

[382]

but you know how she is, once her mind is made up."

"She might have consulted me first," Karsten said. "Who are the men?"

"Our congressman, Rigwold. And Baynes and Fleet. They're all in with Roald and Arne on some public utilities deal. I guess it's honest enough, or Arne wouldn't have anything to do with it."

Karsten laughed. "Thanks, pa," he said with an old familiarity in his voice. "I guess you and I understand each other well enough to take a little dig now and then."

Ivar's face colored a little. "I didn't mean it that way, my boy."

"Of course not. I don't even know what you think about my part in that dirty business in Minneapolis."

"A man can do foolish things to please a woman," Ivar said mildly. "But he can start over again and do what's right. And he doesn't have to go to the Philippines to make the start. That way, you run away from yourself only—and you meet yourself again. Or maybe"—his clear eyes twinkled beneath his weathered brows—"maybe you meet Edna Cole again in one o' them hay skirts the women wear out there!"

Karsten laughed with ease for the first time in many months. There was no evaluating his father's belief in his integrity that still lay beneath all the glittering scum of the past few years. To Karsten it was a new lease on life itself. But they were both shy men, not given to hand-gripping and loud protestations of gratitude. Karsten's laugh was thanks enough to his father.

And when they left the table, Karsten was sure that he was prepared to withstand the violent force that had sprung toward him from the thin body of Rose this afternoon. They would meet, they would talk and reason it all out together on the river bank tonight, and they would part good friends, with a wistfulness, perhaps, for something that should have been and now could never be. But they would part as friends—not as burning and clandestine lovers.

June passed, and July, and the August evening was misty and starless, rain not quite falling on the thick, murmurous black of the river.

Karsten had stayed late in his new office above Roald's bank in Wing, listening patiently to the tedious claims of a client who had far more money than brains. Listening patiently, but on the surface only. Beneath the keen interest which had already in less than three months justified his supporters who had helped to establish him here, abode a frenzy to be waiting under the oak in the river woods before Rose came to him. He had always been there first, through these delirious weeks of their meetings. Chivalry insisted on that. And tonight Rose was to tell him what had come of her appeal to Gideon to free her from their marriage, an appeal she was to have made this morning. Not a soul knew of those secret meetings in the river woods, of that Karsten was confident. Gideon had known nothing even of their young romance, years ago. And it was only on nights when he was in Moorhead or elsewhere on business that Karsten and Rose contrived to be together. Tonight Gideon was to attend a bank meeting involving a new policy toward farm loans.

Karsten hastened from his father's house, where he still had his old room with its brown-floored washstand set, and strode west across the field to the river timber. The smell of fresh stubble came up tonic through the ground fog. He breathed deep, relishing it in his very blood. Rose was like that, he thought. And she had blossomed out into her young beauty again, this summer. Love—the moon of the tides, the tides of the sea, the sea drawing the rivers, and the rivers drawing the creeks and the brooks—all toward the moon of the tides! *I'm light-headed,* Karsten thought happily. *In five minutes, now, Rose will be in my arms again. We'll stretch out long, both of us, in the secret blackness under the tree, and she won't talk for a while, but then she'll have to tell me what Gideon said when she went to him this morning and asked him for her freedom.*

Two minutes later, the sharp report of a gun split in Karsten's ears. He stood numbed from head to foot and stared into the mist towards the woods, while the echoes broke about him, crashing from the trees near by, growing fainter as they hurried up and down the river—but moving on and on forever.

He started running then, in the direction from which the sound of the shot had come. But a moment later a second shot rang out, and Karsten seemed to feel rather than hear the dull thud of a falling body as it struck the ground.

"Rose—oh, Rose Shaleen!" he whispered.

Gideon Gaffley had made his reply to Rose, and for the manner of that reply he would not have to answer to anyone on this earth. He had with mathematical precision followed Rose out of this life, since he had always believed that one and one make two.

Karsten Wing found himself looking up at the gloomy fullness of the summer trees. Just over there, he remembered, a streamer of red silk had fluttered for an instant—and then hung motionless one sunlit summer day.

I

THERE had been a light snowfall the night before, and now the early Sunday afternoon glittered under a cloudless and jewel-blue sky. The air gave April to the senses, but December lay gaunt on old Ivar Wing's fields and woodlands.

Norma paused before an open window of her bedroom and looked southward over the whitened stubble patched in spots with the moist dark of melted snow. She had come upstairs to rest for a little while—or so she had politely given old Ivar and Dr. Phillips to believe. Dr. Phillips, rosily content after one of Eudora's matchless chicken dinners, had patted Norma's hand as she excused herself.

"Little Ivar likes to relax, too, after a feast like that," he had joked. "Go and take your rest. You're looking well, my dear. When you come back down, you'll have a glass of that fine old port I brought out with me. Little Ivar won't mind a bit of encouragement on the last two months of waiting."

But Norma had not come upstairs to rest. She had eaten lightly of the massive noon meal, and she felt electrically awake. She had experienced an inscrutable compulsion to come up here to this room that had been hers and Brill's during his brief leave after their marriage last July. It had been young Karsten Wing's room years ago, and Solveig had slept here on her visit to her father after Magdali's death in 1928. Solveig's lovely daughter, Olina, had been with her.

And now, as she stood looking out of the window across the white fields toward the modest frame farmhouse where she was born, it came to her that she had not wanted to leave this room at all today. All day she had felt some pulling from the past, from the days when her father Loren had walked those fields alone, his blue eyes leveled toward the horizon of his far thoughts. A past less remote, too, had held her strangely. On waking at dawn, she had felt Brill's arms about her with a secure and sensuous reality unattributable to dream. She had smiled and sighed over on the pillow against the strong rampart of his breast. She had thought—or had she dreamt?—that word. Rampart! "The ramparts we watch." And then she had come fully awake, and had sat up in a chilled room, startled and alone.

But once more within it now, she felt peculiarly not alone. The sun was shining directly upon Brill's photograph, lighting the deep, grave laughter of his eyes—eyes that were not like those of his banker father, Arne, but like those of his grandfather, Ivar Wing. The sun was shining on the nameless brown Victorian flowers of the crockery water pitcher on the cherry washstand, and they seemed to bloom and glow beyond their inanimate captivity. The room enveloped Norma and the new life she bore with a sun-drenched and seasonless warmth, and she stood still for a full minute, letting it caress her with its mysterious peace.

"Brill," she whispered at last. "Thank you, my darling— thank you for being here today. You—and those others—all of those others who loved and lived so long ago!"

Now she would have to go downstairs again and listen to the doctor exclaim upon this and that—Brill's good fortune in having his play accepted by that New York producer, a play which the doctor hoped to see when he went to New York this winter to a medical convention—and the wisdom Norma had shown in her decision not to go to San Diego with Brill after their marriage. All the uncertainties of military orders, living quarters, and so forth, were unsettling to an expectant mother.

[390]

. . . She had never told Dr. Phillips of how Brill had begged her to come with him, of how she had kissed his mouth hard and said, "No, Brill—I'll stay here and keep this place for old Ivar and little Ivar and you and me."

Norma moved carefully down the stairs in her long paisley wool housecoat.

Old Ivar and the doctor sat before the glowing birch log fire in the cosy sitting room at the rear of the house. A decanter and glasses stood on a small maple table near by. The doctor rose and set the old red-velvet wing chair closer to the fire for Norma as she came into the room. She seated herself and reached toward the silver box on the table that held cigarettes.

"That's your third since dinner, young woman," Dr. Phillips reproved gently. "I thought you were cutting down on cigarettes."

Norma laughed penitently and folded her hands in her lap. "I'm sort of absent-minded today," she said.

The doctor nodded comfortably and decanted a glass of wine for her. "I've got to be on my way in a minute," he told her. "I think one of your Tridd great-grandsons is coming down with the mumps, Ivar. His mother is having conniptions."

"Nothing new for Dorothy Tridd," Ivar remarked, undisturbed. "I often wonder how I came by a granddaughter like her. I s'pose she takes after her mother, Cecily. A good woman, of course—and a fine wife and mother. But it strikes me she gets more like Frank Tridd's Glass Block every day. All fuss and feathers. Have you any explanation for that, Doctor Joe?"

The doctor laughed. "If I had, I wouldn't give it to you, Ivar. Professional ethics would prevent me!"

He drew placidly on his cigar.

"I suppose it's something like professional ethics that keeps us from knowing what's really going on in Washington these days," Norma said suddenly. "All those polite talks with the

[391]

Japanese envoys—what do they mean?"

Ivar picked up his cane and leaned forward to brush a feather of ash from the carpet back to the stone hearth.

"They will tell us in their own time, my girl," he said. "It will do you no good to worry about it."

"Kurusu and Nomura sound like reliable men," Doctor Phillips observed. "I think they'll avert a crisis and patch the business up. The Japs have enough on their hands right now, with China and maybe Russia."

Old Ivar's eyebrows rose quizzically, and he picked up his pipe and began scraping its redolent bowl.

"Brill is in Hawaii," Norma said softly, and moved a little in the old red-velvet chair so as to ease the new down-pull of her heaviness. "The letter I had from him yesterday—I dreamt last night that I read it all over again, and I remembered it word for word."

"Well, that's understandable," Dr. Phillips said. "You're keyed up, of course. But it's nothing to concern yourself about, my dear."

There was a tap, rather excited, at the door back of them, and Eudora Spragg strode into the room.

"I wanted you should be in by the radio in the front room!" she babbled, her eyes full of wrath. "Them heathen Japs has bombed Pearl Harbor, and the whole place has sunk right into the ocean!"

"Woman!" old Ivar said, his cane bringing him erect on his feet. "What way is that to talk? Have you got no sense?"

His cane smote the floor, and Eudora burst into tears.

"Two o' my nephews is in the Navy somewhere in them outlandish parts!" she cried.

Norma got up and placed her arm about the woman's heaving shoulders. "Your nephews will be all right, Eudora, I know they will. You'd better go to your room and lie down for a while. Doctor, give her a glass of wine, will you, please?"

The doctor poured out the wine, and as he watched his hand to see that it was steady, he thought of his own two sons, a few years out of college. They had seemed to mean so much more to him since his wife's death. The last drop of wine filling the glass, dimpled oddly, as if it did not want to stay there.

He lifted the glass carefully and gave it to Eudora. "Drink it down, Eudora," he said, doing his best to sound jovial. "This old world isn't going to smash yet for a while. Generations, once begun, go on and on forever."

Norma stood for a moment at the window, looking westward across the tranquil field to the woods where the last of the autumn foliage screened the river in thin, rusty gold. *Generations, once begun. . . .*

"Grandpa Ivar," she said, turning to smile steadily up at the old man, "give me your arm, and we'll go in and listen to the radio. There'll be more, I think, than Eudora has told us."

Ivar's eyes, suddenly and penetratingly young, searched her face for a long moment. Then he, too, smiled as his shoulders lifted in a proud, rugged gesture. He left his cane standing against a chair as Norma slipped her hand into the crook of his elbow, and together they walked out of the room.